NO STONE
UNTURNED

Previously published Worldwide Mystery titles by
JULIE MOFFETT

NO ONE LIVES TWICE
NO TEST FOR THE WICKED
NO WOMAN LEFT BEHIND
NO ROOM FOR ERROR
NO STRINGS ATTACHED
NO LIVING SOUL
NO ONE TO TRUST
NO REGRETS

NO STONE UNTURNED

JULIE MOFFETT

W⦿RLDWIDE®

TORONTO • NEW YORK • LONDON
AMSTERDAM • PARIS • SYDNEY • HAMBURG
STOCKHOLM • ATHENS • TOKYO • MILAN
MADRID • WARSAW • BUDAPEST • AUCKLAND

Recycling programs
for this product may
not exist in your area.

No Stone Unturned

A Worldwide Mystery/August 2019

First published by Carina Press, an imprint of
Harlequin Enterprises Limited.

ISBN-13: 978-1-335-45554-3

Copyright © 2019 by Julie Moffett

All rights reserved. No part of this book may be reproduced or
transmitted in any form or by any means, electronic or mechanical,
including photocopying, recording or by any information storage and
retrieval system, without permission in writing from the publisher. For
information, contact: Harlequin Enterprises Limited, 22 Adelaide St.
West, 40th Floor, Toronto, ON M5H 4E3, Canada.

This is a work of fiction. Names, characters, places and incidents are
either the product of the author's imagination or are used fictitiously,
and any resemblance to actual persons, living or dead, business
establishments, events or locales is entirely coincidental.

® and ™ are trademarks of Harlequin Enterprises Limited.
Trademarks indicated with ® are registered in the United States
Patent and Trademark Office, the Canadian Intellectual Property Office
and in other countries.

Printed in U.S.A.

This one is for you, Beth Moffett! Thanks for ALL you do for me, the kids and our family. You're an amazing person and the best sister-in-law and friend ever! Love you!

ONE

Lexi

IF MY MOM texted me a picture of my own engagement ring one more time, I was going to lose it.

Apparently she was trying to send them to her best friend, Candi Schmidt, but Mom and her new phone were still coming to an understanding, so she'd texted me the same picture seven times in the last five minutes. It was my picture to start with, and I'd only sent it to her after she bugged me for a week, threatening that if she didn't get a photo, she'd post an engagement announcement on my behalf in the *Washington Post.* That horrified me enough to snap a photo of my ring and send it to her. Unfortunately she now wanted to share it with all her friends, which essentially meant the entire greater DC area. I had seriously been considering hacking her phone so it went exactly nowhere, but it seemed that wasn't necessary. For now, I gritted my teeth and tried to be happy that the photo was coming back to me, over and over, instead of to her ginormous circle of friends.

My phone dinged again, but I ignored it. Mom was just excited for me, but she was telling *everyone* about my engagement, while I've struggled with telling *anyone*, even close friends and family. Her enthusiasm was starting to make me feel weird about the mixed-up feelings I was having about getting engaged. I'm a geek girl who loathes attention, and telling people that Slash and I are engaged inevitably leads to screams, hugs and a thousand questions about a wedding I haven't even thought about yet. The stress was getting so acute that not even reciting Carl Friedrich Gauss's Theory of Reciprocity could take the edge off my social anxiety.

My name is Lexi Carmichael and my life was a bit weird even before I got engaged. My fiancé and I are both uberhackers—me for a private cyber intelligence company called X-Corp and Slash for the NSA. His nickname is short for backslash in hacker lingo, and only a few people know his real name because of the covert nature of his intelligence work. He's recently taken a much more visible position, and is now the youngest director of the Information Assurance Directorate in NSA history, followed around the clock by his own special Secret Service detail.

My own job isn't exactly lacking in excitement either. X-Corp is based in DC, but despite the virtual nature of my job, I travel a lot to secure my clients' assets. I used to think that being an expert in cybersecurity meant a safe, quiet job behind a desk. I've discovered that couldn't be further from the truth. It's a new world out there, and security is more often than not managed by strokes on a keyboard. Since humans are often the weak link in cybersecurity, I've had to do considerable work with people to keep data safe and secure. All that means both Slash and I are at the forefront of protecting national security, as well as business interests. It sometimes puts a strain on our relationship, but we decided to take it to the next level and commit ourselves to each other anyway.

At this particular moment, national security wasn't

even on my radar. Instead I was focused on the engagement party Slash had informed me was inevitable. As the news of our engagement filtered out, our friends and family wanted to see us in person to congratulate us and see the new house we'd recently moved into together. Although we'd planned the party for this Friday, I was obsessing and stressing because this would be the first one I'd ever thrown in my own house. Slash was helping, which meant we were muddling along, trying not to kill each other in the process.

"Do we really have to allow people to bring a guest?" I asked him for the third time, studying the spreadsheet while chewing on the eraser at the top of my pencil. We were sitting at the counter with mugs of coffee and a printed spreadsheet of all the things we had to do for the party. I'd carefully divided the spreadsheet into three parts—my responsibilities, Slash's jobs and our joint tasks. Inviting people was part of our joint-task column, so here we were, hammering it out.

He glanced up from the spreadsheet and my breath caught in my throat. He was unquestionably the best-looking guy I'd ever dated. Okay, he was pretty much the *only* guy I'd ever dated seriously. Still, when he spoke with his sexy Italian accent and gazed at me with his deep brown eyes, all logic left my brain. I knew that sometimes he used that to his advantage.

His mouth quirked slightly at the corner, probably because he could see the glazed look coming into my eyes. Yep, Seduction 101, that's exactly what he was doing. Even though I was fully aware of it, it was still working.

"Your brothers have girlfriends, right?" he replied. "Guest plus one is standard."

"Who cares about plus one?" I groused. "I don't even know who their girlfriends are this week."

He didn't respond, so I let out a loud huff of annoyance before reluctantly adding two extra people as the unknown guests of my brothers. "We've already got sixteen people, including my parents. It's too many guests. We'll never fit them all."

"We have a big house, *cara*. We'll fit and have room to spare. Besides, it's possible some people won't come. You can stop worrying."

I'd never stop worrying, because I'd rather endure a dozen Microsoft patches than attend a party. But here we were—party planning central.

Forcing myself to keep my mind on the task at hand, I resumed studying the spreadsheets. "Do I have to iron napkins?" I asked.

Slash looked up from the spreadsheet. "What?"

"The napkins. The book said formal events required ironed napkins. But now that I think about it, we don't *have* napkins to be ironed."

Slash started to say something and then shut his mouth. After another beat, he asked, "What book?"

"*Party Planning for Dummies*. They have separate chapters for formal and informal events. Formal events require cloth napkins. Do I need to buy some? More importantly, I've never ironed a napkin before and the book isn't terribly clear on how to do it properly."

Slash put his hand over mine, stopping me before I could write it down. "We are *not* buying or ironing cloth napkins. This is *not* a formal gathering. This is a casual party with close friends and family. It's being catered, so we need to do little more than show up."

"Easy for you to say. You don't mind the showing up part."

"I like it better than the party planning part, I admit." He put a hand on my back and made circles with his fingers. "We've got this. We'll email the invites, pay the caterer, keep the house clean, and we're done. People will come, congratulate us, look at the house, eat, drink and make small talk. One evening—over and out."

He made it sound easy. I only hoped he was right. In hindsight, I should have known better.

Nothing is ever easy when it involves me.

TWO

Lexi

EVERY TIME THERE was an occasion that called for something fancier than jeans or work clothes, my anxiety skyrocketed. Part of the problem was I don't understand fashion. At. All. Hemlines, necklines, and sleeves—short, half-length, or otherwise—completely mystify me. Trying to match shoes and purses scares me. Being in a room with people looking completely put together with expertly applied makeup and perfectly coiffured hair is like my own personal hell.

But sometimes, it was time to suck it up and deal. My engagement party was one of those times. Sighing, I pushed away the doubts and pulled on a white sundress that Basia helped me pick out, along with a cropped baby-blue cardigan that was remarkably close to the color of the rare blue diamond in my engagement ring. I added a small pair of silver earrings and debated whether to pull my long brown hair up in a ponytail. I wanted to, but since this was an informally formal event, I left it down. I swiped on some lip gloss and mascara, then paced nervously while Slash finished shaving. He patted on some aftershave and stepped into the bedroom, pulling on a white, short-sleeved button-up shirt, watching me with an amused look on his face.

"You're lovely."

I looked at myself in the mirror for the millionth time and tried to tug the neckline higher. "I'm overdressed and I'm in white. I'm a disaster waiting to happen. I should have worn jeans." I stuffed my hands in the dress pockets so I wouldn't bite my nails.

"You're *not* overdressed, I promise." Our eyes met in the mirror and he smiled. "*Cara*, look, if you're feeling overwhelmed at the party, just squeeze my hand twice, and I'll figure a way to extract you. Remember, close friends and family, okay?"

"And unnamed guests." Anxiety coursed through me. "I don't understand how we got so many friends in such a short period of time. I was perfectly fine with only three friends for the past two years. The ratio had better not grow at the same rate over the next year or so, or we'll need two houses to hold everyone."

He thought I was joking, but only partially. I really did require a lot of personal space.

He chuckled and walked over to me while buttoning his shirt. Cupping my chin in his hand, he lowered his lips to mine, kissing me. Mmmm…he smelled like after-shave and soap. When he leaned back, I wound my arms around his waist, pressing my head against his chest.

"Want to cancel?" he murmured.

"Yes. I really do. But we won't. I really do like all of our friends, it's just that I'm not sure I like them all here at the same time. If you're with me, I'll make it through."

"Okay, then. Let me finish dressing and we'll go downstairs. People will be arriving shortly."

My parents were the first to arrive, twenty minutes early. No surprise there. My dad was a high-powered attorney in Georgetown and he's habitually early to ensure he's punctual. He's also wicked observant, which helped hone his interrogation skills, but also meant I never got away with anything growing up.

After a lot of awkward hugs and a grand tour of the house, Slash and my dad disappeared into the kitchen to get beer. That left me alone with my mom, a former beauty pageant queen and social butterfly. If there was a television show for the Rich Housewives of Georgetown, she'd be one of the stars. I turned toward her, trying to look like I was totally excited about the party and having everyone over. After that failed, I decided to modify and aim for looking like I didn't want to run out of the house screaming. *That* was far more achievable.

"Oh, you look so pretty, Lexi." She fussed with my hair, arranging it on my shoulders. After that she studied my ring for a long time, then beamed with happiness. "Love looks good on you. Have you and Slash set a date for the wedding yet?"

"No."

"So we're clear—you are *not* eloping, young lady." She narrowed her eyes at me. "I would never forgive you."

It was scary how accurate my mom was at reading my mind. I tried not to look guilty, but she probably saw through that. "Mom, we haven't even *thought* about the wedding yet. We've got a lot of other stuff going on right now."

"What could be more important than a wedding? Your house is beautiful, the furniture is lovely—although a bit modern for my taste—and you both have well-paying jobs. Get on with it already. Although, it is kind of strange those people follow you around all the time."

"They're Secret Service agents, and they're just doing their job." It was hard for me to be annoyed about this comment when I was still coming to terms with them being parked in front of our house whenever Slash was home. I automatically looked toward the window, wondering which team was on duty tonight.

"If you say so. Look, darling, let me give you a piece of advice. Don't make Slash wait forever."

I tried to keep the exasperation out of my voice. "Mom, we just got engaged a few weeks ago. Can't we enjoy that for a while?"

"Of course you can enjoy it. Just enjoy it *while* you're planning your wedding." She reached forward, adjusting one of my earrings, then stepped back and examined me. Mom was a perfectionist. Her blonde hair was long, shiny and expertly styled and she always knew just what clothes to wear to show off her best features. Tonight she wore a form-fitting red dress with a scoop back and dangling diamond earrings that caught the light and sparkled every time she moved. She was gorgeous. Sometimes it was hard being her daughter, because people who hadn't met me expected a lot more than a lanky, brown-haired girl who was into math and computers and didn't care much about clothes and makeup.

"Remember, the best wedding venues fill up fast," she continued as if she hadn't heard my protest. "Your father and I have a lot of social contacts, but we'll need plenty of lead time to get you what you want."

"We don't even know *what* we want." That was true, but we were both one-hundred percent certain whatever it was we wanted, it would *not* be what my mom had in mind. She was all about pomp and pageantry, while Slash and I were way too private and minimalist for that.

"Well, at least we'll go shopping for your wedding dress soon," she said. "I've already bought several bridal magazines for us to flip through so we can determine what you're thinking about in terms of style."

The mere thought of flipping through a bridal magazine filled me with such dread, I shuddered.

"I also sent you that link to the online wedding dress style quiz last week," she continued, oblivious to my horror. "Why haven't you taken it yet?"

Jeez! That was it! I had to get out of there right now.

"Ah, excuse me, Mom. I need a drink." I executed a sharp turn and made a beeline for the kitchen.

My dad and Slash were leaning against the kitchen counter, drinking beer and laughing about something. Ever since Slash proposed, my dad had relaxed his constant interrogation tactics and had started to enjoy Slash's company. Thank God for small miracles. It did make things between us a lot more comfortable. I still had to be on my guard, though, because while my dad understands me a lot better than my mom, I knew he wouldn't side with me on any wedding-related drama. I was on my own for that, and prepared for lots of it, because everyone knew that *nothing* brought out the family drama more than a wedding.

Thank God Slash was from Italy where most of his family resided, except for his mom and stepfather—who I'd never met. Yet. They'd moved from Italy to London when Slash started working at the Vatican. Either way, their location in another country was a plus for me, and possibly for him, too. An ocean away was a comfortable distance, in my opinion. In my case, it meant I had to deal with only one set of relatives at a time.

I reached for the wine when the doorbell rang. Slash and I exchanged a glance. He held out a hand and I took it. Together we walked into the foyer and opened the door. Grayson Reese stood there smiling. She was a CIA analyst and one of the few people willing to discuss quantitative research with me. Maybe we could hide in a corner and talk about the new trends in research statistics and evaluation. Just *anything* non-wedding related. Her brown hair was loose and curled and she wore a cute black dress and heeled strappy sandals. Her boyfriend, Hands—his Navy SEAL nickname—was nowhere in sight.

"Lexi! Slash!" She launched herself into our arms for a hug, and I caught the faint scent of strawberries. "It's been way too long since I've seen you guys. Congratulations on your engagement and the new house. I can't wait to hear all about your wedding plans."

I swallowed my disappointment as my dream of huddling in the corner with her and talking about anything *except* a wedding vanished in a poof. "So, where's Hands?" I distinctly remembered him being on the list that had RSVP'd for this evening.

"I'm sorry," she said shoving a bottle of wine into my hands. "He got deployed unexpectedly. I hope it's okay I came solo."

"It's more than okay," Slash said with a smile, ushering her into the house. "We're glad you could make it."

The next half hour was a whirlwind as people continued to arrive in clusters. Suddenly my house was full of people and more were still arriving and I had to recite the periodic table backward so I didn't freak out. Slash handled everything with amazing calm and charm, so I gladly let him do most of the talking. I envied him that, in spite of his own deep introversion, he could dazzle people so effortlessly.

I disappeared into the kitchen to chat a while with

my older brother, Beau, a detective for Baltimore Police Department, about a case he was working that had some interesting cyber elements. When I walked out into the living room again, I clutched my wineglass and looked for Slash. He immediately made eye contact with me, clearly assessing my mood. It warmed my heart that he could gauge my anxiety level so well without us even having to speak.

He smiled as I approached and slid an arm around my waist, pulling me close and taking my hand, giving me the chance to squeeze my way out of the party. I was doing okay, so I didn't signal, but I loved him for thinking of it. I gave him a brave smile, leaning into him and soaking up his warmth. He brushed a kiss against my cheek. When he did that, it felt like it was just the two of us in the room.

He'd been speaking in Italian to a couple who were friends of Slash's family. As soon as I arrived, they switched effortlessly to English. I admired people who could do that without missing a beat. I chatted with them for a bit until my mom and dad pulled me aside.

"Lexi, you and Slash did a lovely job with the party," my mom said. "I have to say, the caterer is to die for. The house is lovely as well. You'll have plenty of room to grow here, especially when you have children."

I choked on my wine. "Mom, we haven't even got married yet."

"And your point is? You don't have to be married to get pregnant, you know. Although we'd better not have to go shopping for a maternity-style wedding dress. But as soon as you've walked down that aisle, you should start working on my grandchildren. I don't intend to be an old grandmother." She glanced around the room. "Where's Slash? He needs to hear this, too."

I opened my mouth to respond when I heard a sound like popcorn being popped, only louder.

"Get down," Slash yelled as the lights went off.

I turned toward his voice just before he slammed into me, my mom, and dad, bringing all three of us to the floor in a jumble of limbs.

My elbow smashed into something soft and I heard my dad yelp. I gasped as my hip banged against the floor. "Ouch! Slash, what's going on?"

"Stay down." Slash rolled off me and came to a crouch.

I crawled toward my mom, lying protectively on one side of her, with my dad on the other. She was shaking. I patted her shoulder awkwardly.

"Lexi, are we going to be okay?" she whispered.

As my eyes adjusted to the darkness, I could see Slash creeping toward the window, his hand resting beneath his sports coat, where I knew he had a gun.

Why the heck was someone shooting at us during our engagement party? Did someone want to hurt Slash?

I swallowed my concerns, tried to be the calm and collected hostess. "Don't worry," I whispered to my mom. "Slash has everything under control."

My dad made a noise between a grunt and a sigh. Not quite disbelieving, but not happy either.

I just held my breath and hoped I was right.

THREE

Slash

SLASH SWORE SOFTLY in Italian as he headed for the window. He and Lexi didn't live normal lives, but he'd promised her father he'd keep her safe, and this wasn't helping his case.

"Everyone stay down," he ordered, his hand resting on the gun in the shoulder holster beneath his jacket. He'd already loosened the strap, but he didn't want to draw it and scare everyone. He first needed to determine the level of danger. The noise had faded and all he could hear were faint pops. Not firearms, but something else.

Something familiar.

His phone was vibrating but he ignored it. He figured they were multiple warnings from the security camera feeds warning him that the side perimeter of his house had been penetrated, and the audio and motion-activated feeds he had surrounding the house had been tripped. He also would have received alerts from his Secret Service detail. He didn't read any of them; none of them were more critical than a situational awareness of what was happening at the moment.

As soon as the noise had sounded, someone, probably Beau, had hit the lights in the living room. Someone else had turned off the lights in the dining room and kitchen, plunging the house into darkness.

Offer no easy or illuminated targets—an operational countermeasure.

He scrutinized the front windows, illuminated by the moon outside. No evidence that any bullets had tried to penetrate the glass, not that they would have succeeded. The windows in the house were all bulletproof, one of the concessions he'd made to the government so the agents who followed him around were not also assigned to live in his basement.

"Stay calm and don't move yet," he urged the guests as he approached the window. "I'm just going to check things out."

He cleared his mind, listening and assessing the noise outside. It came from the left front of the house in a rapid staccato before abruptly dying off. He immediately pictured the entire schematics of every inch of his yard, including bushes, hedges, trees, and located the approximate position of the noise.

When he got to the window, he saw what had made the sounds, confirming his earlier suspicion. He rose from his crouch, letting his hand drop from beneath his jacket. "It isn't gunfire."

"Car backfiring?" Beau asked from across the room.

"Firecrackers," he said. He walked away from the window toward the kitchen. It was time to check it out for himself.

"Firecrackers? That's unusual," Beau said. "Not part of the party, I suppose."

"No." Slash considered the potential threat firecrackers could hold. It was little to none, but required investigation just the same. "However, out of an abundance of caution, please stay where you are and keep the lights off until I give the all clear." He strode toward the kitchen and Beau followed him.

"What's going on?" Beau asked him as he rooted around in a drawer for a flashlight and snapped it on.

"I don't know. The Secret Service agents are already checking it out. I'm going out."

"Whoa. Is that your best move?" Beau asked. "Someone could be trying to draw you out."

He withdrew his gun from his shoulder holster. "I'll be ready. Stay here and secure the front and rear accesses to the house. Let's make sure the firecrackers aren't a distraction to something else. You have your service weapon?"

Beau lifted his jacket. "Armed and ready."

"Good."

Slash disabled the alarm on the kitchen door and went out low. As he crept closer to the wooden gate that opened up to the side of the house, the soft voices of the agents became audible.

He spoke quietly, calmly. "It's me, code-named Capri. I came out to see what's going on." He carefully opened the gate and stepped into the side yard.

The two Secret Service agents were waiting for him, John August and Mick Calhoun, their guns aimed his way. As soon as they saw him, they lowered their weapons.

"What are you doing out here, sir?" August asked. He holstered his weapon while taking a defensive position in front of Slash.

"Sorry to startle you, gentlemen," Slash said, keeping his back against the house. "I appreciate your professionalism, but I saw the firecrackers and came to investigate.

I need to be front and center in getting this sorted out as quickly as possible."

The agents stared at him and didn't move. Were they really going to make him say this aloud?

He cleared his throat, glad it was dark and they couldn't see his face well. "My future in-laws are in there, and they aren't impressed."

A look of understanding, perhaps even sympathy, crossed their faces, but they were trained agents and didn't budge from their positions. "I understand, but this isn't protocol, sir," August argued. "You should be inside. We have backup on the way."

He had no intention of going back inside until he had a thorough understanding of what had happened. Even if they didn't like it. "Until backup gets here, let's evaluate the situation. What happened?" A quick glance confirmed there was little left of the fireworks other than a charred box, the soft rise of smoke and the acrid smell of sulfur. His mind rapidly sorted through several things at once. The number of firecrackers, the wooden container and the precise location it had been placed—close enough to the house to be both seen and heard.

Not a threat. A message.

"As you can see, someone set off fireworks," Calhoun said. He kept staring at Slash, as if weighing how successful he'd be if he forcibly tried to drag him back into the house and to safety. Wisely, he decided not to try. "We didn't see any vehicles on the street and no one on foot, but the fireworks didn't set themselves off. Could have been kids."

"Could have been," Slash said, although he didn't agree with that assessment. "I felt the vibration of the perimeter alarms on my phone shortly before the fireworks went off. I'll check the security camera feeds when I go back inside."

"Excellent. We'll wait for the back-up agents, then review them with you, if that would be acceptable."

"It would. For now, let's spread out and see if we can find any clues." Slash clicked on his flashlight.

"You're really not going back inside, sir?" Calhoun asked.

"I am not."

August looked disappointed. "You do know that if anything happens to you, our careers are in the toilet."

He didn't say it aloud, but if he didn't get a handle on this situation, his relationship with his future in-laws would be in the toilet. They had so far dealt with the risks that were a part of his job with as much grace and aplomb as they could. But the additional risk he brought to the table that came with his position at the NSA was proving to be a sticking point, especially with her father.

Slash clapped him on the shoulder. "Then, let's get to work to make sure that doesn't happen."

FOUR

Lexi

GRAYSON CRAWLED OVER to me. "Lexi, what's going on outside?"

"I don't know," I said in a low voice. "But I'd bet money Slash went outside to find out."

"What if he's the target?"

"You think that would stop him?"

"No." Gray lowered her voice. "Don't let Slash see you."

I started to crawl toward the window. "I'm just going to go see if he's okay."

"Whoa, young lady." My dad grabbed my ankle. "Where do you think you're going?"

"I'm checking things out, Dad." I shook my ankle, trying to get free. "Let go."

"Slash said we're supposed to stay where we were."

"I'm not going outside. I'm just going to peek at the window to see what's happening. I'll be careful. I promise." I knew what I was doing. I'd been getting shot at on a surprisingly regular basis these days, so Slash had been working with me to prepare for such occasions, just in case. But I could hardly tell my dad that without freaking him out, so I had to hope he'd take my word for it.

After a moment, he released me, so I continued my crawl. When I got to the window, I peeked over the sill and saw three dark figures. I spotted Slash by the shape of his silhouette. He was standing a bit away from the others, holding a flashlight and looking around on the grass. He picked something off the ground and put it in his pocket. I wondered what he'd found.

A few minutes later, everyone came back in. Slash flipped the lights on. "False alarm, folks. It was fire-crackers. Kids playing around. Everyone can get up."

The guests chuckled in relief, but I didn't. Something wasn't right. My eyes met Slash's across the room. Although he smiled, I saw the tension in his jaw. I stretched out a hand and helped my dad pull Mom off the floor. She stood, brushing down her dress. "Lexi, you do know this kind of environment is not conducive to raising children."

"Mom, this was not my fault! And can we please stop talking about children? Why don't you ask Beau or Rock why they haven't produced any yet?"

"Neither of your brothers are engaged yet," my mother pointed out.

"You just told me that wasn't a prerequisite for children!"

Before she could answer, Slash came up beside me, slipping an arm around my waist. "How's everyone doing?"

"Peachy," I said, glaring at my mom.

"We're fine." My dad straightened his tie. "So, it was some kids playing with firecrackers on your lawn?"

"Looks like it," Slash said. "I apologize for bringing you all down, but safety is always my first concern."

"Of course," my dad replied. "Although at this point, we're almost expecting it every time we get together."

"Don't be ridiculous, Dad," I said heatedly. "Not *every* time."

"I'm glad we didn't have a real threat to worry about this time," Slash said smoothly, but his arm around me tightened slightly.

"Well, I'll wear my kneepads next time...just in case." Dad gave me a peck on the cheek before he moved away to talk to my other brother, Rock, and his new girlfriend, Paulina. The poor girl looked kind of freaked out about what had happened. I guess hitting the floor because of potential gunfire wasn't the norm for most parties, not that I'd been at a lot of parties for comparison. Still, I felt sorry for Rock. I wasn't sure how long she'd stick around after this.

I turned to Slash. He was staring into the backyard, his expression distant. I wanted to ask if he was okay, but a guest chose that exact moment to put on some dance music in an apparent effort to lighten things up. I couldn't even hear myself think, let alone carry on a conversation.

The furniture in our living room was pushed to the wall and people started dancing. I should have been relieved that the party was revived, but I wasn't. I was worried. Although Slash was as gracious, charming and attentive as always, his thoughts were clearly elsewhere.

At one point, he excused himself to speak with an additional detail of Secret Service agents who arrived to discuss the incident and review the security camera tapes from our alarm system. They disappeared upstairs with Slash, presumably to review in our home office. Twenty minutes later, the agents left and Slash rejoined the party.

I was dying to find out what they'd seen and discussed, but from the look on Slash's face, I had to wait until the party was over. I was even more curious about what he'd found on the ground and slipped into his pocket without showing the agents.

A part of me hoped all of this was just a couple of kids playing around. But it was wishful thinking, and I knew it.

Our life would never be that simple.

FIVE

Lexi

As soon as we closed the door on our last guest, I turned around and leaned back against the frame. "So, what did you see on the security camera?" I asked Slash.

He stacked several paper plates and a couple of plastic cups and carried them toward the kitchen. "A dark figure entering the yard from the side of the house and setting off the firecrackers. He, or she, already had them in a box."

"So, it was clearly thought out." I followed him into the kitchen, snagging two empty beer bottles on the way.

"Apparently. A single figure, well-prepared."

"That rules out kids or random teens, right?"

"I would say that's a fair assessment."

I dumped the bottles into the recycling bin and studied him, thinking about what that meant. "Well, that certainly raises a lot of questions, but foremost in my mind is what would be the point of the firecrackers? And is it aimed at getting my or your attention?"

"It doesn't matter. Someone put you, your parents and our close friends at risk, and that got my attention. Not in a good way."

I waited, but he didn't say anything further. Finally, I spread out my hands. "Slash, when were you going to tell me? Or were you *ever* going to tell me?"

He had one hell of a poker face, but I knew disingenuity when I saw it. And it pissed me off. "Tell you what?"

"What you picked up off the ground near the firecrackers."

He shot me an exasperated look. "I presume that to mean you didn't stay on the floor as I asked." He crossed his arms and regarded me.

"Of course not. I thought you knew me better than that."

He was totally busted, so he reached into his pocket and pulled out a folded piece of paper, then passed it over to me. I tried not to be mad he hadn't shown it to me right away, but I was.

I unfolded it and read aloud. "Daniel 9:5. Come home." I looked up. "What does it mean?"

"It's a message."

"From whom?"

He didn't answer, so I tugged on his arm. "Slash. What is it?"

He braced himself with one arm on the counter, looking like he didn't want to be having this conversation. I wished the same thing, but I needed to know what was going on.

"It's a Bible verse," he said.

"I *know* it's a Bible verse." I tried to keep the exasperation out of my voice and wasn't sure I succeeded. "Do you know what the verse says?"

I assumed he'd know, given his time as an altar boy in Sperlonga and the work he'd done for the Vatican before he came to the States. Given my nonexistent church experience, I would have to rely on Google if he didn't know.

He pushed his fingers through his hair and avoided

my gaze. "It says: 'We have sinned and done wrong. We have been wicked and rebelled; we have turned away from Your commands and laws.'"

"What the heck does that mean?" Nothing good, I presumed, based on the way he was still refusing to look at me.

"I don't know. My best guess it's connected to the letter I received a couple of weeks ago."

That letter had arrived by mail the day Slash and I returned from an assignment in the British Virgin Islands. It contained five words and no signature.

I KNOW WHO YOU ARE.

Slash had followed protocol and turned the letter over to the NSA. They'd tried unsuccessfully to track it down, but other than keeping a close eye on our mail, there wasn't much more they could do about it.

"Did you show the Secret Service agents?" I asked.

He remained silent.

I crossed my arms and stared at him, not letting him off the hook. "Slash, why didn't you show them?"

"Because they can't help me with this," he said quietly.

"What's *this*?" This conversation was not going the way I expected it should between two people who were engaged. Why was he being so evasive and ambiguous with his answers? This was me he was talking to—his fiancée—not some stranger.

"I'm going to find out," he said.

There it was again. He was answering my questions, but he'd told me exactly nothing. I pressed on, more determined. "Why would someone want you to come home? Or, more specifically, to Italy."

His expression turned thoughtful. "I don't know."

"So, are you?" I paused, disconcerted at the thought. "You know, going home?"

He took me by the shoulders, looking into my eyes. "I *am* home. I'm not going anywhere."

Relief swept through me, but also concern. Someone seemed intent on escalating this situation…whatever this situation was. Slash knew more than he was telling me, but he was either unwilling or unable to share. I felt conflicted between confronting him about it and understanding that, given the secrecy of his job in various intelligence agencies, as well as a former member of the Vatican intelligence *sodalitium pianum*—a group that didn't officially exist—he might not be able to tell me.

Ever.

I wasn't sure how that made me feel. Upset, yes, but also angry that someone would go to such lengths to torment him in this way. What could possibly be the point of dragging him back into his old life—a life he told me he'd left behind?

For now, there was little more I could do except support him. I just hoped we'd figure it out. Soon.

SIX

Slash

"YOUR FATHER DOESN'T like me."

Lexi raised her head from his bare chest, her hair brushing against his stomach. This was his favorite time of the day—just the two of them alone, in perfect sync, holding each other. She looked at him thoughtfully. He knew she was trying to choose the right words. Any number of wild things came out of Lexi's mouth on a daily basis, but she was careful and deliberate when it counted, one of the things he loved best about her.

"He likes you just fine. He's just not sure he likes you *with* me."

"Great." He blew out a breath, put a hand across his forehead.

Her hazel eyes filled with sympathy. "Give him time. He's still in the alpha-male-I'm-protecting-my-only-daughter mode."

"Things were progressing, and then those damn fireworks."

"Those weren't your fault."

"I know. But that hardly matters at this point."

She fell silent, returning her head to his chest. He liked that she didn't try to change his mind with false assurances. Still, he wasn't sure what he'd do about her father, so his mind added it to the part of his brain assigned to work on long-term problems. That was going to take time, finesse, and perhaps an entirely different approach.

He stroked a hand down her arm. Soft skin, a brilliant mind, and a kind heart. When he bent to kiss the top of her head, the sparkle of his Nonna's engagement ring caught his eye. Emotion tightened his throat. He'd asked her to be his wife and soon she'd be part of his family. As far as he was concerned, it couldn't happen fast enough.

"Slash, I'm still thinking about the firecrackers and the Bible verse," she suddenly said. "Those are just really odd ways of getting your attention. Almost theatrical. Do you know what I mean?"

He continued to stroke her hair. "I know what you mean."

"If it were someone from your past, like from the Vatican or something, wouldn't there be a specific protocol if they had to reach out to you?"

"There is, and this is not it." Messages were always sent through approved channels with specific passwords and clear instructions. Fireworks seen by dozens of people and a Bible verse left out in the open where anyone could have found it were not approved methods.

"So, who *would* approach you this way?" she probed. "Who would cite a Bible verse insinuating you're wicked and have lost your way, shaming you into returning to Italy?"

He dropped his hand from her hair and rested it on her shoulder. He'd considered many possibilities, but discarded them all. None of it made sense. He'd done many things in his life he wasn't proud of. But those were done under orders, to serve a higher power and bigger purpose. His work at the *sodalitium pianum*, the top-secret intelligence agency whose existence the Vatican still publicly denied, had hardened him, made him into the man he was today. He was a dangerous man with a past that, if exposed, could hurt a lot of people. A possible chess piece in a game he knew nothing about.

Yet.

But who would summon him like that, and for what purpose?

"It's someone who can't, or doesn't know how, to reach me through normal protocol," he finally answered. "Someone who thinks I'm susceptible to intimidation."

"Well then, clearly someone who doesn't know you well."

He smiled at the conviction in her voice. "Possibly."

She sat up, crossing her legs and pulling the sheet against her chest. He immediately missed the skin-to-skin connection. "Slash, do you trust me?" she asked.

He paused, wary of the question and yet intrigued as to why she asked. "With my life."

"Good. Because when I accepted your proposal, I signed up to work through the hard stuff. This letter, Bible verse, firecracker thing could turn into hard stuff. So, I want you to know you can count on me. That's part of the couple deal, right?"

Her sincerity gutted him. He didn't deserve this woman. "Right. Now, I want *you* to know something, *cara*." He gently cupped one of her cheeks in his hand. "I'm deeply and intentionally in love with you. You can rest assured I'm not going to let anything touch what we have. You—our life—it means everything to me."

He kept his voice calm, but his insides were churning. Their relationship was on the line and something, or *someone*, was coming for him. For what purpose, he didn't know.

She studied his eyes, looking for any double meanings or perhaps trying too hard to interpret what he meant by that. Thankfully, she didn't ask. He would never lie to her and they were veering dangerously close to topics he didn't want to discuss.

She furrowed her brow in an expression of disapproval, which meant this discussion wasn't over. Lexi was like that when she encountered a problem—deliberate and incredibly reluctant to let something go until she'd discovered all its secrets.

Mio Dio.

How would he keep her out of this? That part of his life was over, and he couldn't stand for her to know any of the details. He'd been a soldier of God, had always done as he was asked to serve the greater good, even when his actions left him riddled with guilt and shame. But that was before he had anything to lose. This life with Lexi—he'd earned it. So as far as he was concerned, the greater good could be damned from this point forward.

"I'll take care of everything," he said firmly. "I promise you that."

He didn't give her a chance to respond. Lowering his head, he softened his mouth against hers, sinking into the comfort that was her. After a moment of hesitation, she relaxed against him and wound her arms around his neck, threading her fingers through his hair.

For once in his life, he had something precious to protect. That meant only one thing.

He'd never let anyone touch what he had with her.

Ever.

SEVEN

Lexi

I DREAMT I was in Italy with Slash's grandmother, Nonna, chasing me around the kitchen table with a wooden spatula telling me I was leading her grandson down the path of perdition for living in sin with him. Church bells rang loudly, bringing both of us to a sudden halt at the table, staring at each other in surprise. Then, with a gasp, I woke and realized it was Slash's phone that had been ringing and he'd already picked it up and was talking.

I shook my head because I couldn't understand what he was saying, until I realized he was speaking in Italian. His voice had seemed happy at first, but now he sounded concerned. He spoke a bit longer and then hung up. He sat on the edge of the bed with his back toward me. I sat up and crawled across the bed, putting a hand on his shoulder.

"Slash, who was it?"

"Giorgio."

I'd met Slash's younger brother in Papua New Guinea a few months ago. He was handsome, like a younger version of Slash with wavy dark hair, olive complexion, a square jaw and buff physique.

"Is everything okay?"

"He's getting married."

"That's great." I paused, considering. "Right?"

"Right." He pushed a hand through his hair. "Except there's a problem."

I swung my feet over the side of the bed to sit beside him. He'd leaned forward, resting his elbows on his thighs, still holding the phone. "What kind of problem?"

"He's been denied his request to get married in the church."

"Why?"

"That's the thing, he doesn't know. He wants to get married in Sperlonga, but says the church has denied his marriage petition. Apparently the denial comes from Rome. He wants me to look into it."

I took a blanket from the foot of the bed and draped it around our shoulders. I could sense his distress and confusion on behalf of his younger brother. "Why would the church block his marriage? Can they do that?"

"Not legally." Slash straightened and slid an arm around my waist beneath the blanket, pulling me closer. I liked our close connection, the physical affection he showed me so easily. "You don't have to get married in the church, but most people do. The church can block anyone they want from getting married, and for a variety of reasons. The priest might decide they're not ready to make a lasting commitment. There might be legal or moral issues, too, but those are usually decided by the parish priest at the local level. Only a supreme authority in the church can forbid a marriage in the church. Apparently in this case, this directive came from Rome, and they didn't give Gio a reason for the denial. Even the parish priest is mystified."

"That's just weird."

"Exactly. Gio submitted a formal protest, but that

takes time. They want the wedding to happen soon. His fiancée, Vitoria, is pregnant."

"Oh. Maybe that's why they can't get married in the church?" I wondered how Slash's grandmother, Nonna, would feel about the child being conceived out of wedlock.

"No. That decision would be handled at the parish level. It would not involve Rome. A denial from Rome is extremely unusual."

I had to take his word on that, so I considered the implication here. "You're worried this is connected to the things that have been happening to you. The firecrackers, the note saying they know who you are, the Bible verse, and the instructions to come home."

"*Si*," he said quietly.

"So, what's happening to you, and now your family, must somehow be connected. What are you going to do?"

"I'm going to make some calls. It's almost five o'clock in the morning here, which makes it about eleven o'clock in Rome. I'll see if I can find out what's going on."

I shifted on the bed so that I faced him. His dark hair was tousled from sleep, but his brown eyes were alert and assessing. "Where will you start?"

"Where else?" He looked at me. "Father Armando."

EIGHT

Slash

LEXI WENT BACK to sleep, but he was done for the night, so he headed down to the kitchen with his phone in his hand. After drinking a glass of water, he picked up the phone and tapped on the number for Father Armando's office. It would be morning in Rome by now, and he hoped to catch the priest in the office. He didn't have any expectations he would be put through immediately. As the Archbishop of Genoa, as well as the Vatican's newest cardinal, Father Armando was an important and busy man. He was also the closest thing to a father Slash had ever had, as much as a Catholic priest could fill such a role.

As expected, a clerk answered the phone in Italian. Slash requested to speak with Father Armando, then provided his name and waited patiently as he was put on hold, imagining the priest's face in his mind.

Spiritual advisor, teacher and supporter, Father Armando had played many significant roles in his life, including the most important one. Father Armando had been the person to find him, abandoned as an infant, in a basket under the church organ. Their bond had started at that moment and had somehow held and strengthened over the years.

He leaned back in his chair and rolled his neck. It had

felt good to speak Italian. While he considered himself fully fluent in English, Italian was his first language, and the language of his heart. In addition to Italian and English, he also had a pretty good command of French, German and Latin. Not that anyone spoke Latin these days except during mass, but he considered it a useful language just the same.

The clerk returned within three minutes, and he was immediately put through to Father Armando.

"Nicolo, it's good to hear your voice." Slash held the phone away from his ear and smiled at the priest's booming voice. "It's been too long since we spoke, and yet, I pray for you every day."

Nicolo was the name Father Armando had given him as an infant. One of a long list of names Slash had gone by in his life, and one of the ones he loved best.

"I apologize for letting a few months slip past since we last spoke," Slash said. "It's been a busy time for me."

The priest laughed. "No worries, of course. You're an important man."

"Not nearly as important as you." In fact, more important than most people outside the Vatican knew. As a close friend of the pope, Father Armando was widely seen among many other priests and cardinals as the new, forward-thinking conscience of the Vatican. The father, however, would be appalled to be identified as such, considering himself a humble man, but Slash thought it true just the same.

Father Armando laughed. "I am but a servant of God. How are you?"

They exchanged pleasantries for a few more minutes, with Slash asking the priest about his new responsibilities and getting an earful about the numerous duties and complexities of being both an archbishop and a cardinal.

"And I thought I was busy," Slash finally said.

"You certainly are. Now, Nicolo, tell me: to what do I *really* owe the honor of this call? There's something on your mind."

"You do know me well. It's happy news, Father. I wanted to let you know I'm engaged."

"Engaged? Oh, I'm absolutely delighted. Congratulations. Is it with the young woman you were telling me about?"

"*Si.* Her name is Lexi."

"I look forward to meeting her. When's the wedding?"

"We haven't gotten that far yet, but I'd like you to be there. It would mean a lot to me. To both of us actually."

"It would be my honor and privilege to attend. I can't tell you how glad this news makes me. You deserve every moment of joy that comes your way, Nicolo."

"She makes me happy, Father. It's a rare person who can do that."

The father's laughter boomed through the phone, and Slash removed it from his ear again. "Forgive me for sounding cliché, but God works in mysterious ways. He *will* reward those who are faithful."

Slash slipped the gold cross from beneath his shirt and kissed it. "Thank you."

"When do you plan on visiting Italy again?" the priest asked. "Will I get to meet her soon?"

He hadn't realized how much he wanted that to happen until this moment. "We haven't planned a trip in the immediate future, but as you know, things often change. However, there's an additional reason I called." Slash caught him up quickly on the situation with Giorgio.

"That's quite unusual," Father Armando said after he'd finished. "What was the reason offered?"

"That's the strange part. There was no reasoning for the denial. Just that it came from Rome. Gio has filed a petition, and while I know it's not your jurisdiction, I wondered if you might be able to find out what's going on."

"Of course. I shall make it a priority."

"Thank you, Father. I'd greatly appreciate it."

The priest's voice lowered and softened with affection. "For you, my son, anything."

NINE

Lexi

SINCE SLASH WASN'T there when I got home from work, I started dinner. Mondays were my nights to cook anyway, so I pulled out my phone, checked my dinner spreadsheet—the one I always completed Sunday night with attached recipes and exact nutritional value. Slash preferred to eat healthy meals, but since I loved sweets, we'd compromised by always having dessert with dinner. Tonight, the menu called for grilled salmon, asparagus and brown rice. For desert, it was chocolate ice cream with rainbow sprinkles. I fixed myself a small bowl of the ice cream to ensure it would complement the rest of the meal.

After I licked the bowl clean, I decided it would.

I marinated the salmon and let it sit a bit while I started the rice. We were low on rice, so I took the grocery list off the refrigerator to jot it down, when I realized Slash had ordered the grocery list all wrong. I was fixing it when he walked in the door.

He dropped his briefcase and set a package on the table by the door before walking into the kitchen and kissing the back of my head. "How was your day, *cara*?"

I turned around, pencil still in my hand. "Not bad. We completed two penetration testings, which convinced clients they needed to hire us, and I finished up an article on fileless attacks for *Cybersecurity This Week*. The article should be out in two months."

"Sounds fascinating, and I want to hear all about it at dinner." He peered over my shoulder at the grocery list. "What are you doing?"

"I'm fixing the grocery list."

"What's wrong with it?"

"It's not in the same order of where the items are shelved in the grocery store. Trust me, our shopping time will be shortened by at least seventeen percent if we list the items by their placement in the store."

He opened his mouth to say something, then shut it. Instead he pressed me against the counter, giving me a long, lingering kiss.

When he lifted his mouth from mine, I blinked at him a bit dazed. "Wow. What was that for? Grocery lists don't usually inspire this much affection. Although, if it's a turn-on for you, I can incorporate it into our everyday routine." I grabbed the lapels of his black sports coat and pulled him in for another kiss.

After a moment, he rested a hand on the side of my right cheek, the hard planes of his face softening. "I love you, *cara*. You know that, right?"

I knew that, but something in the way he said that set off an inner alarm. I'm not the most intuitive of people in regards to emotions, but I'd come to know Slash fairly well. Something was off, although my brain was still trying to figure out what.

I studied him carefully. "Slash, is something wrong?"

He released me, took a step back. "There's something I want to show you." Retrieving the package he'd set on the table, he brought it to the counter. The box was already open. Reaching in, he pulled out a small wooden statue and held it up. "Have you ever seen anything like this before?"

It was a figure of a man with crossed arms standing on a small wooden base. He wore a headdress and a tunic, and had several nails or spikes stuck into his body at different angles. The statue both fascinated and scared me.

"What is it?" I asked.

"It's a *nkondi* idol. Folklore holds that the *nkondi* are the most powerful of the *nkisi* spirits—spirits which the people of the Congo believed could seek out evil people and destroy them."

"Where did you get it?"

"It came in the mail today. Addressed to you."

"Me?" That made absolutely no sense. Surely it was a mistake. "Who sent me a statue like that?"

"There was no return address."

I took a closer look at it, but I was one-hundred percent sure I'd never seen anything like it. I finally lifted my gaze to meet his. "Why would someone send me a statue from the Congo? And, following that train of thought, how did you get it if it was addressed to me?"

"As part of our new security, our mail is being diverted through a security center and vetted before being sent on to us. It's still being delivered to our house, but with a safety stop first. Security passed this package on to me this afternoon at the NSA after it had been flagged for not having a return address."

"Oh." I had to digest that for a minute. It was weird to think there were agents pawing through my mail. Even if I hardly received anything by snail mail these days, it was still disconcerting that if I ordered something online, secret service agents would review it before I got my hands on it. That kind of creeped me out. "So, we don't know who sent it?"

"No. There was no return address on the box. But the postmark was Rome."

"I don't get it." I racked my brain, but nothing came up. "Do you?"

He avoided eye contact with me, putting the statue back in his briefcase. "*Si*. I know."

"So, what is it?" Why was he avoiding me like this? I put my hand on his arm. "Slash, what does it mean?"

"It means I'm going to Rome."

"*What?*" I took a step back. He hadn't included me in the decision process, which couldn't be a good sign. I needed him to talk to me, and he was closing himself off. "Why?"

"Something's going down, *cara*, and I need to be there."

"You said you could handle it from here."

"I thought I could. But apparently, I'm going to need to get a bit closer."

"What exactly does the statue represent? Slash, you need to talk to me." Fierce, protective anger rose inside me. I wanted to help, to stand with him against whoever was putting that look on his face, but right now, it seemed like he wanted to be anywhere except in our kitchen with me.

He sighed. "The statue is said to contain the *nkondi*, spirits who root out evil and enforce an oath or a promise made. Legend says the nails activate the spirits inside the statue. Those nails have been recently added." He pulled one out and held it up. He was right. The nail was new and mostly unblemished.

I looked between the nail and him. "An oath? Why do you know so much about this? What does it symbolize?"

He placed his hands on my shoulders, looked me in the eye. "You are going to have to have faith in me, *cara*. I don't like that your name was on the package. I'm going to go to Rome for a short time to check things out and have a few conversations."

What? He was going to Rome after he'd told me he wasn't? I didn't understand what was going on. I'd thought we were past all this. He'd always been respectful, as had I, that we both had potentially dangerous jobs and we'd worked through our issues on that front, or at least I'd thought so. But now—without warning or discussion—he was shutting me out. Something deeper was going on, something ominous, and he wasn't sharing. I wanted to be calm and logical in my response, but the lack of trust hurt. A lot.

Still, my brain raced to find the right words to argue effectively. "You do realize that by going to Rome, you'll be doing exactly what they want—whoever *they* is. You'll be walking right into whatever trap or scenario they've created for you."

He calmly opened the refrigerator and took out a chilled bottle of water. Twisting off the top, he took a long drink. "I realize that and I will not go in blind. But they are escalating this. If I don't go now, it's only a matter of time before they do something else to get my attention. I'm not waiting until that happens."

"You're doing this to protect me." The expression on his face proved it clear as day.

"No. I'm doing this to protect *us*."

"This is crazy." I threw up my hands, desperation setting in. "So, you've already decided to go?"

He set the bottle on the counter and took two steps toward me. "The statue decided it for me. I'm going to Rome to find out what's going on. That's all."

My stomach churned uncomfortably as I tried to get him to see clearly. "You're not thinking logically. How can you be sure I'm even in danger? Firecrackers, statues and notes. Those are hardly death-defying. Can't you see? They're manipulating you—escalating things to get you to do what *they* want."

"I know." His voice remained calm, agitating me even more. "I'll be careful, but I've got to take care of it. Trust me, okay?"

Every word heightened my anxiety. Why hadn't he discussed this with me before making his decision? We were a team and now, suddenly...we weren't. But I wasn't giving in so easy. "What about your work at IAD?"

"As far as they are concerned, I'm taking a short vacation to resolve a family matter. Charlie will manage things for me while I'm gone."

"How can they just agree to that? What about your security detail? Are they going with you, too?"

"Not this time. The department is actually facing severe budget cuts. We may even lose our constant tails as a result of it. They're discussing the possibility of relying solely on this for most of us." He held up his left wrist where a tracker had been implanted. It was both a GPS and medical alert so the people who were watching it could monitor his every heartbeat. Although he'd never acknowledge it, I also knew it could provide an electric shock that would stop his heart if he fell into the wrong hands. That's how important he was. His knowledge of the architecture of America's most sensitive networks, as well as his extensive insight to a great deal of US cyber vulnerabilities, made him a priceless commodity to American national security. The fact that he might be walking straight into danger despite that upset me more than I cared to admit.

"*Cara*, I'm going to be fine. *Everything* is going to be fine."

I tried to swallow, but my mouth was dry. Why wasn't he listening to me? He always listened to me.

"The embassy in Rome has already been notified of my arrival," he continued. "I'll have any resources I need through them. It will be okay."

But it wasn't okay, and yet, it was a done deal. I could see it in his eyes, in the hard set of his jaw. He'd informed his work, the embassy and now me. He wouldn't back down no matter what I said.

I closed my eyes. I wanted to believe this conversation wasn't taking place, but it was. "When do you leave?"

He pulled me close, rested his cheek against mine. "Tomorrow afternoon, but I'll be back before you have time to miss me."

He didn't know how wrong he'd be.

TEN

Slash

WHAT THE HELL am I doing?

He shoved his hand through his hair, looking at the empty passenger seats on the jet he'd chartered. He'd violated a sacred relationship rule. He hadn't accepted any consultation or input from Lexi before he made his decision to return to Rome. They hadn't come to a mutual agreement, nor had they engaged in a give-and-take discussion. He'd simply dictated to her what he was going to do and left.

It hadn't been his finest moment. But it had to be done for her sake.

As soon as he'd seen the statue from the Congo addressed to her, he'd run a series of comparative risk analyses, exhaustively examined every potential outcome, every tradeoff he'd have to make by returning to Rome, and considered the danger to Lexi, to himself and to their relationship. In the end, he had to select the option that reduced the most risk. That meant he had to go to Rome alone and shut her out temporarily. It was far safer than her discovering what he'd done in the Congo. She didn't understand how he'd come to this decision, and that it was truly based in logic. But seeing the hurt look on her face hadn't set well with him. Still, he could manage the problem if he handled it right. He only had to keep his head in the game and approach this situation like all others—analytically and carefully. He couldn't even contemplate the possibility of failing to solve it or what it might mean to their relationship.

He looked around the plane, thinking it was strange to be traveling without her. At this moment, he was truly alone. He hadn't felt that way for some time, not since he'd met Lexi. Now that he'd shut her out and surrounded himself with his habitual cloak of isolation, he felt the loneliness engulf him. At one time, he'd accepted those feelings. Now they choked him.

He tugged at the collar of his shirt even though he wore no tie and had unbuttoned the top two buttons of his dress shirt.

The flight to Rome seemed to be taking longer than usual, although it was exactly the same route he always took. He was restless, unable to rest, concentrate on work, or relax. He paced the aisle, drank too many cups of coffee, and thought of Lexi constantly.

He'd told her he'd be careful, and he meant it. He'd gone from a man with nothing to lose to a man who would do *anything* to protect the life he'd built. But this was about her. It had become *all* about her. Whoever had summoned him had marked her. That made him not only pissed, but extremely dangerous.

He settled into the heavily upholstered seat, his gaze drifting out the window to the dark sky. He couldn't figure out who was summoning him or why. But the reference to the *nkondi* and the Congo made it clear that the summons came from high up. Someone who knew things that were closely guarded at the top echelon of the Vatican.

There were plenty of people who knew of his particular skills, but only a few knew what he'd done in the Congo. Most of his colleagues in the *sodalitium pianum* had burned out, washed out or simply checked out. A few had become addicted to the danger, adrenaline, and excitement of the hunt. When it ended, they had no idea how to fit back into society again. He'd been lucky to avoid that by having other talents to fall back on, and by having someone shepherd him in another direction.

Loneliness had become a way of life for most of them, himself included. It was safer and a lot less complicated that way. He'd been lonely for a long time, although never without company if he'd wanted it. Yet he couldn't escape the irony that while he'd traveled all over the world, he'd never really had a home of his own or anyone waiting for him.

Until Lexi.

Until now.

He looked up as the flight attendant asked if she could bring him a drink. His gaze settled on the dazzling glass credenza where an impressive array of alcohol sparkled in crystal decanters. He shook his head, declining the offer. He needed to keep his wits about him, figure out what he could before he landed in Rome. It all came back to the Vatican. Who'd send such a threatening summons, and why? This was a deliberate, provocative and systematic campaign to bring him to Rome. He knew that, understood that, and yet he had no choice but to enter the game. He had too much at stake to do anything else.

He'd moved the first chess piece on the board, although he had no intention of playing by anyone else's rules. Besides, he had a few moves of his own. The answers were out there, and he was confident he would get them.

Soon.

Slash

As soon as he landed and cleared customs, Slash picked up his rental car and made a call.

"Hallo?" The voice was cautious and accented.

"Tito? It's me." Slash spoke in German, Tito's native tongue.

"Nico?"

"*Si.*"

"You're home." Tito's voice was delighted. "It's been a while."

"It has. Since I happen to be in town, are you available for lunch?"

"It's my day off. Where do you want to meet?"

"*Il Bacaro?*" Slash suggested. They'd eaten there before. It was a quiet restaurant, not overly packed with tourists, and had decent food. His stomach grumbled thinking about it, as he'd eaten nothing on the flight.

"I can be there in one hour. See you soon, my friend."

"*Ciao.*" Slash punched off his phone, leaving it on the dashboard.

For a moment, he thought about what Tito had said. *You're home.*

Was he? It was easy to slide back into his old life, like slipping into a comfortable pair of jeans. As the familiar scenery flashed by and the voice on the radio chatted in his native language, the duality of his life hit him. Even though his heart now belonged in America with the woman he loved, it was impossible to wipe clean the slate that had once been his life here in Italy.

Italy was the country where he'd been born, where many members of his family still lived, and where he'd meet the young, widowed mother who would welcome a scared little boy with open arms, raising him along with the son she already had and the one she would have after she remarried. But it was more than that. He knew Italy, and Italy knew him. He fit seamlessly into the country, the landscape. He spoke the language, knew the nuances of the culture, and completely blended in when he walked down the street and ordered a glass of wine or a gelato. There was no effort required, no thinking. He was simply Italian.

It wasn't always that easy for him in the US Moving and assimilating into a new country had been a personal challenge on a number of fronts. Part of him had been thankful for the opportunity. Part of him struggled to fit in. Despite his affinity for languages, the English language had tripped him up on more than one occasion. Some of the cultural references and practices baffled him. Doggy bags in restaurants. Tailgate parties (a barbecue on the back of a truck bed?). No metric system. A somewhat puritan approach to the appreciation of the human body. Ice in every drink.

His first experience with *that* had scarred him. Shortly after he arrived in the US, he'd ordered coffee at a café. They asked him if he wanted it hot or iced. He couldn't even imagine the look of horror that had been on his face. What the hell kind of people drank iced coffee?

He was completely charmed by other aspects of America, though. Americans had a reputation abroad for smiling and laughing a lot. He found that to be an accurate assessment. Americans seemed to deeply appreciate humor, even at their own expense. More importantly, they'd welcomed him when he needed a place to go, and he'd found a home there.

It'd been Lexi who'd told him that home wasn't a

house—not even the brand-new house he'd built for her. He now understood that home wasn't a country either. Home was where your heart belonged, where the people you loved anchored you. Home was where you could be your true self with people who loved you just as you were. That was still a hard concept for him to swallow. There were parts of him, his past, he never wanted known, especially to those he loved. He knew, better than most, that people could hurt or abandon those they loved for reasons that weren't always clearly defined.

He pushed that thinking away for the time being. It was time to prepare himself for the game.

The only problem was, first he had to figure out what game they were playing.

ELEVEN

Lexi

IT WAS HARD to concentrate at work when my mind was on overdrive worrying what was happening with Slash. He'd texted to let me know he'd arrived safely in Rome, but otherwise, I hadn't heard another word. He needed to remain focused, but I didn't like how any of this was playing out. He'd gone to Rome largely out of concern for me, and now he was shutting me out in a misguided attempt to protect me.

It ticked me off.

If he thought I was going to sit at home and play video games while he walked into potential danger, then he hadn't learned enough about me yet. I was going to help him, even if he didn't want it. He wasn't going to go this alone. I needed only to organize my plan of attack. Luckily, I had a light day of work, because I knew exactly where I wanted to start.

The package with the *nkondi* statue.

That package most certainly held clues I needed to track down. At this point, all I had was the label with the shipping number and my home address. That meant a hack on Europin Shipping would be in order.

Taking special precautions, I started the hack. Unfortunately, after conducting a thorough investigation of Europin's defenses, I determined they had recently implemented top-of-the line cybersecurity measures. A hack was possible, but would take triple the time I'd expected.

I'd have to revise my approach in the name of expediency. I jotted down notes and calculations on a pad of paper on my desk. Slash said the postmark had been from Rome, therefore, one certainty regarding the package was that it had been sent from one of three Europin locations there. The fact that it came from Rome meant that although there was no sender listed, there would have to have been a customs form, and by extension, a name and payment method attached in case of a claim.

I briefly toyed with hacking into the US Customs' site to get the information, but that, too, meant a lengthy hack. I rubbed my temples with my fingertips. There had to be a faster way in.

Time to get myself some more coffee. On the way to the kitchen, it occurred to me that if the package had been declared lost, the shipper would be required to notify both the sender and the shipper's insurance company to handle the claim. That meant if I could find out who the shipper's insurance company was, I could penetrate that database and possibly come up with the information I needed.

But first I had to find which company was the shipper's insurer. After another hour of digging around I discovered Carriers' Assurance International, or CAI for short, often worked with Europin. To confirm, I called CAI's local office.

"Hi," I said. "I'm following up on a lost package insured by CAI. Can you let me know the process for filing a claim and which forms I need to fill out?"

"Sure." The guy had a nice, cheerful voice. "You can

get the forms online." He directed me to a URL where all the pertinent forms and information were located.

I spent the afternoon hacking into CAI's systems but never made it all the way into the client database. I didn't have to since I was able to penetrate their email system. It was enough to confirm that CAI was handling the insurance for my package, after I cross—referenced my shipping number.

My next step was to get the two companies to share information about who'd actually shipped the package to me so I could intercept it. I took the claim form and filled it out with the shipping number and my address, declaring it was never delivered. Thankfully I wasn't prompted to provide the shipper's information, which was logical since I assumed they already had information linked to the shipping number.

Unfortunately that was all I could do for the day, given the six-hour time difference between Rome and Washington. No one would read my claim until the morning. Right now everything was closed up and people were sleeping in Italy.

I drove home from work, trying not to feel sad that Slash wouldn't be there. When I got to the house, I made myself a bowl of Cheerios and ate it in front of the computer. It didn't cheer me up. I gamed a bit, but my heart wasn't in it. Feeling like I needed a change of pace, I pulled on a pair of shorts and worked out, running three miles on the treadmill and practicing my Krav Maga self-defense moves until sweat dripped down my face.

After a while, I sat on the mat in the middle of the room, drinking water and feeling sorry for myself. I hated every minute of being alone. How had this happened to me—the girl who used to prefer solitude? I wondered if Slash had felt this way when I'd gone to the British Virgin Islands and he'd been left alone in this big house.

The doorbell rang and I checked my phone app to see who was there. There was only one person I knew who was that short and would wear that particular shade of neon yellow. I ran down the stairs, disengaged the security alarm and opened the door.

"Basia, what are you doing here at this hour?"

"It's nine o'clock." She stepped into the house, shaking her short, dark bob and giving me a once-over. "OMG. Were you working out?"

I felt mildly offended. "Don't look so shocked."

"Are you kidding me?" My best friend pursed her lips and gave me the same affectionate, but slightly bewildered look she'd been giving me since our days as roommates at Georgetown.

I crossed my arms defensively against my chest. "Well, I had to do something."

She kept looking at me, so a confession came tumbling out. "I miss Slash."

"Oh, honey." Basia came in, closed the door behind her. "Finn told me that Slash took off for Rome yesterday. I figured you could use some girl time, but I also wanted to share some good news with you." She held up a bottle of wine.

Good news could mean anything to Basia. It could mean she'd found a fantastic pair of shoes on sale, the neighborhood café was serving triple espresso shot soy lattes or she'd got a raise. It was hard to anticipate. "What kind of good news?"

She hopped on her feet in excitement. "I've been

dying to tell you. Xavier and I found a house. We put an offer on it, and this afternoon, it was accepted."

That was pretty exciting news. "Really? Congratulations."

"Thanks. Now ask me where the house is located."

"Where's it located?"

"Three blocks from here." She clutched my arm and gave a little squeal. "We can walk to each other's house. Isn't that awesome?"

Wait, what? She and Xavier bought a home near ours?

"Your house is in *our* neighborhood?" I asked.

"Yes." She beamed. "Xavier and I love this area so much, and we had the same issues you and Slash have with commuting. Now we're neighbors."

I wasn't sure how I felt about that. On the one hand, I adored Basia and often needed her advice on things ranging from languages (of which she spoke several), to relationships to fashion. On the other hand, I wasn't sure what it meant in terms of how many times a month/week/ day/hour she'd be at my house. I already saw her every day at work. Now I'd have to run some calculations on a spreadsheet to determine how I should feel. For now, I decided to express cautious optimism.

"That's definitely exciting, Basia."

She hugged me. "I'm totally stoked. It's a brand-new chapter in our lives, right?"

"Right." After I reset the alarm, we went into the kitchen. I removed the cork and poured the wine while Basia grabbed some crackers and a block of cheese. We took everything into the living room and sat on the black leather couch.

"Here's to being practically roommates again." Basia

lifted her wineglass. "Isn't it funny how life comes full circle?"

It *was* interesting and perhaps statistically significant that we had remained in such close proximity over the past several years. I raised my glass and offered a toast. "Here's to being neighbors."

We sipped our wine before Basia shifted on the couch, pulling her legs up beneath her. "Do you want to talk? Can you tell me why Slash dashed off so unexpectedly to Italy? Did it have anything to do with the fireworks at the party?"

"Partially." I gave her a quick rundown of the entire situation, including my hack into the shipping company and my hopes I could trace the package back to the sender in Rome.

Her eyes widened. "Do you still have the statue? Can I see it?"

"I do." I retrieved it from the box Slash had left on our entry table, then handed it to Basia who cradled it gingerly.

"Wow. That's crazy scary. Why are there all these nails stuck in it?"

I gave her the rundown on the evil spirits and oath enforcement thing. She set it down carefully on the coffee table. "What does a statue from the Congo have to do with Italy and Slash?"

"I have no idea."

She picked up her wineglass and took a sip while studying the statue. "But he obviously did. That statue worried him enough to return to Rome."

"I know. Do you think that it's symbolic of something?"

"Possibly. It's an angle to explore. Has Slash ever been to the Congo?"

"I don't know." I stopped, looked at her in surprise. "Wait. Are you encouraging me to dig into this?"

She waved a hand. "Of course I'm encouraging you. Do I know you or do I know you? Why suggest prudence or caution when I know you'll never act that way? So, I might as well offer to help."

I felt a lump in my throat. There was family. There were friends, and there were friends who became family. Basia was my family in that way. "If I'm successful in tracking down the sender of the package, I may need your help translating documents or emails from Italian."

"Well, I'm your girl. Italian happens to be one of my favorite languages, after French."

"Thanks, Basia." Emotion hit me again. "You're the best friend ever."

"And now I'm your neighbor." She held up her wineglass, smiling. "So, let the fun begin."

TWELVE

Slash

SOMEONE BRUSHED UP against him as he walked into the restaurant, and before he realized what he was doing, Slash pivoted slightly to his right, instinctively slipping his hand beneath his jacket for a gun he didn't have.

"*Mi scusi.*" A middle-aged man threw the phrase over his shoulder as he herded two young girls, probably twins, into the restaurant where he joined a brown-haired woman who was already seated at a table.

He slowly removed his hand from beneath his jacket and forced himself to relax. Lack of sleep and food were putting him on edge. He needed to settle down, refuel and refocus. Jumping at shadows was not helpful. Situational awareness was key, and his thoughts were distracting him far too much lately.

He'd arrived at the restaurant before Tito, so he requested a table in the back of the room. He took a seat facing all exits so he could see who was coming and going, and who might be paying undue attention to him.

Hot, he removed his sports coat, revealing a white shirt with no shoulder holster. If there had been a problem at the restaurant entrance, he wouldn't have solved it with a gun. He felt naked without it, but he had plenty of weapons stashed in various places around town and could easily get to them, as needed. Right now, he was on an information-gathering assignment only.

He ordered a coffee and a glass of *Gattinara*, a full-blooded red wine, dry and crisp as hell. The coffee came before the wine and the first sip relaxed him immediately.

Tito arrived less than five minutes later. He was tall, with his brown hair close to his scalp in a military cut. Dressed casually in a pair of khaki shorts, a green T-shirt and sandals. He spotted Slash and strode over for a hug and a handshake.

"Good to see you, Nico. What brings you to our side of the world?" He spoke in Italian as a courtesy, but he answered him in Tito's native German. It was safer in the unlikely event of eavesdropping, but it also gave the impression they were tourists. Blending in was always advantageous.

"Figured it had been too long since we had a drink together," he said.

Tito laughed. "Yah, it really has."

They sat and he waved over the waitress to take Tito's order. Tito ordered a glass of white wine and they perused their menus. When the waitress returned with the wine, Tito ordered the *ravioli di capesante*, a thick ravioli made with scallops, and a lettuce pesto. Slash chose the *baccalà*, a salt cod, and the *fiori di zucca*, zucchini flowers. When they were left alone, Tito leaned forward, regarding his friend across the table.

"So, what brings you to Italy, old friend?"

"Personal business." Slash sipped his wine, enjoying the bold taste. "So, how's work?"

Tito Blickensdefer was a Swiss citizen, a good friend and a member of the Swiss Guard, the personal bodyguards of the pope. As a guard, Tito was stationed at the Vatican and sometimes did the changing-of-the-guard thing with high-stepping and fanfare every hour on the hour. However, what many people *didn't* know was that the Swiss Guard also traveled with the pope in plain clothes to protect him from security threats. While they'd been trained for centuries to use a *halberd*—a combination of pike, ax and spear—the guardsmen were also experts at hand-to-hand combat and could adeptly use machine guns and Sig Sauer 9mm pistols. Tito was a regular on the pope's security detail.

Tito picked up his glass of wine and swirled the contents around. "My time is, unfortunately, limited. I turn thirty next month."

Swiss Guards could be no more than thirty years of age, so Tito would have to head home unless he decided to stay and find work in Italy.

Slash smiled and lifted his glass. "Then I wish you a Happy Birthday early. Many good returns."

"It's been a ride." Tito clinked their glasses together. "Now I'm trying to decide what else to do with my life. Being a Swiss Guard is all I've ever known."

"What are your options?"

"Police, military intelligence, counterintelligence or maybe surveillance. I need to give it some more thought."

"You'd be good at any of those. It's a new chapter in your life."

"It really is."

They talked a bit more about Tito's discharge from the Swiss Guard until the waitress brought their food.

Tito leaned forward, wagging a piece of ravioli on his fork. "So, how's our girl?"

"*Our* girl?"

"You still together with Lexi, Nico? Because if not, I may have to make a trip to America and look her up."

Slash smiled easily, but he was pretty sure the humor didn't reach his eyes. "We're engaged."

Tito's eyes widened, his mouth opening in an exaggerated circle. "You? Engaged? You're joking."

Slash laughed at his expression. "Come on. You can't be that surprised."

"I can and I am. But not because I don't think you make a good match. It's because *you* are settling down. I never saw you as a family man."

"I never saw myself as that, either. But I asked her about a month ago."

"And she was crazy enough to say yes? I thought she was smarter than that."

"Apparently she had a moment of lapsed judgement of which I took full advantage." He smiled, remembering how his proposal had gone awry. She'd stuck with him anyway and agreed to be his wife. It had been best day of his life.

"Well, then, hearty congratulations are in order." Tito raised his glass. "To the family man. We may need more alcohol."

"We may." Slash smiled as he touched his glass to Tito's.

After a few minutes, Tito sat back in his chair and studied him. "So, what personal business could take you away from your beguiling fiancée?"

"The troublesome kind."

Tito didn't look surprised at that revelation. "Figured as much. Wherever there's trouble, you can be found. How can I help?"

It meant a lot to him that Tito always had his back and

could be counted on for help. There were just a handful of people in his life he could trust for that. "You could start by letting me know how things are going at the Vatican."

"Well, it's interesting that you ask, and even more intriguing that you show up at this exact moment." Tito leaned forward, studying Slash and lowering his voice. "Things seem tense lately. There's been an unusual amount of activity."

"What kind of activity?"

"Nothing specific. A lot of cardinals coming and going. Secretive meetings at odd hours. Something is going on...and then you show up. I don't see that as a coincidence."

"It's not. Do you know what's going on?"

"No. But I suspect it's something significant."

A lot of cardinals coming and going could signal either the pope was orchestrating something secretly or someone was plotting against the pope. Either way, it was unsettling. He'd likely been summoned to help one side or the other, so the play was to determine which way it would go. He could be a threat to many because he knew things. But he could also be used to harm others. Dozens of possibilities. Until someone played the hand that involved him, he'd have to sit tight.

"It's enough that you've confirmed this for me." Slash lifted his wineglass. "By the way, do you happen to know where Rinaldo Pacini retired?"

Tito stared at him. "Pacini? You're thinking about contacting him?"

Slash swirled the wine, then took a sip. Rinaldo Pacini had ruled the *sodalitium pianum* with an iron fist the entire time Slash had worked there, until the organization had been disbanded shortly after the Congo incident. "I'm thinking about it."

Tito shook his head in disbelief. "Good luck with that. He changed his name, changed his life. You'll have a hard time finding him."

"I won't." It wasn't bragging, it was the truth. The only question was how long would it take him, and whether Pacini knew, or would share, anything useful.

"You think what's going on is connected?" Tito asked.

"It's possible."

"Rumor is he's in Terni, but that could be old news or no news at all."

"Terni is as good a place to start as any." It sat about 104 kilometers northeast of Rome, nestled between two rivers. Once a bustling Roman city, it was now known for its innovative chemical and technological start-ups.

"To be honest, I'm not surprised you've shown up," Tito continued. "When things start to get hot, you are always in the middle of it."

"Apparently, that's my fate in life."

"Well, we all have our destiny." Tito fiddled with his fork. "I'm here to help as needed."

"*Danke*, my friend. I appreciate that, and it goes both ways. If you can't find a job you like, let me know. I have some connections that could be useful."

"Thanks, Nico. It's good to know."

They spent the rest of the meal chatting about friendly topics. Slash hadn't spoken German for a while, and it felt good to use it talking with one of the few friends he had. Already a plan was forming in his head. He wanted to execute it and get home as quickly as possible.

He insisted on paying for the meal. When they stood, Tito thanked him and shook his hand one more time.

"I'm relieved you're here, Nico. I've got a bad feeling about what's going on. Something feels off."

"Agreed. Stand by, old friend. I'm going to get to the bottom of it."

Tito nodded, but a shadow of concern crossed his face. "I've no doubt about that. You're definitely the man for the job, whatever that job may be."

THIRTEEN

Slash

THE DRIVE FROM Rome to Genoa was about four and a half hours in ideal conditions. He wanted to call Lexi, but what could he tell her? She'd want to know what was happening, and he had nothing substantial to report other than a confirmation from Tito that something mysterious was happening at the Vatican. He wondered what she would think of that.

How could he shield Lexi from his past without jeopardizing her trust? Gripping the steering wheel tightly, he considered the three principal issues.

Will she still love me the same way if she knows the things I've done?

Will I lose her respect if I continue to try to hide my past from her?

If I keep secrets, does that mean I am admitting I don't trust her?

He rolled his neck. That last question was moot. He trusted Lexi implicitly. It was himself he didn't trust.

Outside of Florence, traffic crawled past a serious accident. A small car lay partially crushed under a large truck that had spilled construction materials across several lanes of traffic. As he passed the scene, he noted them loading an injured woman on a wheeled stretcher into an ambulance.

So, instead of calling Lexi, he turned on the music and rolled down the window, enjoying the breeze and the last couple hours of the drive. The weather was hot, but it didn't bother him as much as he expected. His body adapted quickly, familiar with the heat and the rhythms of his birth country. Regardless, as soon as he arrived at the church in Genoa, he was relieved to walk into the cool dimness of the administrative offices, located behind the church.

A young priest rose from behind a desk when he entered.

"*Buon pomeriggio*," Slash said. "I'm here to see Father Emilio Armando."

"I'm sorry. Do you have an appointment?"

"I do not. I'm hoping the cardinal will be able to fit me in."

"The cardinal is currently unavailable. He's a busy man."

"I'm sure he is. I'm only requesting that you let him know I'm here. He will either see me or not."

The priest looked doubtful, but asked for Slash's name and then disappeared down a corridor. Slash removed his sunglasses and hooked them on the front of his shirt as he sat in one of the chairs. About two minutes later the priest came back.

He looked at Slash with undisguised curiosity. "His Eminence will see you at once. Please follow me."

"Thank you, Father."

As they headed toward Father Armando's office, an older woman, dressed in a crisp suit of navy blue, her brown hair pulled back in a tight bun, exited his office. She kissed the priest on each cheek and then left, making brief eye contact with Slash as he passed. Slash dipped his head at her, noting her eyes were puffy and red. She'd been crying.

Damn, he'd interrupted something.

Father Armando already stood in the hallway, dressed in an ordinary black cassock and collar. He waved Slash in. His black hair held more gray than last time, but his eyes were filled with happiness and obvious affection.

I wonder what changes he sees in me.

Before Slash could say a word of greeting, the father embraced him with open arms. The young priest who accompanied him quietly closed the door behind them when they stepped into the father's office.

"Nicolo, what a surprise to see you." Father Armando framed Slash's face between his hands and studied him for a long moment, and then gave a satisfied nod before kissing him on both cheeks. "You look well. Why didn't you tell me you were coming?"

"I'm sorry. I've interrupted something."

"It's okay. We were wrapping things up. Please, sit down. To what do I owe this honor? Did you just get in?"

Slash sat as requested and Father Armando took the chair across from him. "I did. I'm sorry I didn't give you advance notice of my arrival. This trip was rather unexpected."

"I see. Is this about Giorgio?"

"Yes…and no."

Seemingly intrigued by that comment, the priest leaned forward. "Well, I've been digging to see if I can figure out what is behind the denial of his marriage request, but found nothing yet. It's highly unusual. I still have more threads to pull, so I will get answers for you."

"I understand, and appreciate your effort. I actually wondered if you wouldn't mind taking a stroll in the church garden. I'd appreciate the opportunity to see how it's grown since the last time I was here."

Father Armando looked at Slash for a long, puzzled moment and then rose. "Of course, I'd be delighted to show you the garden. I've nurtured the most splendid purple wisteria. You will be amazed at the vividness of the color. Come, my son, let us walk."

Father Armando grabbed a Nationals baseball cap from the bookshelf—one Slash had given him—then swept out his hand to indicate Slash should go first. The father closed the door behind them and they walked down the cool, dark corridor until they came to a door. They stepped into the bright sunlight, blinking rapidly. He slipped on his sunglasses while Father Armando jammed the cap on his head to shade his head and face.

"This way," he said.

Slash followed without comment. When they reached the purple wisteria, he lifted a bloom to his nose and noted the sweet fragrance.

"Impressive," he said, releasing the flower. "You've developed quite the green thumb."

"Thank you. I believe that nurturing the environment is a noble endeavor. If you'd like, we can sit on the bench and enjoy the view while you tell me why you really came. I trust there's a reason we cannot speak candidly in my office."

"*Si.* I'm afraid someone may be listening in on your conversations, Father."

Father Armando stumbled, nearly falling onto the bench before Slash caught him by the arm.

"What? My office is bugged? Someone is listening to my private conversations?"

"I think it's a possibility. I prefer to err on the side of caution."

Shaken, the father settled onto the bench. "That's a grave accusation on many different levels. Who exactly would be listening?"

"I'm not sure, but I urge you to be circumspect in what you say from this point on." Slash joined him on the bench. "I'm concerned there's something going on at the Vatican. Something's not right."

"Why would you say that?"

"It's complicated. Suffice it to say, I've been summoned to Rome, and not in a good way." He briefly brought the father up to speed on recent events. Father Armando listened quietly without interruption. When he finished, the priest leaned back on the bench, a contemplative expression on his face.

"The *nkondi* statue means it has to be someone who knows what happened in the Congo," Father Armando said.

"*Si.*" Slash spread his hands. "But who? There are only a handful of us who know. What would be the purpose of revealing such things now?"

"Well, whoever sent the statue is playing dangerously." Father Armando reached up to tap the gold crucifix around his neck. "It's most certainly about power and control. What happened in the Congo… You know your actions were justified as those necessary to the church. You did what you were told. No one could have foreseen what would happen."

The words didn't help. They never did. He looked at the wisteria, its blossoms stretching toward the heat of the sun, yearning to grow. "Intellectually I understand, but my soul remains troubled by the actions and the outcome."

"I know." The priest put a gentle hand on his arm. "Nicolo, your heart is not yet healed, and you continue to seek peace for your past actions. As we have spoken before, what happened there is not on you."

"It will *always* be on me."

The father shook his head sadly. "You have confessed and asked for forgiveness. That forgiveness has been granted to you by those who are closest to God. God forgives those who are repentant for their sins. You know this. This is not your burden to carry alone."

He remained silent.

Father Armando exhaled, lifting his cap and rubbing his right temple with his hand. "I believe this may be the time to bring you in. Come let us sit a moment."

Puzzled, he followed the priest to a shaded bench and sat next to him. Father Armando put the cap in his lap and folded his hands on top of it. "Nicolo, what I'm about to say must stay confidential."

Now he was more concerned than puzzled. But he kept his voice neutral when he answered. "I understand."

The priest hesitated for a moment, then spoke. "The pope is ill."

Dismay and shock shot through him. Whatever he'd been expecting Father Armando to say, that hadn't been it. He took a moment to work through all the emotions before he managed to ask, "How badly?"

"I'm not sure. His Holiness confided in me a few months ago."

The fact that the confidence had taken place did not surprise him. The pope and Father Armando had been close friends for decades, both serving in various, and often overlapping, positions in the Vatican. One of the pope's first official actions had been to elevate Father Armando, the Archbishop of Genoa, to a cardinal.

"I believe His Eminence told me this for a reason," the priest continued. "I also think you being here is not a coincidence."

"Why would you say that?"

"Because when His Holiness told me about his illness, he provided no other detail other than to say I was forbidden to tell anyone of his condition, except for you... and only if the time was right."

"Me?" The Holy Father had permitted Father Armando to confide in him? That was nothing short of unprecedented and a little unsettling. He didn't understand why he would be brought into a matter at the very pinnacle of Vatican power, even when there was a great deal of personal respect and affection between himself and the Holy Father.

"He permitted you to tell me? Why?"

Father Armando shifted on the bench and put a reassuring hand on his back. "At the time, I did not understand why. I know he is quite fond of you, but I thought perhaps the illness had made him confused. It was a lot for me to accept, as it was. However, now you are here and we're speaking of this, I don't believe his comment to me was as offhand as I suspected. The Holy Father is a wise and prudent man. So, I believe he had good reason for this. You need to know, Nicolo. But why, and what it means in the bigger picture of what's going on, I have no idea."

It was a staggering development, and he wondered why the time had to be "right," and how that coincided with what was happening. "Why didn't you summon me at once? You knew I would have come."

"*Si*, I knew. But you, better than anyone, understand the supreme confidentiality of what I've revealed. It is not a simple confidence. If the Holy Father had not specifically said I could share this with you, I would not have. I'm as mystified by all of this as you are. That being said, I think your presence here is expected. By good or bad forces, I do not know. For whatever reason, you've become a player in what's happening."

"What *is* happening?" Many possibilities, mostly bad, raced through his head, culminating with Tito's warning that something big was going down at the Vatican.

"I don't know, but I'm worried."

The deeply concerned expression on Father Armando's face unsettled him. He needed to focus, get his thoughts in order, to figure out how to form a plan of action. "No worries. We can handle this. One place to start is to find out who interfered with Gio's wedding. That might lead me to the person who has brought me here."

"Perhaps, but as I suspect you know, this is not about Giorgio. This is about you. They are using him to get to you."

"Or using me to get to you," Slash added.

Father Armando considered. "Perhaps. But for what purpose?"

"I don't know, but the *nkondi* statue was not sent by benevolent forces."

"I agree. So, what next?"

Slash rubbed the back of his neck, feeling the muscles knotted tightly. "I've already touched base with Tito and I'm thinking a talk with Pacini might be useful."

Surprise crossed the priest's face. "Pacini? He no longer

lives in Rome. Shortly after the organization was dissolved, he cut ties with the Vatican and essentially disappeared, which is understandable given the circumstances."

It *was* totally understandable. All those involved in the mission had been reassigned or moved. Pacini, as head of the *sodalitium pianum*, had a lot more to lose than the rest of them.

"Do you know anyone who might still have contact with him? Tito said he heard rumors that Pacini went to Terni."

"It's possible." The father looked off into the distance, thinking. "He was close to Father Nucci and he's not in Lazo's pocket. I could see what I could find out."

"I'd appreciate it. I also intend to make my presence known at the Vatican and see what plays out. In the meantime, I'll continue my search to see if I can find who's blocking Gio's wedding."

"I'll work on that issue, as well." They both rose from the bench. "Should I alert security to the potential bug in my office?"

"I would urge you to wait, if you feel comfortable doing so. If your office is indeed bugged, then we would tip our hand if we reveal we've found it. We may yet be able to use the bug to our advantage. If there is no bug, we may paint ourselves as paranoid."

"Understood. Then I will say nothing for the time being. But please, Nicolo, be careful."

He smiled. "You sound like a certain someone I know."

"I imagine I do." Father Armando offered a small smile of his own. "Let's wrap this up as quickly as possible so you can get home to her."

He put a hand on the priest's shoulder. "Trust me. There's nothing I want more."

FOURTEEN

Lexi

I SET MY alarm for five o'clock in the morning to get up and check the progress of the claim on the package. Although I'd told Slash I didn't think I was in danger, he clearly believed I was. That meant whoever sent the statue held some kind of power over Slash, which indicated the real threat wasn't against me, but him. To hell with that! I wasn't going to let someone use me to get to him.

After brewing some coffee, I got to work, still in my pjs, and gave myself three hours to snoop online before I had to leave for work.

I reentered the CAI email system to check on my claim. It had been read and the claim's process started, so I typed an email and made it appear to come from one of Europin's staff. I said in the email that data corruption had occurred on several of their claims. Files with multiple addresses had been mistakenly merged with the senders who were filing claims. As a result, I requested that a new list of package numbers and sender information for shipping numbers, that included mine, needed to be generated at once to confirm the correct pairing. I provided a bogus email that I'd created within the system and sat back to wait.

Within forty minutes, I had what I needed and was

grateful for CAI's efficiency. In order to hide my tracks, I cancelled the claim, so I didn't alert the sender I was on to him.

Now I had to track down the sender. I had a name but was about ninety-nine percent sure it would be bogus. It took me another half hour to confirm that, but I still had to rule it out. The sender used an electronic wallet to pay anonymously, but it didn't matter. I had a number and that was all I needed. It did mean, however, I would have to cruise the murky alleys of the Dark Web looking for what I needed, and that was extremely dangerous because I was searching for a credit card number and that was illegal. I didn't intend to use the card number for nefarious reasons, but that didn't make it any more legal. Plus, most of the agencies like the FBI and the NSA had penetrated the Dark Web and had agents who were pretending to be sellers, buyers or offering goods and services. They were clever, so I had to be smarter. I had been one of those agents once, so I was experienced and knowledgeable about their methods, but I still had to be exceptionally careful not to trigger any alarms or get noticed in ways I shouldn't.

Cloaked in anonymity and using a special browser that hid my IP address, I plunged into the Dark Web, my heart accelerating. It was truly nerve-racking work, even for an experienced hacker like me. My experience worked in my favor. Thirty-two minutes later I had a name.

Julian Koenhein.

Meant nothing to me, but I disconnected from the Dark Web, then stretched my arms above my head and rolled my neck. Time to get ready for work, but I wanted to do a quick search on Mr. Koenhein first. A brief overview provided quite a bit of interesting information. Julian Koenhein happened to be a priest at the Vatican. He apparently worked as a clerk for Cardinal Jacopo Lazo. No way did I think that a coincidence, especially because Cardinal Lazo was the current president of the Vatican, a position I didn't know existed.

"Holy conclave," I muttered. I didn't need Basia to translate the significance of that. Slash needed to know as soon as possible what I'd discovered. A clerk from the office of the president of the Vatican had sent a statue from the Congo to me. I had no idea what it meant or what kind of importance it held for Slash, if any.

I checked the time. It was almost eight o'clock in the morning, which meant it would be about two o'clock in the afternoon Slash's time. Hoping that after I gave him the info, we could try to talk and sort things out, I swiped open my phone and called him. It went to voice mail immediately, which meant he likely had his phone turned off. Swallowing my disappointment, I left a message.

"Hi, Slash, it's me. Call me back when you get a chance. I've got something important to tell you."

I hung up, letting out a deep breath. I wasn't sure how my information would impact him, but the sooner he found out what I'd discovered, the better.

FIFTEEN

Slash

HE NEEDED ACCESS to a weapon.

In truth, he felt fine most of the time with just his hands and training, but he had no idea what was going on, and it was always prudent to be prepared. Keeping that in mind, he'd secured some specialized equipment that he felt might be needed and assembled the unlicensed and unregistered weapons in a spot more central to his planned location in Rome. He didn't carry anything on his person yet because at this stage of the game, he couldn't afford to be caught with unlicensed and unregistered guns. But he'd secreted what he needed in close proximity to his current area of operations, so they would be available as needed.

As he drove up toward the hotel, his phone vibrated. It was a text from Father Armando with nothing more than a phone number. He knew what it was.

Father Nucci had come through with a number. That'd been fast.

While scanning his phone, he noticed he'd missed a call from Lexi, and she'd left him a message. He'd figured she'd be busy at work, so he'd ring her later. For now, he instructed his phone to call the number Father Armando had sent.

The phone rang several times before it was picked up.

An irate male voice spoke. "Who is this?"

"*Vipera.*"

There was a long silence. "This phone is not secure." He didn't ask how Slash had got the number. Nucci had probably tipped him off that he'd be calling.

"I need to talk to you." He had no expectations that his former boss would speak to him, but he risked nothing in trying.

The silence stretched on for an uncomfortable amount of time. Still Slash waited.

"The usual place?" Pacini finally spoke. "One hour?"

The usual place was Piazza della Madonna dei Monti at a place near the sixteenth-century fountain. They'd met there several times for private discussions outside the Vatican.

"I'll be there," Slash said.

Pacini hung up without another word.

Slash reorganized his plans for the afternoon in his head, then listened to the message from Lexi. He told his phone to call her immediately, but it rang several times before her voice mail kicked in. Although he hated the wasted effort of phone tag, he left her a message.

"It's me, *cara.* Sorry I missed your call. You're probably in a meeting. I'll call you back this evening. *Ti amo.*"

It took him thirty minutes to arrive at the piazza, but he drove past and parked about a half-mile away. Though he had little reason to suspect a problem, since he had the time, he used the thirty minutes to reconnoiter the area around the fountain.

He walked slowly, blending in with the local population, and bought a coffee to go. Just another local on his way to work. While the area wasn't overrun with tourists, it wasn't devoid of them, either, which provided cover for those who might otherwise look out of place surveilling them.

The area surrounding the piazza was filled with kiosks, shops and stores. Feral cats ran wild here, as they did in many parts of Rome. He strolled, seemingly unconcerned, along the uneven sidewalks and narrow alleys, the façades lined with stone and Roman stucco—old ruins mixed in with new, more modern structures. He passed a couple of stalls with striped awnings selling colorful vegetables. The butcher shop that sold the best pork he'd ever eaten still stood in its same spot, the meat hooks showing the slabs visible in the shop window.

He meandered into the piazza, doing a visual sweep of the crowd, looking for an averted gaze or someone who met his eyes and looked away too quickly. An old woman fed pigeons from a paper bag while sitting on the edge of the fountain. Japanese tourists took pictures of each other. People passed by, some chatting with friends, others talking on their cell phones. An older man sat in front of one of the buildings, sketching on a pad. Nothing triggered his instincts.

Just in case, he made two more sweeps before slipping into a seat at an empty table at a café. He positioned himself behind other diners, but with a decent view of the fountain. His field instincts remained calm, so he ordered two glasses of the local white wine, and paid when the server brought them.

Ten minutes later Pacini slipped into the chair across from him with a grin. He had aged considerably in the seven years since Slash had seen him. His jet-black hair had been dusted with gray, but now it had turned completely white, and the lines on his face were carved deeper, especially around the eyes and on the forehead.

But his physique remained fit and defined, and his handshake was firm when he reached across the table to shake Slash's hand.

"It's good to see you," Pacini spoke in Italian. His expression looked reluctantly impressed. "You haven't aged a day."

"Flattery doesn't suit you," Slash responded.

"No, it doesn't, which is why I don't engage in it." Pacini picked up the wine and took a sip. "*Novello Superiore*. Excellent choice."

"I remembered it was your favorite." Slash lifted his own glass in a salute. "Hopefully that hasn't changed."

"It hasn't." He tapped his glass to Slash's and took a sip, sighing in pleasure. "I need to take a bottle or ten of these home with me."

"I appreciate you coming."

"Just saved us some time. Figured you would have found me by tomorrow anyway. Better we meet on neutral ground." Pacini's fingers played with the wine stem. He was clearly uncomfortable with the summons, as he should be. He took another sip, then regarded Slash. "What do you want?"

That was Pacini for you. Blunt, direct and honest. He liked that. No wasted conversation, no wasted time.

"Information on the Congo."

Pacini's hand with the wineglass stilled inches from his mouth. He carefully set it down, narrowing his eyes. "What kind of information?"

"Someone sent a *nkondi* statue to my fiancée. That was preceded by an anonymous note that said, 'I know who you are,' the refusal of the church to marry my younger brother, and a firecracker display with a Bible verse referring to my wickedness and a so-called betrayal of my oath."

Pacini lowered his hand. "What the hell?"

"Someone wanted me here. So, here I am. Happen to know what's going on?"

He stared at Slash, thinking, then shook his head. "Ah, I'm afraid I'm long retired from such intrigue. I drink coffee and brandy during the day and spend my nights with whomever is willing to stay with me."

Slash didn't believe that for a minute. Pacini's eyes remained sharp, assessing. As much as Pacini might have wanted to deny it, Slash saw the interest their conversation had sparked. He also knew the man had many deep and important connections at the Vatican. In many ways, Pacini was still a very dangerous man. As head of the *sodalitium pianum* for so many years, he held a lot of important secrets.

Slash leaned forward. "Who else knew about the operation? As far as I know, there were only a few of us in the know."

Pacini looked at the fountain, thinking. "It was the tightest held secret of the organization. Only you, me, Carmelo and Manna were officially in the know regarding the details. Carmelo passed away two years ago from liver cancer, and Manna is rarely sober these days. I assure you, even if he was, he wouldn't remember you. About a year after the Congo, he overdosed. He survived, but it addled him. These days he seeks solace in the bottle. That leaves you and me."

Manna was a good man, and Carmelo had been, too. The operation had hurt all of them. "No one else knew about the mission?"

Pacini shook his head. "No one."

He ran a hand through his hair, considering. Father Armando and the pope both knew, as a result of his confessions, but Father Armando hadn't been a cardinal yet, and the current pope hadn't yet been elected pope. Besides, he trusted both of them to respect the vows of his confession even among other priests. It was possible Manna and Carmelo had also confessed, which brought in any number of priests who could know and might not be as circumspect as the pope and Father Armando. Still, there had to be a deeper connection somewhere.

"Perhaps someone is just fishing," he mused aloud. "If so, they won't get anything from me."

But Pacini was no longer listening. He stared out at the piazza as if frozen deep in thought, then snapped his fingers. "Wait. When we disbanded the *sodalitium*, I borrowed a couple of Vatican clerks to help me close down things. It'd be unlikely they saw or understood anything of value, but it's possible."

He wanted to believe him, but he didn't. Swallowing the frustration, he kept his voice even. "What about my file? Could they have seen that?"

Pacini's eyes shifted slightly, just enough to raise doubt. "I doubt it."

"But it's possible."

Pacini reluctantly nodded. "All things are possible, but I sincerely don't think so. Besides, priests are sworn to secrecy. What would be the point? Revealing information on the Congo operation would only hurt the church."

"Maybe someone doesn't want to hurt the church."

Pacini paused, gave him a long, hard stare. "Are you saying you're the target?"

"Blackmail." That made the most sense. "But I'm not

sure to what end. Any chance you remember the names of those clerks?"

"Not off the top of my head." He drained the last of his wine. "But I'll get them to you."

"I'd appreciate that."

Pacini stood, resting both hands on the back of his chair. "In the meantime, be careful, Viper. I share your sense of concern. I suspect there are layers of complex motivations at work, and those behind this will not be eager to see you picking at them. They clearly know more about you at this moment than you know about them, so be careful who you trust. People who say they've got your back may be simply positioning themselves for an easy stabbing."

"I'm ready." He could handle whatever they threw at him, as long as it stayed directed at him. "I can play this game, too. But I'm not going away without answers."

Pacini dipped his head in acknowledgment. "I figured as much. Good luck and I'll send you what I find."

SIXTEEN

Lexi

I'D JUST WALKED in the door at home when my cell rang. I recognized the tone, so I dropped the keys trying to get the phone out of my purse. When I bent down to get the keys, my briefcase dropped on my foot, causing me to hop around on one leg, cursing while finally retrieving my cell.

"Slash?" I slammed the front door shut and tapped in the code on the alarm.

"*Cara.* Is everything okay?"

It was so good to hear his voice, I momentarily forgot why I had called him in the first place. So, I stood there dumbly in the foyer of our house, the purse hanging drunkenly off my arm, my brain freezing. "Uh, I…"

"*Cara?*"

"Slash, hi. I'm fine." I closed my eyes. "No, actually, I'm *not* fine. I miss you. A lot."

He let out a breath. "I miss you, too. More than you know."

We both fell silent as an unusual awkwardness descended on us. We were engaged to be married, and yet, we were suddenly talking like strangers. Mysterious secrets, hidden agendas and an unknown past were coming between us with no end in sight.

I walked into the living room and dropped my purse

on the couch. "Slash, I have something to tell you. I was, ah, hanging around online, and decided to see if I could track down the sender of the statue package."

No response. I pressed my hand against my forehead. "Okay. Fine. I wasn't just hanging around. I deliberately and intentionally tracked down the sender on your behalf. I wasn't just going to sit around and worry about you. I'm perfectly capable of helping you with or without your permission."

He said nothing. I figured he was thinking what to say. We were on seriously shaky ground after all. Since I didn't know what else to say, I waited.

"Thank you."

It was a small step, but it was forward progress. Thank God for that. Still, I was so nervous, my words came out fast. "Do you want to know what I found out?"

"I do."

Was it wishful thinking or did I hear a hint of hopefulness in his voice? I gave him a brief rundown of how I tracked the sender of the package through the claims company and by extension, the insurance company. "I was able to secure the electronic wallet number, but I needed to know to whom it belonged. I went through the Dark Web and came up with a name, thank goodness."

"That was smart thinking, *cara*. No mishaps on the Dark Web?"

"None to my knowledge."

"Did you get a name?" he asked, and now I was sure I heard a tinge of excitement.

"I did. It's a guy named Julian Koenhein. Have you heard of him before?"

"No. It sounds German."

I hadn't even wondered. "I don't know his ethnicity, but he works at the Vatican."

Slash was quiet for a moment. "Where at the Vatican?"

I braced myself for the revelation. "In the office of Cardinal Jacopo Lazo. Lazo is the president of the Vatican."

"I know who Lazo is. Are you sure about this, *cara*?"

"I'm sure. Does it mean anything to you?"

"It might."

"Well, personally, I didn't know the Vatican had a president. However, in hindsight, it makes perfect sense since the Vatican is technically a country, albeit the smallest in the world in terms of both population and area." I was babbling, but I was afraid he'd shut me out again and say he had to go.

To my surprise, he explained further. "You're right. The Vatican has a president appointed to the position by the pope for a five-year term."

"Does the president work with a congress, or a parliament or something like that?"

"No. It's not a democracy. The president is served by a secretary general and a vice secretary general, both of whom are also appointed by the pope for five years. The appointment is extremely delicate in terms of how the pope selects them. Often it's to appease or strengthen certain political alliances."

"Sounds complicated."

"It is. Even then, the president's actions must be approved by a commission. The pope can remove any person at any time, although a move like that without good reason would be quite dangerous politically. The president is considered the most powerful position in the Vatican behind the pope."

I thought that over. "Okay, then. So, the fact that Lazo's clerk is sending me a statue from the Congo is not a good thing, right?"

"It's not. But it gives me a lot to think about."

He sounded tired—so tired it made my heart hurt. I had no idea what was going on in his head or what was bothering him so badly. "Slash, are you okay?"

"No. I'm not okay without you, *cara*. But I hope to get to the bottom of this soon and come home."

"You're not in danger, are you?"

"Don't worry. I can handle myself."

That wasn't an answer. "I know you can." I pressed the phone harder to my ear, as if it would bring him closer. "I also know you feel like you have to keep me out of the loop on this one. But if I can help…"

"You *have* helped."

"Good." I could hear some noise in the background, as if he sat near an open window. I wondered what he was doing…what he was feeling. I'd never felt so far away from him.

"This is a difficult situation," he finally said.

"Which is all the more reason I should be there helping you."

"I don't want you involved in this."

"I'm already involved, Slash." I closed my eyes. He didn't get it. From this point on, when it came to him, I'd always be involved.

He said nothing, and for a moment, neither did I. I finally spoke. "Call me if you need anything, okay?"

"I will. I love you, *cara*. More than the decimal value of pi."

He was clever and sweet, that fiancé of mine. "That happens to be infinite."

"That it is."

I glanced down at my engagement ring, rubbed it with my thumb. "I love you, too."

"I'll be home soon. I promise."

"I'll be waiting." I disconnected and set my phone on the desk. I didn't know what *soon* meant in terms of days, hours and minutes, but it didn't really matter. I hoped that we'd get through whatever this was in one piece, and that things didn't permanently change between us.

Although, if I was perfectly honest with myself, I wasn't feeling terribly optimistic at the moment.

SEVENTEEN

Cardinal Jacopo Lazo

"So, HE GOT the message?" Jacopo leaned back in his chair, steepled his fingers together.

"Yes, Your Eminence. He landed in Rome yesterday and has now apparently gone straight to Genoa."

Jacopo smiled, feeling more encouraged by recent developments than he had in days. "Excellent. I couldn't have choreographed this better myself. Except I did." He chuckled at his cleverness. "You'll inform me of his return to Rome."

"Certainly. We're carefully monitoring the situation in Genoa, as well."

"Perfect. At last, the truth will be revealed." He sat back, satisfied. His clerk was efficient and exceptionally loyal, having served him for nearly three decades. The older he got, the harder it was to find good assistants who were both resourceful and malleable.

"Do you think the truth will come out before the Holy Father passes?" Father Koenhein asked him tentatively. "His Eminence does not appear well. Reports are that his health is failing noticeably."

Jacopo felt a leap of excitement. "Yes, the Holy Father appears frailer by the day. But I'm confident this will play out in time. We need to move expeditiously, but without tipping our hand, so they will not see it coming.

If the Holy Father passes shortly after everything comes to light, so much the better."

"As God wills it, of course," the priest agreed, lowering his eyes.

"Oh, trust me, my son," Jacopo said, turning his chair to look out the window. "God wills it."

Lexi

I TOOK A SIP of coffee, enjoying the perk of having my office in downtown Crystal City, near several excellent restaurants and cafés. This new mom-and-pop café had recently opened two blocks from X-Corp, and it had outstanding coffee and an even better selection of desserts.

"Thanks for meeting for me, Gray."

"Of course. Why wouldn't I?"

"I don't know. Maybe because I've never invited you for coffee. I guess I should have. That's probably what friends do to keep in touch."

She laid a napkin across her lap and regarded me, perhaps with a little exasperation. Maybe that hadn't been the right thing to say. "I just saw you at your engagement party, so it's not like we've been strangers. Besides, it's my day off and I can't think of a better way to spend it, having coffee and—" she looked down at her plate "—this amazing-looking Bavarian crème éclair."

I licked chocolate frosting off my fingers, not wanting to waste a smudge on a napkin. "I appreciate it. I just didn't give you much lead time on this one. That's socially inappropriate, right? How much lead time do you generally prefer when being invited for coffee? Basia usually needs three hours to get ready if it's going to happen on the same day, but I know you're busy and often work on the weekends, so what's good for you? I'll add it to my spreadsheet and then next time I go to invite you to coffee or conversation, I will give you the appropriate amount of lead time."

Gray picked up her fork and knife and neatly cut the éclair in half. I looked at my fingers and the mashed éclair on my plate and felt like a barbarian. But we are who we are.

"I'm here, Lexi, so obviously it wasn't a problem. I'm pretty spontaneous, so just ask when it's convenient for you. What's up?"

I really liked Gray and not just because she showed up to see me on her day off. In addition to her smarts and excellent analysis abilities which were well-utilized at the CIA, I was especially impressed with her research skills. We'd been through a lot together on one of my foreign assignments for X-Corp—surviving an insanely intense and life-threatening experience that had bonded us in a way that transcended normal friendship. Not that I had a lot of experience with friendship, but those I had were special, and Gray counted among them. Even with all of that in our favor, I still needed courage to work up to what I wanted to ask her.

"Slash had to take an emergency trip to Rome."

She paused with a bite of the éclair millimeters from her mouth. After a moment, she returned it to her plate uneaten. "I see. Does it have anything to do with the firecracker show at your party?"

I wound an end of the napkin around my finger, my anxiety surfacing. "Yes, that's part of it. Also, the church is denying his younger brother Giorgio's request to get married in the church, and someone sent me a threatening statue from the Congo." As her eyes widened, I gave her a quick rundown on all that had happened.

"Slash didn't like any of it, so he went to Rome to sort it out," I continued. "He thinks someone is trying to get to him through me and he isn't having any of it. But—"

"But what?"

"I need to ask you for a favor. One I'm not entirely comfortable doing. I don't like asking for help, even from friends. It's hard for me. But I need assistance and if you can't do it, please say no. I will totally understand."

"Lexi, just tell me what you need."

I swallowed, hesitating. Wow, this was a lot harder than I thought it would be. There was also the mortification factor—the knowledge I couldn't handle this on my own. Forcing myself to ignore my insecurities, I pushed forward. "Would you be willing to take a look at what the Vatican has been doing in the Congo, going back, let's say, six to seven years? Nonclassified sources only. I've already done an open-source search of my own on this topic, but I don't know what I'm looking for. International affairs, diplomatic negotiations and the subtle language that accompanies those things—it's not my skill set. I want to know if something seems off to you or if there's anything that stands out as being overly unusual or dramatic, or makes you wonder if there's more to the story than is officially out there."

She studied me carefully. "The Congo? The Vatican? Lexi, why don't you just ask Slash? This is totally his area."

"I know." I glanced down at my hands. "But I can't."

"Because?"

"Because he doesn't know I'm looking into this. Frankly, I'm not sure he'd approve. He wants me to stay out of his past, but there are things going on that have me really worried about him. I'm only looking for information at this point. I haven't decided what, if anything, I'll do when, and if, I get it. You may not find anything of interest. I want another set of eyes on my hunch. Something about the Congo is key here. Your eyes and analytical skill in this area are the best I know, so that's why I came to you."

She leaned both elbows on the table, rested her hands beneath her chin. I could tell she had a lot of questions and the thought of having to answer one, or any of them, was stressing me out. But I'd asked her for help, and it was only fair she knew what she was dealing with. "Are you ready for what you might find?"

It was a logical and good question that gave me cause to examine my motivations for my search. Why did I need the answers? For Slash? For me? For both of us? Things began to get murky when I really thought about it.

"Honestly, Gray, I don't know. But right now, *not* knowing is worse. It's a conundrum for me. On the one hand, I'm worried I'm overstepping an imaginary boundary by trying to help Slash. I mean, if this was an NSA job-related issue, the boundary is clear. Unless he asked, I would keep my distance and respect his work. But this is a personal issue—possibly a threat—which, by extension, is a threat against me, too. We're supposed to be a unit, right?"

"Right."

Feeling validated, I continued. "I know he'd respond the same way if our roles were reversed—and he has done, in the past. But here's the thing. I don't want to set an unusual precedent for our relationship. It's not in my nature to force people to confide in me. Most of the time, I sincerely hope they *don't.* However, a threat to him is a threat to me, and I can't fight or help him if he won't let me in. He can be so stubborn sometimes."

A look of understanding crossed her face and I realized she probably had some of the same issues with her Navy SEAL boyfriend. Between his job and hers at the CIA, there was bound to be secrets. So how did they deal?

"I totally get that, Lexi. When Hands has a planned mission, meaning one of the rare few he knows about in advance, he often gets pissy a couple of days before departure."

"Pissy?"

"Yeah, he's grumpy and pushes me away. At first I didn't get what the problem was. Then I figured it out. He's putting space between us. He needs to do that to focus. But it's more than that. It's important for him to know I'll be okay in his absence. He needs to know I can take care of myself, and that he doesn't have to worry about me when he's gone. To him, that's a certain kind of peace that can allow him to focus on getting the job done."

I thought about the gun Slash gave me for Christmas, the GPS-locator earrings he'd given me so he could track me if I got into trouble, the shooting range lessons and the Krav Maga self-defense moves we'd been working on for several weeks. Suddenly, things began to make a lot more sense.

"I still don't understand why he doesn't trust me with his past," I said. "If it's bringing danger to him or me, aren't I entitled to know?"

She studied me for a moment. "Is it important for you to know it?"

"I don't know. Maybe. It keeps coming up, coming between us. Will it always be this way?"

She pushed her plate to the side and lowered her voice. "Let me turn that around. Do you feel differently about his past now that you're engaged?"

I had to really think about the question so I could answer honestly. "Maybe," I finally admitted. "I feel more…protective of him—of us—as a couple. Is that strange? I mean, obviously Slash doesn't need my protection. He's perfectly capable of protecting himself. But somehow, his battles have become mine. We're a unit, or at least, we're supposed to be. I should be in Rome helping him. But I don't think he sees it that way." In fact, I *knew* he didn't, and somehow that hurt.

"He likely thinks he's protecting you."

He absolutely did, but that wasn't the point. "That's not fair if we're supposed to be a team in real life."

"I didn't say it was fair. Look, that being said, Slash does not strike me as the kind of guy who does anything without having looked at it in multiple ways. If he's keeping something from you, I would think he has what he considers a good reason. Have faith."

Faith.

I kept circling that word—a concept so foreign to me—to my grounding in science—and yet, it seemed to be taking a prominent role in my life. Faith in my abilities, faith in my relationships and faith in my judgment to help the person I loved, even if he didn't want my help.

I replayed our conversation in my head—the implications, the possible outcomes and my motivations before I came to my decision. "The request still stands," I said, hoping I was doing the right thing. "Will you help me, Gray?"

"Of course I'll help. That's what friends are for."

Wow. Was it really that simple?

Relief swept through me. I'm not sure she had any idea how much it meant that she was willing to step into my mess.

I gave her a shaky smile. Even though I really liked Gray, it had been hard to ask for her help. But it was the smart thing to do, and I'd done it, so that was something—a step forward in the progression of my development as a social being.

"Thanks, Gray. I guess that's something I'm still learning."

EIGHTEEN

Slash

SLASH SPOTTED HIS tail the moment he walked into the lobby of the expensive Hotel *Alimandi Vaticano*. He had expected it, which is why he'd chosen this well-known hotel, close to the Vatican and high-profile enough that he could easily be found. He strolled into the lobby and confirmed his reservation under a name that would be recognized by most people at the Vatican.

He declined the assistance of a bellhop and carried his duffel bag and laptop case to the elevator. On the way up, he ran into a lady with a seeing-eye dog. He murmured a greeting to her as he passed, mentioning she had a beautiful shepherd. She stopped to chat and they spoke for a few moments in Italian about the weather and Rome before she told him he could pet the dog if he desired. He did, so he knelt and the dog gave him a friendly nuzzle.

After he and the woman had parted, he opened his suite after tapping his key card to the opening to his suite. Once inside, he looked around. The suite was furnished with stylish, contemporary furniture, parquet floors, coffered ceilings and kitchenette with an espresso machine, table and refrigerator. He strolled into the bedroom. A walk-in wardrobe, a separate sitting room and a Turkish bath with LED lighting in the bathroom rounded out his accommodations. More importantly, the wifi speed and internet connection were both satisfactory.

He didn't unpack, as he had no intention on staying long. Instead, he settled into a lounge chair with his laptop, figuring he'd have an hour or two to work. He'd only been working for about a half hour when his phone vibrated. A text had arrived from an unknown number and held three names.

Lorenzo Cavallo.

Thomas Pecora.

Julian Koenhein.

His eyes stopped and rested on the third name. The same name Lexi had just given him. The clerk in Cardinal Lazo's office. Not a coincidence.

He tapped back a quick text of thanks and continued his work. Sixty-two minutes later, there was a knock on his hotel door. He quietly approached, then checked the peephole. He recognized the person who stood there, so he opened the door, leaning with one arm braced casually against the doorjamb.

"Julian Koenhein. I've been expecting you." Slash spoke in German, Julian's native tongue.

That comment elicited a squeak of surprise and a visible flinch from the priest. While he figured out what to say, Slash took stock of him. Nervous tics. Mid—fifties. Receding hairline and a bad comb-over. He looked exactly as he had in the Vatican photo Slash had just pulled up. A vein in his neck throbbed as he studied Slash, clearly not sure what to do or say next. As his gaze fell on the gold cross that Slash had purposefully removed from under his shirt and clearly identified him as a member of the Vatican's *sodalitium pianum*, the priest finally spoke.

"Y-you know who I am?" The priest answered Slash in Italian, not German, but his voice shook just the same.

Slash continued in German on purpose, remaining in control of the conversation. "Of course, I do. You sent me the *nkondi*."

Color drained from his face, all but confirming his guilt. "I…don't know what you are talking about."

Slash tapped his fingers against the doorframe, implying impatience and boredom. "Lying, Father? Is this a new trend at the Vatican?"

"How did you know?"

At the least the priest had the good sense to abandon his false protestations. "Does it matter? You've summoned me and I'm here. That's what you wanted, right?"

"I'm only the messenger." He pulled a tissue from beneath his robe and swiped at the sweat on his lip and forehead. "His Eminence, Cardinal Jacopo Lazo, would like to see you."

"I'm sure he would."

Slash's easy tone apparently agitated the priest further, because he shifted nervously on his feet, tugging at his collar as if it were too tight. "He wishes to speak with you about an important matter."

"What makes you, or him, think I will agree to an audience?"

"Excuse me?"

"I don't respond well to threats, Father." He lightly fingered the cross around his neck to drive the point home. "Maybe you've heard that about me."

The priest swallowed hard, his Adam's apple bobbing a few times. "Sir, please. He is the president of the Vatican and he wants to see you. I have a car waiting. I'll take you to him."

Slash studied the father for a long time. The priest was the first to turn his gaze away, shame and fear burning into his cheeks. "I beg you," he whispered after a few moments. "I do as I am told. I am but a lowly servant of God."

"Aren't we all?"

He kept his tone hard and unforgiving because he wanted the priest afraid of what might happen to him now that Slash had confirmed he'd sent the statue. But the clerk was not the root of the problem. That problem was a lot bigger and much more dangerous. He needed to know what Lazo wanted with him.

The priest waited, his eyes remaining downcast until Slash finally dropped his hand from the doorjamb. "Fine. Lead the way, Father."

NINETEEN

Lexi

"OKAY, WHO ARE you and what have you done with my best friend, Lexi?" Basia sat with her elbows resting on my kitchen counter next to a large pizza box, two bottles of wine and a carafe of coffee.

I rolled my eyes. "Is it really that unusual for me to ask you to come over?"

"I didn't just come over." She wagged a finger at me. "I came over for a *girls'* night—arranged, organized and planned by you. That's huge. Momentous. Worthy of noting in the Official Book of Lexi's Life."

"You're totally overreacting."

"I am not." She snapped a selfie, catching the wineglass and part of my scowling face. "Trust me, this is worth marking."

I poured myself some more coffee. "Fine. I initiated a girls' night. I really appreciate you coming over, although I'm not sure it was a good idea to take you away from newly wedded bliss."

"Are you kidding?" Basia carefully extracted two slices of veggie pizza from the box and put them on her plate, licking her fingers. "We've been married a month now. There's only so much bliss you can take, if you know what I mean."

I stopped in midsip, wincing. "No, no. No. You did *not* just put that in my mind."

She laughed and shoved the pizza box at me. "Besides, Xavier won't admit it, but I know he's secretly thrilled to have the evening off to game himself into oblivion."

"Lucky him," I said, totally meaning it. Mindless gaming was a much more appealing option than spending an evening worrying whether your fiancé was in danger and if your relationship would survive it. I took a slice of pizza and ate it without setting it down on my plate once.

Basia neatly closed up one pizza box and handed me a couple of napkins. "So, I assume the real reason for this girls' night is you've discovered who sent that weird statue to you."

"I did. His name is Julian Koenhein. He's a priest who works as a clerk at the Vatican."

"A priest? That doesn't sound like a very priestly thing to do. Can't be a coincidence, though. Especially after Slash takes off for Rome right after you receive it."

"Exactly. So, I've gathered a lot of information about Koenhein and his boss, but a good chunk of it's in Italian. I need help with the translation."

"Sure. What do we know so far about this Koenhein guy? Who does he work for at the Vatican?"

"An Italian cardinal by the name of Jacopo Lazo. Lazo happens to be the president of the Vatican."

She whistled. "Wait. The Vatican has a president? I didn't know that."

"I didn't either." I reached into a folder on the counter and pulled out two photos I'd printed, then pushed them toward her. "But apparently they have one. The first is Julian Koenhein, the clerk. The second photo is Lazo."

Basia studied Lazo's photo. "I think I've seen this guy on television."

"I wouldn't be surprised. Apparently he's pretty important."

Basia took another bite of pizza and wiped her mouth with a napkin. "Okay, so why would the clerk of the president of the Vatican go to all the trouble of summoning Slash in a really bizarre, threatening way by sending you an statue from the Congo?"

"I don't have the slightest idea. Obviously it was a message of some kind. Slash knew what it meant, but he wouldn't tell me. Shortly thereafter, he left for Rome. I think by sending it to me, someone wanted it made clear that if Slash didn't return to the Vatican, something might happen to me."

"Wow." Basia frowned. "Priest or not, I don't like this clerk, and possibly not the Vatican president either." She paused. "I hope lightning doesn't strike me for that."

"No worries, I happen to agree with you. Anyway, that's where I'm at. I've collected data on Koenhein, Lazo, political relations between the Vatican and the Congo, and everything I could find on the *nkondi* statue. I'd like you to review the documents on Lazo and Koenhein in Italian to see if something unusual pops. I've got Grayson reviewing the international developments between the Vatican and Congo relations for the past ten years. It's a lot of material in an area that's not my skill set, so I need some additional eyes on all of this."

"Well then, let's get to work."

I handed Basia the papers and a pad of paper and pen for her to jot notes as needed. We ate pizza and drank coffee and wine while we worked, mostly in silence.

I was deep into reading the English-language sources

about the life of Jacopo Lazo when the doorbell rang. I exchanged a worried glance with Basia.

"You expecting someone at nine o'clock?" she asked.

"I'm not." I pulled out my cell phone and checked the front door camera on the security feed. It was Grayson, dressed in shorts, a T-shirt and sandals.

"It's Gray." I pocketed my phone. "What's she doing here?"

I disengaged the alarm and opened the door. "Hey, Gray, what's up?"

She didn't waste time with any simple niceties. She stepped across the threshold, her expression serious. "Lexi, I've got something important to show you."

"Well, by all means, come in. We're having a girls' night…sort of. Basia is in the kitchen. We're going through some documents while eating pizza and drinking wine—that's my version of a girls' night. There is plenty of pizza left, so please help yourself."

Basia scooted around the counter to give Gray a quick hug. Gray declined the pizza and wine. She seemed worried and that triggered my anxiety. What could be so important that she would drive over at nine o'clock at night without calling me first? The pizza, wine and coffee suddenly rolled around my stomach.

Gray glanced at the documents we had spread out and then pushed them to the side, pulling a laptop out of the bag over her shoulder, setting it on the counter and opening it up. She perched on a stool as she logged in, then tapped some commands before pulling up a document.

"Lexi, you tasked me with finding out what I could about relations between the Vatican and the Congo over the past ten years," she said. "Interestingly enough, there's been a lot of activity on that front."

I pulled a stool around the counter on one side of her and sat while Basia scooted closer to her on the other.

"Like what?" I asked.

"About ten years ago a man by the name of Harun Apeloko overthrew the government in the Congo and seized control. He implemented martial law and began executing anyone who disagreed with him."

"Typical despot," I muttered.

"Exactly. The country plunged into worse poverty while Apeloko built himself lavish palaces and hoarded cars and jewels. It wasn't long before the immense suffering of the people sparked the protest of the Vatican, that has deeply entrenched roots in the country. Apeloko certainly wished to silence the bishops who spoke out against him, but by doing so he threatened his tenuous grip on power. Christian institutions were highly revered by the people and acted as a social and cultural stabilizing force. Removing the bishops would have certainly caused riots and protests. So, instead Apeloko was clever. He placated the population by meeting regularly with the clergy in his country, as well as entertaining Vatican representatives and presenting himself as aligned with them. He pretended to consider progressive concepts like elections and representation."

I took some more milk from the fridge and added it to my coffee. "When you say 'pretend,' I take that to mean he never really considered them."

"He did not," Gray answered. "The Congolese bishops, Vatican priests and local representatives wrote and drew up an accord with a blueprint for free elections, a peaceful transfer of power and other democratic measures, then presented it to Apeloko. Several human rights groups and other governments signed the accord, praising the plan. But there was a problem."

"Which was?" I stuck my coffee mug in the microwave and nuked it for forty-five seconds.

"Apeloko never signed it, nor made any public statements indicating he would abide by it. The situation dragged on for at least two years before the matter came to an end."

"What kind of end?"

"Apeloko and his nineteen-year old son were assassinated in a mysterious attack inside the palace. A Vatican priest who was with them nearly died as well."

I removed my mug from the microwave, carrying it carefully to the counter. "What happened?"

"Apeloko, his son and the priest were poisoned while in his personal study. Two guards who were stationed outside the room heard nothing. No one came in and no one came out of the room. Somehow, the priest who was inside was able to open the door to let security in before collapsing near death. When the guards rushed inside, Apeloko and his son were already dead."

"They didn't catch anyone?"

"They did not. But they think the assassin and the son both came in through a previously unknown secret passage into the study. Apeloko's security apparently knew nothing about it."

I thought it odd that the security detail knew nothing of the passage, but perhaps it wasn't so outrageous considering despots were typically unhinged and obsessively paranoid. "Maybe the son wanted to kill the father to take power for himself, so he got help doing so. He opens the hidden passage to a killer to get the job done. Instead, the assassin wants the power for himself or someone who paid him more. So, he takes them both out and the priest is collateral damage."

Basia looked at me in shock, perhaps concerned I'd so rapidly formed such a morbid scenario. It kind of surprised me, too, but I'd have to wonder about the state of my mind at another, more private, interval.

An intrigued expression on her face, Gray entertained my scenario. "It's possible, but no one knows for sure. It could have been the assassin kidnaps the son, forces him through the passage into the room, and then poisons everyone once he was in the study."

"What was the priest's accounting of what happened?" I asked. "The one who survived."

"Apparently the priest was permanently injured—mentally incapacitated from the poisoning—and unable to tell investigators anything useful."

"That's horrible," Basia said. She'd pushed aside her food, placed her elbows on the counter. "Seriously."

"But none of it makes sense from an operational standpoint." I frowned, working it out in my head. "Why poison them? Why not slit their throats or snap their necks? Do something fast and permanent."

Basia held up a hand. "Please, Lexi, I just ate."

Gray, however, seemed interested by my train of thought. "That's a good question, Lexi. As far as I can see from the open source material, there are no easy answers."

I sorted through the possibilities. "Okay, then let's postulate. For example, how did the assassin keep three people quiet while forcing them to take poison?"

"Hard to say." Gray rolled her shoulders. Not surprisingly, she was much more comfortable discussing assassination methods than Basia. "The prevailing theory is the priest had already been knocked out and the assassin put the poison in his mouth while he was unconscious. Somehow, the priest came to after the assassin had left and was able to raise an alarm before passing out again."

"That's just bizarre."

"Right?" Gray reached into her pocket and pulled out a thumb drive. "But that's not all I found, Lexi. You need to check this out." She plugged the drive into the laptop and angled the screen toward me. "By the way, this isn't classified information. I found it on my own. Just so we're clear."

"We're clear," I said. "And appreciative. What is it?"

"A BBC video of a news report on the afternoon of September 17, the day of the assassination."

I leaned over closer to the screen as the video played. It was grainy footage of three priests getting out of a car in front of the palace steps, greeting a man I assumed was Apeloko. The four men talked for a moment with armed security forces ringing them, until Apeloko motioned they were all to enter the palace. Apeloko pulled aside one priest, putting an arm around him, giving him a favored position at his side as they walked first toward the palace. The other two priests followed behind. For a brief moment, the priest at the president's side glanced over his shoulder, directly at the camera. Gray froze the clip and enlarged the frame by three hundred percent.

"So, this is the interesting part," she said, tapping her finger against the screen.

My breath caught in my throat. The priest in the photo was Slash.

TWENTY

Slash

SLASH WASN'T IN the habit of terrifying priests, but today he was in an unusually poor mood.

After they passed security, where he was required to leave his phone and laptop, they walked through the echoing corridors of the *Palazzo del Governatorato*. Father Koenhein carefully kept his distance. Every time he dared to glance at Slash, he'd cringe at the look he'd receive in return. Once they reached a doorway at the same time, and Slash slapped a hand on the door before opening it. The priest jumped back so violently, he nearly tripped.

Any other time, he might have been amused, but he wasn't. He didn't want to be here, didn't want to be dragged back into a life he thought he'd left long ago. A quick glance at his reflection in the mirrors that lined the walls showed an unshaven jaw and dark circles under his eyes. They passed through one more checkpoint before Father Koenhein led him into the president's office. Slash was instructed to wait in a chair while the father went through one more door, closing it behind him.

Minutes later, he exited, sweeping his hand toward the room. "His Eminence will see you now."

Slash entered the room, met by Cardinal Lazo, dressed in an ordinary black cassock with a heavy silver cross around his neck. Lazo was a tall man—possibly an inch and a half taller than Slash—and had thick black hair peppered with gray. He stood rigidly with the confidence, or perhaps arrogance, of his station. His pretend intellectualism and an ill-hidden disdain for those he considered beneath him were just a couple of the reasons Slash, and many members of the *sodalitium pianum*, had always disliked him. Lazo used his position as a cardinal and the president of the Vatican as a means to serve his own ambition, rather than the good of the flock. He'd derailed several worthy progressive initiatives—especially those supporting the poor—hiding behind the excuse of fiscal responsibility. That, of course, hadn't stopped Lazo from spending exorbitant amounts of money on anything that involved his personal comfort or security.

Lazo remained a dangerous man for many reasons. In addition to the significant power he wielded, he was the key to several important Vatican coalitions, including ones he'd formed within the Foreign Office, the finance department, and a group including several important Italian bishops, minus Father Armando. All of which, Slash was certain, added up to a carefully orchestrated plan to ensure Lazo one day ascended to the papacy.

Regardless, Slash had no intention of playing the game on Lazo's terms, whatever the game might be. But he had to factor in the variables.

"I appreciate you meeting with me on such short notice." Lazo spoke with a slight accent from the southwest region of Campania near Naples, where he'd been born. Father Koenhein discreetly disappeared into the outer office, closing the door behind him.

The cardinal held out a hand, clearly expecting Slash to take it or kneel. He did neither. President of the Vatican or cardinal, he would never kneel to this man. Respect and devotion was earned, and Lazo had done nothing to deserve his.

Displeasure flashed in the cardinal's eyes as he dropped his hand before walking toward a small refrigerator. "Can I offer you a refreshment? Coffee? Chilled water?" His voice remained light, unfailingly polite, but Slash could hear the steel in the undercurrents.

He didn't respond. Better Lazo understood from the start he would not be malleable to his demands. Lazo took two bottles of water out of the refrigerator anyway, and handed one over. Slash accepted it, but offered no thanks.

Perhaps finally understanding that his station or intimidation would have no effect, Lazo waved at a chair. "Please have a seat. Let's start over."

Slash considered a moment before setting his duffel next to the chair and sitting. Lazo took the chair across from him, leaning back and crossing his legs. He noticed at once his chair was slightly lower than Lazo's, certainly not an oversight. However, instead of projecting the intended authority and dominance, it signaled blatant insecurity. That meant Lazo needed something and wasn't sure he had enough power to force Slash's compliance.

"Thank you for coming," the cardinal finally said. "I'm sure you're wondering why I invited you here."

Anger leapt and simmered. The audacity and arrogance of the man was astounding. "Sending unsigned, threatening notes and packages, blocking my brother's request for marriage in the church, and providing an unusual display of fireworks on my front lawn can hardly be considered an invitation," he finally said. "An email or a phone call would have sufficed."

Amusement crossed the cardinal's face, as if he were

delighted by his imagined cleverness. "Oh, I'm afraid I have no idea what you're talking about. I simply heard you'd arrived in town, so I asked Father Koenhein to find you and request a meeting."

Slash had to fight the urge to wipe the smirk off of the cardinal's face. It wasn't easy. "Don't waste my time pretending ignorance. What's so urgent that it requires my physical presence?"

"It's really quite a simple matter, but it's delicate, and not something that can be discussed over the phone. I'm fortunate you happen to be in Rome to discuss this in person with me."

The fingers on one hand curled into a fist, but he deliberately opened them and wrapped them around the bottled water instead. *Breathe in, breathe out. Invite the calm.* Lazo had to play his cards, and Slash had to wait for them.

"So, discuss, Cardinal." He hoped his voice sounded like he couldn't care less, instead of wishing he could plow his fist through Lazo's self-serving grin.

Probably believing he had him on the hook, Lazo leaned forward eagerly. "I have a special and quite important request for you."

"Which is?"

"I want you to publicly acknowledge your biological father."

For a second, Slash couldn't breathe.

His biological father?

Surprise, anger and disbelief coursed through him in a tangled rush. He knew his background was a source of interest to many at the Vatican. There had been plenty of people who'd assumed he had special connections that had helped catapult him to the highest echelons in such a short period of time. But he knew differently. It was skill, not heritage, that propelled him upward. He'd earned every damn thing he'd ever received. So, why did Lazo want him to reveal his parentage now, and how did it fit into his grand scheme?

When he felt in control of his emotions, he spoke. "Why do you care who my father is?"

"Why?" The cardinal lifted his hands. "Oh, my child. Because it's quite important to the church, of course."

Slash didn't believe that for a minute. Everything the cardinal said and did served only one purpose—his own positioning for the papacy. But he pressed on, needing more information. "How exactly does my so-called acknowledgment of my father assist you or the church?"

"It will help me take the church in a new direction."

"What's wrong with the direction it's going in now?"

The cardinal pressed his fingers together as he studied Slash. "I'm afraid it's moving too far away from traditional values. I intend to bring us back."

It was such an absurd statement, he laughed. "To the Dark Ages?"

Cardinal Lazo was not a man used to being mocked, which made it all the more pleasant to watch him seethe. "I would advise caution, my son. You and your loved ones are more vulnerable than you think."

Mention of his family made his response all the more ominous. Slash leaned forward, making sure he crossed into the cardinal's personal space. "Was that a threat, Your Eminence?"

"Of course not." The cardinal pressed a hand to his chest in mock disbelief that Slash had suggested such a thing. But he also moved back a bit in his seat, indicating Slash's message had been received. "It was a promise. I have asked you for a simple request in the name of the church. That's all. After all, an exposed truth must stand on its own merits."

Move and countermove. He had to make his next step carefully. "Well, if you want me to acknowledge my father, I'm afraid you're going to have to tell me who is he is."

"Really?" The cardinal regarded him with interest. "You want to play it this way? Come now. You've always known, haven't you? You've been his secret for far too long."

Time to signal an end to the conversation. Slash stood, reaching for his duffel. "We're done here. I'm not playing your game anymore. Take me out of the equation."

"Father Emilio Armando," Lazo spat out, watching Slash for any hint of reaction.

Slash almost laughed, but caught himself. He'd suspected, but now he knew. *That* was endgame. Father Armando had become Lazo's greatest threat to the papacy, and Lazo was looking for a way to neutralize or even remove him from contention. Father Armando was close to the current pope, was popular and widely viewed as a priest of the people, and was rapidly becoming known as the conscience of the church for his forward-thinking social initiatives and work with the poor and disenfranchised. No wonder Lazo was worried.

So, Lazo's goal was to use Slash against Father Armando. But Lazo wasn't stupid. He knew Slash would never willingly agree to do something like this unless he had irrefutable proof of parentage or a way of extracting Slash's cooperation. Now, he just had to figure out which one it was.

He turned around slowly and regarded the cardinal. "Emilio Armando is my father? Says who?"

"Says me. And says you."

He seemed unusually confident Slash would agree, which made him wary. He hadn't lied to Lazo. He had no idea who his biological parents were. He'd often wondered, and sometimes wished he knew, but he hadn't ever really considered Father Armando a contender for his father. Too many things didn't make sense with that scenario. Regardless, he hated that it had been Lazo to shove that possibility front and center.

Lazo suddenly laughed. "Wait. He didn't tell you? Well, this is certainly an interesting development. I'd assumed he had. After all, you've maintained a close relationship all these years."

Slash masked the disgust, but couldn't keep the derision from his voice. "We're close friends, so now you assume he's my father?"

"Not assume. Know. I have evidence."

Now came the moment of truth. Would it be blackmail or proof? His stomach clenched, but he responded calmly. "Such as?"

"I'm afraid I cannot reveal that. Sanctity of the confessional and all that, of course." Lazo couldn't quite keep the smirk from his face.

Anger coiled even tighter in Slash's gut, but he kept his expression neutral as he needled for more information. "Come now, Cardinal. Did you really expect me to play your little game? You summon me to Italy by threatening my family, then insist I make a statement about Father Armando being my biological father? Apparently you haven't read enough of my file. It isn't wise to piss me off."

Lazo's nostrils flared. "I know exactly who you are. You are a man without conscience, without regret. You want people to think you've turned your life around, but

I know better. Men like you are irredeemable. So, I'd suggest you carefully consider how you answer me. I'm a powerful man with a long reach. You help me, your family stays protected. Cross me, and I promise nothing."

So, there it was—blackmail. Cold and ugly. Slash leaned forward, his tone matching the cardinal's. "Let me make one thing perfectly clear, Cardinal. Stay away from my family. You get one warning, and that's only as a professional courtesy. You touch them, *any* of them, and you'll never see me coming."

"How *dare* you speak to me like that." Fury rolled off Lazo, but not fear. He still believed himself to be untouchable. "Are you aware of who I am?"

"A man who is so weak he has to resort to blackmailing former Vatican employees."

"Oh, please." Lazo waved a hand dismissively. "You think I care about your insults? We both know I'm going to be the next pope. The question is whose side will you choose? I will do whatever it takes to protect the church from this destructive path the current pope is leading us down, so I advise you to consider your words carefully. I'm in a position to help you in ways you can't imagine. And all I need from you is a simple acknowledgment that he's your father."

"Or what? You come after me and my family?"

Lazo spread his hands in a gesture of pretend noncommittal. "Or things from your past, including the Congo, may inadvertently come to light. Things that could change your life for the worse."

There it was. Lazo thought he held an ace in the hole with the Congo operation. While it wasn't an ace, it was still a high card, and Slash had to be careful how he handled this. Without knowing exactly how much Lazo knew about the operation, the safest way to play was to assume he knew it all.

"I thought you wanted to protect the church," he finally said.

"I do, and I will."

"Revealing the details of that operation would help the church exactly how?" He paused, curious how Lazo would respond. "We both know I was acting as an agent of the church."

"Were you?" He paused, steepling his fingers together. "I hope you're confident the documents will back you up on that. After all, a renegade operative is a serious danger to the church and to society. If there were an unfortunate leak about that operation that portrayed you in a bad light, it could cost you your new job at the NSA. Or perhaps adversely affect your newfound love with your talented fiancée. Congratulations on your engagement, by the way. The church approves…so far. You do like your life as it is now, don't you… Viper?"

So Lazo *had* read his file and wasn't just repeating rumors about the Congo mission. The use of his code name confirmed it. Still, he didn't want Lazo to know he was concerned.

He lifted the water to his lips and finished it off. As he screwed the lid back on the empty bottle, he permitted himself a small smile. "You're more worried than I thought. Good. Deal not accepted. I'm not going to lie for you or for anyone."

The cardinal's eyes were chillingly cold. "Ah, but we both know I'm not asking you to lie. As a man of the cloth, such a request would be abhorrent to me. I'm simply asking you to tell the truth."

"You already know my truth."

Lazo's hands clenched tighter around his water bottle. "I suggest you reconsider. You *will* lose this battle, and in the process, it will cost you everything you hold dear. Is it really worth it? Can you handle the trouble coming your way?"

Slash stood and took the position of power, leaning forward until his face was inches from the cardinal's. "You misunderstand me, Cardinal. I *am* the trouble, the variable you can't control. You've no idea what you've unleashed here."

Surprise and perhaps fear—finally—flashed in the cardinal's eyes, but he quickly composed himself. "I'll give you a couple of days to think it over. You have a lot to lose. When I say I will go to extraordinary lengths to ensure the future of the church, I mean it. Consider that carefully when you're deciding." He saw the empty bottle in Slash's hand and dipped his head to the side of the room. "The trash can is over there."

Slash stuck the empty bottle in his duffel instead. "You've made a significant miscalculation, Cardinal. It wasn't a wise move to poke the snake."

"Oppose me and I will crush you," Lazo warned in a low voice, abandoning all pretense of civility. "Don't make a mistake here, son."

"I assure you, I won't make a mistake." Slash lifted the strap of his bag to his shoulder and turned to face the cardinal for one last comment. "If you were a true man of the cloth, you'd concede the future of the church is not up to you, but to a higher power. I'm going to give you one final piece of advice before I leave. If you try to play God, you're going to burn. And I'll be the one to personally see to it."

TWENTY-ONE

Lexi

"Wait. What? Slash was a priest?" Basia said. "I never knew that."

Gray, Basia and I sat, transfixed by the enlarged image of Slash dressed as a priest. My brain had somehow frozen on the photo and couldn't move on from it. I wanted to reach out and turn off the monitor, but I couldn't seem to move or feel anything except the uncomfortable churning of my stomach.

"Lexi, do you know if Slash was ever a priest?" Gray asked gently.

I blinked, trying to bring my thoughts back to the present. It felt weird having my friends revealing things I didn't know about a man I was going to marry. It was completely backward. I should be the one knowing important things about the man I was going to spend the rest of my life with, but I didn't.

"I'm...not sure of anything right now." Anxiety had started to interfere with my thinking. I mentally ran through a couple of rows of Fermat's Last Theorem to calm myself. "You said this picture was taken on September 17th? The same day of Apeloko's assassination?"

"Yes." Gray looked at me with sympathetic eyes.

That look was almost more than I could stand. I

pressed my lips together and kept my mind solely on the facts.

"That would mean Slash was likely in residence when the assassination happened," I said.

"That's a reasonable assumption," said Gray.

"And they never caught who poisoned Apeloko, his son and the priest, right?" Basia asked.

"Correct," Gray answered. "The murders remain unsolved to this day."

I closed my eyes. I didn't like where my thoughts were headed, but I needed more data. "What else do we know about the assassination?"

Gray reached around the laptop for an empty wineglass. "Can I have some of that Malbec first? I could use a drink after all."

"I think we all could use a refill," Basia said.

We held out our glasses, and Basia poured the wine.

"Better," Gray said after a few sips. "So, we know the Catholic Church was in the Congo acting as an intermediary in political negotiations, promoting peace between the various factions. Lexi, do you know if Slash was working for the Vatican in any capacity when he lived in Italy?"

"Yes," I confirmed. "He was working for the Vatican, but I don't know exactly what he did."

That was the truth. Sort of. Only a few people knew about Slash's top-secret connection to the Vatican's intelligence service, the *sodalitium pianum*. But that wasn't my secret to share, so I didn't provide details.

Basia hopped off her stool and came around to put a hand on my shoulder. "Lexi, if you're worried Slash was involved in the assassination, what does it matter?

I mean, this Apeloko guy was a total scumbag. He got what he deserved."

I wasn't sure if I should be shocked or thankful for her words. After considering, I wished she hadn't said anything. It wasn't helping.

"What about the son and the priest?" I asked. "Did they get what they deserved?"

Gray and Basia fell quiet.

I pinched the bridge of my nose with my fingertips, willing myself to think rationally. I was stressing out, which wasn't logical since I knew nothing of political assassinations and their ramifications. As a computer geek, I never expected to have to deliberate such weighty thoughts in my lifetime. While I knew and understood intellectually that Slash's work might involve killing or hurting people, being faced with concrete examples was a different experience altogether.

"I don't know, guys," I finally said. "Despite that photo, I don't think Slash was ever a priest. At least not officially. He once told me once he'd considered the priesthood, but he felt his talents would be better used elsewhere."

"That's no kidding." Basia waved a hand. "I mean, how many times have you and he saved the world in the past year?"

I rolled my eyes at her attempted humor, but I still wasn't feeling any better.

"Well, my best guess is that if Slash were working for the Vatican, he was there on an intelligence-gathering mission," Gray speculated between sips of her wine. "Undercover as a priest, most likely."

"Perhaps," I said. "Is there any way to find out which

other priests were there on the night of the assassination?"

"Not from facial recognition," Gray said. "Their faces are too obscured. But I can try to pull that thread via different sources."

"Thanks, Gray. I'd appreciate it. That would be helpful." My expression must have worried them because Basia kept her hand on my shoulder and now Gray touched my arm as if in solidarity.

"Lexi, this happened seven years ago," Gray said. "A long time before Slash met you. A person can change a lot in seven years."

I inclined my head. "I know. You guys don't have to worry about me. I'll work this out. I don't intend to be judgmental of a situation and circumstances I know nothing about. Slash told me he's done things he never wants to talk about again—not surprising given his line of work. I'm gathering information solely to help him, not to judge him for what he may, or may not, have done."

Even as I said that, I couldn't deny I *was* worried about my reaction and understanding of the situation and Slash's role, even if I didn't intend to be judgmental.

"We know," Gray said, setting down her wine. "But *suspecting* Slash can do such things and *knowing* he can do such things are two different beasts. I'm saying that because it's something I've had to deal with given Hands's line of work."

"Guys, I appreciate your concern, but I'm okay." I sounded a lot more confident than I felt. "I've got this."

Gray didn't look convinced, and that was probably because my poker face stunk. But thankfully she dropped that subject and moved on. "Lexi, I need to ask you a couple more questions. How much do you really know about Slash? I mean, do you know when he came to the US?"

I thought back to a previous conversation. "He told me it was about six-and-a-half to seven years ago, and yes, I know that puts it shortly after this incident. I don't know the exact date of his arrival, though."

"I've confirmed his arrival in the US at that time, too," Gray said.

I looked at her in surprise. "If you already knew, why did you ask me?"

Gray blinked and looked down into her wineglass. Basia became unusually quiet as well. I looked between them until I figured it out.

"You were checking to see if Slash lied to me."

Gray didn't deny it. "I'm just looking out for you, Lexi. There are a lot of unknowns about Slash. For example, did he already have a job at the NSA when he came from Italy? He couldn't have hooked up with the NSA blindly. There had to be some kind of connection there. One does not simply join the NSA, especially as a foreigner. You, better than most, know it doesn't work that way."

"There was a connection," I said. "He came recommended from someone at the Vatican, I think. Slash told me he was already working at the NSA when he was assigned as part of the team to protect the president's infrastructure and network after Elvis and Xavier left for the private sector. Slash was apparently so good at what he was doing, he became a legend. I worked at the NSA at the time, and I honestly thought 'Slash' was a concept made up by the executive staff to convince everyone that the networks would remain impenetrable after the departure of the Zimmerman twins. I honestly didn't believe Slash was a real person until he showed up in my bedroom one night."

"Slash showed up in your *bedroom*?" Gray said.

Oops, I guess I'd never told her how Slash and I met. "Yeah, but that's a story for another time." I waved my hand. "Anyway, I assumed Slash got the position due to his unique and extraordinary capabilities on the keyboard."

Gray tapped her pencil against the table, thinking. "It's possible, but something about his situation wasn't adding up for me, so I did a little digging of my own. It wasn't easy. Slash has a list of aliases longer than I've ever seen, and I work at the CIA. Anyway, I had to call in a couple of favors, but I finally got the name he's using on his official documents at the NSA. Unfortunately, I don't think it's his real name, because the date it was issued and his age don't add up. He would have been seven years old when this was issued. Something is off."

"He was adopted," I explained, feeling guilty and horrible that I was revealing this, even though Basia and Gray were two of my closest friends and I knew they'd keep it confidential. "He was in foster care in Italy until age seven. He vanished with his foster family—fell off the radar completely. Something happened to him during those seven years. Eventually he turned up in a hospital in Sperlonga, a city on Italy's coast. He…has no memory of those seven years. I don't think anyone was ever able to track down what happened to the foster family who'd taken him in. A nurse who treated him in the hospital adopted him. She gave him a new name and a family he took as his own. That would account for the discrepancy in the years."

Basia and Gray both had stricken expressions on their

faces. Slash was exceptionally private, and I'd never said anything about it, so, of course they hadn't known. He would have hated that I had divulged this, but I needed to be straight with both of them if they were going to help me help him. His safety was paramount at this stage. Still, I had to look away to keep my composure, but I cleared my throat and continued. "Anyway, I assumed his naturalization process and security clearances were put on the fast track due to his specialized skill and the critical needs of the US government. That makes the most sense."

"It does, but there's something else, Lexi. Something significant." Gray spoke, almost hesitantly. "Slash didn't go through the naturalization process."

"What?" It was inconceivable. Naturalization was the law, and no one would be exempt, not even Slash. "How would that be possible?"

Gray leaned forward. "It's possible because he didn't *need* to go through it. Slash was already a US citizen. According to his records on file at the NSA, he's been one all his life."

TWENTY-TWO

Cardinal Jacopo Lazo

JACOPO WATCHED SLASH walk out the door without a backward glance. That man was going to be a lot harder to handle than he'd expected. No matter, there were other methods to get what he wanted, if Slash refused to cooperate. The man had serious demons, so he needed to play those to his advantage.

Father Koenhein knocked a few minutes later and stuck his head in the door. "He's gone, Your Eminence. The driver is taking him back to his hotel. Did he agree?"

"He did not. Yet. But it doesn't matter. We'll get what we need with or without his cooperation."

"Did he leave the water bottle?"

"No. He didn't fall for it. He took it with him. Unfortunately, he's a lot smarter than that. Did we get anything from the hotel?"

"No, sir. We found no luggage, nor any evidence he had used the facilities. The room was pristine. But we'll try again tomorrow. We'll get something."

"You'd better. I need that DNA sample. His house in the US is a fortress with top-notch alarms and agents following him everywhere. He works at the most secret agency in the world. But now, we've finally got him where we want him. If he's not going to cooperate willingly, we'll *have* to get something from him while he's here. Do you understand what I mean by that?" He hated having to repeat himself, and usually Koenhein was good about things, but he seemed to be slipping up lately.

"I understand."

"Good. A strand of hair, saliva, anything. Get me a sample."

"Of course, Your Eminence. We have our best people on it."

"I'm counting on that." He paused and tossed his own water bottle into the trash. "Oh, Father, be aware of one more thing."

"Yes?" Father Koenhein said turning around. "What is it?"

"Be careful. He's a dangerous man, but he can serve us well."

The priest lowered his eyes. "I understand, Your Eminence. I will take all necessary precautions."

"I'm counting on it. Remember, eggs have no business dancing with stones. If our people aren't capable and prepared, he will break them. I don't want to see that happen."

Slash

INTRIGUE, SCANDAL AND innuendo were nothing new in the history of the Vatican. Slash wasn't surprised by it, he'd just never expected to be a part of it.

Now he was front and center at a struggle for power in the Vatican. How did he intend to handle it?

Father Koenhein didn't accompany him for the return ride, which suited Slash just fine. For the entire drive, he'd been analyzing and creating various scenarios for the game's end. That was the way his mind worked. Start at the desired result and work backward until the path forward became clear. But first he had to think like Lazo to get a feel for his agenda.

Given the pope's failing health, Lazo would certainly be making a hard play for the papacy. He'd been positioning himself for this opportunity for his entire career, so he'd definitely have a plan in the works. He'd just revealed his first step—removing the competition. That meant for the immediate future, he'd be hyper-focused on Father Armando and anyone else he saw as a threat. Good. While Lazo was working on that, Slash had a plan to disrupt things just enough to slow Lazo's current operation without him even realizing it.

On the way up to his hotel room, he once again ran into the blind woman and the seeing-eye German shepherd as they exited the room two doors down from him. With her permission, he stopped to pet the dog, who was panting heavily, suffering from the Italian heat.

"How long are you in Rome?" he asked the woman conversationally, as he scratched the dog behind the ears.

"I'm visiting relatives," she answered. "I'll be here a few more days."

"Enjoy your visit. Both of you."

"I will. Thank you, sir."

An idea suddenly occurred to him, and he waited until she passed. Tapping his key card to the door pad, he went inside. As expected, both of his internal wire traps were tripped. They wouldn't have found anything, but he was certain they'd be back. This time, he'd make sure they found something. Now he knew the game, he was ready to make his first move.

But first, he had a lot to do.

TWENTY-THREE

Lexi

GRAY AND BASIA left well past midnight. After they were
gone, I gathered up all the papers and Gray's thumb
drive, which she'd left for me, then slipped my laptop
under my arm and climbed the stairs to the home office
Slash and I now shared. I was stressed and exhausted,
but my mind was on overload, churning with an endless stream of information that needed sorting, clarifi-
cation and organization. Before I could sleep, I had to
determine what pieces of information were important
and which ones to discard.

What I needed was a spreadsheet and a clear strategy.

I tapped in the security code for the office and blinked
into the retinal scanner until the door clicked open, the
lights automatically turning on as I entered. I loved this
space. We had filled it with the things we cherished
most—top-of-the-line computer hardware and software.
We had not spared any expense in this room, which in
our case meant we pretty much had the virtual world at
our fingertips.

Slash had his desk and work area on one side of the
room, and mine was on the other. Not because we wanted
to be apart, but to help us focus on the work and not each
other. That was difficult when we were in close proximity. We'd chosen sleek module furniture, and Slash had

wired the entire house to handle the most optimal speed. His black desk had three large plasma monitors, two vertical and one horizontal on his desk, with two more on a nearby table. We had a cluster of laptops dedicated to various tasks, completely customizable, depending on what we needed. My desk was white with two oversize monitors and a laptop, which I now held under my arm. I set it on the desk and slipped on the sweater draped over the back of my chair because we kept the room arctic cold as a result of the equipment. I reattached the laptop to a large monitor on my desk before I got to work.

Several hours later, I'd printed and taped a series of spreadsheets to the wall with all the pertinent information I'd gathered, creating a visual timeline of Slash's life. Unfortunately, I needed more information, which meant one thing—it was time to hack. But I needed help for this one. Powerful help.

I glanced at the clock. It was already five in the morning. Thank God it was Saturday. I shot a quick text to Elvis, asking him if he'd have time for a consult later today.

He texted back almost immediately, which was unusual since he told me he'd been working on a big project and going to bed early so he could function during the day when he led a team.

Just heading to bed. Looks like we are both keeping hacker hours. Let's meet at my place at two o'clock. Does that work for you?

I smiled. He was one of my best friends, and somehow it was comforting that our schedules were back in sync. When we both worked at the NSA, before we left for the less restrictive private sector, we typically kept hacker hours. But now we both had significant others, which meant less time to game and hack at night. So, it surprised me he was awake now.

I tapped out a text stating my agreement before standing up and yawning. I desperately needed some sleep to function properly. I got into my pajamas, washed my face and brushed my teeth. Before I fell asleep, I realized I hadn't talked to Slash today. He hadn't called me, and I hadn't called him. When was the last time we'd gone twenty-four hours without speaking to each other?

I looked down at my engagement ring, and pressed my thumb against the band. Part of me wanted to call him right at this moment and be damned with time zones and painful secrets, but part of me was afraid.

As I was summoning my courage to call him, I fell asleep. Another day passed without us talking to each other.

Lexi

IT WAS EXACTLY 1:58 p.m. when I pulled up in front of the Zimmermans' house. I wasn't feeling awake or well— stress and lack of sleep were all playing a big role in that. I rang the doorbell and Gwen, Elvis's girlfriend, answered.

"Hey, Lexi." Gwen ushered me in. She looked cute in a navy T-shirt, jean shorts and bare feet. Her flaming red hair was loose around her shoulders, her face void of makeup, full of freckles.

"Elvis said you were coming over," she said cheerfully. "He's getting out of the shower. Guess he had a late night on the computer."

"Yeah. Me, too." I strolled into the twins' command center, which was a converted dining room where they worked and kept all their equipment and computers.

I stopped in the doorway. It was the same room, but it looked...different. The couch had been pushed against one of the walls and now had pretty throw pillows and there was a new rug spreading color across the wooden floor. The cords on the curtains had been neatly gathered and tied. Holy cow! Were there curtains on the windows?

"Wow." I did a three-sixty revolution. "You fixed things up."

"Just a little. I've been staying here an awful lot, and Elvis encouraged me to do it, so I did." Gwen tucked her hair behind her ears. "Do you like it?"

"Yeah, I do. It looks great." I spotted a small table to the side with a chair on either side covered in Legos and what looked like a half-finished project. I spied the box nearby on the floor. "No way. Is that the Taj Mahal Lego set?"

She smiled. "Elvis bought it and we're spending our free time building it. Cool, right?"

"Totally cool. Gwen, everything looks really nice. Seriously." She'd been careful not to change up anything big, just small, homey touches. I spotted a little plant on Elvis's desk. Plus, the Lego area was prime, and I knew Elvis had to love it.

Gwen picked up one of two blankets draped over the back of the couch and handed it to me. "You still have your own blanket here. I had to get one, too, because they keep it so cold in here, but this one is still the Lexi blanket."

"Thanks." I took the blanket, surprisingly touched by the gesture.

I draped it around my shoulders as Elvis walked in. His hair was still damp from the shower. Dressed in shorts and a black T-shirt, he slid his glasses on his nose as he came into the room.

"Hey, Lexi." He looked rested and relaxed, and maybe even a couple of pounds heavier. Gwen was probably cooking for him, because he was about as good a cook as I was.

"Hey, back at you," I said. "Thanks for seeing me today." I studied his face and manners. He seemed content. I liked that. He and Gwen hadn't been dating long, but things were clearly going great.

As if to prove my point, he walked over to Gwen and slid an arm around her waist, then kissed her on the cheek. They were a cute unit, and seeing them together warmed my heart.

"So, geek princess, I understand you need a consult," he said to me.

"I do."

"I hope it involves some serious hacking. I've been busy on a project that's leaving me no time to spread my wings. I could use a good hack."

"Well, I've got one for you."

Gwen lifted a hand. "Okay, you two continue your geek speak. That's my cue to leave. Elvis, I've got your coffee and some breakfast in the kitchen, although already it's past lunchtime. I'll bring it to you." She turned to me. "You want something, Lexi?"

"Coffee would be great. Lots of milk."

"Coming up."

She headed into the kitchen and Elvis went around to the couch and sat down. He tapped the spot next to him. "Talk to me."

I decided to get right to the point. "I want to hack the Vatican archives."

"*What?* Are you out of your everlasting mind?"

Really? He didn't have to be so dramatic. "I want to hack into the Vatican archives," I repeated. "We hacked them before—you know, as part of our job—so it's do-able."

"No, we hacked a *file* from the Vatican," he corrected. "The file had already been extracted from the archives, and it was heavily encrypted. It took the four of us—you, me, Slash and Xavier, as well as some heavy equipment—about forty-eight hours to get into it."

"I know, but we're familiar with the coding, the style," I argued. "I think we can do it."

He leaned forward, his elbows on his thighs. "Lexi, come on. You know better than this. You don't walk into a guy's house and say 'Let's hack the Vatican.' Besides, Slash would be the guy for this job anyway. Why didn't you ask him? What's really going on?"

I tugged nervously on my ponytail. "It's Slash. I think he's in trouble."

"What kind of trouble?"

"I'm not sure." I gave him a brief update on the cryptic note, the note from the fireworks, Slash's brother, Giorgio, and the *nkondi* statue.

Elvis whistled when I finished. "Wow. Slash won't tell you what's going on?"

"He can't or won't. I don't know which one it is."

His brows drew together as he processed that. Elvis liked relationship talk as much as I did—which was not at all—but he'd initiate it if he thought I wanted it. Right now, I definitely didn't, so I asked him, "So, will you help?"

He seemed undecided as to whether to push for more information, but then he changed tactics. "Are you looking for a particular file in the Vatican?"

"Yes. It has to do with the assassination of President Apeloko of the Congo, seven years ago. The Catholic Church was involved in the negotiations between Apeloko and the Congolese bishops who were trying to ease the iron fist of his despotism."

"I remember reading about that." Elvis ran his hand through his hair. "Didn't the guy and his son get assassinated, presumably by some of their associates?"

"Yes, that's the one."

His brow furrowed together as it did when he thought. "Does it have to be the Vatican archives? There might be useful intelligence on that situation elsewhere."

"I need to know exactly who within the Catholic Church was involved and how. Specifically, I want to know if Slash was involved. The Vatican would be the ones with the file, right?"

"Well, yes, but they might not be the only ones with intelligence on the assassination." He shifted on the couch so he could look at me directly. "What about taking this down a notch, at least at first? We'd have a better chance of getting the information you need if we come at it from a different angle."

"What angle?"

"The CIA angle. I guarantee you, they'll have intelligence on what went down in the Congo. That would be much more familiar hacking for both of us, although a lot more dangerous this close to home. Still, we'd have a better chance to get at this in a timely fashion if we go that route."

I pressed my hand against my forehead. "It's a good

idea, Elvis. I'm not thinking properly. I'm too close to this."

He put an arm around my shoulder, pulled me in for a hug. "Look, I get it. You love him, which means you've got a lot invested in his safety. So do I. Slash saved my life on more than one occasion. If he's in trouble, I've got his back. Besides, I may have a trick or two up my sleeve. Come on, let's get hacking."

"I don't know what to say. Thanks, Elvis."

"No thanks necessary. You can count on me anytime."

TWENTY-FOUR

Lexi

ELVIS HAD MORE than a trick; he had a freaking back door into the CIA, which saved us, at minimum, forty-eight hours of work. Possibly more. We drank coffee, ate snacks and hacked our hearts out rooting around in the system. We proceeded cautiously, so as not to draw the attention of their security monitoring software. It was extremely tedious work, unlike in the movies when after three dramatic clicks, the desired information popped up. Finding a specific file without using the search query function—which inevitably tipped off the security software—was like finding a special magic sword in multiplayer game world. There were lots of promising leads and even more dead ends.

Around dinnertime Basia and Xavier returned from purchasing furniture for their new house, on which they would close next Tuesday. Xavier joined the hack after Elvis quickly brought him up to speed. The backdoor was starting to get crowded. Basia and Gwen went out on the back porch to drink lemonade and enjoy the warm evening while dinner cooked.

"Bingo!" Elvis finally exclaimed. "I've found a folder that appears to correspond to the target years and countries. Give me a minute to poke around in the subfolders." He spent a bit of time investigating. "This looks like the right stuff, but the security processes are pretty lame. There's no use of code names, just regular text subfolder headings Africa, Congo, Vatican, and Apeloko. I would have expected something more innocuous like Project 19 or Continent X."

Inner alarms were going off in my head, and I sensed Elvis's growing unease, as well.

"Okay, we need to assume there might be a security tripwire associated with this information that we need to avoid," I said. "Hopefully we haven't already tripped it. We can't back out now that we're so close, but we don't want create an uproar that will bring attention to this information if, in fact, it's damaging to Slash."

"So what's the plan?" Elvis asked.

I considered the options. "Well, it looks like there's an audio file, a large video file, a couple of photos, and some documents. All encrypted, naturally. It will be difficult to copy the video or audio files because of their size without alerting the monitoring software, but we might swing it. We could also attempt it in two stages, grabbing some documents and getting out, seeing if we can crack the encryption, and confirming that it contains the material we're looking for, then going back for the rest if we need to do so."

"You got a plan, geek princess?" Xavier asked.

I considered the options. It might be trap to find out who might be interested in this material and it might just be a honey pot that was established with false or fictional information to convince an interested party to stop looking while alerting the authorities to the presence of prowlers. But I didn't believe anyone would go to the trouble of creating audio and video files in a honey pot. Too much time and wasted effort. So, my gut was telling me it had to be the stuff we wanted. We just had to be very careful and a lot smarter than the defenders.

"Yeah, follow my lead." I tapped on some keys. "We're going to go in real slow. If we detect a trap, we shift gears and try to buy enough time to grab what we can and get out."

I handed Xavier and Elvis their assignments. "Xavier, I want you to monitor the back door to make sure that we get some warning of any activity that might try and close it before we can get out. Elvis, you have the security monitoring software. Do whatever you can to keep it asleep or distracted long enough so we can get out. I'll also need you to make sure that we can't be backtracked afterward in the activity logs if they do detect our presence. I'm going to grab as many of the documents as I dare, and perhaps a photo or two if things are going well. That shouldn't take too long, and we'll just have to hope that it's enough. I want to do this in just one try, so let's put our best game faces on."

"Got it," Elvis said. "Be advised it will take me about fifteen minutes to set up so I can monitor the security software and temporarily suspend the activity logging." His fingers raced across the keys.

While he was doing that, Xavier reported he was in position, monitoring the back door. I spent the next fifteen minutes planning my exact steps so I'd be as quick as possible in case we did set off an alarm.

"Okay, I'm ready," Elvis said. "Just give me a heads-up right before you start to actually copy the files. I'm going to create an error loop that will effectively block the security software and make any file transfer logs that do get saved look like a malfunction."

"Understood." I began with the penetration, taking

my time and going as carefully as I could. After about five minutes, Xavier interrupted my train of thought.

"Lexi, we have something going on with the back door," he said. "It's subtle, but the traffic through the access point has increased in the last two minutes. Are either of you doing anything that would cause that?"

"Nope," Elvis said. "Not me."

"Me neither," I said. "Did we trip an alarm?"

"I don't think so," Xavier mused. "It appears most of the traffic right now is from the outside coming in."

I watched the data scroll across my screen looking for answers or anomalies. Something was off. "That's strange. Elvis, who else would know about this back door?"

"No one except for Xavier and me. If someone else does, we'll have to close it down after this."

"Understood. Keep monitoring it. I want to get this done and get out of here." I navigated to the subfolder and started to select the files in order to copy them when they suddenly disappeared. I refreshed my directory and caught a glimpse of them before they vanished again.

My hands flew across the keyboard. "Elvis, what's going on? Is the security system onto us? It looks like it is randomly renaming the files." I refreshed the directory and everything changed again.

"No." His voice sounded puzzled. "There is no indication the security system is aware of our presence at all."

"Once again, the back door is showing increased unknown activity," Xavier offered. "Can't explain it, but it's definitely there."

What the heck is going on?

I jumped out of the hack to write a quick script and

readied it for my next attempt. "Elvis, I am going to try and copy a file in about ten seconds. Are you ready?"

"You're good. Go for it."

I ran the script, then hit refresh. Immediately I received a message confirming I'd retrieved the file. But when I went to where the copied file was supposed to be, the directory was blank. My log showed I'd copied the file, but somehow my copy had been routed to some unknown directory.

"What's going on?" I asked, mystified.

"Back door activity spiked about fifteen seconds ago and has since gone back down," Xavier stated calmly.

"No change in the security software," Elvis reported.

Frustrated, I revised the script to make two copies instead of one, routing the first to the same new temporary subdirectory I tried to use last time. Concurrently, I secretly sent a second copy directly back to my laptop through the back door. I alerted Xavier and Elvis of my planned maneuver and ran the script. Abruptly, I was kicked out of the system.

"Back door just went down and then came back up," Xavier said.

"I'm knocked out," said Elvis.

A quick check confirmed my copy of the file did not make it through the back door before it went down. That meant only one thing. There was no automatic software that could be responding in this sophisticated a fashion.

We were facing a human opponent. Someone who was good.

Very good.

"Holy crap!" I breathed. "There's someone on the other side in real time, and they aren't using the regular security software. We must have tripped a hidden alarm when we first started looking for the files. Who could it be?"

"No idea," Xavier said. "But it's weird. The defensive activities are being directed from outside the back door and corresponding with the activity spikes."

No way was that right. "That's…impossible!" I stared at the screen. "Outside protection on files that are seven years old? Through a hidden back door supposedly only known by you and Elvis and being handled by an incredibly talented hacker?"

"Crazy." Elvis's shoulders were tense, but I heard a note of excitement in his voice. He wasn't used to meeting anyone approaching his level of skill. "Who the heck are they hiring at the CIA these days?"

"It just doesn't make sense." My brain hurt. Someone had anticipated and counter opposed my moves effortlessly. "It's bizarre. It's like whoever is on the other side can read my mind and knows what I'll do before I even do it."

Xavier swore when the back door suddenly dropped offline again. "I know, right? This is wizard-level planning and execution. With the exception of a few Russian and Chinese hackers, there isn't anybody I know with moves like this outside our group."

My fingers froze on the keyboard. OMG. The pieces suddenly fit together.

Gwen, who must have been in the kitchen, ran in to see what all the excitement was about. "What's going on?"

"We're close to our prize," Elvis said. "Come on, come on. Xavier, get that back door open again."

"Lexi," Xavier barked, snapping me out of my trance. "The door is open. What do you want us to do now?"

Nothing. I was numb. There was only one person in

the world who would know about the Zimmermans' back door and would know my moves, our moves, like that.

"Abort," I said quietly.

"*What?*" Elvis threw a wild glance over his shoulder at me. He had the hacker glaze, a look we got when we get close to the target of the hack. "Are you kidding? We're so close."

"Abort. Please." I said it louder this time, trying to keep the panic out of my voice.

"Why?" Elvis's face scrunched up in confusion. "The security software has no idea we're inside. We're just fighting with another hacker who wants the information for himself. We can beat him. We don't want to let him get there first. It puts Slash at further risk."

"Elvis, it's Slash on the other side." My nerves, stretched to the breaking point, were causing queasy twitches in my stomach. "He doesn't want me to see what's in there. He knows if we're determined he can't keep all three of us out at the same time, especially when we're using the same back door. He can't shut that down permanently or he shuts himself out, too. He also knows he can't do too much or he'll alert the authorities and jeopardize the back door. But he's still trying anyway, hoping we will quit." I couldn't believe I was saying this. How had it come to this—Slash and I on opposing sides? We were actively working against each other, like enemies. The queasiness in my stomach was turning into full-fledged nausea.

Elvis was as floored by the situation as I was, color rising in his cheeks. "Are you kidding me? We're hacking against Slash? Why the hell would he try to stop us? I thought you were trying to help him."

"I am. It's complicated." How could I explain it to Elvis when I was just working it out myself?

"Lexi, does he know it's you?" Xavier asked.

"I think so."

"And he's still blocking you?" Elvis asked, his voice incredulous. "What's going on with you two?"

My throat was so tight, I could barely squeak out the words. "I think he's protecting me."

For a moment, Elvis stared at me and then shook his head. "That's not cool. Not cool at all." Then he turned, tapped something on the keyboard and stood up. "I sure hope you know what you're doing."

I didn't.

Without another word, he turned and left the room. I let him go. I couldn't deal with his feelings when I was still fighting my own.

"Okay. I'm closing up," Xavier said, his hands busy on the keyboard. "At least it was Slash coming in through our back door and not someone else. Guess I must have mentioned it to him before. That guy has a mind like a steel trap."

As he shut down, I sat in front of my laptop, staring blankly at the screen. I felt sick.

Xavier stood, flexed and shook out his hands. "Don't worry, Lexi. Everything will work out." As he walked past, he put his hand on my shoulder, letting the solid weight linger for a moment. He didn't ask what was going on with Slash and me or why I'd made the decision I had. I suppose neither mattered at this point.

Xavier disappeared into the kitchen, and I heard a door open and close. He'd gone out to the back porch, presumably to find Basia.

I glanced up when I heard a shuffling noise. Gwen.

I'd forgotten she was still here. She looked at me sympathetically. "Lexi, are you okay?"

Was she kidding? I'd just had a serious hack-off against my fiancé. We'd been officially on opposing sides, working hard to thwart each other. It wasn't a drill. It wasn't a game. We'd been aggressive opponents, fighting a brutal, virtual duel against each other.

How had this happened to us?

"No, I'm not okay," I admitted. "I just hacked against the man I love. He shut me out, and I let him."

"Why?" she asked. Her question was innocent and concerned, and it helped me focus.

"I don't know, Gwen. I think he's afraid of losing me. Whatever is in those files, he must have known I'd come after them, and that's why he set a trap…why he was waiting for me." The fact that he'd planned the tripwire and trap in advance, knowing I'd come for them, hurt more than I could articulate.

I held up my left hand where the blue diamond in my engagement ring sparkled. "It doesn't make sense. Why is he fighting me so hard on this? We're committed to spending the rest of our lives together. He's not going to lose me because of what's in a file."

I wouldn't let that happen.

Gwen's voice softened. "I think what's important is that you loved him enough to stop the hack. You stopped it because you were protecting Slash, just like he was protecting you. That's what people who really love each other do. They stick together. They figure it out. I know you will."

Sudden clarity descended on me and I abruptly stood. "Gwen, you're absolutely right." I knew exactly what I had to do.

I shoved my laptop into my bag. "Tell Elvis and Xavier I'm sorry I wasted their time. I'll make it up to them. I promise."

Alarm crossed her face. "Of course, I'll tell them. But Lexi...what are you doing?"

I added the power cord to my bag and zipped it up. I slung it over my shoulder, my voice steady, my mind made up.

"Doing what I should have done in the first place. I'm going to Italy."

TWENTY-FIVE

Slash

A THOUSAND MILES and an ocean away in his Rome hotel, Slash closed his laptop, resting his elbows atop it and placing his forehead in his hands. She'd found the files. He had no doubt it was Lexi the second the alarm had been triggered. She'd been faster than he expected, and he should have known better than to underestimate her. As soon as he saw the hacker's methods, his suspicions were confirmed. He'd hacked enough times with her to know her style. He also knew Xavier and Elvis were helping her. It was their back door, after all. It's what he would have done—brought in the best to get the information. If only they knew this was the one time he didn't want their help. He didn't want any of them to know what those files held.

He'd known he'd never be able to hold all three of them off in a hotel without special equipment and top-notch wifi speed. But he had to try. Then, without warning, they'd suddenly backed off when they were within seconds of getting the files they wanted.

Why?

He wasn't sure of the answer. But he had his suspicions. Did they know it was him on the other side?

A headache brewed behind his eyes. His shoulders ached, and he felt swamped with a sense of wasted time and useless futility. Why was he doing this? He'd placed his fiancée and his closest friends on the opposing side. How the hell had that happened? How had he let that happen?

What is it that gives meaning to your life? That's your direction, Nicolo.

Father Armando's words echoed in his head. He'd asked Slash that very question when he'd sought counsel from the father about a transfer after the incident in the Congo. Slash had truly believed the work he could do behind the computer would give his life meaning, but now he knew he'd been wrong. His work gave him *purpose*, but it was Lexi who gave his life *meaning*.

He'd thought he could leave his past behind, take ahold of the life he'd always wanted. Lexi had offered him a new start, a chance at genuine happiness. He wanted to have that more than he'd ever wanted anything in his life.

Now they were worlds apart and it was his fault.

His past would always haunt them. He didn't know how to fix that, wasn't sure it was even possible. He picked up his phone, held it in his hand. After a moment, he tapped out a quick text, saying the only thing he could at this moment.

I love you, *cara*. I always will.

He stared at the text for a long time before sending it, then slipped his phone back into his pocket. As he was about to stand, he felt his phone vibrate. He pulled it out and opened it. She'd already responded to his text.

I know you love me. Now you're going to have to trust me.

He stared at the message for a long time, wondering what she meant and how he should respond. He waited for questions that never came—questions he wouldn't know how to answer. But his phone remained silent. After a minute, he set the phone aside, poured himself some coffee, then sat down to resume the work on his laptop.

He had important things to do before he left for Genoa again.

TWENTY-SIX

Slash

SLASH SLIPPED THE concierge a two-hundred dollar tip to have maid service first thing in the morning. He also tipped the maid well, ensuring she would do a good job. The cardinal's team would be back, and he wanted to make sure they found only what he wanted them to find. As soon as the maid finished cleaning and left, he made some small adjustments, then took one look around the room and headed out. His visit at the Vatican, coupled with the hack on the Africa file, made it clear that time was ticking for him to get the answers he needed. And he fully intended to get them.

He ran several errands in Rome, so by the time he arrived in Genoa it was dusk. He parked two blocks away from the small brown apartment building next door to the Cathedral of San Lorenzo and entered the building along with a young woman who let him in after he smiled at her. She gave him a long once-over, which he politely acknowledged with a slight nod before he quickly climbed the two floors to Father Armando's apartment.

He pushed the buzzer and waited patiently until the priest came to the door and looked through the peephole. The lock clicked and Father Armando swung open the door, looking concerned.

"Nicolo, you've returned so soon? Are you okay? What happened?"

"Emilio, can we talk?"

His use of the father's familiar name, as well as the grim look on Slash's face, surprised him. But it also alerted him that something was afoot, and Father Armando was an astute man.

"Of course. Forgive me. I'm surprised to see you. Come in." He opened the door and Slash walked inside, waiting in the foyer until Father Armando had relocked the door.

"To what do I owe this visit?" he asked, ushering Slash into the small living room. A radio was on in the background. From the sound of it, the father had been listening to a program about detoxifying the Christian soul.

"I couldn't pass up the chance to visit you again while I was in Italy. Please continue listening to your program. I'll wait."

The father looked confused, but Slash shook his head and held a finger to his lips as he removed a radio frequency detector from his bag. Slash liked this model because not only could it detect most wireless cameras and microphones, it could also detect wireless bugs, and he needed to make certain the apartment was completely clean before they started talking.

He started in the living room, stopping beneath a ceiling light fixture. Setting down the detector, he took a chair and placed it beneath the light. A couple of quick turns on the light fixture and he found what he was looking for.

Holding the micro transmitter between his fingers, Slash snapped it as the father looked on in shock. Slash resumed his search through the rest of the apartment, but it was clean. He returned to the living room where Father Armando sat on the couch, holding a bottle of cognac and pouring a generous amount into two glasses.

"So, it's true," he said, his hand shaking slightly as he poured. "Spying on me in the office and now at home. For what purpose would someone want to eavesdrop on me in my own home?"

Slash sank into a chair across from the couch. "There's a game being played in Rome and it involves you and me."

The father set the bottle down and handed Slash a glass. "What in the world would either of us have to do with any of the machinations in Rome?"

"A lot, apparently." Slash swirled the cognac for a moment and took long a drink, fortifying himself. "You're a threat."

Father Armando pointed to himself as if he'd heard Slash incorrectly. "Me? How am I a threat and to whom?"

"Cardinal Lazo. He has eyes on the papacy."

"Well, that's no secret. But what does that have to do with me?"

"Do you really have no idea?" Slash studied him, looking for any signs of deception, but saw none. Thank God. Father Armando was as guileless in this matter as he'd suspected.

"I do not."

"You're a popular man, Father. There are a lot of powerful people who would like to see the papacy returned to the Italians. Right now, you have a strong coalition building in Rome. Imagine what you could do with that if the pope were to pass."

"That's ridiculous. I'm a new cardinal, and nothing more than a fierce and loyal follower of the Holy Father.

Besides, I happen to be Italian, but that does not matter to God. He looks into my heart, not my ethnicity. I have no desire to return the papacy to Italians. I wish nothing more than the next pope is a true man of God and a defender of the people and poor."

That was exactly what he'd believed Father Armando would say. Now that he had, it made him more convinced to protect him. "But you could still be voted in if the Holy Father were to pass." He rested his elbows on his thighs. "Listen to me, Emilio. You would have the pope's following, as well as those who favor his more progressive agenda. Lazo, he's no fan of the Holy Father or progress."

"Well, if Lazo is threatened by me, then he's certainly desperate." Father Armando took a swallow of his cognac.

Slash tried to temper his frustration. The father clearly didn't believe himself to be a threat, and Slash needed to change his perception on that.

"He's not desperate, Emilio. He's shrewd, and in this case, he's right. You could rally the pope's forces. You're his single greatest threat."

"Nonsense. I told you, I am not seeking the papacy."

"It is possible, and Lazo sees it. He's the best positioned of all the cardinals right now to take the papacy, and he knows it. He could easily consolidate the Italians and go that route, but only if you are out of his way. So, unfortunately, we'll have to play his game, at least for a little bit."

Father Armando looked up sharply. "Play his game? What does that mean?"

Setting his glass on the table, Slash looked directly into the priest's eyes. A fist squeezed his heart, a suffo-

cating sensation. He wanted to know the truth, but part of him didn't. There was safety in not knowing, because knowing might change the dynamic between them, and Slash didn't want to venture into that kind of unknown territory. But Cardinal Lazo had forced his hand, and now he needed to know. He steadied himself internally, preparing himself for the question, as well as the answer.

"I need to ask you a question, and I pray you will tell me the truth. It may matter, it may not. But I need to have the information." He cleared his throat a couple of times before he could continue. Why was this so hard after all these years?

"Emilio, are you my father?"

A myriad of expressions—stunned, shocked, scared—crossed Father Armando's face. For an endless moment, the question hung in the air, suspended between them. Cars zoomed past on the street below, and there was faint laughter from the adjoining flat where a neighbor had the television turned up too loudly.

They stared at each other, neither speaking. It was a simple question, but given the length of time it was taking the priest to speak, apparently the answer wasn't quite as straightforward.

"Nicolo, why would you ask me that?" Father Armando finally asked. Sadness and regret tinged his voice.

It was neither the answer nor the reaction Slash expected. Hurt and confusion swept through him. "I need to know if it's true. It's just a question." But he knew it wasn't that simple. This was his life they were discussing. His identity.

Who am I?

"Where did you get that idea?" the priest asked. "Lazo?"

Slash dipped his head in acknowledgment. "He wants me to publicly acknowledge you as my biological father."

The priest stared at him for a moment, when, to Slash's astonishment, he started to laugh. "Oh, heaven help me. What is this? He wants to reveal you as my secret love child to remove me from contention for the papacy? Not that I believe I'm *in* contention for the papacy. I assume he's the one holding up Giorgio's wedding in order to bring you here and force a confession."

Slash picked up his glass again. He hadn't realized how much this conversation would upset him, but it had. It shouldn't even matter who was his father at this point in his life, but somehow it did.

It mattered a lot.

"I don't know who is holding up Gio's wedding," he answered. "But my question remains on the table, Emilio. I need to know if you're my father."

A shadow fell over the priest's face. "I don't want to play this game. Don't let Lazo drive a wedge between us."

Slash curled his hands into fists, not because he was angry, but because they were shaking. He was on uneven ground right now, unsure of his judgment, confused by Father Armando's evasion of the question, and hurting from the conflict in his heart regarding possible answers. He badly needed a shower, sleep and processing time to work through his emotions. But he needed answers more, so he pressed on.

"This is no longer about Lazo." His voice sounded more strained than expected. "Please, Emilio, just tell me the truth. Are you my father or not?"

Another long silence ensued, the cars and the television set providing an uneasy soundtrack for their con-

versation. He didn't know how much time had passed
before Father Armando seemed to come to a decision.
The priest straightened on the couch, squaring his shoulders and lifting his chin.

"Just so we're clear, this answer is for you, not Lazo.
I want you to look at me when I say this, Nicolo, so you
know I speak the truth."

Slash met and held the gaze of the man he'd always
trusted, a man he'd considered his father, whether they
were related by blood or not. Emilio had been connected
to him since birth. While he owed everything to the kind
nurse who had become his mother, Father Armando had
been an influential male figure in his teenage years, before his mother had remarried, and had served as his
confidant and supporter during his time at the Vatican
and for some of the most important moments of his life.

"Yes, you're my son." Father Armando spoke quietly.
"In all ways except blood. You always have been my
child. I may not be your biological father, but I love you
as if you were my own, and I always will."

The fist around his heart eased, releasing a flood of
emotion so powerful he needed a moment to regain his
composure. He wasn't sure what he'd expected to hear,
but he felt enormous relief at the priest's declaration because it meant this man he'd come to care greatly about
wasn't the same person who'd abandoned him at birth.

"Lazo said he has evidence you are my father," Slash
finally said.

"He has nothing." Father Armando shook his head, a
pensive expression on his face. "Because there's nothing to be had."

Slash nodded, satisfied with the answer. He was a
trained interrogator and Father Armando spoke the truth.

He could see it in his face, eyes and demeanor. "He's trying to get my DNA. Presumably to link me to you, but perhaps for more nefarious reasons."

"That's truly despicable."

Slash shoved his hand through his hair, still shaken by their conversation. "Still, something isn't adding up for me about this. Lazo is focused on me for some reason."

"He's using you to get to me. I'm so sorry."

Slash rose from his chair and went to stand beneath a picture of the Madonna and child. Was it more than just the Congo operation? What did Lazo know that he didn't? Was there something else about his past that Lazo could use against him? He studied the picture of the Madonna for a long moment before turning to the priest. "Emilio, did you really find me beneath the organ at the church?"

Father Armando started so abruptly, he nearly dropped his glass of cognac. Guilt streaked across his face. He blinked a couple of times as if he hadn't heard Slash right. "What did you ask?"

Pain lanced Slash's heart. He already had his answer, but he steeled himself and pressed on anyway. "Because I'm trying to get to the truth about a great deal of things."

Guilt and indecision played clearly on Emilio's face, hurting Slash even more. But he said nothing and waited for an answer.

Father Armando spoke softly. "Why are these details so important after all this time?"

"I need to have all the information to make sure I make the right decisions."

"What decisions?" The priest couldn't keep the alarm from his voice.

Slash closed his eyes. He couldn't do this. He just

couldn't. And yet, here he was, once again pitting himself against someone he loved. What was *wrong* with him? He was bone-tired—emotionally, physically and mentally. Still, deep within him, a white-hot anger simmered and boiled against Lazo, the man who'd brought them all to this.

"I have reasons for asking what I do," Slash said quietly. "Did you find me beneath the organ at the church?"

Sorrow flickered in Father Armando's eyes. "No. But you often sat there in a basket at my feet. You were still a child when I told you that, not yet healed from your trauma. I thought it was the kindest, the softest way, to present it like that."

So, he'd lied. Damn, that hurt. In a relationship that had always been strong and harmonious, this conversation had become excruciatingly painful for both of them. Still, Slash had to finish it.

"I was sixteen, Emilio."

"Sixteen is still a child. I adjusted the truth to protect you."

Slash gritted his teeth, fighting the urge to shout at the man he considered his father. How much more didn't he know about his own life? "I don't need your protection or adjustments any longer. I need answers. Who brought me to you?"

Misery swamped the priest's face. "You were brought to the church by someone who couldn't keep you. Why does it matter now?"

"I'm not sure." Slash studied him for a longer time, wondering if he even really knew this man. "You say you're not my biological father, but do you know who is?"

Father Armando held up a hand. "Please. Let's not go down this road."

"We should have gone down it a long time ago." Slash's voice came out much harder than he intended. Feelings of betrayal were swamping him, hurting him.

"I don't understand." Father Armando was pleading now. "Why do you want to drag out the past? It won't change anything. It is what it is."

"So, why does everyone want to hide my past from me? I want the truth, Emilio. That's all I want. That shouldn't be too much to ask from you. Not from you. Never from you." His voice broke on the last word, and he hated that his emotions were so raw and close to the surface.

The priest spread his arms and shook his head. "Nicolo, I cannot say who brought you to the church. I am bound by my vows and by an important promise. I am deeply sorry, and I love you. If I could, I would tell you. You know that."

He wasn't sure *what* he knew anymore. How the hell was it possible that in one hour, everything he thought he'd known about his birth had turned out to be a lie?

"I don't know why I never thought to ask you directly before," he said, his voice cool. "Maybe I wasn't ready, or maybe I didn't really want to know."

"I promise you, a name would change nothing." Father Armando's voice broke a little, too.

"That not for you to decide, is it?" Slash said harshly. "You *lied* to me."

"You were a child," Father Armando protested. "I was protecting you."

Slash looked away, emotion choking him. "You could end this now, by telling me the truth."

"That's not fair," the priest said emphatically. "You know better than anyone what I can and can't divulge."

"You said I was like a son to you. If that were true, you would tell me."

"You *are* a son to me," Father Armando protested. "And I've been as honest as I can and still protect you. You have to believe me."

"I don't know what I believe anymore." Slash held up a hand, stopping the father before he could say something else. "Please, don't explain further or try to find me. I need time to think about this." He headed for the door.

"Wait, Nicolo," Father Armando pleaded. "Please don't go like this. I beg you."

Slash paused, then, without looking back, opened the apartment door and walked out into the night.

TWENTY-SEVEN

Lexi

I WAS JET-LAGGED, had a stomachache and my teeth felt as though something fuzzy was growing on them as the taxi pulled up in front of an enormous stone church. I turned my phone around for the taxi driver to see and pointed to the address.

"Cathedral of San Lorenzo?"

"*Si.*" The taxi driver pointed vigorously at the church.

I peered out the open window in the blinding sun at the Romanesque structure. The façade was made of black-and-white stripes of marble with three arched entrances, the one in the middle larger than the others. Each entrance had towering double doors. Two stone lions guarded the church front on the opposing banisters of the stone staircase. My research had indicated the Cathedral of San Lorenzo was the seat of Father Emilio Armando, Archbishop of Genoa, and exactly the person I'd come to see. Whether he'd agree to see me was the tricky part, because I wasn't sure he knew who I was. But that wouldn't stop me now. I'd flown over four thousand miles to see him, and I hated flying. I was on a mission.

"Okay." I swiped my credit card in the taxi's machine, and virtually signed on the dotted line, adding a decent tip. "*Grazie.*"

The taxi driver dipped his head at me. "*Prego.*"

I grabbed my backpack and laptop bag and climbed out. Tourists streamed in and out of the church. I fought my way through the crowd, trying to get to the entrance, but as I reached the main doors, someone in a suit blocked me and said something in Italian.

I shook my head. I'd been learning some Italian, but he spoke quickly, and I was too tired to understand it. "Ah, sorry. I didn't catch that."

The man switched to English. "You may not enter the church with the backpack or luggage."

Terrorism. Duh.

"Oh, I get it. Okay." Unfortunately, now I had to figure out what to do with my stuff or I'd never get into the church.

I headed back down the stairs toward a priest who stood on the steps talking to someone. I waited until they finished and then I approached the priest.

"Excuse me. Do you speak English?"

"Yes," the priest replied with a smile. "How can I help you?"

"I'm looking for Archbishop Emilio Armando. Do you know where I can find him?"

"I'm sorry. You must make an appointment to see the archbishop. He is a very busy man."

"I'm sure he is, but could you let him know that Lexi Carmichael is here, on the steps of the church, all the way from America? If you could mention I'm a friend of a person named Slash. He's a family friend of the archbishop." I sincerely hoped Slash had mentioned my name at least once when he talked to Father Armando or things were going to get tough really fast.

"I'm afraid I can't do that," the priest said.

"Please, I know this is an unusual request. You don't

have a clue who I am. But could you ask him this once, please? If he says no, I'll leave right away. I promise you, it's very important. I think he'll see me."

I'm not sure if my disheveled appearance, the note of desperation in my voice or whether divine intervention stepped in, but the priest told me to wait and disappeared into the church. I waited on the steps, trying to stay in the cool shadows as much as possible. I was dressed in jeans and a T-shirt, but I was sweating like crazy from the sun and humidity. The security guy kept an eagle eye on me, too, which made me uncomfortable, but at least he didn't take me down. I guess as long as I didn't try to approach the door again with my backpack, we were cool.

While waiting, I took the time to study the church. I wondered what the banners stretched across the front of the church said. There were photos of a good-looking man and woman on the banners, complete with crosses and text. Religious figures of some kind, I presumed. There were lots of tourists taking photos of them, and I heard a few of them speaking English, so I asked a guy with a big camera around his neck what the deal was with the banners.

"The pope will be reviewing the sainthood of the two individuals this weekend," he said, snapping a couple more photos of the façade. "People are showing their support for the candidates. There's a big parade here in town tonight, and parades all week long throughout Italy."

"Really? You mean people can support candidates for sainthood? Like voting?"

The guy laughed, clearly thinking I was an idiot.

Maybe I was. My knowledge of sainthood procedures was exactly zero.

"No, not voting," he said. "The Vatican is not a democracy. The pope has the final say on who is and isn't a saint. But the people can show their support and admiration for those under consideration, to help the pope decide."

"Oh," I said. "Well, that's fascinating." I guess I'd have to read up on the sainthood thing.

The guy moved on and still I waited. After what seemed like forever, but was probably only thirty minutes or so, the priest returned. "Please, Ms. Carmichael, can you come with me?"

I breathed a sigh of relief as the priest said something to the security guy. After a cursory glance in my backpack and laptop case, he let me pass. I took off my sunglasses as soon as we entered the dimly lit church. Thankfully, the air was significantly cooler inside.

"Wow, it's beautiful," I said in a hushed voice, stopping for a minute to admire the dark wooden pews and gorgeous stained-glass windows.

"The side altars, nave, dome and apse were built in the fourteenth and fifteenth centuries," the priest explained. "The cathedral itself was finished in the seventeenth century."

"It's stunning." I tried to take in everything at once. "The ceiling fresco is exquisite."

The priest smiled. "Did you know San Lorenzo also preserves the ashes of St. John the Baptist, which arrived here at the end of the First Crusade? He is the patron saint of our city."

"I didn't know that. So much fascinating history here."

"I hope you will enjoy your stay."

He led me down the left side of the church. He unlocked a door and ushered me into an annex. We walked farther down a corridor lined with more breathtaking paintings before stopping in front of a door. After a knock, I heard a voice from inside say something in Italian. The priest opened the door and ushered me in.

A tall man rose from behind an ornate desk. He was dressed in a black cassock with a cross around his neck and had thick, dark hair. Suddenly I realized I had no idea of the protocol for greeting an archbishop, not to mention a cardinal. I probably should have changed clothes or something, but that hadn't occurred to me until this exact moment. Panicked, I curtseyed—probably the most awkward curtsey in the universe—then bowed, and finally knelt in the middle of the room, still wearing my backpack and laptop bag. Hopefully, I'd covered all the bases.

"Archbishop, esteemed Father, thank you for seeing me." I stayed on my knees.

He strode toward me, his eyes twinkling with amusement. Apparently the kneeling had been a step too far. "Please, call me Emilio. So, you are Lexi." He took my hand in his and lifted me to my feet. "It is an honor to finally meet you."

"Thank you for seeing me. I guess that means Slash mentioned me."

"Of course. You're the girl who won his heart."

A tiny bubble of happiness surfaced inside me. It meant a lot to me that Slash had told Father Armando about our relationship. I figured the priest would be grateful to hear the same words. "Slash talks about you, too, Father. You're very important to him."

For some reason, instead of happiness, my comment

caused a sad expression to cross his face. Before I could wonder why, he gently took my bags from me, setting them on an empty chair.

"Come, Miss Carmichael, let us take a walk in the garden."

I thought it an odd request, especially since it was beyond hot outside and he was in a heavy cassock, but I was so grateful he'd agreed to see me, I'd go wherever he wanted. Taking only my purse, I followed him down the hallway toward a wooden door at a side entrance to the church. As we stepped outside, I blinked in the harsh light and slipped my sunglasses back on.

We wandered deeper into the garden before the priest spoke again. "I apologize for the abrupt change of location. I wanted to be able to speak confidentially with you, and my office is not the place to do it."

I looked at him in surprise. "You can't speak confidentially in your own office?"

"Unfortunately, I cannot." He didn't offer any more explanation and I wasn't brave enough to pry further. "Would you like to sit or walk?"

"Walk." I rolled my neck and shoulders, trying to get the kinks out. "I've been sitting for hours on an airplane."

"Then walk we shall."

The garden was fragrant, and several trees offered us shade from the relentless rays of the sun. The garden path was made of stone and wound through perfectly symmetrical box hedges, past benches, stone birdbaths, and flowers like roses and hydrangeas.

We were both silent as we strolled. I was trying to figure out how to ask him what I wanted to know, and he seemed to be waiting on me to speak. Thankfully, he didn't rush me. It was hard for me, not only because I'm an extreme introvert who sucks at small talk, but because I'd never spoken with an archbishop before.

"The garden is lovely," I finally said.

"It is well loved by both those who work here and those who come here for a moment of peace," he answered.

"I imagine you come here often."

"I do." He stopped and turned to face me. "Forgive me. I completely forgot to congratulate you on your engagement. It is the most wonderful news."

"Oh, thank you." He looked down at my hand, and I held it up so he could see the ring.

The father examined the ring with interest. "A blue diamond. A rare stone. Did you know the blue diamond is believed to foster rebirth?"

"I hadn't heard that before."

"It's a bit of cultural trivia. The setting is beautiful. Antique, certainly."

"It was Slash's grandmother's. The proposal came as a surprise to me."

He smiled. "I've never known Nicolo to be rash about anything in his entire life. Although it may seem sudden to you, I'm sure the decision was considered quite carefully on his end."

"You called him Nicolo. His friend from the Vatican, Tito, calls him Nico. His adopted mother calls him Romeo, and everyone in the States calls him Slash. Why do you call him Nicolo, if I may ask?"

"I named him Nicolo after he was left at my church. Nicolo was my father's name, so it was to honor him. We were together for three days before child services came to take him away. That's a long time to call a baby nothing but *bambino*. I do not know why his friend calls him that, but I suspect it's because he used the name Nicolo at the Vatican."

"He did?"

"He did." Father Armando's face stretched into a smile. "He asked to be called Nicolo when he entered the seminary because the name Romeo, combined with his exceptional good looks by the time he was an older teenager, resulted in quite a bit of teasing."

It made sense, but it was yet another thing I hadn't known about Slash. How long would I be peeling away the layers of the man I was going to marry?

We strolled for a bit more before the father spoke again. "So, Miss Carmichael, what brings you to Genoa?"

I guess he'd gotten tired of waiting for me to get to the point. I figured I'd better take the opening. Archbishops were likely very busy people.

"I'm worried about Slash," I blurted out. So much for my plan to ease into my questions.

"I'm worried about him, too," the father said. "Right now he is deeply confused, conflicted and hurt."

"Why? What's happening?" It pained me to have to ask someone else, since I was supposed to be the person closest to him. My cheeks burned, but either Father Armando didn't notice or was too nice to point it out.

"There are people who are trying to hurt me through him. Unfortunately, in the process, I've hurt him, too. I've made mistakes I can't undo."

"Oh." I fell quiet a moment. "I suppose you can't tell me any more than that."

"I'm sorry. I cannot."

I fiddled with my sunglasses, summoning the courage I needed. "Father, maybe you can help me with something else. I have a couple of important questions. I understand the confidentiality thing, so you can always decline to answer. But will you at least entertain my questions?"

"Of course."

We stopped beneath the shade of a tree, facing each other. Sweat trickled down the back of my neck from the humidity. "I want to go back to when you found Slash. He told me he was abandoned at your church when he was a few days old. Is that correct?"

"It is."

"Is it common in Italy to leave babies at churches?"

"It's not commonplace, but it's not rare either. In rural areas it happens more often than you might think."

"Where was the church located?"

"San Mauro Cilento, a small hamlet with less than a thousand residents."

"You never saw who left the baby?"

The priest fell silent. I waited, but he didn't answer. In a way, that was an answer in itself. I had to think about that later, but for now I continued. "How long was it before child services showed up?"

"We had terrible weather that night. It was the worst storms and flooding Italy had seen in decades. Until the representatives from Salerno were able to reach us, I took care of him. We spent almost every moment together. He was a good baby. Angelic. I could always soothe him with music, especially music from a particular pianist— a favorite of mine."

"Hai Tsang."

"Yes. He told you." The father smiled, his face softening. "I'm glad."

"He did. We saw Tsang perform in New York City

several months ago. He was amazing. Slash still listens to his music, and now, so do I."

"I used to play Tsang's music for him on the organ. He was remarkably soothed by the melodies." He cleared his throat. "I will tell you a heartfelt truth. I fell in love with that baby. It was an instant bonding orchestrated by God. I have no other explanation for it. I can't tell you how much it broke my heart to give him up."

"What happened to him?"

"Child services took him to Salerno, and he was taken in by a foster family. To this day, that remains my greatest regret."

"Is fostering the normal route, as opposed to an orphanage or something?"

"It's quite normal. Some people believe giving the baby to the church is their only way to save them. They don't always understand, or have the luxury of caring, that the church has to turn the children over to the state."

"What happened after the foster family took charge of Slash?"

"They vanished for seven years."

"Vanished? How could that happen?"

"Somehow, the information on the forms had been falsified, and it went undiscovered until after they disappeared. By the time it was discovered, they were long gone with Nicolo."

"Did you ever meet this foster family?"

He shook his head, regret heavy in his voice. "I did not."

"Wasn't there a background check?"

"Several, but the falsification was done well, and Nicolo fell through the cracks. I searched for him every day for seven years and begged God over and over to let me find him alive—to try and make amends. I eventually found him in a Sperlonga hospital. Thankfully, he'd been fingerprinted as part of the foster process, so when he arrived at the hospital, not able to speak, they ran his prints. I went to him immediately, but Nicolo had been traumatized, rendered mute. The experts weren't sure what was wrong with him, other than that he'd been beaten. At first, they thought he was on the autism spectrum, but that was eventually ruled out. He'd been traumatized and he'd adopted similar techniques to calm himself. After that first year, the doctors and psychologists realized his silence was self-imposed."

Just hearing this story again, in more detail, hurt more than I could say. I couldn't imagine him as a small boy, so alone and afraid, with no one to turn to for help. I wondered if he felt that way right now, and it made me even more determined to find him and let him know he didn't have to face any of this alone.

"Nicolo was terrified of strangers, so I stayed back. But there was a nurse there, tending him. He responded to her."

"Juliette," I supplied. The only mother Slash had ever known, and the woman who had opened her heart and home to a scared little boy.

"*Si.* She fell in love with him, much as I had. She quickly requested permission to adopt him, which was unusual, as she was a single mother herself. But people are drawn to him. He's a blessed child."

I was sure Slash wouldn't have considered himself blessed, given all he'd been through. I pushed my sunglasses to the top of my head so I could look at Father Armando with an unfiltered view. "So, Juliette adopted him, and he grew up in Sperlonga with his new family."

"Correct. I did not stand in the way of his adoption. How could I? I've never said this to another person, but I was ready to give up the priesthood to take care of him. It was difficult for me to step back, to let someone else take charge of his life once again. But Juliette, she is a wonderful woman with a kind and compassionate heart. It was the right thing to do. Nicolo needed a mother, and now he had a brother, too. My decision was validated when, a year later, he started talking again and making great strides. Juliette, bless her, let me keep in touch with him after I told her my story of how he'd once been mine. When Nicolo was sixteen years old, she permitted me to tell him of our connection at birth. That's how he came into my life. We have always been connected at the heart, Nicolo and I. He's truly been my greatest gift from God."

I lifted my ponytail from my neck, wishing I could dump a bottle of cold water on my head. "Is that why you groomed him for the church?"

The question appeared to catch the father by surprise. "Groom him? I never considered that for him. I didn't even talk to him about the priesthood. He came to me when he was eighteen and said he'd seen a vision. He wanted to ask me about the church, God and how he could serve." The father slipped his fingers behind a white blossom and inhaled the fragrance. "I was hesitant at first, but he'd had a calling, and he was persistent. That's Nicolo for you. When he wants something, he can be singularly persuasive. I could not refuse him anything."

No one could, it seemed. Not even me. "His mother, Juliette, she didn't mind that he was interested in the priesthood?"

"She did not. She, like me, let him follow his heart."

Juliette lived in London now, and I hadn't met her yet. I already liked her anyway. A lot. "What happened next?"

"He began training for the priesthood. Not under my tutelage, but I kept a careful watch on him. It quickly became apparent that Nicolo had important talents."

"Computer skills."

"Not only. Analytical, mathematical, logic and visual-spatial skills that were off the charts. He also had an extraordinary ability to code. All those who witnessed his skill agreed he was astonishingly gifted. He quickly outstripped everything his teachers could offer him. We had to bring in special tutors and, even then, it wasn't enough. He soon became the teacher. Not surprisingly, word got back to the Vatican."

"They had other uses for him," I said, stating the obvious. Of course, they did. Slash was so talented, he would have excelled at nearly any challenge they could have given him. But in the end, they had used him for darker, more nefarious, purposes, and he had apparently surpassed expectations with those, too. How much of his life had ever gone the way he wanted?

Perhaps Father Armando was thinking along the same lines, because sadness settled into his face and mouth. I steered the topic to safer ground.

"Slash studied while he worked at the Vatican, right?"

"He did. He obtained several degrees, no surprise for a very talented young man."

Nope, no surprise at all. "Father, do you happen to know what year Slash went to the United States?"

Father Armando considered. "Seven or eight years ago, I think. I'm sorry. I'm not sure exactly when."

I watched him carefully, trying to gauge his reaction. "To your knowledge, had he ever been to the US before that?"

"Not before he began his training at the Vatican. After that, I don't know. At a certain point, I was no longer apprised of his activities. I suppose it's possible, given his line of work, but I cannot confirm that."

I was satisfied he was telling the truth. "Have you ever seen a birth certificate for him?"

"I have. One issued by child services shortly after he was taken from me and fostered."

"What exactly was his name on the birth certificate, if I may ask?"

"Nicolo Cilento. Cilento after the hamlet where the church I was working at was located. However, when he was adopted by Juliette, she changed his name to Romeo—a poetic gesture, perhaps—his Romeo to her Juliette. Nicolo took her last name, too, which, at the time, was Fortunato. She eventually remarried and took her new husband's name, but as far as I know, Nicolo did not. So growing up, he was Romeo Fortunato. As I already mentioned, he chose to be known as Nicolo Cilento at the Vatican, but at some point, he asked to be called Slash. I admit it was quite bewildering to me at first, but he assured me it was a nickname of his own choosing. He said it was a computer term, shortened for the backslash on the keyboard. At the time, I didn't understand the significance of it, but later it occurred to me that for him, the backslash was incredibly symbolic. It was as if he were putting a hard stop, or a backslash, to his old life. From that moment on, he was his own man. For the first time in his life, he'd given himself a name and identity of his own choosing."

A lump settled in my throat. I had no idea there was so much history behind his nickname. So much I didn't know about him.

"But old habits die hard, and he permitted me to continue to call him Nicolo," Father Armando continued, the memory chasing away the sadness on his face. "I guess it's hard to teach an old dog new tricks, as you Americans are fond of saying."

"Did he ever ask you about how he was found at the church?"

"Yes." Pain crossed the father's face. "We discussed it, but that's not my story to tell."

This totally sucked. I hated that I was dredging up a painful past, hurting him by making him remember and relive it, but I needed to know as much as I could in order to help Slash.

He was my first priority.

We resumed walking again. Father Armando strolled with his hands behind his back, deep in thought. I was sorting through all the information I'd learned, trying to fill in the blanks.

"When was the last time you saw Slash in person?" I finally asked.

"Yesterday."

I tripped over my feet, almost face-planting into the hydrangeas. I would have, except for the steadying hand on my elbow Father Armando offered. "What? Slash was here in Genoa? Yesterday?"

"*Si*—at my home. We had a conversation. It did not go well. He's conflicted and hurt. I am complicit in that."

"What happened?" Alarm coursed through me.

It was if the priest had to force the words from his

mouth. "It is not for me to say. You must ask him your-self."

I'd no idea what had happened between them, but Father Armando looked so miserable, I had to assume it was something awful. I glanced away, staring instead at the imposing stone wall of the church that formed a protective barrier on one side of the garden. "Do you know how I can find him?"

"Doesn't he know you're here?"

Well, I'd successfully brought us to a supremely awkward moment. Until now, I'd managed to avoid telling him that Slash and I were having issues and barely talking to each other. Now I'd have to confess.

I looked down at my hands and realized I'd been anxiously twisting my T-shirt. "No, he doesn't know I'm here. He's trying to keep me out of this, whatever *this* is, but I'm not going to let him do that. He shouldn't have to face this alone."

He let out a huge sigh of relief. "Bless you, child. Thank God he's chosen a strong individual to share his life. You will need every bit of that strength. The truth is, I don't know if Nicolo wants to be found, even by you. As you are discovering, Nicolo is not an easy man to know. Trusting does not come easy to him. Perhaps now you'll understand that a little better."

I did, but I wasn't sure what good it would do us if I couldn't find him.

"If you do find him, please be careful in what you say, Miss Carmichael. There are important reasons Nicolo is keeping you out of this. He loves you desperately and fears what you will think of him if certain things come out."

"I'm not here to judge him. I'm here to help him, if

he'll let me." I meant it, and by the look on Father Armando's face, he believed me.

"I don't know if he'll permit you to help." He hesitated, choosing his words. "He prefers to handle things alone, and it's no surprise. He's been traumatized and used by others, and as a result, he doesn't have a high opinion of most people. Those he does trust, myself included, have hurt him in one way or the other, even if it was unintentional. He needs someone who can see through that and love him for the man he is."

"I *already* love that man," I said. "Father Armando, please, if you can tell me where I can find him, I will do everything in my power to help him."

"I know you will. But the truth is, I don't know where he's at right now. If he's still here in Genoa, he often stays at the Hotel Meliá. He would want to be alone, so if he's there, he's likely under an assumed name. On the other hand, he may have already gone back to Rome or somewhere else. Nicolo is not a man of idleness. When he wants something, he will be single-minded about it."

I knew firsthand that was true. "What's he single-minded about right now, Father Armando?"

The priest paused and then decided to answer me. "Bringing down Cardinal Jacopo Lazo. Do you know who he is?"

Did I know who he was? I'd pointed Slash in that direction, so if anything happened on that front, it was on me. "Um, yes, I know who he is. President of the Vatican, right?"

"Right."

"Well, I guess I can start my search for Slash at the Hotel Meliá. Thank you, Father, for agreeing to speak to me and for being so candid." At this point, my brain was nearing the shutdown point. I needed a shower, a nap and a decent meal. If Slash was not at the hotel, at the very least I hoped to get a room, some sleep and try to plot my next move.

"It was my pleasure," he answered. "Remember, Nicolo does not feel worthy of you. As a result of his abandonment and pain, he's spent his entire life trying to prove his worth to others. That's why he is so incredibly driven and successful. But it comes at a price. He desperately needs peace—something he told me he finds with you."

"I know," I answered. "The ironic thing is, he doesn't have to prove his worth to me. I already know it, and love him for it."

TWENTY-EIGHT

Slash

SLASH LOVED A good challenge, but hacking into the personal finances of Cardinal Lazo, stored on the cardinal's home computer, was so laughably easy a teenager could have done it. Lazo's arrogance and sense that he was untouchable made him careless and stupid.

He intended to take full advantage of that.

He sat in his hotel suite, working on his laptop, sitting by an open window, the desk angled so he had a nice view of the city. The sounds from below, cars honking, people talking and the smells from the nearby bakery, all soothed him. He was neck-deep in a review of Lazo's bank account when his phone vibrated.

I'm currently standing in the lobby of the Hotel Meliá in Genoa. Father Armando says you sometimes stay here. I just met with him, asking him if he knew where you were. He didn't know, but suggested I start here. I know you didn't want me in Italy, but I came anyway. Whatever demons you are facing, you don't have to face them alone. Not anymore. I won't give up until I find you, even if I have to petition the pope himself, so please, don't put me through that awkwardness. Tell me where you are and I'll come to you.

For a moment, he stared in astonishment before he closed his eyes and leaned his forehead against the phone. She'd come after him. He blocked her, shut her out, hurt her, and yet she'd flown all the way across the ocean to find him anyway, not knowing where he was.

My girl.

My incredible, extraordinary woman.

He couldn't have stayed away from her even if he'd wanted to. His feet were already carrying him to the door and down the hallway. Skipping the elevator, he took the stairs, his stride quickening as he approached the lobby.

He opened the stairwell door and saw her, his heart slamming against his chest. Standing there, he took a moment to drink in the sight of her—the long brown hair pulled back into the ponytail she was so fond of, and a small furrow between her brow. She sat on the edge of one of the high-backed chairs, staring at her phone and waiting for him to return her text. In a simple white T-shirt, jeans and sneakers, she was the most beautiful woman he'd ever seen. His gaze fell on her hand and relief swept through him when he saw she still wore the engagement ring he'd given her—thank God.

"*Cara,*" he choked out, striding across the lobby in a few steps.

She rose at the sight of him, her mouth forming a small O of surprise. He pulled her into his arms with a hard yank, savoring the warmth of her, the solidness. The one thing that could steady him. Her arms wrapped around his waist as he closed his eyes and buried his face in her hair, not fully understanding how badly he'd missed her until this moment.

For a minute, they didn't speak. He didn't bother to ask what she was doing here. He already knew. She'd come for him because, despite his efforts to push her away, to protect her from his ugly past, she loved him. *Still* loved him. God only knew how or why, but he never ever wanted to question the miracle of it.

He finally drew back, cupping her cheeks with his hands, his eyes searching hers. "You came." It wasn't a question, but a statement.

"Yes." She hesitated, seemingly uncertain how he'd feel about her presence. "I didn't want to be intrusive, but I thought you might need some help."

He couldn't help but smile. "You came all this way… to help me?"

"You've flown across oceans to help me. It seemed only fair I return the favor."

He kissed her long and hard, not giving a damn who was watching them. When he lifted his mouth, she looked a little dazed.

"Um, I guess that means it's okay I came," she finally said, sounding a bit breathless.

He smiled, winding a strand of her hair around his finger. He couldn't explain how much it meant that she'd come and still loved him—he hoped—but his brain was raising an alarm that she was too close now. The fact that he loved her didn't mean he was suddenly okay with her finding out his secrets, which was why he'd come alone in the first place. But he couldn't bring himself to say anything about it at this point. The fact that she was physically here, in his arms, made his world right. The rest he would deal with later.

"It's better than okay. Thank you for coming." He stared at her for a moment longer and then smiled. "Come on. You look like you could use a nap."

"I'm a little jet-lagged," she admitted. "And hot. I

think the humidity is one hundred and ten percent. A shower and some food might be good, too. I can't decide what I need most at this point."

He grabbed her backpack and holding her hand, they headed to the elevator. "What about work?" he asked her. "Finn let you come?"

"I'm taking unpaid leave right now. I'd just wrapped things up with a client and I'm not working on anything I couldn't hand off. I'm lucky he puts up with me."

Slash squeezed her hand. "Trust me on this, *cara*. He's got a good deal with you and he knows it."

When they got to his suite, Lexi dropped her laptop bag by the door and went directly to the window. She stared out at the bustling city below. "Wow. You've got a great view of the city."

He came up behind her, sliding his hands around her waist. "You always do that."

"Do what?"

"Notice the view first. Not the suite nor the amenities. You walk into a room and your mind goes beyond that. It focuses on a vantage point, a window to the world. I love that about you."

She said nothing, but he felt her relax against him.

"The suite has another surprise, but I'll show you that later," Slash said. "What do you want first? Nap, food or shower?"

She turned in his arms. "I want you, Slash. You have no idea how much I've missed you."

He leaned over and trailed kisses along her cheek until his mouth grazed the curve of her jaw and rested there. She leaned into him, a perfect fit of mind and body. Her fingers lightly touched the stubble on his cheeks.

When had he shaved last?

"*Tu me manques*," he murmured, slipping his hands under her T-shirt and flattening his palms against her back. Her skin was warm and soft.

"That didn't sound like Italian," she said, pressing tighter against him.

"It's French. The French don't say 'I miss you.' They say '*tu me manques*,' which means 'you are missing from me.' That's what it feels like when you're not with me. A part of me is missing. The *best* part of me. The last time we were in Italy together, we weren't dating yet, although I was already in love with you."

She lifted her head, smiling tiredly. "Well, we're together and in love now. And, you know the saying, 'When in Rome, do as the Romans do...'"

He pressed his lips against her temple and left them there, smiling against her skin. "Ah, but unfortunately, we're in Genoa not Rome."

"No worries. I'll make a geographic exception for you."

He laughed, the tightly coiled tension of so many days releasing. "Oh, *cara*, how I adore you."

"*Ti amo*, Slash," she murmured.

"*Sei la mia vita*," he whispered against her cheek before he reached around her and pulled the curtain closed. "Come to bed, my love. We'll sort everything out after a nap."

TWENTY-NINE

Cardinal Jacopo Lazo

"WE'VE GOT a new development." Father Koenhein stood by the door. "His fiancée has arrived in Italy. She was spotted in Genoa, talking to Father Armando."

Jacopo looked up from the document he was reviewing on his computer screen. "Well, isn't that interesting? We'll have to see how he plays that. Do we have a transcript of their conversation?"

"We do not."

"Why not?"

"They did not stay in his office, but went outside to the garden."

"That's unfortunate."

"Also unfortunate is we've lost our surveillance capability at Cardinal Armando's home. It's no longer working."

He didn't like what that implied. "That can't be a coincidence. He must know."

"I don't think so, Your Eminence. I believe it to be a malfunction. He's neither removed nor reported the one in his office. I have someone working on replacing the one in his home now."

Jacopo thought for a moment. He didn't like the fact that they had gaps in surveillance. "When did we lose contact at Father Armando's apartment?"

"Shortly after Slash arrived to speak with him. So, we heard nothing of their conversation."

Jacopo gritted his teeth. Was he the only intelligent one in a sea of idiots? It couldn't have been sheer coincidence that the bug stopped working just as Slash arrived. Yet, Father Armando had not reported it, nor had he found or removed the one in his office. Why? Was there a purpose, a strategy for that? Disinformation? A lure? He had strategies in place if the bugs were found, so he wasn't worried about that, but if Slash had found them, why hadn't he done anything about it? He'd have to think that through, but for now, he had other pressing matters with which to deal.

"Where's the fiancée now?" he asked.

Father Koenhein straightened his two guests' chairs. "I presume still in Genoa. We weren't expecting her, so she got away before we could put a tail on her. We're not sure where she is at this point, but we'll find her."

"Good. When will the DNA results be in?"

"Soon. Forty-eight hours, possibly earlier, is the window we were given. We requested the highest level of expediency, of course."

"The sooner the better."

"Understood. But, sir, what if Slash doesn't cooperate?" Father Koenhein's voice was tenuous, worried. "What will we do?"

Jacopo gave his clerk a reassuring smile. He was a powerful man, and he knew when he held all the cards. "He'll cooperate. For the first time in his life, he has something important to lose. He'll do it, and even if he doesn't, we'll have what we need to crush him if he gets in our way. I will not risk the future of this church to a man like him."

"Yes, of course, you're right, Your Eminence."

Jacopo smiled. "By the grace of God, I always am."

Lexi

I WOKE A FEW hours later feeling significantly better. Slash slept beside me, his arm draped over my hip. I shifted slightly, wanting to look at him but not wanting to wake him. The curtain was blowing from the open balcony door, and the gentle breeze felt good. Dusk was falling. There was still enough light to see his face, the long column of his throat, the dark smudges under his eyes, and raspy cheeks. His chest rose and fell with each breath. The fact that he slept so deeply likely meant he hadn't been sleeping well. I understood that.

Still, even in exhaustion, he was a beautiful sight. Father Armando was right, Slash was extraordinarily handsome. Midnight-black hair and a face nearly perfect in its symmetry—a generous mouth, aquiline nose and square jaw. I ran my fingertips down a well-muscled biceps to his long, strong fingers. Classic and strong features from the ancient Roman tradition. I wondered if his shoulders ever wearied of the burdens he carried.

I watched Slash sleep for a few more minutes, then slipped out from beneath his arm and headed to the bathroom. I grabbed my backpack as I went, making sure I had a toothbrush, shampoo and a clean change of clothes.

When I came out of the bathroom, Slash was awake, dressed and sitting on the side of the bed. He was putting on his shoes and smiled when he saw me. It lit up his whole face.

"Better?" he asked.

"Significantly." I dropped my backpack on the bed. "But I'm starving."

"Luckily, I've got dinner all planned."

"I hope it involved lots and lots of incredible Italian food."

"It does. It also involves that surprise I was telling you about earlier."

I looked down at my stretchy blue cotton sundress and flat sandals. "Is this good enough in terms of the dress code? I didn't pack anything fancier."

"It's perfect. Let me shave and we'll go."

Surprisingly, we didn't go far. He led me up the hotel stairs to a rooftop terrace restaurant. There were about twenty-five small tables. Small torch lights ringed the roof. Candles flickered on tables covered with crisp white tablecloths. It was still warm, but with the sun having set and a nice breeze stirring the air, it was almost pleasant.

Slash had reserved a table for two in one corner and we followed the maître d' to our seats.

"This is really nice," I said as we were seated. "You can see all of Genoa from up here." Lights twinkled below us while cars made noises on the streets as they passed.

"I knew you'd like it. You can't see all of Genoa, but most of it. There's the bell tower of the Cathedral of San Lorenzo, where I presume you met with Father Armando. You can see the people gathering there for the candlelight vigil in honor of the saints-to-be."

"An English tourist told me about the sainthood thing. I take it that's a big deal in Italy."

"It is, indeed."

The waiter arrived at our table and asked us if we

wanted anything to drink. Slash asked me if I preferred meat or fish for dinner so he could base the wine selection from that.

"I'm going to let you choose," I said. "Wine and food."

"Okay." He dipped his head, studied the menu, then spoke to the waiter in Italian. The waiter asked him a few questions and then left.

"What are we having?" I asked.

"Creamed *baccalà*, which is a salt cod made with potato and parsley. I selected a local Ligurian wine to go with it. Genoa sits at the center of Liguria's largest wine-producing territory, the *Liguria Riviera di Ponente*. Excellent wines are made here. My favorite is a white wine made from *albarola* grapes, which will go well with our dinner. Do you approve?"

"It sounds delicious. I can't wait to try it."

He reached across the table and took my hand, linking our fingers and holding tight. "I can't tell you how much it means to me that you're here."

"I should have come with you from the start."

"That you're here with me now is enough." He lifted my hand to his lips, turned it over and pressed a kiss on the inside of my wrist. "Thank you."

The waiter returned, carrying a bottle of wine. He poured us each about a third of a glass, waiting for us to try it. I took a sip and let it roll around on my tongue. It was light and refreshing without a heavy taste or sweetness.

"It's wonderful," I told him. "Not overpowering, complementary. I like it."

Slash nodded to the waiter, who set the bottle on the table and departed. I decided to keep the conversation on a neutral topic for a few more minutes as we settled.

"So, how does the sainthood process work?" I asked. "Someone performs a miracle and *boom*, they're a saint?"

Slash leaned back in his chair, sipping his wine. "It's not nearly as simple as that. It's actually a long and complicated process."

"Enlighten me."

"Well, first you have to be dead for at least five years before you can be recommended for sainthood."

"That's totally unfair," I protested. "You'd die not knowing you've been nominated."

He seemed amused by my comment. "Saints live a life of extraordinary grace and kindness, not expecting a reward."

"Still." I set my wineglass on the table.

He chuckled. "You have to be considered a true servant of God, and the person must be nominated for sainthood by a bishop, cardinal or the pope himself. After that comes the beatification, followed by the canonization or blessing."

"That's a lot of requirements."

"Oh, that's the easy part. The final steps are the hardest. Saints must perform at least two miracles in front of credible witnesses. A lengthy investigation by church officials is conducted to prove the validity of the miracle before it can be considered valid and true."

"Two miracles? Well, then I guess it's a miracle—pun intended—anyone ever gets approved for sainthood."

Slash chuckled. "The pope, of course, may decide to waive one or any of these requirements as he sees fit. There have been a handful of cases where he's done just that."

Before I could respond, the waiter brought us two

small glasses filled with an unknown liquid and a plate of thick, crusty bread served with several types of cheese.

"What's this liquid?" I asked, examining the glass.

"*Prosecco*." He took a sip. "It's excellent. The cheese and bread are the antipasto."

I'd forgotten the Italians ate several courses before and after the main dish. "God, I love this country." I broke off a piece of bread and took a chunk of cheese, pairing them together. I took a bite, closed my eyes, and may have hummed or purred aloud. Hard to say, as I could hardly hear myself over all the chewing.

When I opened my eyes, Slash was watching me with a smile. I finished chewing and wagged a finger at him. "Italians are the masters of food magic."

"So you're saying we are sorcerers?"

"Food sorcerers?" I corrected him. I liked the way the hard lines of his face had finally softened and relaxed. Had I helped him in that way? If I had, I wanted to keep him engaged. "Tell me more about these saints. Who are the people up for sainthood? The banner on the front of the Cathedral of San Lorenzo had a photo of a man and a woman."

"*Si*, Sister Ana-Paula Núñez from Uruguay and Cristian Descantes from right here in Italy."

"What miracles did they perform?"

"Sister Ana-Paula of Uruguay had two healing miracles back in the 1970s using a relic, which in this case was a bone fragment, from another saint, Padre Pio. Pio had also performed several healings before he was designated a saint. The sister is believed to have cured a little boy from a rural town in Uruguay of brain cancer. The child had undergone three surgeries to remove an aggressive tumor. One of those surgeries had badly damaged part of his brain, rendering him unable to speak or walk. But his parents refused to give up. They contacted Sister Ana-Paula, who traveled out to the countryside to pray for the healing intercession of Saint Pio and rubbed the relic against the boy's skin. Within one week, the tumor suddenly vanished. Even more astonishing, the damaged part of his brain was also healed. Nine days after the intercession of Sister Ana-Paula, the child woke up, walked around and has been in perfect health ever since. An investigation by the Vatican, including several medical doctors and neurologists, confirmed the healing was rapid, complete and lasting, but most importantly, utterly inexplicable in light of current medical science."

"That's incredible," I said. "Surely there had to be some explanation."

"There was none. They examined the X-rays, the medical documentation, and there was no logical explanation for the recession or the healing."

"Wow." That was all I could think of to say. "What was her second miracle?"

"Using that same relic, she cured a child of blindness. Completely. The child can now see perfectly...even though she had no transplant and has no cornea in either eye."

"Get out! That's not possible."

"Exactly. Thus the miracle."

Slash pulled off a chunk of the bread and paired it with a piece of yellow cheese. "Sister Ana-Paula passed away in 1987. There were reportedly other miracles, although they were not investigated since the required two were already verified."

I nibbled on a delicious fig, wondering about the scientific viability of the miracles. "Did the other guy up for sainthood do healing miracles, too?"

Slash shook his head. "No. Cristian Descantes is a saint of another sort. Popularly known as the Savior of Salerno, he singlehandedly saved nineteen children and their driver when their school bus plunged into the Mediterranean Sea."

"Whoa. Not to denigrate that amazing feat, but it seems more heroic than miraculous."

"Except that the bus driver and the children reported that Cristian lifted, bent and snapped pieces of the wreckage with his bare hands to free them." Slash sipped his wine and speared a piece of melon. "This was later confirmed when the bus was retrieved."

"Isn't it more plausible to presume the structural integrity of the bus was weakened by the crash to permit him to break things?" I suggested.

"The wreckage was intensely scrutinized. There were several breaks that could not be explained away by the accident trajectory. However, of a more miraculous nature, the bus driver and three of the children were underwater for more than fifteen minutes. There was no air trapped in the bus, as the bus split upon impact, yet all the passengers survived, with not a single one of them suffering any lasting damage from the accident."

"Okay, now that's impossible."

"Except the timing was confirmed by the rescue crew, who arrived exactly twelve minutes after the accident. Three minutes after that, they witnessed Cristian surfacing with the last three children from the bus wreckage. He then went down one last time and saved the bus driver, who also fully recovered after being underwater for fifteen minutes. And there you have it." Slash pulled off a piece of the bread and ate it, watching my reaction.

I was floored. "Wow. What was his second miracle?"

Slash refilled our wineglasses and handed me mine. "The second one is much more tragic, and not a miracle, really. Once again, it involved children. In 1979, an anti-Semitic group calling themselves the *Combattenti Della Libertà Ariana*, which roughly translated means the Aryan Freedom Fighters, occupied a Jewish day school in a small town near Milan."

"Oh, no. What happened?"

"Cristian had become profoundly affected by his experience saving the children and the bus driver. Like the others, he believed he'd been chosen by God to perform a miracle and perhaps spread the word. As a result, he joined the priesthood. He was widely beloved in Italy. He offered himself in exchange for the children. This group hated the Catholics almost as much as they hated Jews. Since Cristian was a popular and much revered figure in Italy, they agreed. They released all the children and most teachers, except for the headmaster and two rabbis who were connected to the school."

"I'm afraid to ask what happened next," I said.

"They blew up the school, killing themselves and everyone inside. Cristian saved seventy-four children and sixteen adults that day but lost his own life in the process."

I looked down at my wine. "Okay, that counts as a miracle in my book."

"I agree. Since the pope, at his discretion, can waive the requirement of a second miracle, people are hoping that's what he'll do in this case."

"I hope he does, too."

The waiter brought the cod and took away the now-empty plate that once held the bread and cheese, as well as our empty *aperitivo* glasses.

I took a bite of the fish. I closed my eyes, savoring the taste. "I don't know how the Italians make the most exquisite food, but I could die happy after every meal."

"You'd better not die anytime soon," Slash warned.

"Trust me. I'm not planning on it. I'm hoping for a long life so I can eat my way through Italy for years to come."

He grinned and we finished our dinner, sitting back in our chairs completely satiated.

"Best dinner ever," I said.

"You say that about every meal in Italy," Slash pointed out.

I rubbed my stomach and beamed. "True, except every meal seems to be better than the last. Except for Nonna's. That is cooking on an entirely different level."

"That it is."

After the waiter cleared the dishes, we sipped the last bit of our wine. Slash's face became serious as he set his glass down on the table. "So, *cara*, are you ready to talk?"

I'd been dreading this moment because I wasn't. I sucked at relationship conversation, and I was worse at confrontation. But it was time we cleared the air, and we both knew it.

Steadying myself, I set my fork down and mustered a smile. "I thought you'd never ask."

THIRTY

Slash

HE HATED THE space that had grown between them—the
chasm he'd created—separating them in ways he never
imagined. Even as he told her they had to talk, he wasn't
sure how he'd fix this with her. But he was going to try.

"Let's start with Father Armando." He wasn't ready
to broach the hacking matter. He might *never* be ready
to deal with that. Small steps first. "I never anticipated
you'd meet him without an introduction from me."

She looked down at her plate. "I was lucky he agreed
to see me. He's a busy man."

"He knows all about you. I told him of our engagement, but I'd mentioned you long before that. I told him
how special you are to me."

She seemed embarrassed by my comment, the color
rising in her cheeks. "I'm not sure I made the best of
impressions showing up at the church unannounced in
jeans and a T-shirt, looking for you. I curtseyed, bowed
and *knelt* to make sure I covered all bases."

A smile touched his lips as he pictured that. He could
see her marching up the steps of the church, insisting
the archbishop see her. She'd likely made a lasting impression on the archbishop, and if he knew Emilio, a
good one at that.

"He wouldn't have told you where I usually stay when

I'm in Genoa if he didn't like you." He lifted the wine bottle to pour more wine into their glasses.

"He calls you Nicolo."

"He named me that at the church when I was left there. It was also one of the names I used when I worked at the Vatican…to honor him and his father."

"Is that why Tito calls you Nico?"

"It is."

She fell silent, while he poured the wine. When he was finished she reached for the glass, her fingers wrapping around the stem, but she made no move to drink it. "Slash, can you tell me what's going on with you and Father Armando? He wouldn't say much, just that you two had a falling out of sorts. What happened?"

Slash didn't see any sense in keeping her out of what had happened so far, as long as it didn't move into a discussion of other things he couldn't, *wouldn't*, discuss with her. Lowering his voice, he told her about his lunch with Tito, the summons to Cardinal Lazo's office and what Father Armando had told him about the night he was brought to the church. He omitted only the meeting with Pacini and anything connected to the issue of the Congo.

She listened intently without interrupting. When he was finished he sat back and watched her think. It felt surprisingly good to tell her, and he waited to see what she would think of it. He'd missed this, her thoughtful perspective on things. She was analyzing and sorting every word he'd said, sifting through the information he'd dumped on her. He understood, because that's exactly how he processed information.

"So, it wasn't true you were found under the organ at

the church?" she finally asked. "Someone brought you in and he met them?"

"That's the new story."

"But you don't know who brought you, and he won't tell you."

He looked at the twinkling lights of the city, ignoring the tightness in his gut. "Something like that."

Her fingers drummed on the tabletop. "Slash, there's something I need to ask you. It may help me make sense of things. If you can't tell me, say so, okay?"

He visibly tensed, unable to stop himself. He had no idea what she'd ask, and whether by denying her any answers he'd widen the gap between them. However, when she finally spoke, it wasn't the question he'd been expecting.

"Do you remember when you became a naturalized US citizen?"

"What?" He frowned, rearranged his thoughts. "Naturalized?"

"Yes. When did you become a US citizen?"

He thought back. "It was shortly before I started work at the NSA. I filled out some forms and they came back rather quickly—in about three weeks, if I recall correctly. I was told it had been expedited."

"Didn't you have to take a test and have a ceremony where you recited your pledge of loyalty to the country or something like that?"

"No."

"Well, that's interesting because I asked Gray to help me with some stuff I was looking at to help you figure out what's going on. At my direction, she did some digging around and called in some favors to friends at the

CIA. She discovered you weren't naturalized as a US citizen."

He stared at her for a long moment. Grayson's research was always meticulously sourced, but this time she was incorrect. "That's impossible. It must be classified. I have a passport and a security clearance at the highest level. I'm the Director of IAD at the NSA. It's incomprehensible that I wouldn't be naturalized."

"I know, right?" She spread her hands, then pressed her palms against the tablecloth. "But that's not all. Here's the kicker. Gray found out you weren't naturalized because you *already* had American citizenship."

"What?" Astonishment, disbelief swept through him. "That's not possible. I was born in Italy."

"Are you sure? Then how have you had American citizenship since birth?"

"I haven't."

"But Gray says you do."

"Did she see my so-called American birth certificate?"

"She didn't. But her source told her it's there, and it's legit."

He considered the implication and how soon he could get hacking to confirm this. "Maybe the birth certificate is manufactured. Doctored."

"Why? What would be the point?"

He lifted his shoulders, unsure. He really had no idea what would be the point. He'd had plenty of manufactured passports and identity documents made for him, but none had been under his real name.

"I don't know," he admitted.

They both fell silent and she put her hand on top of his, linking their fingers. "Slash, I didn't bring this up to upset you. Obviously neither one of us has the answers. But the more data we have, the closer we can get to the truth. If we ever want to get to the bottom of this, we need to start at the beginning. The *very* beginning."

He studied her thoughtfully. "Are you thinking the church at San Mauro? Where I was brought as an infant?"

"That's exactly what I'm thinking. In case you didn't already know, there are no digital records of the church online. I checked. But maybe we could find something useful in the documents there, if there's a library and the priests would be willing to let us take a look."

"It's a good idea, *cara*. The church will likely have handwritten books of visitors, major events, and possibly birth and death records. It's a decent starting point." He considered location, time and comfort, then made a decision. "It's too far to drive from Genoa to San Mauro Cilento. It would take us about eight hours. We can fly to Salerno in the morning, rent a car at the airport and drive to San Mauro. It will be much faster."

She hated flying, but she didn't balk at accompanying him. Instead she thought ahead. "Maybe we'll get lucky and find something in the church records. Or someone will remember you being brought there."

"Someone *does* remember me being brought there," he said, a trace of bitterness creeping into his voice. "But he's not helping."

She looked down at her plate and Slash cursed himself for his sharp comment. That wound was still too close to the surface, and it wasn't fair of him to put her in the middle. He wondered what he could say to smooth it over, but she spoke first.

"I can't pretend to understand the dynamic between

you and Father Armando. But if he took a vow or heard a confession, he can't tell you that information, Slash. No matter how important you are to him or he is to you. You *know* that."

He did know that, but he remained silent. There was more than a just a vow at stake here, there were feelings of betrayal and broken trust from which he wasn't sure they could recover.

He picked up his wine. She thought she didn't read people well, but she was becoming scarily accurate at reading him. Most men would consider it a sign of the strength of their relationship—but he wasn't used to having to work so hard to keep things from anyone. He didn't like hiding things from her, either. She was too smart and had too much integrity to take that kind of crap from him. He added this issue to the long-term problem compartment of his brain to work on later.

Perhaps realizing she wasn't going to get anywhere with that line of discussion, she didn't pursue it further. Instead she asked, "What time do you want to head out in the morning?"

Tension uncoiled in his gut, replaced by relief for the temporary reprieve. "As soon as possible," he said. "I'll make the reservations as soon as we get back to the room. We need answers."

"We do," she said. "And I firmly believe it's in our best interest to get them as soon as possible."

THIRTY-ONE

Lexi

WE'D SPENT THE night looking through the records at the NSA for Slash's supposed American birth certificate.

As a high-ranking official of the NSA, Slash didn't need to hack to get the information. The problem was the birth certificate that was supposed to exist confirming his American citizenship couldn't be found. It had either been deleted, moved or fabricated by Gray's contact, because we couldn't find a trace of it. Equally as disturbing, no record of his naturalization could be found either.

Another Slash mystery without easy answers.

I yawned, bleary-eyed and exhausted as we headed to the airport. My body was completely out of sync with Italy. I'd had a hard time falling asleep and a hard time getting up. I was hungry when I wasn't supposed to be and full when I should be hungry. Still, I put my game face on and tried to wake my tired brain.

Slash dropped off his rental car at the airport, and we headed to our gate. On the way we bought coffee and a loaf of warm crusty bread, pairing it with taleggio cheese and cacciatore salami—a perfect breakfast. I dozed on the plane, my head resting on Slash's shoulder, our hands linked. Last night we'd only scratched the surface of the issues that lay between us, but that was okay…for now. I was fine going at his pace. Hopefully, he'd share when he was ready, and I was willing to give him more time to get there.

We landed at the Salerno Costa d'Amalfi Airport at about eleven thirty in the morning. Slash rented a sleek convertible, set the GPS on his phone, and we headed out for San Mauro.

"Tell me what you know about the church," I said as we drove.

He had the top down and the sun was warm on my shoulders. I'd carefully slathered my white skin with suntan lotion. I was wearing the same cotton sundress I'd had on last night and Slash had bought me a wide-brimmed straw hat in the hotel lobby to keep the blistering sun off my face. It had a long white ribbon that kept whipping around and getting in my eyes and mouth, but I held on to the hat with both hands, grateful its wide brim was keeping my fair skin from getting sunburned.

Slash had his sunglasses on and his dark hair was also blowing in the wind. "The Church of San Mauro Martyr is located in the town of San Mauro in the region of Cilento," he explained. "It's an ancient village surrounded by a national park. The village sits on a high hill with a breathtaking panoramic view of the surrounding forest, the mountains and stunning beaches below."

He sounded like a brochure, and it was just too early. "Oh, no. Not the beach," I groaned.

I had a history with beaches. While I didn't particularly enjoy the setting—too hot, too many people and too much sand in places better not mentioned—many of the most transformative moments of my life seemed to happen at the beach.

Slash grinned as we took a tight curve. "The village has been historically divided into two parts, Casalsoprano and Casalsottano. The church is located in the Casalsottano part of the village. It dates back to the twelfth century. The Chapel of the Holy Spirit was added on in the fifteenth century."

"So, a medieval church."

"Beautiful, simple and holy."

We didn't talk much after that, both of us enjoying the scenery as we drove into the mountains. When we got closer to the town, I spotted several quaint houses nestled closely together at the top of the hill. Slash followed the directions into town, but it wasn't hard to spot the spire of the church.

Pretty stone houses and flowerboxes peppered the street as we wound our way through the town. Slash pulled up near the church and we got out of the car. There were a few people walking around, but it was hardly a crowd like it had been in Genoa.

Slash read my mind. "San Mauro Cilento is largely untouched by tourism. The population remains small, less than one thousand residents."

Before we went inside, I took a minute to study the outside of the church. It was a simple stone structure made of three interconnected buildings. Slash pulled open a heavy wooden door on the largest structure. The door squeaked and groaned, but he motioned for me to enter, so I stepped inside.

Inside, the church was stunning, with heavy wooden pews, exposed beams, medieval paintings and thick stained glass. Slash had started his life here, possibly spent time near that gorgeous antique organ that sat to the right of the altar.

"Wow," I whispered. There was a quiet reverence, beauty and holiness to the old structure.

"That was my first impression, too," Slash said. He dipped his fingers into a small bowl near the entrance and crossed himself. "It's exquisite in its simplicity."

"So, you've come back since you were an infant?" He seemed familiar with the church and its layout.

"*Si.* I've driven through the town a few times over the years and checked out the church. Curiosity, I guess. I never spoke with any of the staff, though. Father Armando had already left his post here."

He put his hand in the small of my back, guiding me forward. The church was dim, with lighted candles beneath several statues and small altars off to the side. A gorgeous medieval tapestry of a battle hung on one wall and, although faded, provided lovely splashes of gold and red. The church itself was empty except for a sole priest dressed in a black cassock, who was moving items around on the altar.

Slash dipped his head toward the priest, so I headed in that direction. The priest saw us coming and lifted a hand in greeting.

"*Buon pomeriggio,*" he said with a smile. He had wiry gray hair, his skin dark and wrinkled from the hot Italian sun.

Slash responded to him in Italian and soon they were deeply involved in conversation. Since I couldn't understand what they were saying, I wandered toward one of the apses where a lovely display of fresh flowers and flickering votive candles had been placed beneath a framed photograph of a woman. I recognized her from the banner in Genoa. It was Ana-Paula, the Uruguayan woman up for sainthood.

A few minutes later Slash walked up behind me as I was studying the photograph. "Are you intending to become an expert on sainthood?" Amusement was in his voice.

"I might. Why are people already praying to them?" I pointed to the lit candles and the padded kneeling bench in front of the framed photo. "Shouldn't they wait until they're officially saints?"

"Ah, *cara*, many people consider them already blessed, official sainthood or not. Requesting their assistance and intercession with a problem or prayer is quite normal."

I didn't get it, but I refrained from saying so aloud. Instead I glanced over at the priest who had resumed rearranging items on the altar. "Did you find out anything interesting from him?"

"I did. His name is Father Adam Bianachi. He's worked at the church for the past thirty-six years. He and Father Armando are friends. He knew who I was. Well, not me exactly, but the baby. He remembers when I was brought in during the great storm, and how I stayed with them for three days until the regional child services were able to reach here."

"That's promising. Did Father Bianachi happen to see the person who brought you in?"

"Unfortunately, he did not. The first he saw of me was when I was already in Father Armando's arms."

Slash pulled out his wallet and slipped some bills into an offering box near several unlit votive candles. He picked up a couple of matches and struck one to flame before lighting two wicks.

"So, did he say anything else?" I asked.

Slash straightened. "Father Bianachi says that it wasn't just he and Father Armando who were working here at the church when I was brought in. There were two others. One was an associate priest by the name of Father Daniel Opizzi, and the other was a young acolyte from Rome who was visiting for the summer. Father Bianachi doesn't know if Father Opizzi is still alive, he recalls him being in his forties, which would put him in his seventies now."

"What about the acolyte?" I asked.

"He doesn't remember the kid's name, but says he was an extraordinarily handsome young man who happened to leave a few weeks after I arrived at the church."

"That's interesting. Did Father Bianachi know how we can reach Father Opizzi? Maybe he'll remember something about that night or, at the very least, the acolyte's name."

"That would be ideal. Unfortunately, Father Bianachi does not know how to reach him, but we should be able to track the father down online if he's still alive."

"What happens if Father Opizzi doesn't remember the acolyte's name?"

"I already thought of that. Father Bianachi has granted us access to the church library for a few hours to see if he's mentioned anywhere in the records. How about we split this task up? You do a search online to see if you find Father Opizzi, and I'll go through the ledgers and journals to see if I can locate the acolyte's name."

"Deal." Finally we had two good leads. Maybe we could get some answers to Slash's past.

"That was nice of Father Bianachi to give us access to the library," I said. "Would he have done that for just anyone?"

"Without the personal connection to Father Armando, I doubt it."

"Well, then, let's not waste any time. We don't want him to change his mind."

"And this is why I love you, my single-minded woman. Let's go get your laptop. You can use your hotspot to work, as it's doubtful they'll have decent wifi here."

After we returned from the car with my computer, Slash introduced me properly to Father Bianachi. The priest shook my hand and welcomed me to the church in broken English. I thanked him in broken Italian before he led us through a door to the right of the altar, revealing a stone corridor. We followed him down the passage until he stopped at a door. Using a key on a keychain attached to his belt, he let us into a small room with a thick stained-glass window that didn't allow in much light. Leaning over, he switched on a lamp sitting in the middle of a round wooden table with four chairs. The walls were lined with bookshelves and crammed with books, ledgers, papers and boxes.

The priest said something to Slash in Italian and then left, keeping the door slightly ajar.

The minute he left, I started sneezing. "Wow, it's dusty in here." I looked at all the books and papers. "Where in the world do we start?"

"The year of my birth. Go ahead and get started on-line. I'll see if there is any rhyme or reason to this anti-quated filing system." Slash started pulling boxes and books from the shelves.

I sat at the table, sneezed some more and opened up my laptop.

An idea suddenly occurred to me. "Hey, Slash, do you know if you were baptized in this church?"

He was already seated on the floor in front of the bookshelf, a box between his legs, flipping through a blue leather journal. He had his phone out and was using it as a flashlight to view the papers. "*Si*. Father Armando told me he baptized me on the second day."

"Wouldn't the attending priests be noted somewhere?"

Slash looked up. "Not necessarily on the baptism certificate, which by the way, I've never seen, but it might be noted on an official event record for the church. I'm not sure how official my baptism was. Still, that's a good idea, *cara*."

I flexed my fingers and got to work. It took me over two hours to track down the former Father Daniel Opizzi. The wifi, even with my hotspot and an enhancer, was as slow as molasses.

"Bingo!" I finally exclaimed. "I've found him."

Slash looked up from some papers he was reading. "Alive?"

"Alive." I paused for a moment, scanning the information. "He retired from the priesthood about five years ago. He lives fifty minutes away from here in a small coastal town called Licosa."

"I know where Licosa is. Are you sure that's him?"

I studied his passport photo. "Pretty sure. He's listed as having spent several years working at this church. You could, of course, call him to confirm."

"I will. But I think we'd have a better chance of obtaining potentially helpful information if we were able to see him in person. If he's only an hour away, it might be worth the trip."

"Your call. How's it going with the search for the acolyte?"

Slash set aside the papers and stood, stretching out his back. "In terms of finding a name, terrible. The church's filing structure leaves a lot to be desired. I did, however, find my baptism certificate. As luck would have it, only Father Armando's name is on it." He held up a piece of paper between his fingers.

"No parents' names by chance?"

"I'm not that lucky."

I pursed my lips. "Hey, you got me, didn't you?" I was rewarded with a laugh, so I stood and walked over to get a look at the certificate.

"Did you get a photo of it?"

He tapped his phone. "I did."

"Good." I studied the photo, enlarging it on the date. "Well, at least this confirms you're thirty-three."

"Almost thirty-four."

I studied Father Armando's looped signature on the certificate. "It was nice of Father Armando to baptize you, wasn't it?"

Slash didn't respond. Apparently that hurt was still too fresh to address. Instead he sat down in front of my laptop and studied the photo of Father Opizzi.

"Does he look familiar?" I asked.

Slash shook his head and pulled out his phone. "No, but let's see if he's willing to talk."

Slash tapped out Father's Opizzi's number on his phone and waited. Someone must have answered on the other end because Slash started speaking in Italian. There was a short conversation, then Slash hung up.

"Well?" I looked at him hopefully. "Was it him?"

"It was him. He's agreed to see us today."

"Finally, some luck goes our way." I closed my laptop, rested my hands on top of it. "How much did you tell him?"

"Not much. I need to gauge his reaction when I tell him I'm the baby who was brought into the church, if he even remembers it. I said only that I wanted to talk to him about his time at the church of San Mauro. I told him I'd worked at the Vatican and was trying to track down one of the priests who used to work there."

"Does he remember the acolyte's name?"

"No. But he remembers him. He said he kept personal journals while at the church. He's going to look for the name and let us know if he's found anything by the time we get there."

"That would be great." I pulled off the power cord and began winding it up. "So, should we head out now?"

"*Si*. But let's have a quick bite to eat first."

"Great idea, because I'm famished."

Slash began to pick up the books, papers and boxes strewn across the floor while I packed up my laptop.

"I guess if Father Opizzi doesn't know who the acolyte is, we can always find him in the Vatican records, right?" I asked.

"Possibly." Slash gathered some papers and stacked them neatly in a box. "But I'm not sure how to go about finding that information. I'll have to think about it and that will take time." He put a final box on the shelf and brushed his hands together to remove the dust.

"Well, let's hope Father Opizzi has a good memory," I said. "Then we won't have to worry about that."

Slash smiled. "My experience is that priests are only second to nuns in regards to their memories. Want to bet he'll remember?"

I slapped my hand into his, sealing the bet. "You've got a deal."

THIRTY-TWO

Slash

SLASH THANKED FATHER BIANACHI for letting them look through the records, then they left the church. On the way to the car, he and Lexi stopped in a small Italian bakery where they ate a quiet lunch of risotto and drank espresso. She was quiet, probably wondering what information the visit with Father Opizzi would bring. He wondered that, too.

He finally leaned forward and tapped her arm. "Ready?"

"Yes. Let's go." She took the last sip of her espresso and stood.

The drive to Licosa took only forty-five minutes, but it had a killer view of the coastline, as well as breathtaking glimpses of the Tyrrhenian Sea. Lexi snapped several photos with her phone, her enthusiasm for the view making him smile.

He followed the GPS into Licosa and through the town. According to the small map, Father Opizzi's house was located in a rural area near the cliffs on the other side of the town. The directions eventually took them down a dirt road toward a house made of pretty stucco walls and a red tile and clay roof. They drove past a meadow with a couple of goats and a horse comingling together in the shade of a large tree. The tires kicked up rocks from the road, and the strong smell of sea air

confirmed the house was indeed located near the water.
Apparently Father Opizzi lived a quiet, retired existence
in a heavenly setting.

Slash pulled to a stop in front of the rustic house and
cut the engine. There was no car outside the house, but
there was a bicycle that looked well-tended. Although
the priest had sounded kind on the phone, Slash had no
idea if the father would answer his questions or remember anything useful about his time spent at the church
in San Mauro. But it was a lead that needed exploring.

Regardless, he remained conflicted about tracking
down his paternity. There was a part of him that wanted
to know about his past and a part that didn't. What if
the knowledge turned out to be damaging to his career
or his relationship with Lexi? What if the information
changed him as a person or affected his outlook on life?
But they'd come this far, so they'd talk to the priest and
see what he could tell them.

He turned to Lexi. "Are you ready, *cara*?"

"I'm ready." She unbuckled her seatbelt. "Let's do this."

They walked to the front door and Slash knocked.
The sounds of someone moving around could be heard
from inside.

A man with gray hair and a cane opened the door. He
wore dark slacks and a white T-shirt, his feet in brown
sandals. He squinted in the sunlight and cupped his hand
over his eyes as he surveyed them.

"Father Daniel Opizzi?" Slash said in Italian. "I'm
the one who called you from the church at San Mauro
Cilento."

"Yes, please come in."

Slash put a hand on the small of Lexi's back, ushering her forward so he could introduce her. "This is my

fiancée, Lexi Carmichael, from America. She doesn't speak Italian."

"That's okay," the priest answered. "I know English, and I'm happy to speak in a language you both understand."

"That's kind of you," Slash responded in English. "Thank you for agreeing to see us."

"Of course. Please come in." He ushered them inside the house.

Once inside, Lexi removed her hat. She was sweating, as was he. Even though the house had no air-conditioning, the shade was a welcome relief from the direct heat of the sun.

Slash did a quick survey of the room. Two visible exits, three windows, a television, a couch, a small desk with a small laptop, a round table and four chairs. The balcony doors, which were an exit to the back, were open and offered a slight cross breeze.

Religious artifacts and pictures of Jesus and numerous other saints hung on the wall, including the two new candidates for sainthood. The candles in the small makeshift shrine beneath them were currently lit.

The priest invited them to sit at the table. The table had a colorful woven mat with an open bottle of red wine on it. Lexi sat in the chair next to Slash.

"Would you like something to drink?" Father Opizzi asked them.

"Coffee would be wonderful. Lexi?"

"Do you have anything cold?" she asked. "I don't think I could bear to drink something hot in this heat."

The priest's smile stretched wider. "Coca-Cola?"

"Perfect. Thank you."

He shuffled off to the kitchen and returned a few

minutes later with two coffees and a Coke without ice. Lexi thanked him and Slash noticed she didn't mention the missing ice. His American girl was learning the European way.

Slash took a sip of his coffee and closed his eyes. "*Eccellente.*"

The priest put a spoonful of sugar into his cup and stirred it. "I'm glad it suits you. Now, how can I help you?"

Slash set his mug on the table. "If you don't mind, I'd like to know more about the time you spent at the church at San Mauro Cilento."

"Ah, yes. I enjoyed that year very much. Father Emilio Armando, who was the lead priest at the time, is a dear friend of mine. He's now a cardinal, in case you hadn't heard."

"I've heard."

"Then you've heard the rumors that he might be our next pope. I understand he is quite popular in Genoa, and with the other cardinals, as well."

"I've heard that, too," Slash said.

"Well, largely because of Emilio, my time spent in San Mauro was most memorable. Working in a small parish can be quite rewarding."

Slash pushed his cup aside. "When you were there, do you remember the night of one of the worst rain and lightning storms Italy had experienced in decades? There was widespread flooding and some roads were washed away. A baby boy was left at the church that night."

"Oh, yes. I remember that night and the baby quite clearly."

"*Veramente?*" As soon as he said it, Slash realized he'd slipped back into Italian. He flashed Lexi a grin that said, 'I told you so,' and added in English, "Really?"

The father met his smile, his eyes curious. He had to be wondering about Slash's reasons for a stroll down memory lane, but graciously let Slash lead the way. "Really. Mostly because Emilio took a special interest in the baby. We all did. We had to take care of him ourselves for several days due to the storm. We agreed the experience was a God-given gift to all of us."

"Why was the experience a gift?" he asked. "Surely it had to have been an unexpected burden to be faced with caring for an infant just a few days old."

"Oh, no! It wasn't a burden at all even though none of us had ever taken care of an infant before. There was something truly illuminating about the experience. We could not help but draw comparisons to how it must have been to care for Jesus as an infant. This poor, abandoned baby was such a sweet child. He rarely cried or fussed. But when he did, he could be soothed by a cuddle or singing. The baby seemed especially fond of the music of a pianist whose name escapes me at the moment."

"Hai Tsang," Lexi supplied and then pressed her fingers against her lips. "Oops. Sorry to interrupt."

"No, it's quite alright," Father Opizzi said looking at her in surprise. "You're correct. It *was* the Chinese pianist Tsang. How did you know?"

Lexi glanced at Slash with an apology in her eyes, but he shook his head slightly, wanting her to know it was okay.

"I'm that baby," he admitted. "I'm sorry I didn't tell you that from the start, but I wanted to hear your version of the story without being aware the infant being discussed was me."

The father studied Slash with undisguised interest. "Well, it makes sense. I was wondering where you were going with that line of questioning. This is quite a surprise. A pleasant surprise, of course."

"I'm sorry if I made you uncomfortable."

"No, no, you haven't. By God, I heard you went missing shortly after you were placed with a family. Emilio looked for you for so long. Did he ever find you?"

"He did." Slash didn't offer more information and the father didn't pry even though he had to be curious. "Sir, did you happen to find the name of the other priest who was there at the same time you were? The young acolyte assigned to the church from Rome during the summer?"

"I did, and I should mention he was quite the handsome lad. The young ladies of the village attended mass far more often when he was assisting."

"Father Bianachi also mentioned his physical appearance."

"Oh, yes." The priest set his coffee down and leaned back in the chair, crossing his legs. "That young man looked as if God had created an angel on earth. The proverbial tall, dark and handsome man, if you will forgive my indulgence."

"His name?"

"His name was Manuel de Rosa. He returned to Rome not too long after that big storm."

"Wasn't he supposed to be assigned there for the entire summer?"

"He was. His departure was unexpected, as I recall. He left the priesthood shortly thereafter, much to my disappointment, as I thought he had great promise, and of course, loads of charisma."

"Any idea why he left?"

"I'm afraid the holy life is not for everyone. Leaving

the priesthood is not that an unusual occurrence for aco-lytes, especially one who stood out as much as he did."

Slash knew that truth firsthand. "Do you know where Manuel was from? What city or region? Did he have an accent? Did he ever talk about his family?"

"I'm afraid we didn't talk much socially, and he rather kept to himself. But he was Italian. I don't know anything else about him other than he was assigned from Rome. He could have been from anywhere in Italy."

Slash stood, offering a hand. "Thank you very much for your time, Father. I greatly appreciate you speak-ing with us."

"It was my pleasure. I do not receive a lot of visitors and I quite enjoy it. I am glad God has brought you to my doorstep if for nothing else than closure. May I say one thing more?"

"Of course."

"You were in my life for three days, but your pres-ence stayed with me for my entire life. I'll never forget those days of caring for you. It was one of those experi-ences that last a lifetime."

How odd that his birth and subsequent drop-off at the church had touched the lives of several priests des-tined to never have children of their own. It was a small thing, but knowing his life had served them in that way was unexpectedly gratifying.

Slash felt a lump in his throat. "Thank you for tell-ing me that, Father."

As they headed for the door, Lexi stopped to look at the pictures of the two candidate saints on the wall.

"They are soon to become saints, we hope," Father Opizzi told her.

"That's what I hear," she said. "You've lit the candles beneath their photos. Does that mean you're praying for them?"

"It does. But I'm not just praying for their souls, I'm asking them to guide me by their example so I may become a better person."

"That's quite admirable, especially given your lifetime of service."

He laughed. "Even retired priests need all the help they can get."

She laughed, too, and Slash wondered if she realized how beautiful she looked with a smile on her face. "Thank you for your kindness and hospitality, Father," she said. "By the way, your English is excellent."

"I'm humbled by your evaluation. I do enjoy watching mysteries and the news on the BBC. It's been fun practicing my English with you. I do not often have the opportunity to do so. Now, go with God, my children, and please come back and visit anytime. It would be my pleasure to see you both again."

"We might do that," Slash said and meant it. "We very well might."

THIRTY-THREE

Father Julian Koenhein

THE CARDINAL WAS going to be extremely angry with the statement on the piece of paper he held in one hand, and Julian didn't have a clue how to break it to him in a way that would prevent that fury. Usually he was good at smoothing ruffled feathers and keeping Cardinal Lazo calm by working behind the scenes to keep things moving efficiently and quietly.

But events of late had been bringing him out of his comfort zone on a regular basis and that was unsettling.

Julian hesitated with his hand poised to knock, wishing he could think of a way to deliver the news and vanish, at least until the cardinal's anger had passed. Unfortunately, no amount of thinking and no magic solution presented itself to him, so he knocked on the door.

He heard the cardinal's voice tell him to enter. It sounded irritated, as Julian had expected. Summoning an inner courage and calm, Julian walked into the cardinal's office.

"I told you I didn't want to be disturbed," the cardinal snapped without looking up from his writing. "I'm busy."

"I beg your pardon, Your Eminence, but we have received an email from… Slash."

The cardinal lifted his head. "Do we finally know where he is?"

"We do not, although, at least, we know he hasn't left Italy. Anyway, you received this correspondence from him two hours ago."

"Two hours ago? Why didn't you notify me immediately?"

Julian wanted to answer that it was because the cardinal had told him not to disturb him, but he said instead, "I wanted to be sure of the authenticity of the email. After reviewing it, I believe it's legitimate. But we may have a problem."

"What kind of problem?"

"Slash said he's willing to make a statement about his father, but it may not be what you expected."

The cardinal's set his pen down and swiveled his chair to face Julian directly. "Is that so? What did I expect?"

"I don't know, but not this."

"Read it to me," the cardinal demanded.

Julian cleared his throat. "Cardinal Lazo, if you issue a statement using my name without my permission, I will go viral with a statement you will never be able to stop. In that statement, I will acknowledge *you* as my father." He looked up from the email. "That's it."

"What?" The cardinal's expression darkened. "Give me that paper."

Julian quickly handed it over to the cardinal. Lazo read it, then angrily crumpled it in his fist before tossing it across the room. "Where are those DNA results from the hotel?"

"I received a call a few minutes ago, Your Eminence. The results should be in my inbox by the end of the day."

"They better be, because I want answers and I want them *now*."

Lexi

I SAT IN THE car in front of Father Opizzi's house, my face positioned inches from the car's air-conditioning vent. I was beyond grateful Slash had it on full blast so I could think of something other than the fact that I was melting into a puddle of sweat.

"What do we do now?" I asked, putting the hat back on and cupping my hands around the vent to funnel the cool air toward me in a more efficient way.

"We need to find Manuel de Rosa."

"Okay. Where will home base be for said searching? Do we find a hotel here in Licosa?"

"No. We go to Salerno. It's the closest big city, and the wifi will be significantly better. I know an excellent hotel where we can work comfortably. I'll see if they have a room available."

He pulled up a number and dialed it, and I was quiet while he spoke rapidly to someone. "We got lucky. Someone cancelled their room an hour ago."

"Great. I hope it has air-conditioning."

"It doesn't, but it does have a beautiful sea view. The breeze coming off the water will feel refreshing."

I sighed, my hopes for a cool evening dashed. "What's your plan for finding de Rosa?"

"Open sources first," he said. "It might be that simple."

"Or not." I hated playing devil's advocate, but sometimes things weren't simple. "Slash, he could be anywhere in the world."

"I know. But Italy is the best place to start. We'll find him wherever he is. It's just a matter of time."

"But we're short on time."

"Then we put our heads together and figure a faster way."

I looked out the window at the bicycle and thought of the kindly priest sitting inside, praying in front of the small shrine to the saints. Then I thought of Slash and everything he'd been through in his life. I felt like I was missing something right in front of my face.

"Slash, don't you think it's strange that de Rosa left the priesthood right after you are brought to the church? Father Opizzi said he was exceptionally handsome. There are some potentially uncomfortable lines to be drawn here. Do you think he could be your father?"

He stiffened, but I knew he was too smart not to have considered it. "I have no idea. But until we can rule it out, we keep it on the table for my sake as well as Father Armando's." He glanced at me. "What was your impression of Father Armando, anyway? Did you like him?"

I leaned back against the seat. This was a delicate question and required a delicate answer. "You know I'm not the kind of person who gets warm, fuzzy feelings after meeting people only once, but the truth is, I did like him. I think he has a lot of regret for what happened to you. He wants to help, but instead he feels like he keeps hurting you. That's got to be tough on both of you."

Slash didn't respond. Instead, he programmed the GPS, then slid his hand behind my seat, putting the car in Reverse. Apparently we wouldn't be discussing the issue any further. I wondered if they could ever get past whatever Lazo had shoved between them.

I waited until we pulled out onto the road before I spoke again. "Slash, even if we find Manuel de Rosa, it could be a dead end, or he might not be willing to talk to us. There's a chance he might not be alive. We could be chasing a ghost here. We may never find out who your father is."

Slash's eyes were hidden behind his sunglasses, but his mouth tightened. "I know. But ghost or not, we keep hunting."

THIRTY-FOUR

Lexi

"Don't look." Slash took his hand off the steering wheel to pat my knee.

"Closing my eyes doesn't help," I protested. "My imagination is worse than the road."

"Then keep your eyes focused ahead. I promise to keep you safe, okay? We'll get to Salerno in one piece."

Slash drove carefully along the winding road barely large enough to fit two cars. He filled me in on the history of Salerno as we drove, perhaps to take my mind off the scary cliffs hugging the side of the route.

"How soon until we get there?" I looked to my right where there was no guard rail—just one long drop. I gulped and snapped my gaze back to the road in front of me.

"Not too much longer."

True to his word, we safely made it to Salerno, but I wasn't so sure about my stomach. As we entered the town, we were met with more banners picturing the saints stretched across buildings and streets. Souvenir stands were selling tea towels, keychains and mugs with their images, and posters of the two were plastered on buildings, street signs and houses. You couldn't turn your head without seeing them.

"Wow." I glanced around in surprise. "I had no idea how big a deal this sainthood thing is."

"It's a big deal, especially when one of the saints happens to be from your city."

"Yes, of course, the Savior of Salerno. A hometown boy makes it big."

"Exactly."

We drove up a winding street until we reached a stunning white building built right into the cliffs.

"Holy cow," I said. "That's the hotel? The building inside the cliff? I've never seen anything like that."

"It's the Hotel *La Lucertola*. It has a stunning view, so I knew you'd appreciate it." He smiled as he parked the car and cut the ignition. "And, in addition to the view, it's only a two-minute walk to the beach."

My step faltered. "The beach? But… I, ah, didn't bring my bathing suit."

He chuckled. "You can swim topless here, *cara*. Everyone does."

"*What?*"

The chuckle turned into a full-throated laugh. "*Mio Dio*. Don't look so worried. Unfortunately, we don't currently have swimming on the agenda, although if you change your mind about the topless part, I could be persuaded."

Still grinning at the horrified expression on my face, he grabbed my hand and tucked it into his elbow as we entered the hotel. I waited in a chair in the lobby with our bags while he registered us. He retrieved me once he had the keys.

"What name did you register us under?" I asked in a low voice.

"Mr. and Mrs. Allegretti."

"Allegretti? What if someone speaks Italian to me?"

"You're my American wife. No worries."

"Oh, right."

Our room was on the second floor, so we had to take only one flight of stairs. The room was bright and sleek with a balcony and a gorgeous sea view, as Slash had promised. I dropped my bags and hat on the bed and headed to the balcony, my hands resting on a smooth white railing. The sapphire sea sparkled as the late afternoon sun cast a reddish, golden glow over the water. Sailboats dotted the horizon. To my left and right, the cliffs of the town were wedged with brightly colored houses and buildings built right into the stone like the hotel.

"This may be one of the most beautiful views I've ever seen," I said in a hushed tone.

He came up behind me, circling his arms around my waist. "The Amalfi coast is one of my favorite places in the world. There is a certain quiet here that rests my soul."

"I can see why."

I'm not sure how long we stood there admiring the view, but when we finally moved back into the room, my stomach growled loudly.

I pressed a hand to my abdomen. "Ugh. My body is all out of sorts with the time change."

"I'm hungry, too," Slash said. "Let's get the computers set up and I'll order room service. We'll eat dinner on the balcony, if that works for you."

"That totally works for me. Can we have seafood?"

"We can. I highly recommend the seafood and pasta from this region."

"Perfect."

I set up the computers while Slash called room service. It took me a few minutes to create an automatic search for all males named Manuel de Rosa in Italy, narrowing the parameters to include a specific age range. Slash joined me, creating a duplicate search, but focusing on all Italian males named Manuel de Rosa who were associated with seminary training or the priesthood. We would cross reference later to see who, if anyone, popped.

Sooner than expected, room service arrived with our dinner. I went into the bathroom to wash up and was met with a stunning interior of white-and-earth-toned tiles, including a gorgeous white marble bowl sink. When I came out, room service had departed and Slash was placing our dinner on the small balcony table. I finished setting the table while he was in the bathroom. By the time he returned, everything was ready.

"I ordered two separate dishes and thought we could share," he said, pulling out my chair. I sat down and lifted the top covering one of the plates. "I ordered a variety of stone fruits, *manteca del Cilento* and pecorino cheese, black olives, fresh figs and bread."

It was an amazing spread and only the first course. I was in heaven.

He sat and we loaded our plates. As the first bite of the pecorino cheese exploded on my tongue, I closed my eyes to savor the experience. "Best. Food. Ever."

We both gorged on figs, fruit and cheese before Slash opened a couple of Italian craft beers for us to try. Like everything else, the beer was delicious.

"I can see why people love Italy so much," I said, munching on a piece of bread. "Carbs for every meal of the day."

He smiled. "Life does revolve around food in Italy."

"I hope I can stay awake after we eat. I'm going to need a nap after this."

"Then we'll take a nap."

I needed to stay up and get adjusted to Italian time, but I didn't want to pass up the chance to let him hold me, so I reserved the right to take a nap if I needed one.

After the antipasto, we shared an excellent meal of spaghetti with clam sauce and eggplant parmigiana. For dessert, we drank coffee and nibbled on lemon *delizie*, a spongy cake filled with lemon custard. A couple of times while we were eating, I got up and checked on the progress of our search for Manuel de Rosa.

"It's looking good so far," I said, sitting back down. "We'll have decent data to work with."

"Good. I'm anticipating narrowing it down fairly quickly. I want to move rapidly on this. Either he's a good lead or he's not."

"True." I took another bite of the cake and finally put down my fork, sitting back in my chair. "I can't eat another bite. Being this full reminds me of eating at Nonna's house. Will we get to see her while we're here?"

"I'd be in serious fear for my life if she found out I was in Italy and didn't stop by. Besides, she's excited about the engagement, and the fact that you accepted the ring she once wore."

I looked down at my engagement ring. I was scared that a klutz like me was entrusted with such an important family heirloom. Regardless, I loved it and was already used to the feel of it on my finger.

"Well, in that case, we should definitely visit her."

Slash grinned, lifting his coffee cup to me. "You just want to eat her food."

"Hey, I'm not going to deny it. The two of you have

ruined me for all other food. She's got serious mojo in the kitchen. Perhaps the most amazing food mojo in the entire universe."

He smiled, and I noticed how relaxed he'd become since we'd been here. His posture, expression and tone had all eased away from the rigidity that had been present when I'd first seen him in Genoa. The sun was setting, casting a fiery, almost golden glow on the water and cliffs. It was a moment that would burn in my memory for a long time.

"Now that you're family, she might be willing to share some secret recipes with you," he said.

"The recipes would be great, but I would imagine a certain culinary talent would be required to recreate the magic. I can barely fix a bowl of Cheerios."

"Not true. You've been doing an excellent job of cooking on your nights, and you are smart and excellent with measurements and following directions—most of the time. You have legitimate potential."

The thought cheered me. Perhaps there was hope for me yet.

Finally we tore ourselves away from the view and food and headed back inside to our laptops to get to work. It took us under an hour to cull our list and cross-reference it. When we worked together, we were unstoppable.

"Okay, that totals sixty-seven hits within the age and church connection parameters," I said, tapping my screen. "That's not too bad."

"I'm satisfied. Let's split them up and run a tighter cross-reference. One set specifically with the church at San Mauro Cilento, and another with the Vatican."

I looked up at him in surprise. "The Vatican? You

think someone as young as he was worked at the Vatican?"

"I think it's a thread I don't want to leave dangling."

"Your call." I tapped out some commands and watched the data scroll by. About an hour later, Slash pushed back from the desk. "Got him."

I scooted over and peered over his shoulder at his screen. "How did you find him so fast?"

"I did a little dipping in unsecure Vatican files and went through dozens of seminary class lists for the time I estimated he would be there. I focused on a class I knew he would have taken as an acolyte, and boom, there he was. From that point, I was able to track him to the residency at San Mauro."

"So, what we do know about him now? Is he alive? In Italy?"

"He's alive. He's fifty-four years of age and was born right here in Salerno. The time frame for his residency fits exactly with when I was brought to the church."

"He sounds like our guy. Does he still live in Salerno?"

"No. His current residence is in Gaeta, which is about a two-and-a-half hour drive from here, along the coast. He's divorced with no kids. Tends bar at one of the local hotels."

How odd that his life had changed so dramatically. "From acolyte to divorced bartender," I said. "That's a jump."

"Not really. Bartenders and priests are both good listeners."

"True, that." I closed my laptop and stood, as it looked like the search was over, at least for the time being. "Now what, Slash? Do we call him? Go see him?" I watched him carefully to see how he would react to this. I wasn't sure how he would handle coming face-to-face with a guy that might turn out to be the father who had abandoned him.

But he seemed steady when he snapped his laptop shut and sat on the edge of the bed. "I think we go see him in person, without a call first. I don't want to risk him turning us down for a discussion."

"That's probably a wise choice. When do we leave?"

"Tomorrow, probably around noon. He works at night, which means he'll likely be sleeping in the morning. We can wander and play tourist for a few hours before heading out to see him. After that, we'll swing by Nonna's house since Sperlonga is only twenty minutes away from Gaeta."

"Hooray!"

Slash glanced at me with amusement. "You're only thinking of food again."

"Not only, but yes." I grinned at him. "However, right now, I'm also thinking I have to work off this dinner. Do you think you can help me with that?" I put my hands on his shoulders and abruptly pushed him backward onto the bed.

His expression flared with surprise, but within a second, his fingers had wrapped around both my wrists. He flipped and pinned me beneath him, my arms trapped above my head.

He looked down at me, his eyes darkening. "I'm sure a workout can be arranged."

"Oh, thank goodness, Mr. Allegretti," I said in a teasing voice. "I don't even mind going topless for this one."

"Thank God and all the saints. I've always dreamed about you saying that," he said as his mouth crashed down on mine.

THIRTY-FIVE

Lexi

I ENJOYED THE best night of sleep since coming to Italy. Even though things weren't completely right with us, especially the unresolved Congo issue, it felt like we were healing—getting back on the right track as a couple. Perhaps getting stronger. But there was still a ways to go.

Since I'd been in Italy, I'd received four texts from Elvis, one from Finn, and two each from Basia and Gray. I'd answered all of them by saying I'd arrived in Italy, I was fine and I would explain everything later. I'd sent a special apology to Elvis without going into detail, and promised to come see him when I returned. I didn't imagine anyone was satisfied by my abbreviated response. It was difficult to believe I actually had friends who cared that much about me.

I woke before Slash but stayed in bed. The balcony doors were open, the breeze felt wonderful. The curtains fluttered as sunshine dappled across the sheets. I snuggled against him, smiling as he pulled me tighter, resting his face in the crook of my neck. When he finally woke, we spent another hour or so in bed, cuddling and talking about things that had nothing to do with paternity, statues or Vatican intrigue. We'd stolen this time just for ourselves. While I wasn't naive enough to think we could avoid confrontation forever, I wanted to hold these moments close.

When we finally got dressed, we sat on the balcony sipping coffee and watching the boats sail by. Finally Slash suggested we visit the Salerno Cathedral and do a little sightseeing downtown before we left for Gaeta. We packed up our stuff, but I was reluctant to leave our little haven. Slash seemed to sense my reluctance, because he pulled me in for one last lingering kiss on the balcony.

"We'll come back, *cara*, when we have no other cares but each other," he murmured.

I wondered if that would ever happen with us. Even though I doubted it, I touched my engagement ring with my thumb and said, "Deal."

We checked out of the hotel and put our bags in the car. I returned the floppy hat to my head as Slash drove us downtown. We were detoured several times due to a huge city-wide parade in honor of the saints.

"You still want to fight the crowds to see the church?" Slash asked me as we inched along.

"We don't have anything better to do, right? We've got time to kill and you told me the Salerno Cathedral is spectacular."

"It is."

"Then, let's do it."

Slash managed to find a parking spot near the bottom of a hill. We were getting out of the car when Slash's phone rang. He motioned that he needed to take it, so I walked around to the back of the car and leaned against the trunk, waiting for him.

An elderly woman heading to the parade a couple of streets over was pushing a wheeled cart filled with colorful flowers and tacky saint souvenirs. She passed me and started up the path. She was struggling, as the cart was apparently heavy. Several people walked past her, but not one offered to help. I looked over at Slash, but he was still sitting in the car talking, so I approached her.

I spoke to her with a mixture of gestures and the few Italian phrases I knew. She seemed surprised I offered. I took the handles of the cart from her and pointed to me and then the top of the hill.

"I push it for you, okay?" I said.

She looked at me warily and then nodded.

I started pushing it up the hill and immediately understood why she was having problems. It was hard work. A third of the way up, I started panting. She walked beside me, gesturing and offering a constant stream of advice in Italian that I didn't understand. A minute later I got it to the top of the hill, but I was sweating profusely beneath my hat. My T-shirt was dripping with perspiration. I wished I weren't wearing jeans. Moisture slid from my scalp into my eyes, so I blinked rapidly and ignored the burning sensation.

The vantage from the hilltop was great. The parade was in full swing, a trio of musicians were playing an up-tempo song and two white horses with men sitting atop them in uniforms clopped past. A couple of cars with people waving motored by. Behind the cars a bishop in a white cassock and a tall miter on his head was walking, wielding an enormous wooden cross. It had to be made of cardboard or maybe balsa wood, because he seemed to be moving it with ease. Behind him was a choir, singing a religious hymn. Two priests dressed in black cassocks trailed immediately behind him, holding life-size posters of the saints-to-be on long wooden poles.

The old woman said something to me, and I realized

I'd totally forgotten about her. "Oh, I'm sorry. *Scusate*. Here's your cart."

I angled the handles toward her, waiting patiently until she had a firm grasp on them before I let go. She profusely thanked me, and I turned to go back to Slash, feeling proud of my Good Samaritan moment.

At that moment, a teenager on a scooter zoomed past me on the right. He clipped my shoulder hard as he rocketed past, then shouted an apology. I stumbled forward, knocking into the elderly woman, who lost her grip on the cart. She lurched around me trying to grab the handles, but slipped, banging into the cart, which gave it a hard push forward. I managed to catch her beneath her elbow, but the cart started to accelerate down the hill, pausing for only a moment as it came to a slight rise.

Holy runaway cart!

I ensured the lady was stable before I dashed after it, my hat flying off my head. Four steps forward, I collided with another female passerby who must have seen the cart and had decided to stop it, too. Grabbing on to each other for balance, we watched, horrified, as the cart charged even faster downhill, picking up speed and bouncing merrily along toward the parade.

"Oh, crap!" I bolted after the cart.

It wasn't a fair race because (1) the cart had a head start, and (2) I was wearing sandals, but I chased it just the same. I made respectable progress anyway. However, dealing with the sandals made it difficult to calculate whether I could reach the cart in time—especially if I factored in the exhaustion from pushing the cart up the hill in the first place, and adjusting for adrenaline. I also had no idea if I had the mass and distance to stop the cart once I reached it, given the coefficient of friction from the sandals.

My calculations, though admittedly hurried, suggested I had a slim chance, and that gave me an extra burst of speed. Though I was focused on the rampaging cart, I could see people turning and pointing. I wondered if they had heard the cart...or maybe they'd heard me. Was I screaming? Shrieking? Amid the *slap, slap, slap* of my sandals, I wondered under which tab on my Little Black Cloud Spreadsheet this moment would go. Most Humiliating Moments or Most Heroic Save?

The handles were almost within reach when the cart veered slightly and hit a curb. It went airborne, spinning on several axes while raining kitschy flowers, tea towels, keychains and pins across the crowd before it took out the bishop and crashed to a stop upside down on the far side of the street. The wheels kept spinning.

At this point, I was running too fast to stop cleanly, and the sandals fought my best efforts to slow my momentum. I managed to jump over a downed drum and avoid a small dog, but I ricocheted off two musicians, lost a sandal, pirouetted, stumbled and fell face-first into the bishop's lap, slamming my jaw against his knee.

I lay facedown for a moment, trying to catch my breath and process what had happened, when the bishop said something in Italian in a deep voice. I scrambled to a seated position, my cheeks burning hot. I watched in silence as the bishop rearranged the robes in his lap where my face had been, then turned for assistance from a nearby parade-goer for help back to his feet. A small girl picked up, dusted off and returned his miter.

Suddenly I became aware of the pandemonium surrounding me. People were shouting, crying and laughing. I stood, turning around in the middle of the street, apologizing to the bishop and the parade marchers, and trying, in a mixture of English, pantomime and random Italian words, to explain to two policemen what had happened with the wheeled cart and the old woman.

At last Slash appeared, carrying my hat. He looked around at the stopped parade, the scattered instruments, the bishop gathering the pieces of the broken cross, the policemen holding my arm, and everyone talking and shouting at once.

Just then, the old woman shoved her way through the crowd and, to my astonishment, hugged me hard, before she started shouting at the policemen and gesticulating wildly. When anyone tried to get too close to me, she snarled at them like a lioness. Everyone seemed a little afraid of her, even Slash, who wisely kept his distance.

Slash met my gaze across the street and I lifted my hands. "I know this looks bad, but it wasn't my fault... exactly."

He finally stepped forward, but the elderly lady came between us. I tapped her shoulder, pointed at my engagement ring and then Slash. "It's okay. He's with me."

The woman eyed him mistrustfully but stepped aside. Slash gently tipped my chin to the side, examining my jaw. "Are you okay?"

"I'm fine, I think. My jaw, however, got up close and personal with the bishop's knee, and I may or may not have planted my face in his lap."

Slash raised an eyebrow but said nothing, thank God. A kindly gentleman retrieved the lady's wheeled cart—now rolling crookedly—and returned it to her.

Slash tipped his head toward the elderly lady. "She

told the police you helped her with the cart and it's her fault it went barreling down the hill."

"That's somewhat accurate. I handed the cart off to her after I pushed it up the hill, but a guy on a scooter clipped me and I bumped into her. She didn't have a good hold on the handles, so it got away from her. If I'd had my tennis shoes on, and not sandals, I might have caught it."

The policeman started to ask me something in halting English, but Slash interceded, speaking Italian on my behalf, presumably explaining what happened. People started crowding around listening. At one point I heard Slash say "*Americana*" and everyone burst out laughing.

"What's so funny?" I asked him, my hands on my hips.

"Not a thing." He looped an arm around my shoulders. The policemen moved away and Slash began to check out my arms and legs to make sure I was okay.

"Nothing broken," I insisted. "Just my pride."

"I'm glad you're okay, *cara*." He placed the hat on my head.

"I may be okay, but I don't think I made a good impression on the bishop." I glanced nervously over at him. He was examining the cross, but it definitely hadn't survived my onslaught.

The bishop saw us staring, so he started coming our way. Thankfully, Slash moved to intercept him, and they started a conversation. At one point during the discussion, the bishop smiled and waved at me. Slash smiled at me, too, over his shoulder.

What the heck?

I waved back warily, wondering what Slash was saying about me. That I was the biggest dork in the universe? That a little black cloud followed me around nonstop and

I destroyed things and injured myself and others on a regular basis? Planting my face in the bishop's lap might be a new personal low for me, though.

While they were talking, I reached into my purse and pulled out all the euros I had, which equaled $316. I pressed it into the elderly woman's hand. She looked shocked and tried to refuse the money, but I insisted. After a bit of a shoving match, she finally put the money in her purse.

A minute later, Slash returned to my side. People were thankfully starting to lose interest in the sideshow. The elderly woman said something to Slash and he turned to me. "She says you gave her $300."

"Well, it was $316 to be exact, and it was the least I could do. I would have given her more, but that was all I had in my wallet. I feel terrible."

"It wasn't your fault."

I loved him for saying so, but somehow I was involved in a statistically high number of accidents and there had to be some crazy force in the universe that I kept being in the center of them. "Regardless, she lost all her wares and now she has a damaged cart."

Slash took out his wallet and gave her some additional bills. The woman's eyes went wide and she tried to press the money back into his hands, much like she had done with me. But Slash insisted, so she finally hugged him, hugged me again and then shuffled away with her lop-sided cart.

The policemen eventually shooed us and the other by-standers off the road so they could resume the parade. I assumed that meant I wasn't under arrest.

"Everything's okay?" I asked Slash. At least I hadn't been handcuffed or led away in a police car.

"Everything's okay. Accidents happen."

"Especially with me around. What about with the bishop? Is he okay?"

"He's fine. I think it may have been the most excitement he's had in three decades. All is good with you and the Bishop of Salerno."

Yep, this was *definitely* a new low for me. "While I'm relieved, being the sole source of excitement for the Bishop of Salerno over the past three decades does *not* make me feel any better."

Slash smiled as he adjusted his sunglasses on his nose. "I leave you alone for five minutes, and this happens."

"I was trying to help!"

"And help, you did. The elderly woman you helped walked away with significantly more money than she would have made. The bishop has an exciting tale to tell during mass, and the parade viewers had a lot more interesting fare to watch than the Salerno civic choir singing off-key. Good job." He placed a hand on my back, moving me forward. "Now let's go check out the cathedral."

"Fine." I hoisted my purse on my shoulder and took the hand he offered. "As long as it can be done in anonymity, I'm in."

THIRTY-SIX

Lexi

WE FOLLOWED THE parade route toward the church. The crowds were heavy as we pushed our way through the people who had gathered for the celebration. I noticed the stares Slash got as we walked past. Even in a crowd, his presence was compelling.

"So, who called when I was helping the elderly lady?" I asked as we walked.

"Work. It was Charlie. They have an issue and were asking my opinion."

"An issue? Is it safe to talk NSA-business on your phone?"

"No. But we don't talk specifics."

"Do they miss you?"

"Perhaps. I need to get back, but I'm also finding I quite enjoy showing my girl around Italy, despite the less-than-ideal circumstances."

"Well, this girl is enjoying it…minus those particular circumstances and the runaway cart, of course."

He smiled, but said nothing as he guided me through the crowd. When we finally arrived at the cathedral, the first thing that struck me was the bell tower with mullioned windows.

"Wow, that's incredibly intricate," I said.

Slash gazed up, shading his eyes with his hand even

though he wore sunglasses. "There are eight bells, all perfectly tuned. And, if you check out the front façade, you'll see it contains fifty-six panels depicting various stages of Jesus's life."

"Wow. How do you know all that? Is it from your time spent at the Vatican?"

"Nope. I looked it up on Google this morning while you were in the bathroom, so I could impress you." His mouth twitched as if trying to keep from smiling.

"Hey!" I hit him on the arm as he leaned in with a mischievous twinkle in his eye and planted a kiss on my cheek. "Come on, let's go inside."

I took a few more photos before we entered the church. Slash dipped his fingers in the holy water and crossed himself as I removed my hat, thankful for the cool dimness of the church. The cathedral was understandably crowded, but we wandered around, stopping often in apses to admire the paintings, the ceiling frescos and intricate stained-glass windows.

It was hard to explain how being in church made me feel, especially side by side with Slash. The engineering part of my brain was already calculating the loading on the walls and the columns from the golden vaulted ceilings. I tried to imagine how they completed the construction, given the tools and technology of the day. But another part of my brain was reminding me that not everything can, or *should*, be computed. For a moment, I just stopped in wonder and enjoyed the beauty and majesty of the structure.

We made a full circle inside the church before Slash asked me if I wanted to see the tombs. I did, so we descended below, and spent a few minutes jostling with other tourists to get a good view of Matthew's tomb, as well as that of Pope Gregory VII's.

Before we headed back outside, we stopped at the makeshift shrine of the two sainthood candidates. Slash dropped a few bills into the collection box and asked if I wanted to light the votive candles. I lit two, and Slash bowed his head, murmuring a short prayer for them.

The heat and bright sunshine blinded us the second we stepped outside, so we put our sunglasses back on. The parade had ended in the courtyard shortly after the arrival of the bishop, but the celebration was still going strong.

"How long does the celebration last?" I asked Slash.

"As long as it takes. My guess is all day and well into the night. We Italians like a good party." He looked around. "I'm going to find a bathroom. You good?"

"Good, but thirsty." I spotted a food stand with a line of people in front of it. "I'll get us a couple of waters and wait here for you. Sound good?"

"Perfect. Just stay out of trouble." He reached into his wallet and handed me some euros. "Since you gave all your money away."

"Oh, right. Thanks." I tucked the money into my front jeans pocket.

I got in line and did some people watching. Women dancers in colorful skirts and blouses were twirling around in one part of the courtyard with a large crowd gathered to watch them. Musicians were playing, and I found myself enjoying the moment, relaxing and watching the spectacle instead of being a part of it.

As I shuffled forward in line, I saw a group of children forming under the direction of a nun. It looked like I was going to have a front row seat to a performance by a children's choir. For a moment I could feel my little black cloud part with the sunshine of the courtyard.

When there were only two people in front of me, and just as the children's choir began to sing, I pulled the euros out of my pocket. One of the bills fluttered to the ground. I bent down to retrieve it and saw flames licking beneath the food stand. A pool of grease or some other flammable liquid had dripped and caught fire…right next to a propane tank. Grease ran down the side of the tank, and flames were already licking at the bottom of it.

Holy explosion!

I immediately pushed forward through the line, trying to get the attention of the vendor. Unfortunately, the folks in front of me thought I was trying to cut in line, so one guy grabbed me by the arm.

"Fire!" I yelled and pointed under the cart. Either no one understood my English or the noise of the choir was making everything hard to hear. I briefly thought about whipping out my phone to translate, but there was no time.

Another hasty glance beneath the cart confirmed my estimate that we had a few minutes at most before that tank blew sky-high. The explosion would be significant in this tightly packed crowd, even if I couldn't calculate exactly how significant, since I didn't know the ratio of expansion during the ignition of propane gas. But if I used a factor of 10 to 1, hundreds of people—including the entire children's choir—would be within the blast radius. Worse, the metal shards from the tank would act as projectiles, wounding or killing many more.

Time to do something.

Pulling free of the guy's hold on my arm, I ran around the side of the food stand and got down on my knees to get a closer look at the tank. Bits of fat and grease were already burning on the side of the tank, as well as beneath the gas line leading out of it. If that burned through, it could be moments, not minutes, before the tank exploded. Time was shorter than I thought.

People were yelling at me. I ignored them. Instead, I ripped off my T-shirt and used it to protect my hands from the flames as I pulled on the strap holding the tank to the stand. The strap released, but the tank was jammed, and the gas line connecting it to the cart was still connected. Flames were now cresting the top of the tank. I tried to twist the shutoff valve close, but the flame was too intense.

Finally the owner noticed the fire and started running. People panicked and started screaming and shouting.

"Crap!" I wiped the sweat from my eyes, then planted my feet and pulled with all my strength again, but the tank still wouldn't budge.

"Come on," I shouted in frustration.

That's when I felt a cool hand on my back. "*Cara*, move out of the way."

Slash.

Thank God.

He must have spotted me and known immediately what was going on. As Slash reached for the tank, I knew we had to free the tank from the gas line that connected it to the grill in the cart. I spotted a large meat cleaver and grabbed it. Slash's eyes met mine, and our plan was coordinated wordlessly. We both knew I wouldn't have much time once I cut the line. He'd taken off his T-shirt, too, and ripped it in half, planning to hold the handle of the tank with both hands wrapped in the cloth. From firsthand experience, I knew that was almost like having no protection. Slash thrust his hands into the flames, grabbed the handles and heaved as I chopped down. The tank came free, but a blue flame was now coming from the severed line.

Most of the grease fire had gone out after it had been removed from the source of combustion, but the tank was still red-hot and had a jet of flame from the gas line whipping around. Slash's hands had to hurt like crazy, but he stood looking calmly around.

I knew what he was searching for. *Where the heck do we put a bomb in the middle of a street packed with people?*

The crowd around the cart had thinned significantly, but the children's choir was still going full blast, either oblivious to the danger or too afraid of the nun to stop. I abdicated my position next to Slash and ran toward the choir, waving my hands and screaming like a maniac. Fortunately, that caused the children and spectators to finally pay attention. I'm not sure if the crazed look on my face, the smoldering T-shirt in my hands, or Slash, bare-chested and holding a flaming tank, did the job, but they screamed and scattered.

People were panicking in earnest now, running in every direction. Whistles were screeching and I could hear sirens heading our way. They would be too late. I was surprised that the fire hadn't crawled up the gas line to the tank yet, but it had to be close. Slash put the tank down and tried again to twist the shutoff valve closed, but it had expanded from the heat and wasn't budging.

Running toward Slash, I spotted a manhole cover in the street between us, so I raced toward it and tried to pry it up. A lone policeman who had arrived and sized-up the situation quickly ran to help me. He used a clip from his belt to get a grip on the cover and lever it up slightly out of the hole. Together we wrestled the lid sideways, just enough for Slash to toss the tank inside. The three of us managed to get the manhole cover back on and take two steps away before it blew.

A bright flash enveloped us as the ground heaved. Amid the light overwhelming my eyes, I had a momentary image of the manhole cover rocketing straight up, and I sincerely hoped I wouldn't be around when it came back down. But before I could move, the force of the blast tossed me backward onto the asphalt. I heard the crack of my head as it hit the street and had time for one last thought before the world went black.

Was Slash okay?

THIRTY-SEVEN

Father Julian Koenhein

THIS WAS BECOMING a nightmare.

Julian prided himself on his efficiency and competency, but once again he was bringing the cardinal bad news. Swallowing his discomfort, he knocked on the cardinal's door. Once he was ushered in, he shifted nervously on his feet in front of the cardinal's desk, clutching the paper tightly in one hand.

"What is it now?" Cardinal Lazo asked.

"Your Eminence, the DNA results have arrived."

"It's about time. What does it conclude?"

"Well, that's the thing." He cleared his throat, bracing himself for the onslaught that was sure to come. "We're not sure what it means."

Cardinal Lazo set down his pen and rested his elbows on the desk. A frown crossed his face. "Explain yourself."

"The results confirm that the DNA is one-hundred percent German shepherd."

The cardinal stared at him as if he were out of his mind. In a way, he wished he were. That, at least, would make a lot more sense than the skewered results of the testing.

"*What?* Why is a dog the result of his DNA test?"

Julian swallowed hard, his Adam's apple bobbing nervously. "I'm sorry, but that's the DNA that was taken from the water bottle in the trash at his room in the hotel. I don't know why or how it was in his room."

The cardinal slammed his hand on his desk, causing Father Koenhein to jump. The cardinal was well known for his temper, but he'd never been physical before. Julian chalked it up to stress and a sincere concern for the Holy Father.

"He played us, that's how." Rage made the cardinal's voice tremble. "I need a viable DNA sample. Where's Slash now?"

"That's the thing. We don't know, sir. We lost him and his fiancée just outside of Genoa. But we have someone watching his relatives, in case he shows up there."

"Where is *there*?"

"Sperlonga. He has a couple of cousins and a grandmother he's quite fond of who live there."

"What about his parents?"

"His mother and stepfather live in London. Obviously we have the listening devices in Father Armando's office, as well as in his home. If he shows up there, we'll know. Most importantly, he hasn't left Italy. Our contacts at the Foreign Office will let us know if we does."

"Good. Find him. If he shows, I want you to get the word out that his DNA needs to be secured at whatever cost it takes."

"Whatever cost?"

Father Lazo leaned forward, his eyes hard. "You heard me. Get me a DNA sample however you can. This is a matter of extreme importance to the church. Is that understood?"

Father Koenhein lowered his gaze. He would do whatever necessary to protect the church. It was his God-given reason for being on Earth. "Yes, Your Eminence. I understand."

"Good. Don't fail me this time."

"I won't, sir. You have my word on that."

Lexi

I HAD A SPLITTING HEADACHE. The lights seemed abnormally bright and it took me a minute to get my bearings. Classic symptoms of a concussion. I was lying on my back and could see a white ceiling. I blinked a couple of times and heard whispering nearby. Whatever they were saying, I didn't understand it.

"Slash?" I croaked.

"*Cara*, you're awake." Slash's face swam into view as he took my hand. I felt the softness of bandages. Were those on his hand or mine? "How are you feeling?"

"I'm okay. My head hurts a bit." I didn't want him to worry, but I was actually suffering from a Wookie-sized headache. I blinked several more times until things came into better focus. "Where am I?"

"A hospital in Salerno. You got knocked out by the blast."

"The blast." Memories flooded back. I struggled to sit up, but the effort triggered more pain in my head. "Ouch. Did anyone get hurt?"

"No, thank God. It was a true miracle."

"What about the policeman? The one who helped me get the manhole cover off."

"He's fine. How did you happen to see the fire?"

I blinked and got my memories in order. "I was waiting in line to get water and I dropped my money. When I bent down to get it, I spotted the flames underneath the food stand. I tried to warn everyone what was going on, but given my fluency in Italian, it was faster to remove the tank from the fire. But it got stuck and there were grease splats on the tank, so I knew it would keep burning even if I removed it."

"You did good, *cara*. You saved many lives today, including those of a lot of children."

"Not me. *We* saved lives," I corrected him. "If I recall correctly, you were the one holding the tank."

He perched on the side of the bed and held his hand to my cheek. I leaned into his hand, which had a sizeable bandage across his palm and some sort of ointment glistening on his wrists and forearms.

I pulled back. "Oh, Slash, how are your hands? How badly are they hurt?"

I looked down, realizing both of mine were bandaged, too. Thankfully my fingers were free, so I wiggled them and didn't feel any pain. Another miracle, I guess.

"Not badly. Surface burns only. They will heal."

"What about your head? Did you get knocked out, too?"

"No. I didn't lose consciousness. But seeing you lying there, out cold, took another ten years off my life. At this rate, I have about a year left."

"Don't joke about that." I frowned, wincing from the effort. His comment did, however, make me realize I needed to add a bombs/explosions column to my Little Black Cloud Spreadsheet—the same spreadsheet that proved, beyond a shadow of a doubt, I was a trouble magnet. It was clear to me that I absolutely *never* wanted to make another entry under the explosion column again.

"I'm not dying anytime soon. You won't get out of marrying me that easily." He smiled against my lips.

I suddenly gasped in panic. "Oh, Slash, my engagement ring? Do I still have it? I can't feel it on my finger."

"It's not on your finger." He reached into his pocket and pulled it out. "But it's safe and sound."

I exhaled. "And this is exactly why I don't wear jewelry."

"Because you're busy diffusing potential bombs?"

I pursed my lips. "No. Because this kind of stuff happens to me all the time."

"True." He smiled and returned the ring to his pocket, then picked up my floppy hat from a small table. It was a bit smashed on one side and the ribbon had come a bit loose, but it was still wearable. "My badass woman. You were amazing, *cara*. Cool under pressure. Always thinking, never panicking. You saved lives."

"I couldn't have done it without you. You looked a lot like Superman, standing there with sunglasses and no shirt, holding a ticking time bomb while people screamed and ran in the opposite direction."

"That was quick thinking about the manhole. I was out of ideas."

"I happened to spot it on my way back to you. Thankfully it all worked out." I wiggled my fingers again. "When can I get out of here?"

"As soon as you're debriefed by the police and cleared by the doctors. You will need to take it easy for the next twenty-four hours. I've already spoken to the police, so it's a matter of them completing their investigation to confirm it was an accident and not a terrorist incident. The policeman that helped us corroborated our story, as did the owner of the food stand. But they had to check us both out, and it took a bit longer than expected once they figured out who I was."

"Oh, no. Any trouble?"

"No. I had to check in with the director, of course, but all's well on that front. Italian-American relations are secure, and perhaps a little better. Oh, and Finn called to find out what the hell was going on. Gray saw an intelligence report and called him. I gave him a sanitized accounting of the events, and told him he could pass it on to Gray and the others. He says he's not giving you any more time off if you're going to spend it saving the world."

I rolled my eyes, but it hurt. "Ha, ha."

"When you're released, we'll head back to the hotel," he said. "I was able to secure the same room here in Salerno for another night. Are you sure nothing else hurts? Now that you're awake, they can give you additional pain medication for your burns. Trust me, it's worth taking."

I touched my fingertips to the knot at the back of my head. I folded my palms and felt the skin sting. It was painful, but manageable. "Other than the lump on my head, the splitting headache and medium-rare hands, I'm fine. But I'll need new clothes before I can leave the hospital. My jeans and T-shirt are a complete loss and I am not wearing a hospital gown in public. Especially when I can never figure out whether the opening goes in the front or the back."

"It's good to see your sense of humor hasn't been injured." He walked over to a chair, picked up a white plastic bag and pulled out a plain white cotton sundress.

"That's nice," I said, eyeing it. "But it's white. You know white and I don't go together."

"It's all I could find in the gift shop downstairs. One size fits all."

"Thank you. It'll work until I can get to my other clothes." I noticed he wore a tacky white T-shirt with the photos of the saint candidates on it. "I see you have a new shirt, too."

He looked down as if he'd forgotten what he was wearing. "I bought it at the same place as yours. Not much of a selection."

I smiled as he sat on the bed again, leaning back against the headboard and putting his stockinged feet on the bed, next to mine. He put an arm around me and I rested my head against his shoulder.

"I guess we'll have to wait until tomorrow to go to Gaeta," I said.

"That's okay," Slash said. "Another day won't hurt. We'll wait until you're ready."

"I'm ready to get out of here this moment. I hate hospitals."

"The logical solution to that problem is to stop engaging in dangerous activities like helping little old Italian ladies with runaway carts and playing with flaming propane tanks."

"Hilarious. Just get me out of here."

Slash pressed a kiss against my temple. "I'm working on it."

THIRTY-EIGHT

Lexi

WHEN WE FINALLY got back to the hotel, Slash ordered chicken soup for me and grilled *caponata* salad with flatbread for himself to be delivered to our room. I was actually happy to be back at the hotel, in spite of the circumstances. One night and I'd already become attached to the place where we'd been the closest since this mess had started. We ate quietly at the table on the balcony. Afterward Slash wanted me to sleep, but I was too restless, so we watched old movies on television with English subtitles, for my benefit, until we both fell asleep.

When I awoke in the morning, the television was off and Slash was gone. The balcony was open and the sounds of the water hitting the shore and people talking from the beach below could be heard. I sat up. My head felt significantly better than yesterday, but my hands were hurting. A quick glance confirmed Slash's clothes and laptop were still here, so I assumed he'd gone out for fresh air or food. I unwound the bandages from my hands. The burns were tender and raw, but not nearly as bad as I expected. I took a careful shower and when I came out of the bathroom with a towel wrapped around me, Slash was back with coffee and *fette biscottate*. He'd dressed in light tan slacks and a short-sleeved white polo shirt. Both he and the coffee smelled heavenly.

He immediately took my hands and turned them over, examining the burns. "How do they feel?"

"Sore, but I'm sure your burns are much worse."

"Mine are okay. I washed and dressed them this morning. They'll heal." He pressed a gentle kiss against the side of both my hands. "I should warn you, however, the burns may leave some scars."

Scars I could live with. "I'm not one for appearances, anyway. As long as everything is in working order, I'm good."

"My thoughts exactly. Let's get the ointment and bandages on your hands and eat something. How's the head?"

"Still attached to my body, thank God. The headache is gone, too. Good thing I have such a hard head."

He led me to the bathroom where he treated my hands and bandaged them like an expert. After that, we took our breakfast to the balcony. I put on a loose light green skirt and matching white and green T-shirt and joined him barefoot at the small table.

Slash sat reading the paper, leaning back in the chair, his long legs stretched out. He'd thoughtfully put the cream and sugar next to my coffee, so I quickly poured in everything and stirred it with a wooden stick so I could drink it. The bandages felt funny on my hand, but at least they didn't interfere with the mobility of my fingers, which helped enormously.

Taking a sip of coffee, I leaned over to snatch a *biscottate* from the bag when I noticed the picture on the front of the newspaper. I choked on my coffee, and Slash lowered his paper.

"What's wrong?"

I swallowed and pointed to the picture on the front page. "Did you see that?"

Slash and I were standing in the middle of the street at the parade. A photographer had caught Slash holding the burning propane tank, bare-chested and looking like a total badass from a movie set. Thankfully, I was in the background, my face barely visible. Good thing, because I was dressed in just my bra and jeans, pulling the manhole cover off with the policeman.

He set the paper down. "I saw it. We've been dubbed the Second Saviors of Salerno. A second miracle on the very day of the celebration of the first miracle by the Savior of Salerno."

"So much for anonymity."

"I know. I was going to wait until you had breakfast, but I might as well tell you now. We've been asked to swing by the mayor's office before we leave for Gaeta."

"Why?"

"The mayor wants to personally thank us for our quick-thinking actions at the parade."

"Is that necessary?" *Please say no.*

"Apparently, it is. I told them we'd be at city hall about eleven o'clock. Hopefully we'll be in and out. Shake some hands, smile for some photographs and leave. No more sightseeing for us today. We'll go straight to Gaeta. Now that our picture has been plastered everywhere, our location is no longer a secret."

"I guess you're right. I hope this meet and greet at the mayor's goes quickly. You know it's not my thing."

"It's not mine either, but we'll deal."

I took the biscotti from the bag, dipped it in my coffee and took a bite, feeling like a real Italian. "Somehow we always do, Slash."

THIRTY-NINE

Lexi

As soon as we finished breakfast, we packed up our things and checked out of the hotel. Slash drove to Salerno's City Hall, an old, four-storied, stone structure. Upon entering the building, we were met by a policeman, who directed us to a reception area. We showed our IDs, signed in, went through a magnetometer and were instructed to wait. A few minutes later, a young woman from the mayor's office came to escort us to the meeting.

We followed her into a giant hall made of gorgeous polychrome marble, featuring a huge staircase and a crystal chandelier. The woman led us down a corridor and into a large office. There were several people already there, including a man with a camera around his neck who was walking around snapping photographs. I recognized the policeman who'd helped me with the manhole and, to my surprise, I also saw the Bishop of Salerno.

We were spotted the moment we stepped into the room. A woman wearing a crisp navy-blue suit and a white blouse approached us first. Her dark curly hair was loose around her shoulders. She greeted me warmly as she held out a hand.

"Welcome. You must be Lexi Carmichael. I'm Maria Colella, Mayor of Salerno."

I liked the fact that she was so poised *and* spoke flawless English. It did, however, make me feel embarrassed I spoke only one language. I was going to have to up my game on studying Italian.

"Hi." My bandage made it awkward when we shook hands, and she was careful not to squeeze. "Nice to meet you."

She turned to Slash and gently shook his hand, too. "Thank you both for coming. I'm so sorry for your injuries, but incredibly grateful you were where you were yesterday. You saved a lot of people. Did you know people are referring to you as the Second Saviors of Salerno?"

Slash dipped his head graciously, but shook his head. "That's a kind, but inaccurate, label. We did what anyone else would have done if they'd seen the fire."

"I'm not convinced of that," the mayor responded. "You prevented a tragedy of incalculable cost to this city on a very special day to us. I'm of the belief that Salerno has twice been blessed by God. The timing is not a coincidence. Just as we celebrate the first saint of Salerno, two new saints are born."

I winced. Calling Slash and me saints seemed more than a little overkill. In fact, I was feeling pretty uncomfortable being held to such a high standard. "Um, we were in the right place at the right time," I said. "I'm glad we could help."

She motioned to the policeman, who had also helped, to come join us. As he walked over to meet us, I realized how young he was. He didn't look a day over eighteen years old. Regardless, he'd run into the situation, sized it up quickly and hadn't hesitated to help us. If he kept those skills sharp, he'd have a stellar career in law enforcement.

"I believe you've already met Salvi Zullo," the mayor said to us.

"Actually, we never got his name," I said, holding out my bandaged hand to him. "*Grazie*, Salvi. Thank you for your help."

Slash shook his hand and murmured something to him in Italian. Salvi responded with a beaming smile, clearly pleased by whatever Slash said.

"I thanked him for his courage," Slash translated for me. "He's only been on the force six months, and he performed admirably."

"He did, indeed," the mayor said, beaming.

The Bishop of Salerno was talking to someone across the room, but when he saw me look his way, he waved jovially at me. I quickly averted my eyes. My mind kept replaying the exact moment my face went into his lap. I had a terrible urge to rub my jaw, but didn't want to do anything that would remind him of that moment.

Salvi and the mayor walked away, so it was just Slash and me. "By the way, what exactly did you say to the bishop about me?" I asked in a low voice.

"I told him you were helping a little old lady and her cart got away from you. I also told him you were my fiancée."

"So why does he seem so happy to see me?"

Slash's mouth twitched. "Well, he also asked me for your name so he could pray for you. When I told him that your name is Lexi Carmichael, he broke into a large grin."

"Why?"

"Well, he said your name could be interpreted as '*cara* michael' or 'my dearest angel Michael,' since Michael was, of course, God's number one archangel. The bishop said he couldn't possibly be upset about having a lovely angel drop into his lap. Besides, who else could destroy a cross in a single swipe besides an archangel? Anyway, since it was all in the name of helping people, you are completely forgiven, and dare I say, burned into the psyche of the Bishop of Salerno forever."

I stared at him incredulously. "What? That's...completely nuts."

Slash chuckled, brushing a strand of hair from my face. He was totally enjoying this. "Trust me," he said. "He's never going to forget his little *cara* michael. My best guess is you will be often in his prayers, especially now that you've proven to be an actual angel by saving all those people in front of the cathedral."

Just as Slash finished, the bishop joined us. He took my hand and kissed it. "So, Miss Carmichael, we finally meet." He spoke perfect English without the slightest trace of an accent. I was starting to get a complex about being unilingual.

"Well, technically, we already met," I said. "Sort of." My whole face burned, and Slash looked like he was trying not to laugh. I wished I were anywhere but there.

"You and your fiancé are the talk of Salerno today," the bishop said. "You're truly a gift given to us by God. Thank you."

"It was nothing really," I said, growing increasingly uncomfortable. "Anyone could have done it."

The bishop leaned over, lowering his voice. "But they didn't, did they? You were the chosen ones. You are both as humble as you are courageous. I shall pray often for you."

"Oh, well, thanks, I guess." I hoped that was appropriate thing to say.

Slash saved me from further conversation by engaging the bishop in Italian. The mayor chatted with me a bit more while the photographer ran around snapping more photos, asking us to pose together until I was one thin thread from losing it.

At that exact moment, the mayor motioned for Slash, Salvi and me to join her near her desk. The photographer gave her a thumbs-up, so she began to speak.

"I know it's not much, but I would like to present the three of you with this token of our appreciation." She opened up a small blue box and pulled out a medal that was nestled there against blue velvet.

My eyes widened as she approached me first, slipping the medal over my head. "This civic medal is an honor bestowed upon you in a gesture of Salerno's deep appreciation. We cannot thank you enough for your kind and courageous act. Please know that Salerno is now, and forever, your adopted home."

She presented Salvi and Slash with their medals, too, and the photographer snapped a dozen more pictures of us.

"We are deeply honored," Slash said, pressing the medal against his chest with his bandaged hand. "Thank you for your recognition."

After another minute of small talk, we were finally released. We said our goodbyes and headed toward the door. Near the exit, I noticed a large framed photo on the wall and I screeched to a halt.

"Hey, that looks like Father Armando." It appeared to be an official Vatican portrait. The priest was dressed in a black cassock with scarlet piping and buttons, a red sash, a zucchetto and a pectoral cross on a chain.

Slash stepped closer and examined the photo. "It is."

Mayor Colella spoke over our shoulders. "Oh, yes. Father Emilio Armando is a distinguished citizen of Salerno. He's the Archbishop of Genoa, and more recently, he was named a cardinal. He attended Salerno's *Seminario Vescovile di Teggiano*, one of Italy's most prestigious seminaries, and became friends with our current pope there. If you'll indulge me in a moment of bragging, Salerno has nurtured many important Italians throughout history."

"It certainly has," Slash said.

The mayor herself escorted us from the building. As soon as we were alone, I put a hand on Slash's arm. "Did you know Father Armando was from Salerno?"

He slid on his sunglasses. "I did not."

"That's where he met the pope. You should ask him about it sometime."

"I will. Apparently there's a lot I don't know about Father Armando."

There it was again, that hard, inflexible tone which I knew was his way of hiding the hurt the relationship was causing him. Since I didn't know the full story of what'd happened between them, I had no idea how they were ever going to get past that or if it were even possible. But I hoped for both their sakes, they did.

He opened the car door for me and I climbed in. "Now, however, we have more urgent business to attend to," he said.

"Manuel de Rosa." I fastened my seat belt with difficulty because of the bandage. "He's next, right?"

The muscles in his jaw flexed and tightened, the only indication of his inner tension. "*Si*." Slash slipped on his sunglasses and put the key in the ignition. "It's time to finally meet him."

FORTY

Lexi

"Just try to enjoy the scenery," Slash said. "I'm going to get us there safely."

Once again I sat stiffly in the front seat of the convertible, trying hard to ignore the incredibly narrow and winding roads leading to Gaeta. This was the part of the Amalfi coast that I didn't like. In fact, if Slash hadn't handled the car so expertly, I would have already had a heart attack. Every time we passed a bus or large car, I squeezed my legs together to make myself smaller and bit my lip to keep from shouting "Look out!" I would have screamed in terror, except I was too afraid to distract him for even a sliver of a second.

But Slash knew anyway. Maybe the fact that my face was bleached of all color, my knuckles were white from clenching them together in my lap, and I hadn't spoken for the past thirty miles was a giveaway that I was scared witless.

"We're almost there, *cara*," Slash said soothingly. "You can relax now."

I'd decided I would relax only when I was out of the car and could kiss the solid ground beneath my feet. I envied the calm confidence he had behind the wheel.

However, as we got closer to our destination, I could see the tension begin to build in him, too. His fingers gripped the wheel tighter and it had nothing to do with heights and scary cliffs. The meeting with Manuel de Rosa loomed in front of us and neither of us knew what the outcome would be. This entire situation was taking a toll on us.

To complicate matters, the Congo issue and the massive CIA hack-off between us had been festering inside me since I arrived in Italy. I had no idea how to deal with these feelings. The fact that we'd been fierce opponents, with him on one side and me on the other, was just hanging there between us. If I left the issue alone, it would eat at me. On the other hand, Slash already had a lot on his plate at the moment. I didn't need to add to that. For the time being, I'd decided to keep quiet. Still, I wondered if this thing would always be between us, or if I brought it up, whether we could survive it.

Once we pulled into the town, I was distracted from my worries by the charming view. We passed an open market where people were selling everything from trinkets to strings of sausages. Soon, the town roads became so narrow, they could barely fit one car. At least there wasn't a cliff on one side, so I was thankful for the small things. Eventually Slash pulled onto a sidewalk next to another car and cut the engine.

"Wait. This is a parking space?" I asked in surprise. "Half on the sidewalk, half in the road?"

He got out of the car and adjusted his sunglasses. "Welcome to Italy."

He checked the street addresses as we walked along a twisty road lined with lovely stone buildings, most of which had balconies lined with flower boxes spilling over with colorful blooms.

"This is it," he said, stopping in front of a building.

"Do you think he'll be home?" I asked.

"Guess we'll find out."

We entered the building with a couple of old ladies who glanced at us. All Slash had to do was smile at them and they let us in.

"He works from five thirty in the evening to one thirty in the morning," Slash said as we climbed the stairs.

I didn't ask him how he knew that. By this point, Slash probably knew more about him than his proctologist did.

"He worked last night, but will hopefully be awake by now," Slash continued. "Whether he's home or not is another question. If he isn't, we'll wait."

Slash knocked and after a minute a man opened the door, still held shut by a chain. I caught of glimpse of tousled black hair, brown eyes and the dark complexion of southern Italians. His eyes alighted on me first and then flicked to Slash.

"*Cosa vuoi?*" he asked.

Slash answered. "*Sei Manuel de Rosa?*"

"*Si.*"

Slash spoke rapidly with him. After a minute of back and forth, the man shut the door, released the chain, and reopened it. He motioned for us to enter.

When I hesitated, Slash put a hand on the small of my back, encouraging me to go inside. I took a step across the threshold. The apartment was small, but clean and bright. The sun streamed into a small living room with a tiny couch and loveseat, as well as a well-worn coffee table covered with books and a wide-screen television. A kitchenette was situated off to the left. I could smell coffee brewing. There were a few faded paintings hanging on the wall, including a couple of religious items—a

wooden cross with a crucified Jesus, as well as a picture
of the Madonna and child. I didn't, however, see any lit
candles or a shrine to the candidate saints, as we had in
Father Opizzi's place.

The man ushered us into the living room and spoke
with Slash in Italian. Manuel was tall and well-built with
clearly defined muscles, a strong jaw and chiseled chin.
Definitely good-looking. From the data we'd gathered,
I knew he was fifty-three, but he looked like he was in
his thirties.

Manuel asked something, and Slash responded, holding up his bandaged hands and pointing at mine. After
another minute of conversation, Manuel disappeared
into a kitchen.

"What was that all about?" I asked.

"He agreed to talk with us after I told him I was from
the Vatican and had a few questions about his time at the
church in San Mauro," Slash murmured. "He was curious about our bandages, so I told him what happened in
Salerno. He's getting us coffee now."

"Great," I murmured back. "Maybe we'll finally get
some answers."

"Unfortunately, he doesn't speak English, so I'll take
it from here."

"Sounds good to me." I perched nervously on the
couch and Slash took the seat beside me.

Manuel returned with a tray and three steaming mugs
of coffee. I was grateful he brought plenty of cream and
sugar, although neither man put a drop of anything in
their coffee before drinking it. That worked in my favor
because the coffee was so strong I used all of the cream
and most of the sugar to make it palatable. It was a bit

awkward holding the cup with my bandaged hands, but I did my best.

While Slash and Manuel spoke, I studied the former acolyte to see if I could see any resemblance between him and Slash. Hard to tell. They were both exceptionally handsome with dark hair, brown eyes, and were roughly the same height. So were a million other Italian men. That, of course, meant I had insufficient data to determine paternity.

At one point, Manuel spoke rapidly, sounding completely shocked. I looked at Slash, but he remained calm and continued to speak. This went on for several minutes where Slash would say something, and Manuel would look more and more in disbelief. I was dying to know what was going on but didn't want to interrupt.

Slash finally turned to fill me in. "I asked him if he remembered the baby boy brought in during the great storm."

"Did he?"

"He did, and I told him I was that baby."

"And?" My heart skipped a beat.

"He said I was the reason he left the priesthood."

I almost dropped the coffee mug. Luckily I caught it and placed it gingerly on the table. Manuel was watching me curiously. Guess it was his turn to figure out what we were saying. "Why were you the reason he left the priesthood?"

Slash shrugged. "Apparently he connected with me. Well, with the baby. He said that seeing me for those three days at the church made him realize he didn't want to be celibate all his life. He wanted children—a wife and a family. So, he returned to Rome and left the priesthood. He married a few years later. After a long time of he and his wife trying to conceive, he discovered he couldn't have children of his own. His wife didn't want to adopt, so she divorced him. He's been alone ever since. He believes this is his penance for betraying God."

"Oh, no," I murmured. Running through my head was the theory of the Butterfly Effect—the concept that the smallest of events can have nonlinear impacts on a complex world. The theory concluded that a butterfly flapping its wings could serve as a part of an interconnected catalyst that could start a typhoon. Slash was the catalyst here. He was born, brought to the church in San Mauro, and so many lives had been affected as a result, mine included.

"I'm sorry for him. What a painful thing to have endured." I lowered my eyes to my coffee cup because I didn't want Manuel to see the pity and sadness in my eyes.

It was an unfortunate set of circumstances for all of us involved, but especially the two of them. Manuel, because his life had been so dramatically changed by one decision, and for Slash because it meant the hunt for his father was still on. It *also* meant Slash would now add it to the long list of what he perceived were his transgressions against others, regardless of how ridiculous it was to blame himself for being an abandoned baby.

"That's not all," Slash said. "There's more."

I looked up, puzzled. "What more can there be?"

"He remembers the night I was brought in. The night of the storm. He said he was there, in the church, praying in a corner. He thinks no one knew he was there."

My eyes widened. "Did he see who brought in the baby?"

"He did. It was a woman, holding the infant in her

arms. Father Armando came out, as if he'd been waiting for her. They talked for at least ten minutes. This wasn't a simple abandonment."

I took a moment to digest that huge revelation. "Did he recognize the woman?"

"Unfortunately, no. He says she was young with long brown hair. She spoke with Father Armando for some time before she left."

"Did he overhear anything of the conversation?"

"He did. He heard it all. Voices echo in an empty church. However, he didn't understand any of it."

"Why not?" The hurt in Slash's voice was starting to really worry me.

"Because they were speaking English."

FORTY-ONE

Slash

"WHAT?" LEXI BLURTED OUT.

He wondered if his shocked expression mirrored hers. "The woman spoke English?" she asked.

"Apparently so. The woman who brought me to the church in San Mauro wasn't Italian." His mind sorted through the possibilities. Could his biological mother be American? Was that why he supposedly had American citizenship? But if she gave him up for adoption, wouldn't he have forfeited the citizenship? Was that even possible?

What the hell is going on?

They weren't going to find any more answers here. After thanking Manuel for his time and the coffee, he left a business card with his contact information and ushered Lexi out of the apartment. He saw the surprise on her face when he led her toward the beach instead of the car, but he needed some fresh air and a bit of a walk to clear his head and thoughts. Having to drive with the distraction of what was going through his head at the moment was neither wise nor safe. Thankfully, she didn't question him, just followed his lead, understanding that he didn't feel like talking at the moment. He needed time to process first, to figure out what everything meant.

He took her hand as they walked, taking comfort in

her presence. They strolled for nearly a mile in silence, before he spoke.

"I don't know whether to be disappointed or relieved he isn't my biological father," he said. "Not that it matters. That's not why we came."

She'd returned the floppy hat to her head. The ribbon was only half on and the breeze caused it to stream out behind her as they walked. Strange, but he'd become kind of attached to the hat on her.

"Regardless of why we came, I know that finding out the truth about your family is important to you," she said.

"I *know* who my family is. This isn't about that." It came out sharper than he intended, and he tried to temper his tone. "I just want to know who my father is. I can take it from there."

She wasn't going to let him get away with that comment. "Are you sure that's all?" She turned her gaze on him, tucking her arm into his elbow. "You're a mystery, Slash. There are things that don't add up about you. Your citizenship, your missing past and why the president of the Vatican is so obsessed with your paternity. But having said that, yes, you do know who your family is, and that includes me. Unfortunately we're back to square one. Manuel de Rosa isn't your father, but he did give us useful information. Your biological mother, or at least the woman who brought you to Father Armando, spoke English. That alone could account for the American citizenship you didn't know about."

"Perhaps. But who is she and how can we know for sure if she was my mother?" He sounded irritable, testy, because he was. He was used to getting immediate results, setting his mind to something and taking care of it. Instead, he'd faced disappointment after disappointment since he'd arrived, and they seemed no closer to the answers to their questions they sought.

"Other than the fact that you somehow have American citizenship without naturalization, I don't think we can know for sure yet."

God help him, there was a reason he'd never opened this can of worms. Now that the can had been pried open, he wanted nothing more than to toss it into the sea. But he couldn't. Not if he wanted to stop Cardinal Lazo. Not if he was going to fix things with the woman he loved. That meant the search for his father stayed on. One thing was certain, however, he did *not* want to dig into the past of his biological mother. He'd shut out any thought of her for so long that opening that door was not somewhere he wanted to go. He was still not able to fathom how she could have left him and gone on with her life, while he'd lost the first seven years of his to events so awful he couldn't remember them.

Regardless, a part of him argued that line of reasoning wasn't logical. It wasn't fair to judge his mother when he had no idea of her circumstances. He also couldn't afford to keep her out of the equation. His mother's identity could be an important clue to the identity of his father, perhaps the only way he could get the answers he sought.

So, he had to stay focused and objective—look at it the way Lexi was doing—logically, clinically and without the uncomfortable emotions that were coloring his judgment.

He wouldn't get the answers or the truth any other way.

They walked along a path that paralleled the shore, passing a couple of joggers, a mother pushing a pram and some teenagers. The crash of the waves, the sound of the seagulls and Lexi's presence calmed him, helped him think.

"You're right, *cara*," he finally said. "The American connection would make sense *if* the woman who brought me to Father Armando actually was my mother. How do we know it wasn't someone else acting as a proxy on her behalf?"

"It could have been, but it still doesn't change the fact that in order for you to get the citizenship your mother would have to have been American." Her brow furrowed as she looked out at the water, thinking.

"If my American citizenship is a real thing," he said.

She wound a strand of hair around her finger, still thinking. "Whether we like it or not, Slash, we're at a dead end. We can hack anywhere in the world, but without the name of either your biological mother or father, we have nowhere to start and we have to get back to our lives in the States."

"I know." Examining these truths about his childhood was more difficult than he'd expected. He'd believed that if he ignored them, their significance would fade. But that hadn't happened. Instead they'd surfaced, driving an ugly wedge between him and the one person he loved more than anyone in the world.

"Do you have any idea how many people stare at you?" she suddenly asked, snapping him out of his thoughts.

"Hmmm?"

"People look at you, Slash. I mean, really look at you. Father Armando said something interesting about you when I spoke with him. He said you have a compelling way about you—a certain magnetism. I think he was onto something. People are drawn to you, Slash. Even when you were a baby."

He shrugged. "Babies are helpless and physical attributes are surface-deep. People like looking at pretty things. It means nothing."

"That's not what I meant. Magnetism isn't physical. It's chemical. People *feel* something when they look at you."

"Is that so? Then how did you resist me for so long?"

She rolled her eyes. "Because you refrained, mostly, from seducing me with your stellar good looks and charm, although you could have easily done so. You approached me differently. You said so yourself."

"That's true," he conceded. "You were completely different from any other woman I'd ever met. I didn't want you to come to me the way most people did. But it also meant I wasn't sure how to go about getting you to love me."

"That makes no sense. You just had to be yourself. Obviously, that was enough for me."

He lifted her hand to his lips and kissed an exposed finger. "A miracle. I thank God for you every day."

She stopped walking and looked at him, her expression troubled. "Slash, what do we do next?"

He reached out and touched her cheek. He left his palm resting against her face, wishing he could freeze time. Just the two of them, like this, forever. But inside he knew what he needed to do.

"There's something I need to tell you, *cara.*"

He watched as anxiety and fear crossed her face. He hated that he had contributed to that expression. But he was finished with trying to outrun his past.

The time had come for him to stand and face it. Otherwise, there would be no going on together.

FORTY-TWO

Slash

HE FOUND AN empty bench, and they sat side by side, watching the ocean and listening to the waves crash and recede. An oversize yacht sailed past, and a few sailboats dotted the horizon. Lexi removed her hat and placed it in her lap, playing with the ribbon and waiting for him to speak. He thought he'd figured out exactly what he was going to say, but he kept revising the plan until he lost track of the starting point. He was overthinking things to distraction. He needed to start, get it out, and trust she would understand.

"You tried to hack into a file at the CIA a few days ago," he finally said.

He felt her jolt in surprise, then steady herself. "Yes." There was no accusation, hurt or defensiveness in her tone, just a simple answer. "Elvis and Xavier were helping me."

"That was me on the other side, trying to stop you. Did you know?"

She still didn't look at him, and he hated himself for how much he'd hurt her. "I knew. Not at first, but eventually."

He turned to her, pushed his sunglasses to the top of his head. He had to know. "You had the file in your grasp. You were moments from taking it. Why did you back off?"

She turned her gaze from the sea to look at him. "Because the moment I realized it was you on the other side, taking on all three of us by yourself, I knew it was something you desperately didn't want me to know."

"That's why you stopped?" He thought it over. "Because I didn't want you to know?"

"Yes. And because I love you. We're not on opposing sides, Slash. I'm trying to help you, not hurt you. If you don't want me know what's in that file, or in any other files you have hidden away somewhere, I won't press further. But I'm not going to let anyone drive you from me. If you want to walk away from this—from us—do it on your own terms, not because you're trying to protect me from something in your past. I'm not a child, and I'm aware of the kinds of things men who have jobs like you are required to do. I can make my own decisions in regard to my safety and life. Just so we're clear on that."

He deserved that dressing-down, but it didn't make things any easier. He looked back out to the sea. His chest tightened, so he relied on his training for responding to high-stress situations. *Deep breaths. Focus on the moment and avoid worrying about the future. Invite the calm. Get enough information to move forward and be decisive.* He forced the muscles in his neck and shoulders to relax.

She waited for an answer, but no matter how hard he tried, he still couldn't say what was in his heart. But he had to say something.

God help him, why couldn't he do this?

She must have sensed the indecision warring within him, because she rested a bandaged hand on his knee and left it there, not saying anything, but linking them and letting him know she was there.

Wherever the hell *there* was.

Her small gesture calmed him and gave him the opening to reflect further and work it out in his head.

Can I risk the truth with her?

Can I risk our relationship with the truth?

Am I unworthy of her love if I reveal all of myself? How will I know unless I tell her?

The risk was incalculable. The loss would be catastrophic.

He blinked and looked out at the sea. How long had they been sitting there in silence? He'd lost track of time, yet she waited patiently for him.

Finally, he exhaled and leaned back on the bench. "How much do you know about the situation in the Congo? I assume you know something since you knew right where to look."

"Just the basics," she said. "About your exact role in the situation—very little. Gray found a news clip of the day of the assassination and we saw you dressed as a priest at the presidential palace. All of which means I know enough to speculate, but not have any definitive answers."

So, Grayson had been brought into this, too. He should have known Lexi would be resourceful when asking their friends for help. It shamed him that while he'd been keeping secrets from her, she'd always been forthright with him. He had no excuse for that other than he'd been keeping and chasing secrets his entire life. It was a part of who he was. But was it a part of who he wanted to be?

He kept his eyes on the sea and the timeless push and

pull of the water. Seagulls circled and swooped down to skim the waves, looking for their next meal. The world could go to hell, but the sea would remain a constant force—the peaceful waves masking the dangerous turmoil beneath. Yet even the sea grew and adapted as new environments were forged.

"You came to Italy," he finally said. "To me. Why?"

The question surprised her. "Why? Slash, do you really have to ask me that? When you gave me this ring, I understood it to mean we're a team in all parts of our lives. The good and the bad. We may not have had the wedding yet, but this ring means everything we face, we face together."

He leaned forward, elbows on his knees. "It wasn't supposed to be like this. I wanted to start fresh with you. I didn't want this to touch you…touch us."

"It's too late for that," she said. "If it touches you, it touches me. It already has. We all have a past, Slash. The question is, are you going to remain a prisoner to yours?"

He considered her words. Emotions, responsibilities, fear and wariness still raged within him. If he decided to change, he would do it *with* her—and go wherever that led them. But it started by sharing his worst secret, a part of him he'd never wanted her to know.

"Several years ago the Vatican was brokering a deal in the Congo to promote a peaceful transition to democracy," he said quietly. "We were working with Congolese bishops to form a deal between the leader—an embattled dictator by the name of Harun Apeloko—and rebel forces. The deal was that Apeloko would step down after elections were held to ensure a smooth democratic transition. The problem was that Apeloko didn't officially agree to the deal. He never signed anything or made an official pronouncement. He made some vague promises, but was careful to never put his signature on anything. He was quite clever—a cruel despot, but far from stupid. He was a well-educated, charming man, who spent most of his years in power carefully destroying or controlling every major institution in the country. Except for one."

"The Catholic Church," Lexi said quietly.

"*Si*. The church was holding together the very fabric of the country. People were dying, *cara*, the elderly were in unimaginable pain, and children were succumbing to starvation and disease. They looked to the church for their salvation, and the church tried to help them. The Vatican did everything they could to oust Apeloko. Secret offers of money, safe haven, whatever he might want. Anything and everything was on the table."

"What happened?"

"Apeloko enjoyed matching wits with the bishops and the Vatican delegations that came to broker the deals. He threw lavish parties and dinners, and, at some point, he took a special interest in a young Italian priest with whom he used to fiercely debate matters of the world. Apeloko apparently found the priest witty and interesting. The Vatican noticed the budding interest and asked the priest to cultivate a friendship in the hopes that one day that priest could convince Apeloko to agree to a peaceful transition."

"But it didn't work," Lexi said.

"It didn't work. First of all, the young priest wasn't a priest, although he was forced to listen to Apeloko's horrific, gleeful confessions. The priest was a Vatican operative and Apeloko was his mission."

Lexi inclined her head to show she was following, but said nothing.

"Despite the operative's best efforts," Slash continued, "Apeloko refused to sign any agreement and escalated his murderous reign. It became quite evident he had no intention of stepping down. The discussions with the bishops, with the Vatican, it was all a distraction. In the meantime, his people remained locked in unimaginable poverty and suffering while Apeloko lived in grotesque wealth. He killed indiscriminately and tortured millions of men, women and children. The Vatican was helpless to bring about change, to stop the suffering."

Her hand tightened on his knee, but she remained silent. He kept his focus on the sea and the waves that crashed against the shore.

"There was a rebel leader by the name of Joseph Jakande," he continued after a minute. "He'd united most of the rural tribes against Apeloko. The Congolese bishops, and by extension the Vatican, were supporting him. Jakande was powerful and charismatic. He was poised to take control of the country from Apeloko. He promised to lead the people to a democratic society, if Apeloko would step down peacefully. But it was clear that was never going to happen. So, a decision was made in the highest echelons of the Vatican. Apeloko had to go."

He risked a sideways glance at Lexi. She was looking at the sea, just as he had been, her expression calm and thoughtful. Her hand stayed reassuringly on his knee, waiting for him to get through it. If he could.

"As is true with most despots, Apeloko was extraordinarily paranoid. He had food tasters and bodyguards near him constantly. He'd installed his eldest son, a boy barely nineteen, as head of the national army. The boy was as sadistic and cruel as his father, but he made sure his father was well protected. The only time Apeloko was without his guards present was at night while he was sleeping and after dinner when he retired to his study to drink and read. Guards were always posted outside of his locations, even if he wasn't in actual sight. So, one day, while the Vatican was figuring out the best way to conduct the assassination, a heaven-sent opportunity fell into their laps. One evening, Apeloko invited the young priest to accompany him to his study to play chess and continue their discussion on worldly matters."

He glanced at Lexi. She sat so motionless, he wondered what she was thinking.

"The session lasted several hours and the guards did not enter the study once," he continued. "After the priest reported back, a tightly held group of bishops at the Vatican made the difficult decision to save many more people, if the priest was invited into the study again. So, he was given orders to assassinate Apeloko if he could. The operative resisted, as this was not normal protocol. Options were discussed and alternative scenarios evaluated. But there was no other way, so in the end, the operative agreed to move forward if an invitation to the study came again."

"How long until that happened?" Lexi asked, her voice so soft it was almost a whisper.

"Nearly three weeks. That night, as the others watched the young priest disappear with Apeloko into the study, their plan was put into motion."

Slash leaned forward more, his hand inches from hers, but not daring to touch her. "It was easier than expected. Trust had been built, so Apeloko was careless. When Apeloko went to the bathroom, which was located inside the study, the operative slipped poison into his drink. It was a fast-acting agent, so Apeloko began to die with seconds of ingestion. He slipped from his chair, clutching his throat and foaming at the mouth, gasping for air as the blood coagulated around his heart and lungs. The operative knelt over Apeloko, ensuring his heart had stopped, when he heard a sound from behind him. It was Apeloko's nineteen-year-old son, Thako. He'd come in from a hidden entrance behind a bookcase."

Slash exhaled, willing himself to finish. He didn't dare to pause for long. "Many things rushed through the operative's mind at that moment, but first and foremost was the absolute certainty that the boy would have to die as well."

Lexi clenched her hands together in her lap so tightly the knuckles were stretched pale. He waited until a couple walked past and resumed speaking. "The operative stood with an anxious look on his face, and waved Thako over. 'Something happened to your father,' he said. When Thako bent over his father, the operative hit him from behind, knocking him to the ground. The operative rolled him over and pressed a hand over his mouth and nose. For what might have been a minute or perhaps only seconds, the operative and the boy locked eyes. Thako lay helpless on his back, barely conscious, outmatched and outweighed. Tears leaked from the boy's eyes as the operative's hand pressed harder. At that moment, he didn't look more than twelve years old."

He swallowed, then continued. "The operative racked his brain for a solution that would save this boy's life. He pleaded with God to let him spare this boy, to escape the unfairness of the situation in which they both found themselves. But God was silent, so the priest took another vial from beneath his robe and forced the poison down the boy's throat, holding his nose until he had no choice but to swallow. When the boy died, the operative flushed the small plastic vials down the toilet, washed his hands and popped a harmless foaming pill and sedative into his mouth. The operative staggered to the door and flung it open, collapsing in the hallway. The guards rushed into the room to find their leader and his eldest son dead. The Vatican quickly collected their gravely injured priest and whisked him back to Rome for medical treatment. Mission complete."

He stopped, waited for her to say something, but she was silent. The silence stretched on for so long, his stomach churned with anxiety.

"So, the operative was never actually poisoned. It was an act."

"It was an act," he confirmed.

"He was never near death or brain damaged?"

"No. That was a cover story. He was examined by a so-called Vatican doctor, who was actually just another operative."

She fell silent again. He had no idea how much time had passed before she finally spoke again. "Is this the information I would have found in the CIA file?"

"Yes, although it was largely speculation on the CIA's part. Obviously, the Vatican would never admit to sponsoring an assassination, and, as far as I know, the pope at the time was never told. But it would have been enough for you to figure out the truth."

A pensive look crossed her face. "Was the mission considered a success?"

Slash shook his head. "I wish it were that simple. Joseph Jakande took power as expected, but within weeks, he'd shelved the idea of a democracy. Instead, he became a worse despot than Apeloko. Hundreds of thousands of additional innocent people were murdered, while countless others were starved and tortured. It was all for nothing. The negotiations, the plans, the assassination—everything was a failure. We simply replaced one despot with another, and that blood is on our hands. Jakande remains in power to this day, still subjecting people to horrific atrocities, while we do nothing and let the people suffer."

Another heavy silence ensued, but Slash waited. He had no idea what was going through Lexi's head.

"This operative—the priest who wasn't a priest who killed Apeloko—what happened to him after the mission?" Lexi asked.

"He requested, and was permitted, to go abroad to use his other talents to protect people in ways he hadn't been able to before."

She considered that. "Okay. So, that operative, the one who went abroad, did he use his talents to help others? Save others even?"

"He did. He is."

"Good." She turned on the bench to face him. "Because here's the thing, Slash. We don't live in a black-and-white world, as much as I wish we did. I used to be that person who saw only black-and-white. But you, more than anyone, taught me about the gray. The gray isn't logical or linear or fair. Most of the time, it doesn't make sense. But at some point, the operative who killed Apeloko and his son has to make a decision. Let go and stop reliving the past, or continue to punish himself and never move forward."

The tightness in his chest was suffocating. "This was not the only isolated incident, *cara*. This operative has worn many faces and hurt many people. How much more can you stomach?"

To his surprise, she neither flinched nor shied away from him. "I can stomach them all, if you want to tell me."

To this point, he'd been unable to refer to himself as the operative. It was a protective mechanism, something he'd had to learn early. Detachment. Dispassion. Distance. The three cardinal rules for this kind of work.

Yet, she'd known, perhaps all along, the operative was him and she hadn't bolted. How could she be willing to stay and listen, knowing the kinds of things he had done?

"Why aren't you appalled?" He needed to understand. "How can you just accept those things about me?"

She turned and framed his face with her hands. "Because, Slash, when you trust someone, *love* someone, you believe in their integrity."

He'd never wanted anything more than for her believe in him—to be worthy of her. But he feared she didn't understand. "Did you hear what I said?" He looked at her incredulously. "I killed a child with my own hands."

Her voice remained calm. "The church asked you to protect the people of the country, who were suffering greatly and had no one else to stand up for them. If anything was unjust, it was what was asked of you. They had to know it would hurt you. But apparently they felt there was no other choice. They must have had enormous trust in you to ask you to do that. Why can't I, who love you even more, have that same trust?"

Disbelief swept through him. "You still don't get it. It wouldn't have mattered if Thako were nineteen and the head of the army or if he'd been ten and completely innocent. Whoever entered the room at that moment would have died. I would have killed them regardless of age." He could hear the self-loathing in his voice. "I didn't know how long Thako had been watching or if he saw me slip the poison in his father's glass. I couldn't have risked it. He was a liability the second he walked into that room, and I had to preserve the integrity of the mission. *That's* what I was thinking. That's *all* I was thinking. If I'd been thinking about the people I was saving, it might have been different."

She dropped her hands and shook her head. "You can't keep doing this to yourself, Slash. It's nothing short of torture. You were tasked with an exceptionally difficult job that, if successful, might have saved thousands, maybe millions, of lives. It was an incredibly complicated choice that had to be made in a split-second in the course of a dangerous mission."

"I don't know how else to say it to you, *cara*. I'm good at killing people. It's a talent, a skill that, even now, despite my new position at the NSA, I'm still occasionally tapped to use. I didn't want you to know that about me. I never wanted you to know."

She flinched at the vehemence in his voice, but she still didn't back down or back away from him. What the hell was he doing? Was he *trying* to drive her away?

She kept winding and unwinding the ribbon of her hat around her finger without saying anything, so he had no idea was going on in that mind of hers. Yet no matter how many different ways he viewed it, he couldn't see how she could come to any conclusion other than he was monster.

His head snapped up when she finally spoke. "Why do they tap you, Slash? Surely the CIA has its own cadre of assassins. Why would they risk someone as valuable as you on dangerous missions? I don't get it."

He was grateful she hadn't leaped to any conclusions and had given him the benefit of the doubt. He took a moment to put his thoughts in order, to explain it to her without divulging anything he shouldn't.

"It's a different world out there, *cara*, and it's changing every day. You know better than most that our wars are moving from the physical to the virtual. Today, everyone, from the terrorist on up to the worst despot, has a computer, a smartphone and highly evolved security systems surrounding their homes and offices. Unfortunately, those people who are the most dangerous are often funded by those who can afford to give them those items to make them impenetrable. The hard truth is you can't just send in an assassin anymore to take care of things. It has to be someone who has skills on multiple fronts, including language and cyber skills, and is able to execute those skills on a moment's notice while in the field, and usually while completely isolated."

She closed her eyes. "Oh, Slash. No wonder they come to you." She sounded sad, but not horrified.

He leaned forward, trying to ignore a headache that felt like an ice pick stabbing him behind the eyes. "I came to the US thinking this was behind me. But it's not. I don't think it ever will be."

"So why do you keep doing it?" she asked him quietly. "Why don't you say no?"

He considered a number of different answers, but settled on the truth because he loved her. "Because I can't stop making amends. If I think it will help people, make up for what I've done, I'm in."

She sighed and sat back on the bench, resting her

head against his shoulder without speaking. He didn't know if it were a good or bad sign, so he waited to hear her thoughts.

The silence stretched on before she spoke again. "Look, I understand why you do what you do, Slash. That's part of why I love you. I also understand that inner conflict better than you might think, having made some unpleasant choices of my own while in Somalia."

He didn't know why that hadn't occurred to him before, but now he realized that mission had taken a significant toll on her, too. He frowned, looking at her in a different light. A fiercely intelligent woman who had taken on one of the most brutal cyber mercenaries in the world and won. She'd seen her share of what happened on a battlefield and understood the difficult choices. That bullet he'd put through Broodryk's head on her behalf wasn't one he regretted.

She *did* understand.

"For people like us, it's in the details," she continued. "I struggled with this myself. Hands once told me after every mission he asks himself: Did I do right by that person, by that situation, by the mission? Was my heart in the right place? Did I do everything in my power to save or help as many people as I could? There are no right or wrong answers. If you believe there's a Judgment Day, then you will have to atone, because what's done is done. No one can change the past, not even you, Slash. All you can do—all *any* of us can do—is to try to make each day count moving forward."

She was correct…about all of it. He put his arm around her, pulling her close and seeking the comfort that was her. "I just want peace. But I don't know if I deserve it."

"You do." Her voice caught as she said it, twisting his heart in his chest. "But you have to forgive yourself first. I can forgive you. Father Armando can forgive you. Even the pope can forgive you. But you won't move on unless you forgive yourself. Forgiveness isn't a sign of weakness. It's simply acknowledging that sometimes bad things happen to good people, and we're faced with impossible choices."

He wanted that to be the end of it, but it wasn't. "I wish it were that easy. It's more complicated than that. There's a dark part of me, *cara*, a cold, ugly piece that isn't going away. When it comes to that which is mine— my family, country or innocent people—I won't play nice. I *can't* be nice. I need to be clear about that. It's not something that can change about me. It's how I'll ensure Lazo—or others like him—go down…one way or the other. The only question is whether or not you can live with that."

Her fingers started nervously winding and unwinding the hat ribbon again. He'd never been this honest with anyone before. She knew more about him than anyone ever had, than anyone ever would. It was both liberating and terrifying, because he believed it was the final test for them as a couple. He tried to calm the pressure building in his gut by reminding himself of the principles of tai chi. Be mindful of the present. Embrace the calm, accept the outcome, whatever it may be.

"I may not be entirely comfortable with that part, but I appreciate your honesty," she finally said. "I have one request. If you're going to accept missions that will put you in those kinds of situations, then accept self-reflection as part of the deal and be sure your conscience is in the right place with the mission and the possible outcome.

You can't save everyone, Slash. You just can't. Don't let the guilt and pain become your identity, because you're so much more than that to me."

For a moment, he just stared at her, stunned by her words. She wasn't condemning him. She wasn't pushing him away.

She's not going to leave me.

After a moment, he pulled her close and buried his face in her hair, his throat thick with emotion. She was both his comfort and strength. "Thank you, *cara*," he murmured.

The lines of a letter written by F. Scott Fitzgerald ran through his mind.

I fell in love with her courage, her sincerity and her flaming self-respect. And it's these things I'd believe in, even if the whole world indulged in wild suspicions that she wasn't all she should be. I love her and that is the beginning of everything.

"You're the beginning of my everything," he whispered. "I promise you that by my actions, or inactions, I will not purposely hurt you. That would be a wound to myself from which I could not recover. I'll work on the matter of forgiveness, too, if you'll stand by me."

Lexi tightened her arms around him. "That's what I've been trying to tell you from the moment I set foot in Italy. You're not alone, Slash, and I'm not going anywhere."

FORTY-THREE

Lexi

WE STAYED IN Gaeta for another two hours, catching what Slash called a snack—but it was a full meal to me. We shared a plate of red shrimp pasta at an outdoor café overlooking the water, and I drank a glass of fruity red wine called Rosso Piceno. Slash skipped the wine and opted for coffee. He was a lot more relaxed than he had been an hour ago. Unloading that difficult inner turmoil, sharing a burden that deep, had to have offered him some relief. I couldn't imagine how hard and lonely it must have been to keep the guilt, regret and pain locked inside him all this time.

He downed the last of his coffee, looking out at the ocean. "It's time to go." His voice sounded reluctant, like he didn't want to leave, but knew we had to. It was how I'd felt leaving Salerno. We'd now forged a unique and important piece of our relationship in both cities, so leaving when our connection was fragile was hard for both of us.

"Where are we going?" I asked.

"Sperlonga. I could use some downtime to review the data and figure out a good strategy to move forward."

"I'm with you on that," I said. We desperately needed to regroup and focus our efforts. Nonna's house was the perfect place to do that. She represented good memories of family life, and would remind him of the love and stability his adoptive family had offered when he needed it most.

We didn't talk as we drove along the Amalfi coast, enjoying the spectacular views. The sun was softening over the horizon as the afternoon deepened, the cobalt sky adding a gorgeous backdrop to the setting. I glanced at Slash as he drove. His dark sunglasses hid his eyes, but his black hair was tousled by the wind, and a five-o'clock shadow covered most of his cheeks and jaw. He was probably the most strikingly handsome man I'd ever seen in real life. But it was what lay beneath—the complex, driven and caring person who'd been through so much in his thirty-three years—that I responded to the most.

I was looking forward to seeing Nonna again. The only downside to the visit would be her cat, Principessa, who hated me and refused to use her litter box when I was around—something I was assured never happened with anyone else. I wasn't sure why animals acted so strangely around me. My hypothesis was I must emit an odd vibe, because they either hated me, wanted to dominate me or slobbered all over me. There didn't seem to be a middle ground.

As we drove into town, I admired the gorgeous stretch of white beach and rocky cliffs. Much like the towns of Gaeta and Licosa, tourists didn't overly crowd the streets of Sperlonga. Slash stopped at the market on the way to Nonna's house, picking up some flowers, a bottle of wine and catnip for Principessa.

We finally pulled into the driveway of a small house with yellow trim. Colorful flowers spilled out of the window boxes in the front. When I got out of the car, Slash came around and offered me his elbow. I tucked my bandaged hand into the crook of his arm and, as a united front, we headed to the door. Slash didn't knock, he just went in.

"Nonna?" he called out from the foyer.

"*Chierchetto?*" She stepped out of the kitchen into the foyer, astonishment on her face. Slash's grandmother was a tiny bundle of energy, her silver hair pulled back in a tight bun. She wore a cheerful yellow apron with red flowers and red sandals. From an earlier visit, I knew *chierchetto* was her favorite nickname for him and meant "little altar boy."

With a cry of delight, she rushed forward and cupped Slash's cheeks, kissing them with an abundance of enthusiasm, then she turned to me with laser intensity. Before I could decide if this were a good thing or not, she threw her arms around me and squeezed me with the strength of ten linebackers. Just when I was sure I'd die of asphyxiation, she enthusiastically kissed my face. I'd barely recovered when she snatched my hand, presumably to examine the engagement ring. Instead she saw the bandage.

She looked back and forth between us, noting Slash's bandages, too.

Slash started to speak, and I presumed he was explaining what had happened. She must have asked a dozen questions before he finally pulled my engagement ring out of his pocket where he was keeping it safe. She examined it, then pressed her hand to her breast, her eyes filling with tears.

"*Sono così felice per voi.*"

Slash translated. "She's so happy for us both. She's also sorry to hear about our injuries, proud of us for saving the people at the parade, thrilled to hear of our engagement, and honored that you accepted her wedding ring and the ring of her grandmother before her."

"Please tell her I'm honored to carry on the tradition and I love the ring," I said. "I'm sorry I'm not wearing it at this moment. *Grazie mille*, Nonna."

After Slash told her, it earned me more kisses and squeezes. Then she snatched the flowers and wine from Slash's hand and pushed us toward the kitchen.

"She's going to fix us an early dinner," Slash said.

"We just ate," I reminded him.

Slash raised an eyebrow. "And your point is?"

"Apparently no point whatsoever." If Nonna was cooking, I was eating. I took a seat at the kitchen table and Slash sat next to me. "Something smells heavenly in here. It *always* smells heavenly in Nonna's kitchen."

"That is an indisputable truth," Slash agreed.

Nonna brought us each a chilled glass of wine. I took a sip. The wine had a tart taste, but it was cold, refreshing and surprisingly good.

"Mmmm," I said. "What is this?"

"*Brachetto*." Slash tipped his glass to mine. "*Salute*."

"Can I say I'm really glad you're Italian?"

He grinned as he took another drink and began chatting with Nonna. She was bustling around the kitchen, stirring things on the stove and chopping up vegetables. I noticed a small oxygen tank tucked in one corner of the kitchen and wondered if she were feeling okay. She seemed like she was moving around without a problem, but I wasn't a doctor, so how would I know?

As she and Slash spoke, accompanied by an increasing amount of hand gestures, I heard my name mentioned on and off. I had no idea how much he was telling her about our current situation. I hoped he would update me later, so I knew what he'd said.

Slash helped Nonna with something at the counter when Principessa strolled into the kitchen, holding her gray head high. She sniffed the air, saw me and immediately gave me the evil eye. I'd kind of hoped she had forgotten about the bad history between us but apparently she hadn't. She carefully avoided me, but wound herself around Slash's legs until he picked her up and stroked her beneath her chin. He murmured something to the cat and pulled the catnip out of his pocket. She purred and gave me a triumphant look as if to say, "Ha!"

I almost asked Slash for my engagement ring so I could show her what *I* had, but then I remembered I was dealing with a cat. Luckily, at that moment Nonna put a plate of food in front of me. It smelled so delicious I almost face-planted in it, and I wasn't even hungry.

"Wow, what's this?" I asked, picking up my fork.

"Skillet ravioli and cheese with spicy Italian sausage," Slash said.

"It looks and smells delicious."

Slash translated and Nonna beamed. They both sat there looking at me with anticipation, so I awkwardly scooped up a bite, trying to avoid getting sauce on my bandage. I blew on it and took a taste, a thread of cheese hanging from my chin.

"She's a cooking genius." I chewed, took a moment to savor the taste in my mouth, then swallowed. "Do cheese limits even exist in Italy? Because this food is amazing. Does your mom cook like this, too?"

"She's an excellent cook. I can't wait for you to meet her."

Pleased by my words, Nonna piled a plate for Slash

and set it on the table. He put the cat down, washed his hands the best he could with the bandages on them and joined me in eating. Nonna sat down, too, watching us eat and sipping black coffee. She asked Slash question after question. Finally, he stopped to translate.

"She wants to know when the wedding is going to be held," Slash finally said. "She's asking a lot of questions about the preparation."

"Oh." I stopped in mid-shovel. "What did you say?" There was nothing *to* say. The only planning we'd done had been for the engagement party and I needed a *lot* more downtime—possibly forever—before I planned another social gathering.

"I told her we're working on it."

"But we're not."

He smiled. "But we will."

I set my fork down. "That was a lot of talking for saying we're working on it."

He picked up his wineglass, took a sip. "I'm Italian. I'm providing as much detail to the non-details as possible."

"Wait. You don't think she's going to ask me any awkward questions while we're here, do you?"

He lifted his glass to me, his lips twitching with amusement. "I think there's an excellent chance awkward questions will arise."

I sighed. "I was afraid of that." I finished off the rest of my wine in case I needed the courage. "Did she ask why we're here?"

"She did. I told her we're here to announce our engagement in person, *and* we have a little business as well. She didn't ask further, and I didn't provide additional information."

After we finished lunch, we both drank a glass of limoncello, a lemon-infused vodka that Slash insisted would help me digest. It was so strong it made my eyes water, but I finished it all. By the time I finished that and we helped Nonna clean the kitchen, I was in a complete food coma. I staggered to the living room and collapsed on the couch from the effort.

"I could die happy right now," I said with a sigh.

Slash followed me to the couch, plopping down beside me. Nonna and Principessa joined us. Nonna sat in an armchair with a pretty crocheted blanket and Principessa, not surprisingly, snuggled up in Slash's lap. She made sure her rear end faced me, tail whipping my arm every once in a while as if to remind me Slash had his hands on her, not me.

Nonna and Slash spoke for a few minutes, until Slash suddenly stood and put the cat on the floor, much to her dismay. He headed over to a bookshelf and pulled something off a bottom shelf.

"Hey, *cara*, look at this. Nonna kept my old Xbox."

I had almost fallen asleep, so his words startled me awake. "An Xbox?"

"Not just *an* Xbox. It's an *original* Xbox, European edition, dated 2002. You want to game on it?"

Was that a trick question? Did he even have to ask? "Does it still work?"

"Want to find out?"

"Of course. You got any games for it?"

"I do. Come look."

I sat on the floor next to him sorting through the games. We chose *Halo 2*, and Slash hooked up the machine to Nonna's television. It worked. I hadn't played the game in ages, but once I reminded myself how to use the clunky controller, it was like riding a bike. After a brief warm-up, we started playing in earnest. This was exactly what we needed—mindless fun to clear our heads, to get to a place where we could determine the next best move.

Nonna watched us for a bit, then disappeared back into the kitchen. I hoped she wasn't making a snack. As magical as her cooking was, I was stuffed beyond my limit.

Slash kicked my butt for most of the game, something I blamed on slow reflexes due to the alcohol and food, but I made a steady comeback until I was almost even with him. At some point, he took a break to get something to drink. I was sitting on the floor, so I leaned back against the couch, stretching out my legs. Principessa strolled past me, examining the television, then checking out the Xbox.

She sniffed around and then put her paw on the machine. She stood a little too close for comfort to the eject button for my taste.

"Hey." I waved my hand at her. "Move away from the Xbox." I got on my hands and knees and started crawling toward her, when she suddenly jumped onto the box. One paw landed squarely on the eject button. The game ejected, erasing our progress and scores.

She streaked away as Slash walked back in the room, holding two glasses.

He looked at the television and then me. "Where's our game?"

I tried to calculate the chance that he was going to believe this. "Principessa ejected the disk."

"The cat?"

"Yes, the cat. She jumped on the eject button."

Slash set down the glasses and narrowed his eyes at

me. "Are you sure *you* didn't press the eject button because you were losing?"

"Hey, I was almost even with you, and the momentum was mine. It was the cat. She's got it in for me."

"The cat?"

Principessa strode into the room, wound around Slash's legs and gave me a haughty stare. I pointed at her. "See, she's mocking me."

Slash shook his head, clearly thinking I was nuts. "Come on. Let's start over." He knelt on the floor in front of the machine and pressed the game back in. "Now we go to the best of twenty rounds."

"Fine by me."

I swear the cat was smirking at me as she stalked out of the room and I knew full well what that look meant.

War.

FORTY-FOUR

Lexi

Slash and I took an evening stroll down by the beach.
I'd been doing a lot of thinking and I knew he had, too.

"How long are we staying?" I asked as we walked past
a family of four packing up from a day at the beach. The
father carried one kid in each arm while the mother had
a cooler, a bag of sand toys and an oversize beach bag.
The mother smiled at Slash as we passed, and he murmured a polite hello.

"Just tonight," he said. "I'm needed at the NSA and
I'm sure X-Corp wants you back, too. No matter what,
we both need to be back at work on Monday. I've been
going through Lazo's financials and found some things
that are not exactly aboveboard. But I don't think that's
going to be enough to discredit him."

"Actually, I've been thinking about taking a different approach." I watched him carefully, wondering how
he'd take my suggestion. "As uncomfortable as it may
be learning more about Father Armando's past might be
useful, as well."

His jaw tightened slightly, but he nodded. He was
smart enough to see the value in gathering as much information as we could, no matter how painful. "Agreed.
Let's work on it tonight."

When we came home from our stroll, Nonna was sitting at the kitchen table reading a book while hooked up to her oxygen machine. She set it aside when she saw us.

"Is she okay?" I whispered to Slash in concern.

"She's fine. Her oxygen levels have been low, so the doctor prescribed oxygen whenever her levels fall below a certain threshold."

"But otherwise, she's good?"

"She's good. Don't worry, *cara*. She'll probably outlive us both."

He didn't seem concerned about it, so I dialed back the worry. Somewhere along the line, I had become quite fond of Nonna, and for more than just her cooking. Although we couldn't communicate well, we genuinely seemed to like each other. In my case that was a near miracle, since I generally didn't like most people.

After Nonna retired for the evening, Slash and I set up our computers in the sewing room, which was also my bedroom for the night. Even though Slash and I were officially engaged, out of respect for Nonna, I insisted we sleep in separate bedrooms. We set to work on our respective hacks. Slash already had a good handle on Lazo's financials, but he dug deeper into Lazo's life while I focused on Father Armando. Neither of us was sure exactly what we were looking for, so we set up several automated searches to assist us and hoped something would pop. Unfortunately, neither of us found anything of great interest, so we let the searches continue and decided to call it a night.

"Are you sure I can't stay here with you tonight?" Slash murmured.

"Don't you remember what happened last time?

Nonna walked in on us. Behave yourself for one night. It won't hurt."

"So *she* says," he grumbled, but went off to another room.

I got ready for bed. There was no air-conditioning, so I was sweating by the time I lay down on the bed, which was really Nonna's oversize floral couch. The cushions were lumpy and the door to the room wouldn't close tightly. There wasn't much I could do about it, so I lay atop the sheets in nothing more than a tank top and underwear, and tried not to think about how hot I was. Slash was probably used to it, but I was ready to rip off all my clothes and sleep in a shower of cold water.

I was pretty sure I'd never fall asleep, but while I was wishing I could be eating ice cream while swimming in the Arctic Ocean, I finally drifted off.

Cardinal Jacopo Lazo

JACOPO GOT THE call from Julian Koenhein at about eight thirty at night when he was at his home residence.

"Your Eminence, he has been spotted at his grandmother's house in Sperlonga along with his fiancée."

He flicked the television to mute and sat up straighter on the couch. "Excellent. Do what needs to be done to get that sample. I do not want any excuses or failure this time. Take all precautions and make sure it comes directly from him this time. We can't waste any more time trying to get it off a glass or a hairbrush. Do I make myself clear?"

"Perfectly. I'm putting together a foolproof plan as we speak."

"Just get it done with extreme haste. I don't know how

much more time we have. The pope is looking more frail with every passing day. The future of the church is in our hands. We cannot fail."

"I'll take care of it, Your Eminence. I'll contact you the moment we have anything."

Jacopo hung up the phone, leaning back on the cushions and resting his feet on an ottoman. Everything was falling into place. The coalition had been formed and cemented, the pope's health was rapidly declining, and his biggest threat was about to be neutralized. All he needed was that DNA to seal the deal. He had no doubt Slash was Armando's son and he'd prove it with or without Slash's permission. He wasn't about to let anyone, especially a man as damaged as Viper, stand in the way of his crowning moment.

He was going to lead the Catholic Church into the new age.

FORTY-FIVE

Lexi

WHEN I WOKE in the morning, I felt something heavy on my stomach area. Light streamed in from the window; I'd forgotten to close the curtains. I blinked several times and reached down, feeling around until I picked up the object.

It was a potato.

I turned it over in my hand. A small, ordinary, brown potato.

"Why is there a potato in my bed?" I asked no one in particular.

When I sat up, I spotted Principessa in one corner of the bedroom, licking a paw and staring at me.

"Did you put a potato in my bed?" I wagged the potato at her. "Because that's just weird."

The cat tossed her tail and exited the room with a huffy glance at me.

Sighing, I set the potato on the dresser and got dressed in jeans and a T-shirt. I was going to cook in jeans, but I was out of sundresses, skirts and cool blouses. I needed to do laundry badly.

I was fastening my jeans, which seemed a bit tight, when Slash walked into the room. He pulled me into his arms and nuzzled my neck. "I missed you last night, but I fell asleep faster than I expected."

"Me, too." I looked down and noticed he'd replaced the larger bandages around his hand with slightly thinner ones. "How are your hands?"

"Better. Nonna had some smaller bandages that give me a bit better flexibility. Check your hands after you shower and see if these will work better for you, too." He reached into his pocket and pulled out my engagement ring. "Then you'll be able to wear this again." He set it on the sewing table.

I took it from him, holding it between my fingers. "It seems odd to miss a piece of jewelry, but I do. Do you think we can also do laundry before we leave? I'm getting kind of desperate for clean clothing."

"*Si*. Give me your clothes and I'll get a load of our stuff started. While it's washing, I'm going to go to the store for Nonna." He glanced over at the dresser and then back at me. "Why do you have a potato in here?"

I picked up the potato and tossed it at him. He caught it one-handed. "I have no idea. It was on my stomach when I woke up. I think the cat dragged it in and put it there."

"The cat put a potato on your stomach?"

I loved him, but right now I didn't like the look on his face. "Yes, the cat. Who else would do it? Don't look at me like that. There was no potato on the bed last night, and this morning a potato magically appears on my stomach. Then I see the cat over there in the corner watching me. You have no idea how devious she is. It's like she's stalking me or something."

Slash raised an eyebrow. "The cat?"

"If you say 'the cat' in that tone one more time, I'm going to lose it."

His lips twitched as he scooped Principessa up and

scratched between her ears. The cat meowed and closed her eyes in ecstasy. "I will endeavor to make sure the animal-that-may-not-be-named stays out of your way."

"I think she's jealous."

"The cat?" He held up one hand. "No. Pretend I didn't say that." He slipped out of the room, carrying Principessa and giving me a grin over his shoulder.

That cat was driving me nuts.

I took a quick shower and examined my hands. The burns were still raw and tender, but improving. When I got out, I dried my hands, added the ointment and re-bandaged using the smaller wraps Slash had provided. It felt good to more easily flex my hands and slip the engagement ring back on my finger. I took a minute to admire it before I went downstairs.

Nonna was alone in the kitchen, cooking again. "*Buongiorno*, Lexi!" she said cheerfully.

"*Buongiorno*, Nonna," I looked around the kitchen. "*Dov'è* Slash?"

"*Ah, lui è al mercato*," she answered.

Mercato. Market. Yep, Slash must have already left for the market. She insisted I sit at the table and poured hot milk from an aluminum pot into a mug that sat in front of me. I took a sip. It was hot, delicious and seasoned with some mild spices.

She set a plate of hard biscuits in front of me, mimicking how I should dunk them in the milk to eat. I followed her instructions and ate them, the milk dribbling off my chin. The biscuits were followed by a plate of fresh fruit and what was surely freshly squeezed orange juice. Just like that I was stuffed, and I'd barely got out of bed.

Eventually she joined me at the table, sipping coffee of her own and nibbling on a biscuit. I pulled out my cell phone, thinking about using my phone translator so we could actually have a conversation, when there was an abrupt knock at the back door.

The knock surprised her, and she frowned. Maybe people didn't often knock on her back door. Or knock at all. I wondered if she ever locked her door.

Before she could respond, two men opened the door and stepped in. Possibly neighbors or friends, but I wasn't getting that vibe from Nonna.

She stood and started speaking to them angrily in rapid Italian. I didn't like how this was playing out, so I was coming to my feet as one of the guys shoved her back into the chair.

"Whoa," I said jumping between them and holding out a hand. "What the heck do you think you're doing?"

The guy muscled me aside, pushing me back until my butt was against the stove. I reached behind me, searching for some kind of weapon. I grabbed a wooden spoon dripping with tomato sauce and brandished it at them threateningly.

"Who are you?" I said in English.

They ignored me. The muscled guy stayed where he was, effectively trapping me against the stove while the other disappeared into the house.

"Where are you going?" I shouted after the guy.

No one responded. I debated taking on muscle guy—not that I had much of a chance of winning—but I didn't like what was happening. Still, I considered the option on the table if he made any other move.

The second guy came back almost immediately and said something to muscle guy before whipping a phone out of his pocket and speaking rapidly in Italian. Then he returned the phone and walked over to me. Muscle guy moved aside.

"Where is the man?" he said in halting English.

"The man?" I repeated, pretending not to understand.

He jabbed a finger toward my chest. "Yes. Your man. Where is he?"

Slash. They were looking for Slash. I had to figure a way to stall them. "Look, dude, I'm just visiting my grandmother. I don't know what you're talking about."

He narrowed his eyes, then strode over to Nonna, asking her something in Italian. She spit on him, so he gripped her jaw, and the second he touched her, I'd had enough. I jumped on his back, screeching like a banshee and poking the wooden spoon at the most vulnerable spot of his body, given my position—his eyes.

He shouted and released Nonna, trying to buck me off. Muscle Guy tried to grab me, but my poking was causing his comrade to stagger all over the kitchen, and he couldn't get a good grip. I was pretty sure I scored a hit at least once in the eyes because he roared in pain and slammed me hard between his body and the wall, trying to loosen my grip around his neck. A picture of Jesus and some decorative plates fell, but I held on tight.

Muscle Guy finally managed to grab my arm, when a ten-pound gray missile abruptly shot onto the back of his neck, scratching and biting.

Muscle Guy immediately let go of me, clutching his neck and screaming.

"Get him, Principessa," I shouted as all hell broke loose.

Nonna shrieked at the top of her lungs and started throwing dishes, glasses and whatever was handy at both men. Principessa got her claws tangled in the guy's shirt, so she was slashing at him fiercely to get free, and scratching the hell out of him in the process. Apparently Muscle Guy was allergic or deathly afraid of cats, because he was so panicked he staggered around the kitchen shouting and bumping into everything he could, trying to get her off. I was still hanging on tight around the other guy's neck when we swerved near the stove. I dropped the spoon and grabbed the pot of hot milk, saying a small prayer of thanks that my bandages actually worked as kind of a pot holder. I dumped the milk over his head and jumped off his back.

He screamed as the scalding liquid splashed over him. As he swiped at his face trying to see, I snatched the iron skillet from the stove. It was filled with something that smelled delicious, probably our lunch, so I felt sincere regret when I brained Muscle Guy as he was trying to smash Principessa against the wall. Hot food splattered across him and most of the kitchen. The cat miraculously freed her claws from his clothes and streaked into the living room. Muscle Guy went down like a sack of potatoes, hitting his head on the corner of the kitchen table on the way to the floor.

He stayed down.

I was panting with exertion and adrenaline when the other intruder stalked toward me. His face was burned and raw, his expression murderous. He smelled like cinnamon, tomato sauce and Italian sausage. Taking a step back, I held up the skillet and wielded it like I was at bat.

"Don't do it," I warned, hoping I looked like a badass instead of a scared geek.

Scowling, he pulled out a gun from beneath his shirt. Totally not fair.

Another step backward and my rear end hit the wall.

I was trapped. I held the skillet out in front of me like a shield. I tried to calculate the odds I could accurately deflect a bullet with the skillet at this close range. The odds were so inestimably low, I gave up.

He is going to shoot me dead in Nonna's kitchen.

FORTY-SIX

Lexi

I SQUEEZED MY eyes shut, waiting for the shot. A thud, crack and loud thump sounded, but I didn't feel any pain. When I opened my eyes, I saw the guy lying in a crumpled heap on the floor.

Nonna stood behind him, wielding her oxygen tank and looking supremely pissed off.

"Holy crap!" I gasped, my eyes widening. "You flattened him, Nonna."

She dropped the oxygen tank and said one word, *"Chierchetto!"*

Little altar boy. I got the message loud and clear. They were after Slash, and he was in danger.

I grabbed the guy's gun from the floor and stuck it in the waistband of my jeans. Then I patted down the guy I'd clocked with the skillet. Not surprisingly, he had a gun, too. I handed that one to Nonna and pointed it at the guys on the floor. She understood. Snatching my phone off the table, I punched in Slash's number. After three rings he picked up.

"Cara?"

"Slash!" I shouted. "You're in danger. Two men were here at the house looking for you. Nonna and I took them out, but there might be more out there trying to find you."

There was a long silence before he spoke. "Two men at the house? You and Nonna...took them out?"

"Yes. It's a long story. Where are you? I can come—"

"I've got to go, *cara*," he said suddenly. "I've got company." His phone clicked off.

By this time, Nonna was in the backyard, yelling something at the top of her lungs. I presumed she was alerting the entire neighborhood of our situation. In under a minute, her kitchen was full of neighbors talking at a decibel level higher than a rock concert. Two large guys were checking out our prone intruders, making sure they wouldn't wake and make a run for it. Nonna was front and center, talking in rapid-fire Italian, her hand with the gun waving all over the place. Deciding it would be safer, I took it from her and set it on the kitchen table. A man in the corner of the kitchen was talking loudly on his cell phone. I hoped to God he was talking to the police.

I hated to be rude, but I needed to get everyone's attention. I stood on a kitchen chair and, putting my fingers together in my mouth, whistled loudly. The room fell quiet as everyone stared.

"Nonna, which way to the market?" I yelled. My heart pounded so hard I could barely breathe. "Slash. *Mercato? Dov'è?*"

I tried to keep my voice calm, but I was pretty sure I was seconds from losing it. Our eyes met for a worried moment, then she pointed west.

While the neighbors watched openmouthed, I launched off the chair like Wonder Woman and dashed for the front door, tore it open then flew down the driveway. Our rental car was still there, so Slash had apparently gone to the market on foot. I briefly considered taking the car, but if he were on foot, he might have taken a shortcut and I might miss him. After calculating the approximate distance to the market on both foot and car and figuring it was a difference of only five minutes, I decided by foot would be the best solution.

I ran along the road, panting and sweating, while looking for footpaths that might represent a shortcut to the market. Panic gripped my throat as I bolted past a small meadow and heard shouting coming from a small grove of trees ahead. Veering right, I dashed down a small incline toward the trees to check it out. I screeched to a stop in the shadow of one of the trees, spotting Slash in the middle of a clearing taking on four guys with nothing but his fists. One was already down and unmoving, but the other four were advancing on him, two of them with knives.

Five against one was *not* a fair fight.

I removed the gun from my waistband and held it in front of me like an actor in a bad movie. I wanted to rush toward Slash and start shooting everyone in sight, but I had to calm myself down and do this properly. If I rushed in and lost the gun, or shot Slash by accident, I wouldn't be helping either one of us.

I could hear Slash's voice in my head. *Operational and situational awareness is key.*

A visual sweep of the area didn't reveal anyone else lurking around or a nearby vehicle parked by the side of the road. My best guess would be they'd followed him on foot from the market and that was who the guy in our house had been calling.

A plan came to me, and I yanked the phone out of my back pocket, pushed some buttons, then replaced it.

I looked up as Slash hit one guy hard, bringing him

down. Unfortunately, two others got him from behind and wrestled him to the ground hard, hitting him.

Time to act.

I pulled out the gun, made sure the safety was off and ran out from behind the shadow of the tree with a determined stride.

"Hey, jerkwads!" I yelled.

The guys looked up and stepped back from Slash when they saw I had a gun pointed at them.

"Move away." I waved the gun to the side in case they didn't understand. They hesitated, then the sound of sirens wailed and they abruptly took off running, two of them hooking an arm under the armpits of their unconscious buddy and dragging him along.

The second they were out of sight, I ran to Slash, skidding to my knees on the grass beside him. "Slash, are you okay?"

He gently pushed the gun away from his chest and took it from me, struggling to a sitting position. "Good timing." His bottom lip was split and bleeding, his left jaw bruised. "I'm fine."

"You don't look fine."

"You called the police?"

"No." I pulled my phone out of my pocket and turned off the siren. "I pulled up a European siren on my phone and put it on a timer. I didn't know the Italian version of 9-1-1 and even if I did, I had no way of explaining what was happening or where I was. So, I improvised."

He came to his knees, then winced. "A siren on a cell phone. Clever thinking, *cara*."

"More desperate than clever. I'll be honest, Slash, I was kind of afraid I'd shoot you by accident if they forced me into it. You know my aim isn't great when I'm nervous. Are you bleeding? Should I call an ambulance?"

"No." He touched my arm. "They weren't trying to kill me. They only wanted a souvenir." He rubbed his scalp.

"A souvenir?" It took me a minute to get there. "Wait. They took some of your hair?" I let out an angry hiss. "For DNA?"

"Apparently Lazo has reached the desperation stage."

"They sent five guys to take you down?"

"Five *well-trained* guys. What happened back at the house? Is Nonna okay?"

"Nonna is fine. Slash, you should know she's a complete Italian badass. If we ever get into a fight again, I want her on my side. Two guys strolled into the house from the back door, looking for you. She clocked one guy with her oxygen tank when he was about to shoot me. Took him out completely. I bashed the other guy with an iron skillet off the stove. One small downside about the skillet thing—our lunch was still inside."

He looked at me as if he weren't comprehending what I was saying. "You and Nonna took out two guys?"

"Yes," I said a bit impatiently. "Principessa attacked one of them. Now I owe that stupid cat for saving me."

Slash looked at me in disbelief. "The cat?"

"Yes." I threw up my hands. "*The cat.* Don't start with me on the cat again."

He blinked as if making sure he was actually lucid, then stood up. He touched his ribs and flinched. "You're sure you're okay?"

"I'm fine. You're the one who's banged up. Let's go home. There are, like, twenty neighbors crammed into

Nonna's house, helping her out and hopefully the police are on the way. I left a gun for her, just in case."

"You left Nonna with a gun?"

"Are you going to repeat everything I say and put it into a question?" It wasn't like we had a lot of time here. The bad guys were getting away.

"I might. How did you find me?"

"Nonna said you went to the market. The car was in the driveway, so I knew you went on foot. I didn't know what was happening to you, so I ran all the way here to find you. I heard some yelling, so I came to investigate and that's when I saw you."

"You came to my rescue all by yourself?"

"Of course. They attacked you, me and Nonna in one day. For what? To steal your DNA so they can find out who your father is? What the heck is wrong with these people? They are going down, Slash. I mean it."

He looked at me with a faintly amused expression. "You're scaring me with that tone."

"Good, because I'm completely serious. This has to stop. I don't care if the entire future of the Vatican is at stake. Are you sure you're okay?"

He pulled me into a one-armed hug. "I'm better than okay."

I willed myself to calm down. "We're going to crush him, Slash. Lazo, his allies and whoever else is in his camp. I don't care if he's the president of the Vatican or president of the universe. The gauntlet has been thrown. A line drawn in the sand. You get what I'm saying, right?"

"I'm clear on the analogies, and, *si*, we're going to end this." He reached into his pocket and pulled out his cell. He punched several numbers, hit send and returned the cell to his pocket.

"What was that all about?"

"I'm telling the team reviewing my vital signs that I'm not under duress and not to stop my heart." He tapped his chest with a grin.

I pressed my hand against my mouth. Oh my God. I had totally forgotten about that. "How can you live like that?"

"Very carefully. Come on, let's go home."

I shook my head. "Unfortunately, there won't be any lunch."

"I'm sure Nonna can remedy that." He walked over to a spot where he'd dropped a couple of bags of groceries and picked them up. "Good thing I went to the market."

I took one of the bags from him as we started to jog back toward Nonna's. "Maybe we can get some information from the two guys Nonna and I knocked unconscious."

"Maybe. My guess is they won't talk."

"Then we'll have to give them incentive to do so." I narrowed my eyes.

Slash put a hand in the small of her back, moving her forward. "Good thinking."

FORTY-SEVEN

Father Julian Koenhein

JULIAN ENTERED THE office of the cardinal, relieved he could finally relate some good news. Unfortunately, it wasn't all good, but he was definitely starting with the good and hoping it would balance the bad. Just in case, he offered up a little prayer.

"Your Eminence, the DNA evidence has been secured," he said as the cardinal looked up. "I just got a call. They took it directly off him. It's on the way to the lab with expedited service."

The cardinal's face broke into a huge smile and Julian felt a rush of relief.

"Finally. But it better not be from a dog," the cardinal warned.

"I assure you it's not. But while we were successful in securing a hair sample, there was a tiny mishap."

"Tiny mishap? What does that mean?"

Julian shifted slightly closer to the door. Once, when Julian had shown him an online news article in which the cardinal had been referred to in unflattering terms, Cardinal Lazo had thrown a paperweight at him.

"Two members of the team entered his grandmother's house, looking for Slash, but he wasn't there," Julian said. "I guess he'd left early to go somewhere. When they breached the door, they encountered just the fian-cée and the grandmother."

The cardinal folded his hands atop of the papers. "Okay? So what happened?"

"The women wouldn't say where Slash had gone. They resisted, so two of our guys got hurt."

Julian cringed at the disbelieving look that crossed the cardinal's face. "They got hurt? How?"

"The women attacked them. Viciously."

Color was rising in the cardinal's cheeks, a sure sign that he was getting angry. "You're telling me that two trained security operatives got hurt by women, one of them elderly?"

"Yes, sir. Apparently there was a cat, too. It scratched up Cinelli pretty bad."

"A cat?" The cardinal stared at him.

Julian rushed to explain. "Obviously, Cinelli and Tucci didn't want to hurt the women, or the cat, so they treated them gently and as a result, they got hurt."

The cardinal's tone turned chilly. "Explain exactly how they got hurt."

"Cinelli and Tucci were knocked out somehow. The good news is their injuries are not permanent. They're at the police station in Sperlonga now. Their story is they accidentally wandered into the house and the women attacked them. I'm working to get them released as qui-etly as possible."

The cardinal's face had turned as red as his zucchetto, a sure sign that his blood pressure was skyrocketing. Ju-lian couldn't decide if he should dash out for cardinal's medicine, which he kept in a locked cabinet in the outer office, or whether that would be considered disrespect-ful to disappear in the middle of a conversation.

"Two trained team members wandered into a house by accident, got knocked out by two women, one of them elderly, and now they are at the police station?" he said, repeating the story as if he hadn't heard it correctly. "Where's the rest of the team?"

"They went after Slash and found him alone and on foot coming back from town. They'd just taken him down and were obtaining the sample when the fiancée showed up with a gun."

"Excuse me? The girl, who took down one, or possibly two, of our men came after the team by herself? With a gun?"

Julian hoped the expression on his face was calm and serene because inside his heart pounded against his chest. "Yes, sir. The gun she took off of Tucci."

"You have *got* to be kidding me," Father Lazo exploded. He reached across his desk and picked up the heavy paperweight from atop some papers. "Did she bring the cat, too?"

Julian flinched and stood his ground, but he prepared to duck, just in case. "No, sir, she didn't. Anyway, the good news is, the team got away with a viable DNA sample, which was the primary objective. The sample is on the way to the lab. We should have results in less than forty-eight hours. What do you want me to do about Cinelli and Tucci?"

The cardinal glared at him, but thankfully returned the paperweight to the desk. "Call the police chief in Rome and patch him through to me. I'll work that angle. You clean up the rest of your mess, Julian, and do it quickly. I want those DNA results the second the come in."

Julian murmured a small prayer of thanks the cardinal had controlled his temper this day. Only by the grace of God was he spared.

"Yes, Your Eminence." He bowed his head deferentially. "The very second."

Slash

"NONNA!" SLASH SHOUTED as he dashed into the house followed closely by Lexi.

Relief blasted through him as he saw Nonna sitting at the kitchen table, surrounded by several of their neighbors, seemingly fine. There was also a policeman who appeared to be interviewing some of the neighbors. The kitchen looked like a war zone, with glass and dishes and food everywhere. There was no sign of the intruders.

He quickly identified himself to the policeman and crouched down to check on Nonna.

"Are you okay?" he asked. When she nodded, he gently pulled her frail form into a hug. *Mio Dio.* If anything had happened to her, that would have been on him. He should have never come here and put her in danger.

"I'm fine, *chierchetto*," she said, looking more angry than scared that her house had been invaded. "Lexi did most of the work dispatching the intruders. How are you?" She touched his bruised jaw and split lip, shaking her head at him in exasperation. "Trouble finds you, Romeo."

"I know, Nonna, but I'm fine. Barely a scratch. I'm just glad you're safe."

"I'm always safe with you around." She glanced over at Lexi. "And now with her, too. That girl of yours is worth keeping, and you know I don't say things like that lightly."

"I know, Nonna." He thanked God for her safety, but inwardly his anger ran hot and furious. Lazo would not come out of this unscathed.

He rose to his feet, looked around. "What happened to the intruders?" he asked the policeman.

"They were taken away," he replied. "They'll be checked in at the station and arraigned shortly." He tipped his head toward Lexi. "Can she speak Italian?"

"No, that's my fiancée. She's American. I'll translate for you."

The policeman asked her several questions and Lexi answered them truthfully. Slash occasionally tweaked her answers when he translated, not wanting to implicate Lazo quite yet, especially when he wasn't ready with the evidence. By the time they finished, the policeman had come to the conclusion that it was a home invasion and Slash didn't correct him on that. Yet.

Eventually the policeman and all the neighbors left. Slash helped Nonna up to her room to rest while Lexi began the task of cleaning the kitchen. Once Nonna had settled, he returned to the kitchen help her.

She was emptying some debris into the trash. When she turned around, he set aside the broom and dustpan and pulled her into his arms.

"Thank you, *cara*," he murmured.

"For what?"

"For protecting Nonna. For being here for me. For everything."

She pulled back so she could study his face. "Is Nonna okay? Really?"

"*Si*. She's doing remarkably well considering what she's been through today. She's tough, perhaps the toughest woman I know, other than you."

He could see the words pleased her, but she still didn't want to take all the credit. "Nonna stood up to those guys without a second thought, Slash. She was amazing. From this point on, Nonna is my definition of a badass."

He managed a smile as he released her and took the broom, sweeping the pieces of a broken dish into a pile. "She said you were pretty badass yourself, jumping on one of the guy's back after he put his hands on her."

"That was my threshold for violence." She still had no idea how much it meant to him that she had protected Nonna. "I jumped on his back and attacked him with a wooden spoon aimed at a vulnerable spot on his body—in this case, his eyes—just like you told me to do."

"That training is paying off," he said, tossing Lexi a roll of paper towels. "It will continue."

"That's a good idea." She started to scrub the wall. "At first I thought you were crazy, but you were right. There are ways all of us—regardless of size, gender or strength—can protect ourselves."

"True. You're a good pupil, *cara*."

She threw him a glance over her shoulder and he felt a hard jolt of affection. Yeah, he had it bad for her.

"I suppose it doesn't hurt that I'm being taught by the best either," she said.

Just like that, the tension in his gut eased. Proof that with her around he was likely to live a lot longer.

They worked side by side until they had the kitchen as spotless as possible. It took them nearly three hours. After he changed clothes, he left Lexi at home to watch Nonna while he went to the police station to find out what had happened to the two intruders.

When he got to the police station, the men were already gone.

His irritation rose. "Gone? Where are they?" he asked the detective in charge.

"They were transferred to Rome about an hour ago."

"On whose authority?"

"On the authority of the police chief in Rome himself. Don't worry, sir, they will be handled appropriately. We'll keep you informed as to what happens to them."

In his opinion, their sudden disappearance to Rome, summoned by the police chief himself, did not bode well for justice being served. But that wasn't a matter to be addressed by this detective, and he knew it.

"Can you provide the names of the men who broke into the house?" he asked.

"I'm sorry, sir. We've been told to put a lid on the investigation, as it's being handled in Rome. It seems a bit odd, but perhaps they are involved in something else. They've promised to report back to us, so we can update you on all developments."

There was nothing more to be learned here. He thanked the detective and returned home. When he told Lexi and Nonna the news, Lexi was furious.

"They transferred them?" she said. "Already? They can't do that, can they?"

"They can and they did. It won't stop us. We'll hack into the police department after dinner and get their names."

"Definitely," she said.

He and Nonna prepared a light dinner of focaccia and paired it with a variety of cheeses, honey, grapes and olive oil. Lexi chose a *Lambrusco* wine to go with the dinner.

Nonna said something to her and Slash translated.

"She said you made an excellent choice for dinner. She's impressed."

"It's hard to make a mistake with Italian wine when it's all excellent, but tell her I appreciate her confidence in me," she said.

Nonna retired for the evening after dinner while he and Lexi went to work hacking into the Sperlonga police station. It was easy. Within twenty minutes, they had the two names of the guys.

"Both guys are former military," Slash mused, transferring the information to his hard drive. "Both are also officially unemployed at the moment. Mercenaries-for-hire is my best guess. Lazo will take care of them now they're in Rome. They'll be released shortly, if they haven't been already, and then will vanish. Problem solved…for him."

"I'm starting to intensely dislike this Lazo guy," Lexi said.

"That makes two of us." Slash leaned back in his chair and stretched out his legs. They'd set up their laptops in the sewing room. He wasn't planning on leaving tonight. He'd be damned if he'd sleep one more night without her. She must have sensed his resolve, because she didn't protest too much. After brushing their teeth, they cuddled together on the lumpy couch. She curled up against his side while he stroked her hair and stared up at the ceiling, thinking.

"What are you thinking about?" she finally asked.

"How soon I can buy Nonna a new couch."

"Oh, thank God."

He chuckled and then winced. "Ouch."

She lifted his shirt and took a look at the bruises on

the left side of his rib cage. "Oh, Slash. This looks like it hurts."

"It's tender. One of them was wearing military issue boots. Those boots connected with my ribs a couple of times after I went down."

"I should have come earlier."

"You shouldn't have come at all, but I appreciate it." He turned over his bandaged hands and flexed his fingers a couple of times to see how it felt. "At least our hands are healing."

Her hand brushed against the gold cross he always wore around his neck, but this time she captured it between her fingers and flipped it over, examining it more closely.

"It has a red cross with pointed, not squared, corners engraved on the back." She looked up. "What does it signify?"

"It was given to me upon my induction to the *sodalitium pianum*."

Her eyes widened. "Really?" She studied him quizzically and he wondered what she was thinking. "You never take it off."

"It's a reminder," he said, gently taking it from her fingers and pulling her close, her cheek resting against his. "To make amends."

He felt her sigh against his skin, but she didn't bring it up. Instead she stroked his bruised jaw and lip. "Is there anywhere you aren't hurt?"

He thought about it and pointed to his stomach.

"Your belly button?"

He nipped at her ear. "You asked me where it didn't hurt."

She laughed, lowered her head, then kissed it. "There. Feeling better?"

He pretended to think it over and then shook his head. "I'm afraid not. Apparently I require additional ministrations."

Her hair brushed against his stomach and his abs clenched. "Did you get into a fight so I would do this?" she asked.

He hadn't, but if it got him this kind of attention, he'd sure as hell consider it. "I'm sorry, but that's an operational secret."

"So is this." She reached over him and pulled the chain on the lamp, plunging them into darkness.

An hour later, he could say with great certainty, he was feeling a *lot* better.

FORTY-EIGHT

Lexi

WHEN I WOKE, light was streaming in through the window. I sat up and glanced at the clock next to the sewing machine. Nearly eight o'clock. Slash was missing, which was normal since he was an early riser. He'd probably gone to do tai chi or something, even with burned hands and sore ribs. I burrowed back in the sheets intending to sleep some more, when I realized there was a foul smell in the room.

I bolted upright in the bed, wrinkling my nose and looking around. Then I saw it at the foot of the couch— the carcass of a dead rat.

I opened my mouth to scream, but my voice was frozen in my throat. Panicked, I tried to scramble away, but my foot got caught in the sheets. I rolled off the couch, bringing the sheets and the dead rat with me.

Completely unnerved, I shrieked and fought the sheets like I was Lara in the Tomb Raider game. Slash came running into the room dripping wet, holding a towel around his waist.

"*Cara!*" He stretched out a hand and extracted me from the bedding. I scooted back against the wall. "What's wrong?"

"Dead. Rat." I gasped and pointed at the bedding.

"Where?"

"In there." I pointed to the sheets again.

Slash shook the bedding until the rat fell onto the floor with a splat. I pressed harder into the wall, wishing the room had another six hundred feet of width. "See, I told you."

"How did a rat get in here?" he asked.

At that moment, Principessa strolled into the room with a haughty look at both of us. I pointed at the cat. "She did it. Yesterday a potato, today a rat. She's *escalating.*"

"Principessa? It wasn't there when I got up an hour ago. She's never done anything like that before. Why would she do that now?"

I was going to start rethinking this marriage thing if he sided with the cat one more time. "To scare the crap out of me, maybe?"

Slash considered. "Or maybe she was bringing you a present. A peace offering, perhaps?"

"I am not impressed." I shuddered. "Can you get it out of here?"

Slash reached down and lifted the rat by the tail, taking it out of the room. I exhaled and then hugged my knees, glaring at the cat. "Seriously, a rat? That is *so* not funny."

To my surprise, Principessa strode over to me. I held up my hands, ready to protect my face if she came at me clawing and spitting. Instead she brushed against my leg once and then stalked out of the room.

It wasn't exactly a friendly gesture, but at least she hadn't attacked me.

I slipped on my cotton sundress, thankful we had clean clothes. I didn't think I could survive another day of jeans in the southern Italian heat.

I'd pulled my hair into a ponytail and was putting on my sandals when Slash strolled in, dressed in a short-sleeved shirt and light khaki pants. He had shaved, and looked and smelled like a male model for Gucci. Other than the bruise on his jaw and the small red split on the corner of his mouth, he looked perfect.

"That's not fair." I put my hands on my hips and regarded him critically. "You got beat up yesterday. You're supposed to have the decency to look injured or scruffy."

"Scruffy?" He sounded insulted.

"Yes, you know, like the punches hurt or something."

"They *did* hurt."

"Then why do you look like you're ready to stand on a balcony and blow kisses to thousands of adoring women below you?"

"I only blow kisses to one adoring woman." He lifted his palm and kissed it, blowing in my direction.

"Very funny." I tried to smack his arm, but he pulled me into him and started nuzzling my neck.

"Stop that," I said. "You're distracting me. Why did you take another shower?"

"I went for a run this morning. I needed some time to clear my head."

"You went running? With bruised ribs?"

He ruffled my hair. "I didn't run that fast. I promise."

I knew a lie when I heard one. "What if those guys came back?"

His smile faded. "They aren't coming back. They got what they came for." He took my hand. "Come on. Nonna has breakfast ready. I already briefed her on the rat. Let's go eat something and then go through the data of our overnight searches."

It was a good plan, so I pushed aside the rat and cat

issue. We were leaving shortly, so I didn't see the point of belaboring it. We ate a light breakfast of coffee, hot milk and biscuits and chatted with Nonna. Slash and I were doing the dishes when there was a knock on the front door.

Slash went to get it. I heard him speaking Italian for a minute and then the door closed and he returned to the kitchen. He had a thoughtful look on his face.

"Who was it?" I asked.

"A messenger. We've been summoned to the Vatican for a private audience this afternoon with the pope."

What the heck? Why in the world would the pope summon us to the Vatican? "This afternoon? How did he know we were here?"

"I'm not sure, but I have my suspicions." He quickly translated for Nonna, who gasped and pressed a hand to her breast.

"Is it normal to be summoned for a private audience with the pope?"

"No, it's not. Especially on such short notice. We were offered a driver, but I told him we'd manage on our own. I was told the reason he wants to see us is that he wants to personally thank us for saving the people in Salerno."

"Oh." I thought that over. "Can't he just send a thank-you note?"

"*Cara*." He gave me a warning look.

"Fine." I held up a hand. "I didn't intend to be rude. I know it's an honor to be invited. But first the Mayor of Salerno and now the pope. All this meeting and greeting famous people is stressing me out. Besides, I didn't pack the right clothes to meet the pope."

"We'll do a quick shopping trip here in Sperlonga and

buy you a knee-length, black dress. I have a jacket and tie I can pull out, and we're good to go."

I glanced uneasily over my shoulder. "Slash, I'm really nervous about this."

"Why? You met him before, last time we were here."

"Yes, but I was coached by the monsignor in charge of protocol before we met him. He gave me detailed instructions on social expectation, requirements for genuflection and a list of topics on what I can and can't talk about—all of which I immediately forgot because I was so nervous. Then I blabbered like an idiot."

"You don't need the monsignor to tell you what to do. You've got me this time."

"Well, even you can't make me stop acting like a dork." It was the sad truth.

He rolled his eyes. "You'll be fine."

"Easy for you to say. Maybe I'll get lucky and he won't remember me." I sounded overly hopeful even to myself. "He meets thousands of people every year, right?"

"Right. But don't worry. He'll remember you."

I sighed in exasperation. "You do realize that's not helping, right?"

"It's the truth. You saved the Vatican millions of euros. Besides, he gave you something the last time you met, didn't he? He rarely gifts people anything."

I reached into my purse, unzipping a top pocket, and carefully pulled out a small crucifix on a silver chain. The back of the crucifix was silver, and the front was wooden.

Slash glanced at me in surprise. "You brought it with you?"

"Of course. I always carry it in my purse."

He held it between his fingers, examining it for a moment. "Put it on. He'll appreciate the gesture."

I slipped it over my head and the crucifix fell above the swell of my breasts. "I still don't know why he gave it to me."

"The pope has his reasons for doing what he does. He is guided in ways we don't understand. According to the messenger, the pope has also asked us to bring our medals from Salerno."

"Why?"

He gave me that look which meant I should know better. "One does not question the pope. However, I think we might be expected to stand for more photos."

Groaning inwardly at the thought of more photos and smiling, I pulled the medal out of my purse and put it on. Grumpy or not, I could be a team player when required.

We finished our breakfast and said goodbye to Nonna. She kissed both my cheeks, took one long last look at the engagement ring, before giving me a squeeze that made me wince.

Principessa strolled into the foyer as Slash brought our suitcases down. I knelt on one knee and pulled off a small pink fuzzy ball I had on my keychain. I scooted it across the floor a couple of times before she jumped on it, flicking it back and forth between her paws.

"It's yours," I said. "I owe you for helping me and Nonna in the kitchen. But don't get too excited. It doesn't mean we're buddies or anything. Consider it a peace offering."

Principessa remained focused on the pink ball, so I rose and lifted my purse on my shoulder.

"So, you're friends with the cat now," Slash said.

"No. We are *not* friends. We were momentary allies. There's a difference."

"If you say so. Let's go."

I gave one more hug to Nonna, and she squeezed my cheeks hard and said something to me.

I looked at Slash. "What did she say?"

"She told you to keep taking good care of me."

I gave her a thumbs-up. "Don't worry. I'm on it, Nonna."

FORTY-NINE

Lexi

BEFORE WE LEFT SPERLONGA, we stopped at a boutique clothing store. I had nothing suitable with me to meet the pope, so Slash picked out something for me to try on. It was a simple black dress with a crew neck and a flared skirt that fell well below my knees. Simple but elegant. We added a black cardigan and a pair of medium heels. I wore the outfit out of the store and we were ready to roll in less than thirty minutes. That was good because I hated shopping almost as much as I hated small talk.

The drive from Sperlonga to the Vatican took us a little over two hours. Slash expertly managed the typical Italian traffic, zooming into the city, hugging the curves and going up side streets at what I personally considered an alarming speed. Everything seemed much closer together than in the States. The roads were smaller and tighter, but the cars didn't seem to slow as they passed each other with mere inches to spare.

Slash drove directly to the Vatican entrance. He provided our names and we handed over our passports. The guard stepped into the security house and came back to check inside our car and trunk. Satisfied we were not carrying any weapons or bombs, he provided us with special tags and told us where to park and check in with the next round of security.

Slash drove to where the guard had instructed and parked the car. We got out and Slash opened the trunk, pulling a sky-blue tie and a dark sports jacket out of his duffel bag. While he put on his tie, I carried my sweater over my arm for the time being because it was still hotter than a fifty-percent-off sale on the newest iPhone.

Slash knew where to go, so I followed him as he strode toward the entrance of a building where more security was stationed.

"What's this building?" I asked as we approached.

"The Apostolic Palace," he answered. "It holds most of the Vatican administrative offices. It's called a palace, but it's more like a series of small buildings within a building, all arranged around the Courtyard of Sixtus V. I don't know exactly where we're meeting the pope, but we'll present ourselves and be escorted to the proper location. We're a little early, so we may have to wait."

"Okay. I hope I don't throw up."

He tucked my arm into his elbow. "You'll be fine. Let me do the talking."

"That's not going to be a problem."

"Good. Remember to refer to him as Holy Father."

"Holy Father. Got it."

We were met by security and escorted through what Slash called the *Portone di Bronzo*, a large stone arch with an iron door at the entrance of the Apostolic Palace. The Swiss Guards, the pope's personal security, were stationed at the entrance dressed in their full regality, including the colorful striped pantaloons and berets.

I searched for a familiar face. "Is Tito working today?"

"Maybe. We might run into him."

We had to relinquish our passports and cell phones at another station, went through a magnetometer at another and had a final pat down before we were waved through with our escort.

After talking to someone on a phone, our escort indicated we were to follow him. As we walked, I put my sweater on. We entered a side door into the palace and walked down a long, marbled corridor with cool floors and high ceilings. We took a couple of turns down a few long hallways before he stopped at a door and knocked. A priest dressed in a black cassock and clerical collar answered, spoke briefly with the escort, then dismissed him. He introduced himself as Father Vestini and ushered us into a small reception area. He said something in Italian to Slash and disappeared.

"He told us to take a seat," Slash said, motioning to a fancy, embroidered armchair with gold and red threads. He looked remarkably calm, whereas I felt ready to barf. I perched on the edge of the chair, reciting Fermat's Last Theorem in my head to calm myself.

The priest returned a few minutes later and asked us to follow him. We walked deeper into the palace, our footsteps echoing in the mostly empty corridors. We entered another reception room, a larger one, not unlike the one I was in the last time I'd met the pope. It could have been the same one for all I knew. The rooms were all beautiful, but similar in presentation. Cavernous ceilings, marble floors, scarlet drapes, and golden-trimmed wainscoting and sconces. There were three more priests here, rushing around, arranging three chairs, presumably for us to sit in. We stood in the corner, waiting while another priest walked in with a camera and began testing his camera and fixing the flash attachments.

A few minutes after that, the pope entered the room. He looked shockingly frail and used a cane to walk slowly. His arms were shaking from the effort. Two of the three priests walked nearby, presumably to catch him if he fell.

The pope was wearing a fully buttoned white cassock, sash, red slippers and white skullcap. His face lit up when he saw Slash. The last time I'd seen them together, the pope had hugged him, eliciting surprised gasps from all in the room. They obviously had affection for each other, and some sort of history, but I didn't know any details.

He motioned us toward him. We approached together and Slash knelt to kiss the Fisherman's Ring. I knelt beside him, which wasn't easy in a dress and shoes with a heel, but at least I didn't topple over. The pope touched my head gently, made the sign of the cross over both of us and said something quietly in Italian to Slash. Slash responded and rose. I did, too.

So far, so good.

In accented English, the pope urged us to move toward the chairs. We fell in behind him as he shuffled slowly, leaning heavily on his cane.

The photographer ran around us snapping pictures like crazy. It made me increasingly nervous, since I was certain I had my eyes closed for most of them.

Once the pope was seated, the priests indicated we should also sit. We obliged, and the pope leaned forward. "Thank you both for coming on such short notice. I was delighted to hear you were in Italy." I appreciated the fact that he spoke English to include me in the conversation.

"It is an honor to have the opportunity to speak with you, Holy Father," Slash said quietly.

"Oh, I assure you, the honor is all mine. I understand you are the new Saviors of Salerno. You've created quite a sensation and now the news is racing across Italy. I assure you, it's all anyone could talk about at the Vatican this morning."

I blushed, but I kept my eyes on the floor, trying not to draw attention to myself.

"We were fortunate to be in the right place at the right time," Slash said lightly. "Lexi was the one who first spotted the fire and tried to separate the propane tank from the food cart."

I glanced up to see the pope looking at me, his brown eyes assessing me carefully. "So, it was her. Extraordinary."

It wasn't me who'd been extraordinary. "Slash did all the heavy lifting," I countered. "Without him, we would have had a real problem on our hands. He got the propane tank free and threw it in the manhole. He's the real hero."

"It was Lexi who thought of using the manhole to limit the blast," Slash interjected smoothly.

The pope beamed in delight. "Oh, you both are extraordinary. How wonderful." A twinkle came into his eyes as he pointed at my medal. "So, what do you think of your new elevated status, Ms. Carmichael?"

I looked down at the medal and tried to think of an appropriate response. The problem was I was coming up blank, so I blurted out the first thing on my mind. "Does this put Slash and me halfway to actual sainthood?"

To my surprise, the pope laughed. "Indeed, it does."

I glanced at Slash and saw he, too, was smiling, so maybe that hadn't been a bad answer after all.

After a moment, the pope drummed his fingers against the wooden hand rest on the chair and turned his attention back to Slash. "I desire a firsthand account of what happened. Will you oblige me, please?"

"Of course," Slash said. He briefly explained what had happened in Salerno, sticking to the facts and continuing to downplay his role.

The pope listened intently, asking several questions. When Slash was finished, the pope sat back in his chair, placed his fingers in a steeple and looked back and forth between Slash and me.

"I never cease to be amazed by the way God works in our world. He has such beautiful, wondrous, mysterious ways."

It wasn't a question and he didn't seem to be inviting comment, so neither Slash nor I replied. The pope lifted his hand and waved the photographer over. He spoke for a minute, the photographer listening intently. Slash apparently knew what was going on, because he rose and held out a hand to me. I took it and stood, wondering what was going on.

"The Holy Father would like to take a few official, staged photos with us," Slash explained. "Our assistance to the people of Salerno is a feel-good story for the Vatican, and quite timely given the current candidates for sainthood."

I wanted to get my photo taken as much as I wanted to spend two weeks debugging a new Microsoft patch. But sometimes we do what we have to do.

The pope struggled to stand, wobbling, so Slash put a hand under his elbow to steady him until he took his cane.

"*Grazie*," the pope said, smiling as the photographer snapped a photo of them. It was a nice, unguarded moment and I hoped that Slash could get a copy of it someday.

The photographer told us where to stand and arranged

our positions. He spent an inordinate amount of time on me, fixing my hair, lifting my chin, telling me to stop scowling and hunching my shoulders. He also straightened Slash's tie and collar before shooting us from numerous angles and with different degrees of flash and light. I tried to look like I was happy to be there, enjoying the incredible honor of having my photo taken with the pope. Unfortunately I was becoming increasingly agitated and wishing the entire thing was over yesterday. My face was stretching into less of a smile and into more of a grimace. Finally the pope waved his hand to indicate an end to the session. He called over another of the priests and spoke briefly with him, before the priest bowed and moved away.

The pope and Slash exchanged a long glance, and then they both looked at me. I had no idea what was going on. The pope turned and started shuffling toward another door when Slash put his hand in the small of my back.

"The Holy Father is requesting a private audience with us," Slash murmured. "We're moving into his private study now."

"Oh." I'm sure Slash saw the surprise on my face, but his expression was inscrutable. Together we followed the pope into the adjoining room.

When we were in the study, Slash closed the door behind us. Now it was just the three of us. The pope sank down into a tall chair with a white cushion and gold-plated back. Slash and I took chairs across from him.

"Thank you for agreeing to speak with me in private," the pope said.

Slash lowered his head. "I am deeply honored for the opportunity." He paused and glanced at me.

"Me, too," I added hastily.

The pope balanced his cane against the side of the chair. He straightened, leaning forward, his elbows on his thighs, clasping his hands in front of him.

"Let's speak frankly, Nicolo. If I may be so bold to ask, what really brings you to Italy?"

I looked at Slash, realizing the weight of the question. I knew next to nothing about high-stakes church politics, but even I understood the delicacy of his answer.

"My brother," Slash finally answered. "He was refused the right of marriage in the church."

The surprise on the pope's face seemed genuine. "Stefan?"

Slash shook his head. "No, that's my older brother. My younger brother, Giorgio."

It surprised me that the pope knew and remembered the names of Slash's brothers, which indicated to me that the pope was very interested in Slash's life. Perhaps more than Slash had realized.

The pope asked for more detail, so Slash told him what he knew. Eventually, the pope sat back. "I do not understand why the church won't sanction the marriage. I will personally look into it."

"I am deeply appreciative of your support, Holy Father. Thank you."

"Does Father Armando know of this?"

Slash dipped his head. "He does. He is also investigating the reasons for the refusal."

"Hmmm. That's interesting because I spoke with him yesterday, and he made no mention of this."

"I'm sure he didn't want to bother Your Eminence with such a minor matter. It is not something typically in your purview."

"All matters dealing with a child of God are in my purview. Especially when it deals with holy matrimony."

Slash lowered his head. "Of course. I apologize for suggesting otherwise."

A smile crossed the pope's face. "I am teasing, you know. But, speaking of matrimony, I understand that you two are to be married."

"We are," Slash confirmed.

"I am disappointed that I had to hear this from Father Armando."

"I apologize again. I always intended to tell you personally. The engagement only recently occurred. So, now that I have your undivided attention, I am most pleased to present Lexi Carmichael, my fiancée."

They both looked at me. I sat there frozen, surprised that Slash had so casually mentioned he would call the pope personally to tell him about our engagement, and wondering if I was supposed to stand up, curtsey or do something else. Instead, I held out my engagement ring. Better that everyone look at that instead of me.

"It was Slash's grandmother's," I explained.

I guess it was an okay thing to do because the pope asked me to come closer. I rose and walked over to him. He took my hand, inspecting the ring with great interest. "Congratulations to both of you. It's a lovely ring. A circle is an unbreakable symbol of unity. You two together will be strong in life."

He made the sign of the cross over my hand. "May your union be among the most blessed of God." A smile touched his lips as he looked directly at me. "You do understand I'm anticipating a large Catholic family, Ms. Carmichael."

I froze, struggling with a response—of which there

was none appropriate—when the pope laughed. "I am sincerely happy for you both."

I returned to my seat, embarrassed by his comment, which had apparently amused Slash, because he was grinning, too.

Then, to my utter astonishment, and apparently Slash's as well, the pope stood without the use of his cane and strode over to the French windows. He walked perfectly, without difficulty or shuffle. He looked out the window, standing tall and strong, at the exact spot where he greeted the faithful in St. Peter's Square most Sundays and on special occasions.

"You can walk," I blurted out before I could stop myself.

Slash shot me a warning glance, but it was too late. The words had been said. I clapped a hand over my mouth, wishing I owned duct tape to keep my mouth shut at all times.

The pope turned around from the window, his expression reflective, and perhaps slightly amused. "I can. Are you surprised?"

He directed the question to me. I looked over at Slash, but he didn't attempt to speak on my behalf. He seemed as stunned as I was. I considered my answer carefully before speaking. "You're...acting."

"Let's just say that I may be exaggerating my weakness. Oh, I'm ill, but my immediate situation is not as dire as the Vatican press...or others...might be so inclined to believe."

"But why disguise that you are healthier than you appear?" I asked.

He considered a moment and then returned to the window where he looked out at the people below. "It's not a simple or easy rationale, but I believe it's what I must do. If you will bear with me for a moment, I will explain. When a pope dies, God guides the church leadership in the selection of the next Holy Father, which is the purpose of the conclave. Unfortunately, if you look back over the church's history, the cardinals haven't always listened to God's will when selecting the next pope. For many flawed and undeniably human reasons, cardinals have selected popes for the wrong reasons, reasons that had devastating consequences for our followers, and diverted the church from its true mission—loving one another, lifting up the poor and disenfranchised, and taking care of all of God's children. Obviously, I will not have a voice in selecting the next pope. However, there is yet an important role for me to play. Too often in the past, popes have overlooked their leadership responsibilities in preparing the church for their departure. They've failed to mentor and encourage those cardinals who seem to have God's special blessing and wisdom—qualities that would make them an ideal candidate. Likewise, they often fail to discern and counsel those who would seek the papacy for prideful or selfish reasons. I will not be a pope who fails to prepare the church for my death. When I was a young cardinal, I realized it was easier to discern the intentions of those more focused on their own good than of others, as it corroborated the belief in their own superiority. As I am truly declining, though not as fast as I may appear to be, this allows me to better identify those who would jockey for my position, and thus need to be counseled, versus those who would humbly accept the papacy if it were offered to them."

I took a minute to digest all of this. I couldn't begin to fathom the pressure and difficulty of his position and the responsibilities he held on his shoulders yet, his words about discerning the intentions of the cardinals suddenly made sense in the context of Slash's and my presence.

I looked up at him, understanding dawning. "You already know what's happened to Slash...what's going on with Cardinal Lazo and what's happened to us. You were the one who set this whole thing in motion." Part of me was shocked, while another part of me was impressed, thinking he had the brain of a hacker.

The pope leaned against the corner of his desk. "Yes, and no. I provided the fertile soil from which honest, or dishonest, actions might spring. I, unfortunately, didn't know that both of you would be brought into this. Now that you have, it confirms that my actions were guided by a higher power. God works through us always and shows us the way."

"What does that mean?" I murmured.

I didn't realize I'd spoken aloud until the pope answered. "It means God has chosen both of you for his work. I see it now, and I am deeply humbled by that knowledge. I am convinced that your presence here is divine intervention." He turned to look at Slash. "Now, Nicolo, we shall see it through, shan't we?"

He glanced at Slash and a look of understanding passed between them. "We shall," Slash responded.

"Good. Now, it is my great honor to announce to you that later today I will formally canonize the two candidates for sainthood. Cristian Descantes, the *first* Savior of Salerno, and Sister Ana-Paula Núñez, the Mother of Maldonado. You are the first to know." He held up his hands. "Pray for us, o Holy Mother of God."

"May we be worthy of the promises of Christ," Slash murmured in response.

I bowed my head respectfully and waited.

The pope walked over to Slash and gently rested a hand on the top of his head. "There remains, however, one more important matter between us, Nicolo, and it involves forgiveness. Yours. You must not be afraid of the vulnerability of living in forgiveness. In our violent world, largely abandoned by people of good intention, we must never stop asking for and receiving forgiveness. Those of us who bear the extraordinary weight of the present and future of this church *must* continue to live in forgiveness while praying for guidance and strength. It is not an easy task. Do you understand, my son?"

"I do." Slash kept his head lowered.

"Good." The pope watched him, a contemplative look on his face. "One of my favorite quotes came from one of my predecessors, Saint John Paul the Great. He often said, 'Thanks to the healing power of love, even the most wounded heart can experience a liberating encounter with forgiveness.' So, I ask you to forgive yourself and those who have hurt you. That is an order from your pope."

Slash left the chair and knelt on the floor, taking the pope's hand and kissing the ring. "Thank you for your guidance, Holy Father."

Now the pope glanced at me. "And for you, Miss Carmichael, there is a matter I wish to discuss."

"Me?" I pointed at myself and then looked over my shoulder, as if another Lexi Carmichael might magically appear. I couldn't begin to fathom what the pope could possibly want to discuss with me. Unless it was family planning. In that case, I wished the floor would open up and swallow me whole.

He approached me, putting one hand on my shoulder,

the other pushing aside the Salerno medal and gently holding the crucifix between his fingers.

"You are wearing it. You honor me deeply. Thank you."

Thank goodness Slash had told me to put it on. I opened my mouth intending to say "you're welcome," but instead I blurted out, "Why did you give it me?"

Slash closed his eyes and I interpreted that to mean one didn't question the pope. Oops. But I'd done it, so there you have it. I expected the pope to say he was trying to save my nonbeliever soul or something along those lines, but he didn't.

"This crucifix is very special to me," he said, still holding the cross nestled in his palm. "It was given to my mother by my father. When he proposed, he was too poor to afford even the most inexpensive of rings. So, he gave her a silver crucifix, something that had been handed down in his family for generations. He added the wooden back himself, made from the heartwood of the oldest tree in his neighborhood. My mother wore it until the day she died. She pressed it into my hand and told me to give it to a worthy woman."

I looked at him in dismay. "Oh, if I'd known this was such an important family heirloom, I never would have accepted it. I am not the worthiest of women. In fact, I'm not worthy at all… I'm not even Catholic." I reached for the chain, starting to take it off. "Please, take it back. It belongs in your family."

His hand closed around mine, preventing me from removing it. "Miss Carmichael, I never question the motives of God. I may not always understand them, but I do not question them. I assure you, I'd been waiting for years to give that crucifix to the right person. It'd been my constant companion for more than three decades. The moment I saw you in that room several months ago, although I'd never spoken a word to you, God moved me to present the cross to you. At the time I did not understand why, but I did not question it. That is not my way. Now you are here and in His grace and wisdom, I finally understand why. As always, I am in awe of His goodness and plan. I assure you, this crucifix belongs to you. You must keep it. Please indulge an old man in this request."

I looked at Slash who was watching me, but said nothing. Surely he had to be as stunned as I to hear this story. But either he wouldn't, or couldn't, tell me what to do. It would be up to me to keep it or not. Still uncertain, I turned my gaze back to the pope. He waited patiently for my answer, which paralyzed me more because I was probably violating every sacred rule in regards to interaction with the pope.

Finally, I managed to connect my brain with my mouth. "I don't know what to say, Holy Father, except thank you. I'm deeply honored you've entrusted me with such an important family heirloom. I will cherish it always."

This now made me—the Queen of All that is Awkward and Klutzy—the keeper of two precious family heirlooms, one of them from the pope himself. Me! The woman who had her own personal little black cloud. I wasn't one to question God either, but in the grand scheme of things, this did *not* seem like a good idea even if it came from above.

"Now, there is one final matter," the pope said quietly. He took two steps forward and requested Slash to stand. He withdrew something from beneath his cassock, a small, worn, leather bag the size of his palm. He held it out to Slash.

"Take this to Father Armando and you will get the answers you seek, my child."

Having said that, he pulled Slash into a hug. Slash hugged him back. I wasn't sure where this fell on the proper pope protocol chart, but seeing as how the Holy Father had initiated it and no one else was in the room, I figured it was okay.

There was clearly a palpable affection between the two of them. When the pope finally released Slash, the two spoke quietly in Italian for a minute. Slash knelt to kiss the ring again. The pope retrieved his cane, heading for the door. Then he turned and looked at us with a glint in his eyes before slouching and resuming the familiar, old-man shuffle. Slash opened the door for him, and the three priests waiting outside rushed inside to assist him.

The pope held up a hand stopping the priests as he turned to us one more time. "Go with God, my children, and may the mercy and the blessing of His goodness bring you peace and light always." He blessed both of us with the sign of the cross. "I know you are both destined for great things."

We exited his study and one of the priests took immediate charge of us, leading us through the maze of rooms and corridors back to the security station at the entrance.

After we had retrieved our phones and passports from security control and walked outside, I asked Slash the question burning on my tongue. "What did he say to you before we left?"

Slash slipped on his sunglasses. "He gave me some advice."

"Which was?"

He put an arm around my shoulder. "He told me to take the peace she offers."

"Mother Mary?"

He took my hand. "No. You."

"Me?" I stopped, pointed at myself. "You mean *me* me?"

"You." He continued walking to the car. "And he's right, and not just because he's my pope."

"I'm sensing a pattern here," I joked, but his face remained serious. I'd left my hat in the car and my head was hot. I shaded my forehead with my hand. "Slash, do you think the pope knows who your father is?"

"I do. I think it's why he's sending me to Father Armando with the package, whatever is in it."

"Are you going to peek?" I sure as heck would have opened that package by the time we walked out of the Vatican. But that was me.

"I don't know. Maybe. But not now."

Slash held open my door and I climbed in the car. He came around to his side, getting in and starting the car.

"Does this mean we are heading to Genoa?" I asked my hands on my lap.

"It does. Just not yet. We've got other work to do first. I'm going to get us a room here in Rome for now."

"What other work?"

"I'll explain when we get to the hotel."

I fastened my seat belt and as Slash backed out of the parking lot, I shifted in my seat to face him. "Slash, why do you think the pope gave me his mother's crucifix?"

"You heard him. Because you were meant to have it."

That didn't help my clarity at all. "Did you know it was his mother's?"

"I did not. But when you showed me the crucifix when we were in Rome the last time, before we were even dating, I knew he saw something special in you. It's the same thing I see every day."

I had no idea what he was talking about. It was hard trying to pin down this supposed elusive quality in me that no one could scientifically or rationally explain.

"You do realize there is a lot of pressure to live up to this specialness, whatever it is. I'm the most ordinary person on the planet, with the exception of my abnormal awkwardness and that little black cloud that follows me around. I hope that everyone's belief in me is not misplaced."

"Never." Slash lifted my hand to his mouth as he drove and kissed my knuckles. "There are many things in this world I'm not sure of, *cara*, but trust me, *that* is not one of them."

FIFTY

Father Julian Koenhein

JULIAN WAITED UNTIL the red light on his phone disappeared indicating that Cardinal Lazo had hung up with Cardinal Bertello, the Archbishop of Roselle. He waited another two minutes for good measure and then knocked softly on the cardinal's door.

"Enter."

Julian opened the door and stepped inside tentatively. "Your Eminence, I have news to report."

"It better be information on the DNA sample."

"Yes, it is, but first I wanted to let you know that our sources report that Slash and his fiancée met with the Holy Father this afternoon."

"What? Here at the Vatican?"

"Yes. It was a private audience, initiated by the Holy Father himself."

Cardinal Lazo thought that over. "No doubt prompted by Emilio Armando."

"Perhaps, but the official reason was that Slash and his fiancée saved many paradegoers in Salerno from an explosion. No one was injured except for the fiancée, who received a concussion and was briefly hospitalized."

Julian walked over and laid a copy of the *La Città di Salerno* newspaper on the cardinal's desk. The front page was mostly taken up with a large picture of Slash, wearing no shirt and holding the propane tank in his hands, looking like a Roman god.

"They saved dozens of lives yesterday," Julian explained. "Including an entire children's choir. The press is calling them the new Saviors of Salerno. They were presented medals at the mayor's office."

Cardinal Lazo drummed his fingers against the desk, frowning in displeasure. "What were they doing in Salerno?"

"I don't know."

The cardinal set down the paper. "It doesn't matter. None of this matters. Have we received the results from the DNA sample yet?"

"We have. The good news is that the DNA is not from a dog this time. It's definitely human, and it's Slash's."

"At last. So, what did we discover? Did you cross-reference his DNA with Father Armando's?"

"We did. I'm sorry, Your Eminence, it's not a match."

Father Lazo sat back in his chair, stunned. "What? It's not a match? That's impossible. I was certain. Give me that paper."

Julian handed him the paper. The cardinal took it and studied it for a long time. Finally he leaned back in, turning his chair around to stare out the window.

Julian waited quietly and patiently—behavior that had served him well in the many years he had been with the cardinal. Finally the cardinal turned around. "I want you to have the technician cross-reference this DNA with the Holy Father's."

Julian stared at the cardinal completely aghast. "*What?* We couldn't possibly. Your Eminence…the sacrilege. The technician wouldn't do it."

"Everyone has a price, Father. Find his, and get it done."

"But… I don't think this is a good idea."

"Did I ask for your opinion?"

Julian stammered to find the right words. "N-no. But if this were to get out…"

"It won't. That will be all."

"But, Your Eminence, I must protest—"

"I *said* that will be all, Father. Do your duty."

"Yes, of course." Julian left the room, his stomach churning. He leaned against the closed door, feeling nausea sweep through him.

For the first time in his life, he was deeply concerned about the future of the church.

FIFTY-ONE

Lexi

"I GOT US A suite at the Hotel *Portrait Roma*," Slash said as we drove into the city. "It's three blocks from here and it has parking."

"Works for me. It will feel good to have a shower. All these meetings with important politicians and religious figures has maxed me out. No offense."

"None taken. I'm with you on that."

We found the hotel without incident, turned the car over to a valet and checked into our room. I went straight to the window. The view was a busy street facing another building with gorgeous windows and balconies.

"What's this street?" I asked, pointing below us.

"It's the *Via Condotti*. If you look up there, you can see the famous Spanish steps. They were built in the 1700s by the French to link the Spanish Embassy and the *Trinità dei Monti* church to the Holy See."

"I remember reading about the steps in high school," I said.

He stood next to me, resting his hands on the rail. "Then you'll likely remember that in ancient Roman times, the *Via Condotti* was one of the largest passages that allowed those who traveled the Tiber River to reach Pincio Hill, a coveted spot overlooking the city. The most beautiful villas and gardens were built here. The street is named after those conduits that carried water to the famous baths at Agrippa."

We stood there on the balcony for a few minutes, people watching and thinking about the history of the street below before returning to the room.

"How's the wifi?" I asked, opening my laptop bag and pulling out my computer.

"The wifi is excellent."

"Great, let's get set up." I put my laptop on the desk, reaching for my power cord.

"Did I mention I love a girl with a one-track mind?"

"When it comes to hacking, I'm that girl," I answered, crawling under the desk and plugging in the laptop. "Slash, the pope said you'd finish it. Do you know what he meant?"

"I do." Slash sat in front of his laptop, and handed me his power cord since I was still under the desk. I plugged it in and crawled out while he booted it up. "He's giving me permission to go after Lazo."

"What do you mean 'permission'?"

"I'm going to take him down. Just that."

A twinge of alarm ran through me. "Take him down... how?"

Slash typed some commands on the keyboard. "I'm not going to kill him, if that's what you're worried about. Although I will admit it crossed my mind more than once. I have a plan, one that came to me while we were in Sperlonga. But it means I need to get into his system, so a hack on the Vatican is in order. If something goes wrong, the pope will protect me."

"Hacking into the Vatican," I repeated. "I had this same discussion with Elvis a few days ago." I sat on the edge of the bed, crossed my arms. "How are we going to hack in to the Vatican? Your experience building the system notwithstanding, you don't happen to have a handy backdoor into the system, do you?"

"Unfortunately, I do not. It will take work and time, but with your help, we'll do it."

"I have no doubt about that, but can we discuss the elephant in the room first?"

He typed something and turned the chair around to face me, his keen eyes assessing me. "I'm listening."

I shifted on my feet. "I don't want to play devil's advocate here, for a number of reasons, but what if you being here is exactly what the pope wanted all along? We assumed Lazo summoned you, and maybe he was the one who sent the note and the statue. But what role do you think the pope has in all of this? You're a very powerful weapon, Slash, and he knows that. I want to make sure *you* understand what you're doing and why, even if you've been told what to do by the most powerful religious man in the world."

His astonishment was genuine. "You'd challenge the pope on my behalf?"

Sometimes, I just didn't get men. Okay, I pretty much *never* understood them. How could he be surprised? Of course, I'd challenge anyone who threatened him. I'm his fiancée, and it was logical that I'd stand up for the man I loved. That's what I was doing in Italy in the first place.

"If I think he doesn't have your best interests at heart, I would," I said. "I'm sorry if that upset you."

"Upset me?" He reached out and hauled me from the bed into his arms. "Could I possibly love you more?" He framed my face with his hands and gave me a long, lingering kiss. "God, how I adore you."

I pulled back, studied him. "Don't change the subject. It's a serious question, Slash. Do you trust the pope?"

"I know it's a serious question, *cara*." He rubbed my jawline with his thumbs. "And it's a fair one, too. I trust the pope implicitly. Not just because he's my pope, but because I personally know him to be a man of honor and integrity. I can't say the same about Cardinal Lazo."

"I agree with that. So long as you're sure about it."

"I am."

"Fine. Then what's the plan?"

He dropped his hands, returned to the desk chair. "I'm going to hack into Lazo's work computer. I need to know what he's plotting against Father Armando and the pope. I've already been inside his private computer and had a look at his financials. He's socked away money he shouldn't, and he's taking donations from questionable people, but it's not enough to hang him. I need a smoking gun, for lack of a better analogy."

"Getting into the Vatican network will take some time," I reminded him. "We both know that from first-hand experience."

"I know." He stretched his arms over his head and rolled his neck. "Which is why we need to start as soon as possible. I'll be lucky to get in within forty-eight hours. Seventy-two hours is probably a closer bet, and that's with me having built and secured the Vatican network from the ground up."

I considered for a moment. "You know, that actually gives me an idea. This past year I've learned over and over again that people are the weakest link in cybersecurity. How about we go at this in a two-pronged attack? You on the Vatican hack and me elsewhere. We can see who gets there first."

Slash looked at me curiously. "You have my full attention, *cara*. What do you have in mind?"

Taking a deep breath, I told him.

FIFTY-TWO

Father Julian Koenhein

JULIAN KOENHEIN LOVED ROME. He loved his job. He had his calling to the priesthood at fourteen years old and had never looked back. As the second eldest of seven children, he came from a hard-working Catholic family. His life growing up in Germany revolved around the church from a young age, and he remembered well the catechism, church services, and was enthralled by the mystery and magic of the mass. Unlike most children, who couldn't sit still or fidgeted during the service, he would have spent all day in church, fascinated by the stained glass windows, the breathtaking paintings on the walls, the cavernous ceilings and the smell of incense. He had always felt at home in the church—his safe harbor.

Thankfully, his parents didn't stop him from pursuing his passion. He was an average student, not particularly good-looking, awkward and horribly nearsighted. His parents hadn't been able to afford new glasses, so he'd inherited a beat-up pair from his older brother, Karl. Maybe he was a little too quiet, more of a follower than a leader, but he'd pursued his passion with a devoted single-mindedness. Hadn't his fierce commitment to the church and his work behind the scenes gotten him transferred to the Vatican, his lifelong dream?

Then why did he feel like it was all going wrong?

He'd always been a good team player. He'd always done as he was asked, usually going above and beyond the required duties. He loved the church, but he wasn't naive, and he knew violence was sometimes necessary to preserve peace and further the expansion of the church. There were, of course, the crusaders, but there was also the dark history of the Spanish Inquisition. Sometimes progress required sacrifice. For twenty-seven years he'd been unfailingly loyal to Lazo.

But now he wondered.

Deep in thought, he walked along the street to his small apartment, going through the small neighborhood park. He was admiring some of the colorful summer blooms when he collided with someone walking in the opposite direction. Books scattered everywhere and a young blonde woman fell backward onto her bottom.

"*Mi scusi!*" he said.

"Oh, no, I'm so sorry," she said in English. "I wasn't watching where I was going. Um…*non c'è problema.*"

"It's okay," he said. "I speak English. Are you okay?"

She rose to her knees, putting her hand in his so he could pull her to her feet. He was momentarily taken aback by the gloves on her hand.

"Oh, my. Are you injured?" he asked.

"No. I have psoriasis. The gloves are protection against the sun." She started gathering her books, so Julian knelt and began to help her. As they crawled around, he noticed the beautiful silver crucifix she wore around her neck. He'd seen a cross like that before, but exactly where eluded him.

"I really must apologize again," she said. "I'm such a klutz. Oh, wait, are you a priest? Well, that was a dumb question seeing as you're wearing the cassock."

Julian smiled. "Yes. I'm a priest. Are you visiting Rome?"

She shook her head. "No. Not exactly. I'm a journalism student at the university. Is your church here in the neighborhood?"

"I don't have a parish. I work at the Vatican."

Her eyes widened. "Really? That is so cool."

"Well, I think so." He smiled indulgently.

"Hey, do you think I could interview you? I'm doing a feature article about priests at the Vatican for my college newspaper back in the US It's titled *The Path to the Vatican.* If would be so great to hear all about how you became a priest and how your career led you to the Vatican."

"Oh, I'm afraid I'm just a clerk there."

"That doesn't matter to me, and it won't matter to my readers. I think the kids would be interested in your story."

"Are you sure?"

"I'm positive. Do you have a few minutes? We could sit on that bench over there. It's a nice evening and we could talk."

He looked around. She was right. It was a beautiful summer evening. A couple were strolling hand-in-hand along the path and a woman pushing a pram was not too far behind them. Teenagers sat in the grass, legs tucked under them talking and laughing. There was no reason he had to rush home to an empty apartment. Besides, he enjoyed practicing his English.

"I guess I could spare a few minutes."

"Great! Thank you so much. I really appreciate it."

They sat on the bench. The young woman put her

books on the empty space beside them and pulled out her cell phone.

"Is it okay if I use my cell phone to record our interview?" She smiled at him, and Julian thought she had a really nice smile.

"Sure, I guess that would be fine."

"By the way, my name is Lara. What's your name?"

"I'm Father Julian Koenhein." He spelled his last name when she asked him to do so.

"Okay, let's start at the beginning," she said. "How did you become a priest?"

He walked her through his life, pausing only when she asked follow-up questions. Before he knew it, more than an hour had passed. An hour he'd greatly enjoyed. Maybe this was a sign from God that he needed to get out more—have meaningful conversations with people other than the priests in his office.

She finally clicked off the recorder. "Thank you so much. Do you mind if I take your photo to accompany the article?"

"Of course."

She snapped a couple of photos and frowned as she studied them.

"Something wrong?" Julian asked, wishing he were twenty years younger, thirty pounds lighter and hadn't lost so much hair.

She looked up in surprise. "No. These are good, but they don't really make a powerful statement. I wish I could get a couple of photos of you with the Vatican in the background or, even better, in your office. I mean, I presume you're really busy, but do you think it would be possible for us to meet, maybe during your lunch hour, so I could snap a few more photos? I would promise to take no more than ten minutes of your time. I'd be happy to bring you lunch."

"Well, that would be kind of you. When would you like to come?"

"Would tomorrow work? My deadline is fast approaching and I need time to transcribe the interview and determine word count."

"We'll make it work. Write your name on a piece of paper for me and I'll make sure you are cleared by security to enter around noon. Would that be satisfactory for you?"

"Yes. That would be perfect."

He rattled off the address where she should enter and she recorded it on her phone. She then wrote her name in a notebook and tore off a piece of the paper, handing it to him. "Thank you so much. This has really been great."

"My pleasure," he said, because it really had been.

He returned to his seat on the bench and watched her go, thinking about her silver and wood crucifix and wondering if it were a sign his life was about to change.

FIFTY-THREE

Lexi

"WE'RE A GO," I said when I returned to the hotel room. I pulled the blonde wig off my head and tossed it on the bed. "He didn't recognize me, thankfully. We'll meet at noon tomorrow so I can take photos of him in his office and around the Vatican."

"You make a good agent, *cara*," Slash said from the bed where he sat with his back against the headboard, typing on the computer balanced on his lap.

"If we hadn't practiced ad nauseam what I should say and do, it would have been a disaster."

"You only needed a little training."

I put the books down on the desk and carefully peeled off the gloves. "He was surprised by the gloves, but he swallowed the whole psoriasis thing. You know, it's kind of sad, but I don't think Father Koenhein is a bad guy. He's likable, just misguided."

Slash threw me an exasperated glance. "Do I need to review Operative Rules 101 with you? Do *not* become attached to the target."

"I'm not attached. Just sympathetic. The Vatican is his dream job, something he worked hard at for his whole life, but he ends up a clerk to a guy like Cardinal Lazo."

"We all have our crosses to bear."

"I suppose. So, how's the break-in going?"

"Most of the initial work is being done automatically at this point. I'll need to collect the data first, and see what's in there. I'm almost done with your student ID, however."

"Excellent." I took off my shoes, grabbed my laptop and sat down next to him on the bed. "How can I help?"

"I could use some specific penetration testing. I want to find some vulnerabilities to exploit. You up for it?"

"I'm always up for hacking." I stretched out my legs. "I'll take the keyboard over medals any day."

A crooked grin crossed his face. "Damn, you really *are* the girl of my dreams."

FIFTY-FOUR

Lexi

I SLIPPED THE student identification Slash handed me into my purse, along with the thumb drive, and slipped the strap over my shoulder. I felt the best I had in days. I'd had a long bath, a solid ten hours of sleep, and my body was finally adjusting to the time change. No residual headaches from the concussion, and while the burns on my hands still hurt, they were improving with regular cleaning and application of ointment.

Slash carefully put the gloves on my hand. He tugged a little too hard on one side, and I winced.

"Sorry," he said.

"It's okay. I just hope this works."

"It will," Slash said. "It only needs to be plugged in to any port for ten seconds."

I glanced in the mirror and adjusted my wig. Slash secured it with bobby pins, but I had loosened it by tugging on it. I had to keep my hands off it or the whole thing would slide off. "I can manage ten seconds."

"Yes, you can. But be careful, *cara*."

"I will."

Slash walked me to within a block of the security check near the Apostolic office building before we parted ways. I approached the guard, letting him know I had a meeting with Father Julian Koenhein. One guy took my ID, checked his electronic tablet and made a phone call. After a short conversation, he hung up and handed me the ID.

"Father Koenhein will meet you on the front steps of the building. I'll have to check your purse, please."

"Of course." I handed him my bag. While he searched it, I walked through a magnetometer, and I was in. He returned my purse to me and motioned I was free to walk toward the building.

I thanked him and headed out. By the time I got to the steps of the building, I saw Father Koenhein coming out. I waved cheerfully at him, and he came over to greet me.

"Hello, Lara," he said, taking my hand and shaking it. "It's a beautiful day in Rome."

"Yes, it's not as hot as usual. Thanks for agreeing to meet with me on your lunch hour." I held up a paper bag. "I brought you some fresh bread, salami and cheese. I appreciate you taking the time to help me out."

He took the bag, grinning. "Sounds delicious. It's my pleasure to help you with your school project. Let me know what you need me to do."

"Well, I'd like to get your photo in a variety of shots so I have a lot of photos to choose from."

"Of course."

We walked around and I took several pictures of him in different spots on the grounds of the Vatican. After about thirty minutes, I asked him if we had time to get a few quick shots of him in his office.

"I'd also like to make a short video with you introducing yourself," I added. "You could sit at your desk and talk. These days, videos are worth a hundred words. Would you mind? It'll add another dimension to the on-line version."

He brightened, stood straighter. "I don't mind. Let's go."

"Thank you. This is going to be great."

We went into the same building I'd been in yesterday for the meeting with the pope. The guards were different and no one seemed to recognize me. Regardless, I was sweating beneath the wig. Despite my confidence back at the hotel, I was nervous as heck. This spy stuff was not intuitive for me.

Father Koenhein got me an exception to keep my cell phone for interview purposes, but I was told I could not move around unescorted. He agreed to keep me in his sights at all times. We walked through a series of corridors until we reached his office, where he opened the door and ushered me inside. It was a small, unpretentious room with a desk, two filing cabinets, a bookshelf and a couple of well-watered plants. Several pictures of various cardinals and a portrait of Jesus hung on the wall, alongside the Vatican shield. His desk held a landline phone, an inbox and an old desktop computer connected to a printer that sat on a small adjoining table. Holy crap, how was it possible that the administrative assistant to the president of the Vatican was working on such antiquated technical equipment? On the other hand, it would make the hacking a lot easier.

"Could you sit at your desk and pretend to be typing on your computer?" I asked.

He perched on the edge of his chair and hovered his fingers over the keyboard. I snapped a picture and then shook my head. "It looks funny because the screen is blank. Can you log in and pull up a document, or a website, so it looks like you are really doing something?"

"I can." I made a big deal of looking away as he typed in his login and password. He pulled up a website, so I snapped a couple more and then asked him to arrange his chair so that his back was to the computer.

"Let me adjust the settings on my phone," I said. Instead, I sent Slash a quick text with a single word.

Now.

I took two more pictures when Father Koenhein's phone rang. "Excuse me a minute," he said.

"Of course."

As he scooted his chair forward to pick up the receiver, I slid over to stand next to the printer. I dipped my hand into my purse and palmed the thumb drive. Once I had it secure, I withdrew my hand and set it on the desk, the thumb drive safely beneath.

"*Si?*" Father Koenhein said and then stopped to listen to what was being said on the other end. He glanced over his shoulder and saw me standing there patiently, so he turned his attention back to the phone.

While his attention was elsewhere, I slid my hand with the thumb drive behind the printer, searching for open ports. When my fingertip found the port I was looking for, I slid the thumb drive in. Once it was in, I took out my phone and texted to Slash again.

In.

Father Koenhein said something else in Italian. He sounded irritated, annoyed. I clenched my teeth together in full-on anxiety mode, hoping he would stay on the phone for a few more seconds.

Six, five, four, three.

Father Koenhein said something and moved to replace

the receiver. I snatched the thumb drive, pulling it out and pretending to itch behind my shoulder as he swiveled around in the chair.

"I apologize," he said. "The computer people know better than to call during working hours, but sometimes it's an emergency."

"I totally understand. I know you're busy." I shifted the thumb drive to my palm and brought my arm down by my side. "I think I've got enough material to work with and have taken up quite enough of your time."

"What about the video?" he asked.

Oops. I totally forgot about the video.

"Of course. The video." I reached into my purse, dropping the thumb drive inside and grabbing my phone. "Please tell our audience a little about yourself and what it's like working at the Vatican."

I set up the camera and he spoke for a few minutes. I intended to end the interview after the first question, but when he finished, I impulsively blurted out another question.

"How does it feel to come to work every day when your boss is the pope?" I asked.

He thought about the question and then answered, "It feels great to be a part of history. The new pope is quite refreshing in many ways. He is a man of the people. He does not desire the wealth or status of this position. He lives simply and treats all of us who work at the Vatican as equals. We're never just the butler, the janitor, the driver or the clerk. He's trying to bring about change in the Vatican, but…" He paused, considering. "But change is hard. It takes a lot of courage to stand up to beliefs and standards that are centuries old."

He fell silent for a long moment, then abruptly stood. "Is that enough?"

I lowered the camera, feeling like we'd had a moment. It unnerved me more than I thought it would. "Yes. Thank you." I clicked off my phone and stuck it in my purse. "I've taken up more than enough of your lunch time."

"It was my pleasure. Will you send me a link to your article?"

"Um...sure. I can do that."

As we were walking out of the building, he mentioned the crucifix around my neck. "Do you mind if I ask where you got that?" he asked. "It's beautiful."

I reached up to touch it with my gloved hand. "It was a gift from someone special."

"I've only seen one crucifix like that before. It, too, was special." We stopped on the stairs in front of the building where he made the sign of the cross over me. "Bless you, child. May your heart always be in the right place."

"Thank you, Father. I sincerely wish the same for you."

FIFTY-FIVE

Slash

SLASH WAS ALREADY neck-deep in a review of Cardinal Lazo's email account when Lexi walked in. He looked up, giving her a smile and a thumbs-up.

"Did it work?" she asked him as she set her purse on the bed and took off the wig and gloves.

"It worked. It was close, but you did it. Good work, Agent Carmichael."

"Ha, ha. Thank goodness, because I don't think I could do that again. Way too much talking and smiling. I know I said it before, but I kind of liked him." She came over and stood behind him, one hand on his shoulder, looking at his screen. "Can I help?"

He reached behind him and pinned her hand beneath his. "You already have. The emails are all in Italian. I'll take it from here."

"Okay, if you need me, I'll be on the balcony doing a little work of my own."

He didn't know what she was doing or how many hours passed as he worked steadily, ruthlessly, methodically. Lexi brought him coffee and food, but otherwise didn't interrupt. He appreciated the ability to stay singular in his focus. She understood that was what he needed, and he valued her discretion highly.

When he finally pushed back from the desk, he realized it was dark outside. Lexi had fallen asleep in the balcony chair, a light blanket draped over her torso, the laptop open and running on the small table beside her. One arm hung loosely from the chair, the white bandages on her hands in stark contrast to the night. Her brown hair was loose and spread around her, the slender column of her throat open and vulnerable. His heart stumbled in his chest.

God, I love you.

Not a love of convenience or lust, but a love built on trust, respect and friendship. For a man who had never imagined himself saying, let alone *meaning*, those three words to anyone in his lifetime, saying it to her had become all too easy…and all so true.

She must have sensed him standing there, because her eyes fluttered open and she smiled at him. "Done?"

He lowered himself into the chair next to her and carefully took her hand. "You won't believe what I found."

"Please tell me it's a smoking gun."

He liked when he could please her. "Even better."

She straightened, pushing the blanket off her lap. "Spill."

"Cardinal Lazo's ego knows no bounds. He's been secretly forming a coalition to take control of the Vatican as soon as our current pope passes. While this is nothing new or illegal given Vatican politics, he made it a priority—at any cost—to discredit the one man he sees as his biggest threat."

"Father Armando."

"*Si*, and he will stop at nothing. Yet, he has gone about this with such a disregard for his position and the law that it is sickening. It's all there in his account, a trail that leads directly to his demise."

"I can't say I'm surprised," she said, picking up a water bottle and taking a sip. "His actions toward us have been pretty despicable."

"That, they have. Anyway, this coalition, led by Lazo, has given cartoonish names to all those cardinals who oppose him. For example, he refers to the pope as Slow White. Father Armando is Dopey, Father Tunneli is Sleepy, and so on."

"He wanted to get at Father Armando through you."

"He did. But he's not nearly as smart as he thinks he is."

Lexi drew her knees to her chest, wrapping her arms around her legs. "So, what's the plan?"

Satisfaction and anticipation coursed through him. "Roughly translated, I'm going to sink his ship."

FIFTY-SIX

Cardinal Jacopo Lazo

JACOPO WAS HOLDING a round table discussion with six other cardinals in his office when the knock on his office door sounded.

Irritated at the interruption, he called out, "Come in."

Father Koenhein shuffled in, head bowed, and Jacopo frowned. "I said I didn't want to be disturbed."

"I'm sorry to interrupt, Your Eminence, but there's an important call for you."

"Who is it?"

"Cardinal Tunneli. He says it's very important."

Jacopo looked at the other priests, who suddenly looked overly interested. "This will only take a minute." He walked over to his desk and punched the flashing red button on his phone. "Hello, Father, how can I help you?"

"Jacopo, I was stunned this morning when I received copies of the emails and your subsequent confession and request for forgiveness. I admit I was personally aghast and humiliated by your words. But when I realized your regret was sincere, and after considerable prayer, I reconsidered my stance. I found your willingness to confess your character weaknesses uplifting and inspirational. I want you to know you have my full forgiveness. Godspeed to you."

Before Jacopo could say a word, Father Tunneli hung up. Jacopo looked at the receiver for a long, puzzled moment before he set it down on the cradle.

"What's wrong?" Cardinal Bartini asked.

Jacopo didn't answer, but strode across the room and threw open the door, storming into Julian's office. "That was very strange. Cardinal Tunneli mentioned something about emails, confessing to character weaknesses and forgiving me. What's going on?" he asked between gritted teeth.

Father Koenhein sat in front of the computer, typing madly. "Your Eminence, I don't know. Let me check your email account." He pulled up the account and scanned the documents. "I don't see anything from Cardinal Tunneli, but there is an email from Cardinal Russo."

"What does he say?"

"He appears quite distressed at how you have addressed him and other cardinals in the emails you forwarded to them. He appreciates your humility and transparency in coming clean, but he finds the entire affair sordid and unbecoming of an individual of your stature. The email he is referring to is one from several weeks ago that you sent to Cardinal Bartini discussing what you saw as a character shortcoming among the new cardinal from Portugal. Somehow, it has been forwarded to all of the cardinals."

Jacopo froze, as his brain was having a hard time processing the information. "Forwarded? How is that possible?"

"I think your account has been hacked."

"Hacked?" A frown set to his features. "I thought the Vatican is supposed to have the highest level of information security."

"It is, but Your Eminence, you've now received multiple emails from other cardinals or their staff members. Several are asking me to confirm you sent the email and they are real. What should I tell them?"

"Tell them that they aren't real, of course. It's all a lie and I'm being framed."

He paused, then looked skyward turning slowly. Father Koenhein's computer dinged several times indicating the arrival of more messages.

"How has this happened?"

"I—I don't know how. I've only begun to sort through your account now. It will take me some time to figure out which emails went out, to whom and how it happened."

Fury swept through him. "Slash," he spit out. "He's behind this. What did Cardinal Tunneli mean by he accepts my request for forgiveness?" His voice raised significantly. "Father Koenhein, I'm waiting for answers."

The priest pointed to the printer. "You may sort through them yourself, Your Eminence. I've printed out what I've discovered to this point. The one on top is the most recently sent email issued from your account. It's supposedly written by you and asks the other cardinals' forgiveness for your pettiness and treatment of them, including assigning them derogatory nicknames and disparaging their contributions to the church. You admitted that the guilt over your actions had become too much to bear and that you are begging their forgiveness for your transgressions."

"That's impossible." Jacopo looked at his clerk, stunned.

"It gets worse, sir. Apparently along with your confession, you emailed each of them all the emails where they are mentioned negatively. It will be difficult to deny all of them."

Jacopo's mind was a mixture of despair and rapid-fire searching of scenarios that would rescue him from this situation. His only hope was to convince the pope that it was a deliberate ploy by enemies of the Vatican to weaken the church during the time of his failing health. A plot to drive them apart at a time when the cardinals should all be coming together. It was pretty weak. But if it was going to work, he had to get to the pope before one of the other Cardinals did. Damn Slash. He was going to pay for this, and pay again.

Father Koenhein was still scanning the emails. "Oh, no," he said, and crossed himself.

"I am not in a mood for secrets. What did you find?"

"In your supposed email to the Holy Father, you apologize for disgracing the church, yourself and his Eminence. You say you are willing to humble yourself before God and man and seek forgiveness and absolution."

"The pope? My emails have been forwarded to the pope, too?" This couldn't be happening. It was destroying everything.

"It also appears you offered to resign."

"I *what*?" he roared. He heard a noise behind him and glanced over his shoulder at the other cardinals who were crowding the doorway, listening.

"You said you were resigning, Your Eminence. That's what the email says."

Jacopo snatched the papers from the printer, read the first email and crushed the rest in his fist. His rage burned hot. "This is a travesty. I'm taking this to the Holy Father."

Father Koenhein's computer dinged again and he turned back to read it. "He just requested your presence. He'd like to see you at once. Shall I tell him you're on your way?"

"Absolutely."

Jacopo pushed past the cardinals at the door of his office. "I will go speak with the Holy Father now and clear this up."

Cardinal Bartini stopped him, putting a hand on his arm. "If any of those emails were legitimate, Jacopo, we're in serious trouble. Some of those emails were sent to us, which means our names are attached to this mess. You were careless, very careless."

"I was hacked!"

"Regardless, it shows poor judgment. We will be watching carefully."

Jacopo lowered his voice. "Don't you dare desert me now. I'm what's holding together this coalition."

Cardinal Bartini removed his hand. "We will wait to see how you resolve this. But even if you survive, I believe this will cost you considerable support. I will pray for you."

He walked past Jacopo without any more comment. The other cardinals filed out silently, most avoiding direct eye contact with him.

Jacopo's anger boiled as he snatched his zucchetto and slammed it down on his head. When he stalked out of the room through Julian's office, he saw it was empty. Just as well. He was ready for a fight. He'd been itching for a confrontation with the Holy Father and now he had it. He had no doubt that the pope had a hand in this mess. Now, he'd find out how deep that hand went.

FIFTY-SEVEN

Cardinal Jacopo Lazo

"THE HOLY FATHER will see you now."

Jacopo followed the priest into the Holy Father's office. Once he was ushered in, he approached the pope, kneeling and kissing the ring as he was offered it.

"Father Lazo," the pope said softly. "Please have a seat."

Jacopo sat as instructed, then watched as the pope rested his cane against his chair and sat across from him.

"I'm disappointed by the correspondence I've seen from you but encouraged by your confession and apology in the letter you penned to all of us this afternoon."

Jacopo leaned forward. "I'm afraid none of this is true. I was hacked. Someone was posing as me. I never wrote those emails, and I certainly have no intention of resigning."

"Are you sure about that?"

Jacopo carefully studied the Holy Father's face. "Of course I'm sure."

"It does not suit you to lie, Jacopo."

"I'm *not* lying." Yet, his hands had started to sweat. The Holy Father looked too assured, too calm for his taste.

For a minute the Holy Father didn't speak, just regarded him. Jacopo kept the calm expression on his own face, waiting. Two could play this game. He had to be patient and see in what direction the Holy Father wanted to take this.

"It's no secret we don't share the same views on the future of the church," the pope finally said.

"No, it's not," Jacopo agreed.

"I am greatly concerned by a number of your recent actions. I fear you have lost sight of the true way. You wish for power for the wrong reasons."

"That's an outrageous assumption. None of my actions should trouble you. I have but the purest of intentions when it comes to the future of this church."

"Perhaps you truly believe that. But first, let us discuss your home residence."

"My home?" Jacopo startled, surprised by the abrupt shift of topic. "What does that have to do with anything?"

"Your home recently underwent renovations, did it not?"

"It did, as it is located in quite an old building. It badly needed updating. But what does that have to do with anything?"

"Did that update include a $20,000 bathtub and an 800-square-foot fitness room?"

Jacopo made a dismissive gesture with his hand. "I don't know the exact cost of the bathtub, but I can confirm I did request a fitness room. My body is a vessel of Christ. It's not as if the president of the Vatican can just go to the gym."

The Holy Father regarded him critically. "Or fraternize with the other priests who use the fitness rooms already provided by the Vatican?"

"I prefer to have my own space. That's not a sin."

"Hmmm. Did you not commission a giant iron cross suspended from the ceiling of the new personal chapel that you also had built as an addition to your residence?"

Jacopo leaned forward. "Where are you going with this? You know full well that the president of the Vatican entertains important guests. It is vital for them to see us in settings that reinforce our position."

"Which is why we already have rooms in the Vatican for such purposes."

"I enjoy entertaining from home. It makes the encounters more personal and encourages more investment when done that way."

"I'm afraid the renovation costs of twelve million euros do not outweigh the potential investments from outside sources. It's a travesty, an embarrassment. There are millions of people in this world who are starving, and millions more who have no clean water to drink. And you spend that kind of money to renovate your personal quarters? To improve *your* comfort and status? You have lost sight of what is important, Jacopo. Humility, loyalty, compassion and self-control. *Those* are the characteristics of Jesus that we follow."

Jacopo's face burned. "I have never lost sight of what this church stands for."

"Then how will you explain your transgressions against Father Emilio Armando? Trying to force him into a confession of an illicit affair? Is that an action of a man of God?"

"Why is confronting a sinner with his sin a transgression?" Jacopo argued. "It's vital for the church to have a leader who has the right moral compass."

"Except that's *not* the reason you blackmailed the man you believed to be his son. If you truly had concern for Emilio's soul, you would have approached him privately. Not tried to coerce a man you hoped was his son into making a public confession or forcibly extracting a DNA sample from him."

"I don't know what you're talking about." Jacopo felt his voice rise and fought to temper his emotions. "I didn't blackmail anyone. But the Catholic people have a right to know if one of their own has shown a serious lapse in judgment."

The pope lifted his hands. "Finally, we agree on something." He leaned forward. "I'm issuing a statement tomorrow notifying the press I have accepted your resignation as president of the Vatican."

"*What?*" The Holy Father wouldn't dare risk an uproar at such a sensitive time for the church. Would he? "I won't agree to it."

"I suggest you reconsider. Your actions, including blackmail, the threat of releasing classified Vatican information, employing mercenaries to extract a DNA sample from an unwilling person, and trying to unearth evidence of *my* nonexistent love child, has settled it. You're finished."

"You have no proof that ties me directly to *any* of this other than the request to speak to the man I believed to be Father Armando's son, for which I'm completely justified." Jacopo's mind was whirling, seeking an angle, a way out of this mess. "Your Eminence, this is clearly an unfortunate misunderstanding. I'm a victim here. I was hacked. How does that put me in the wrong?"

"You have lost your way, Jacopo."

"I assure you, I have not. We are not on opposing sides. We both have the interest of the church foremost in our hearts. It is neither fair to condemn me for something I haven't done, nor to punish me for it. That's not the benevolent way."

"It is the right way."

Apprehension coursed through Jacopo. The old man wasn't budging, so he was going to have to adjust his tactics. Removing him as the president of the Vatican would be politically delicate and could cause a possible shift in the pope's own coalition. There would be public outcry, interest and discussion. The pope would have to justify his dismissal, a move that might anger Jacopo's supporters and result in the airing of the Vatican's dirty laundry. That was something he knew the pope would be loath to do. It was time to engage a different strategy.

"Your Eminence, none of this makes sense," Jacopo said in a quieter voice. "Let us take a moment to consider the fallout of my dismissal. You are gravely ill, and the Vatican is at a crossroads. Removing me at this critical juncture would reveal a serious weakness and division within the highest echelons of the church. We cannot risk splitting our believers. You know that. The church requires cohesiveness and solidarity more than ever. You do not want your legacy to be one of divisiveness and scandal. It's obvious I was hacked and those emails were not mine. If I were asked to resign, I would be expected to offer an explanation to the press for my resignation. I would have to express my concerns about the serious divisions and inner turmoil of the church in its present state. That would further weaken your legacy and cause discord among the cardinals and bishops. All that is required to make this go away is that you acknowledge I was hacked, accept my apology for the inconvenience to the cardinals, and we go on. Business as usual."

The pope listened without interrupting, but shook

his head in disappointment. "That sounds dangerously close to blackmail."

"That couldn't be further from the truth. This is about preserving the image of the church, its reach and legacy. We *must* focus on cohesiveness and strength. To show weakness and division would be a grave mistake."

"It would also be a grave mistake to keep you as president of the Vatican. You've engaged in criminal behavior. You crossed the line. You made grievous mistakes while associated with the Church. It will not be tolerated. You have acted outside—and contrary to—the wisdom, doctrines and guidance of our church. Therefore, if you will not resign, I will dismiss you. I will be fully within my rights."

Jacopo's throat burned with fear. "I'll demand a trial. This will go public and your accusations will collapse. You have *no* proof."

"I'm afraid I do." The Holy Father clapped his hands twice and a side door opened.

Father Koenhein shuffled into the room, moving to stand behind beside the pope.

Jacopo stared at Julian in a mixture of disbelief and fury, his mouth twisted in displeasure. "You? You dare to betray me?"

"He dares to stand up for what is right." A thin chill hung on the pope's words.

"I'm sorry, Your Eminence," Father Koenhein said to Jacopo. "I didn't hack your account or send those emails. But the ones where you referred to the other cardinals in such a derogatory manner—those are genuinely yours. As are the instructions to send the notes and package of the statue to the man named Slash. I also hired those men on your request to extract his DNA so you could see if he was Father Armando's child. Then you instructed me to cross-reference his DNA with the pope's."

"Lies," Jacopo hissed. "All of it, lies. None of that happened on my instructions."

"That's not true," Father Koenhein said quietly. "I will swear to that on the Bible and under oath. Cardinal Lazo, I have been loyal to you for more than twenty-seven years. But I could no longer go along with what you wanted me to do because I knew in my heart it wasn't right." He paused, lowering his gaze and plucking nervously at his cassock. "I prayed to God to show me what he wanted me to do right after you told me to cross-reference Slash's DNA with the Holy Father's. Not an hour later, I bumped into a young woman in the park. She was my sign from God. She walked me back through my childhood and the reasons I came to the priesthood. I realized how far I'd strayed from that young man I once was. And that knowledge distressed me greatly."

"Recant, my son," Jacopo said softly. "I will forgive you."

Father Koenhein shook his head, took a shaky breath. "I became a priest to help people, not hurt them. People could have been hurt…because of me. You told me those men *had* to get the DNA at any cost. I agreed, thinking it was justified because it was to protect the church. But my conscience bothered me because I knew it was wrong. They brought weapons into that house. They threatened innocent people who could have been injured or killed. There's no justification for that. I was ashamed of myself, of what I'd let happen in the name of the church. I've confessed everything and begged for forgiveness from the Holy Father."

The pope's voice was cooler than Jacopo had ever

heard it. "I should let you know, I had an interesting discussion with the chief of police in Rome this morning. I'm sure, that if pressed, he, along with the two men he is holding for a crime committed in Sperlonga, will be willing to speak with me, and likely witness against you in a court of law. There is also the matter of two listening devices that were found in Cardinal Ar-mando's office and home. Father Koenhein says they were put there on your instructions."

Jacopo felt everything he'd worked so hard for his entire life slipping through his fingers. He'd been set up and maneuvered into this position, perhaps by the pope himself. But also by Slash. He was so furious he could hardly speak.

"*Judas,*" he seethed, glaring at Julian.

The pope raised a hand. His eyes were angry, distant. "Listen to yourself, Cardinal. You were once a good man. But power has corrupted you. Here's the deal: Your confession and apology to the other cardinals has already been accepted by all, including me, as has your resignation. You *will* remove yourself from Vatican grounds, effective immediately. If you agree, I will ensure your pension and legacy, up to this point, remain fully intact. If you refuse, I will release information regarding what you have done and will consult with our lawyers to decide if we move forward with criminal charges. I give you the choice."

"You did this—all of this—to ensure your legacy continues," Jacopo spat out.

The pope sat back in his chair, tented his fingers. "My purpose, as your pope, is to provide a watchful and loving eye of a father who not only supports but also, when necessary, corrects his children. I will work to ensure that what God has guided me to start, continues. I understand well political maneuvering, a fervent belief in a cause and a willingness to die for what you believe. But what you've done, Jacopo; that is not our way. Throw yourself on the mercy of God and pray for His forgiveness."

Jacopo stood up, bristling with anger. "There are others who will resist you."

The pope dipped his head in acknowledgment. "I know. That, however, is a fight for another day. Goodbye, and may God grant you his everlasting mercy."

Furious, Jacopo whirled around and stormed out the door. Only one thing was on his mind.

Revenge.

FIFTY-EIGHT

Slash

SLASH THOUGHT OF Father Armando as he leaned against the wall in the papal waiting area, arms crossed, waiting for the pope's meeting with Cardinal Lazo to finish. A Bible verse ran through his head.

"And I say to thee, that thou art Peter; and upon this rock I will build my church, and the gates of hell shall not prevail against it."

He wondered if the man he had considered a father for most of his life would someday ascend to the papacy. The Bible was full of instances where God had called upon ordinary men to fulfill extraordinary destinies. As pope, Father Armando would face complex and troubling issues. How would he manage a commitment to tradition while embracing an openness of the tasks God set before him anew? It was important that the church continued to evolve in order to survive. That journey required acknowledging the church's gifts, as well as its mistakes, as it moved forward.

It was Father Armando who had taught him about a life of faith. Adapting, changing, failing, openly acknowledging shortcomings, but never giving up. Always moving in the right direction. Sometimes it meant leaving behind a safe environment and venturing out of one's comfort zone.

It hurt to realize that somewhere along the line, Slash had lost sight of that faith. Hiding his past had been safer than confronting it, and it had almost cost him everything.

At that moment, Cardinal Lazo exited the pope's study. He was livid, his face red with anger, his fists clenched at his side. His shoes slapped the floor as he stormed out. The papal assistants who were waiting outside the pope's study moved inside to attend to him after the cardinal left.

Slash waited until Lazo passed, not even looking his way. When the cardinal strode into the marbled hallway, Slash fell into step beside him.

Lazo stopped, recognizing him immediately. "*You*," he said with barely contained fury. "You did this."

Slash acknowledged the statement with a dip of his head. "I wanted to make sure you knew that."

"You'll never get away with this."

"I believe I already have."

"I will expose you. You will regret this."

The time for the cardinal's threats had ended. Slash cut in front of him, stopping him in his tracks. "I'd advise you never to threaten me again. If you *ever* come after me or mine again, it'll be the last thing you do."

Lazo scoffed at him. "So, you're going to kill me? You're nothing more than a monster. You use violence to get your way, but you go against all that God stands for. You pretend to be sickened by it, but you're not. You're going to burn in hell someday."

"Maybe I will," Slash answered lightly. "But not today." Still, a part of him wondered if Lazo was right. Perhaps violence was an inherent part of his nature. But he wasn't a monster. He'd never used violence as an end to itself. He'd used it only to prevent further violence. That wasn't who he was.

It's never who I was.

The realization hit him hard. Then, just as unexpectedly, he felt lighter—like at least one burden he'd been carrying his entire life had been lifted from his soul.

"You should have sided with me," Lazo continued. "You could have been a great asset to the Vatican."

He looked at Lazo with disgust. "I'm *already* an excellent asset to the Vatican. But you did get one thing right, Cardinal." He clapped a hand on Lazo's shoulder. The gesture was seemingly harmless, but his thumb rested near a particularly vulnerable spot on the cardinal's windpipe. "I'm good at violence. Very good. You, perhaps more than most, know what I'm capable of doing, and I'm just looking for an excuse with you, so don't push me. Are we clear?"

The cardinal's eyes narrowed with hate, but he didn't answer. Slash pressed his thumb down. He wasn't against using the threat of violence if it served a purpose. "I asked if we're clear."

Fear crossed the cardinal's face at the pressure. "Y-yes. We're clear."

"Good. Then we're done here." Slash lifted his hand. "I don't ever want to see you again. Be grateful you have a retirement to enjoy, because I assure you, that wasn't my first choice."

FIFTY-NINE

Lexi

I LOOKED UP worriedly from my laptop as Slash walked in. "How did it go?" I asked.

He pressed a kiss on the top of my head. "Excellent. Lazo is finished." He looked over my shoulder with interest. "What are you doing?"

I tapped on some keys. "A little research of my own. I've found something interesting in my research about Father Armando. Mayor Colella told us he and the pope met at the seminary in Salerno. But did you know *how* they met?"

Slash thought for a moment. "I think the Holy Father had been assigned to teach a class, and Emilio was one of his students."

"Correct. Father Armando was one of the Holy Father's star pupils. They later served on several committees together and became friends. I think the Holy Father was a mentor figure for him."

"That would explain why Emilio was the first new cardinal the Holy Father elevated after becoming pope," Slash said.

"It would. Do you happen to know how old Father Armando was when he became a priest?"

Slash looked at me, clearly puzzled by my line of questioning. "Not exactly. He was young. He told me he knew he wanted to be a priest by the time he was sixteen."

I pulled up a file on my laptop. "Slash, take a look at this photo I found online. Father Armando looks so young in this photo. What does *santo trio* mean?" I angled my laptop toward Slash so he could see it.

"It means holy trio."

He stared at the photo of three young men dressed in black cassocks and laughing. "That's definitely Father Armando on the left, and the Holy Father on the right, but who's that?" He tapped on a young, handsome, dark-haired man who stood between the other two, his face in a wide smile, his arms thrown around the shoulders of his friends.

He didn't see it, but I did. I swallowed hard. I'd seen that smile on the man in the middle before…on Slash and somewhere else.

"Do you know who he is?" I asked quietly.

Slash looked at me for a long moment before sitting down on the bed, sliding my laptop onto his lap. "Not yet, but I will."

WHEN WE ARRIVED in Genoa, it was nearly nine o'clock at night. Slash drove to the apartment and found a parking space about four blocks from Father Armando's apartment. We followed a young man into the complex and found ourselves standing in front of Father Armando's door, looking at each other.

"Do you really want to do this?" I asked Slash. "We stopped Lazo. We don't have to go any further."

He pressed his mouth together, his jaw visibly tensing. After a moment, he raised a fist to the door and knocked once.

Father Armando answered a few moments later, looking exhausted. The age lines around his mouth and eyes had carved deeply into his skin. His thick black hair looked grayer than it had been just a few days prior. This situation hadn't been easy on any of us.

"Nicolo. Lexi," he said, sweeping out an arm. "I've been expecting you. Please, come in."

We crossed the threshold and he ushered us toward the living room couch. Slash and I perched next to each other, our knees touching. Father Armando joined us, choosing a chair directly across from us. For an awkward minute, we sat there looking at each other, and a strained silence enveloped the room as we all waited for someone to speak. I certainly wasn't going to say anything, so I kept quiet, trying to remain calm for Slash's sake.

Slash spoke first. "The Holy Father said you had answers for me." He reached into his pocket and pulled out the small leather pouch the pope had given him, tossing it onto the coffee table. "Do you know what this means?"

For a moment, we all stared at the pouch as if it would detonate. Maybe it would. But instead of vaporizing us, it would blow up what we knew of our lives.

Anguish crossed the priest's face. Apparently, the pouch triggered a strong reaction. "Nicolo, first, I want you to know how deeply sorry I am. For everything."

"I know." Dark smudges of exhaustion were visible beneath Slash's eyes, but his jaw remained set in grim determination. "Let's just do this, okay?"

Father Armando bowed his head in compliance. "Of course. But you should know the Holy Father granted me special dispensation to tell you this information."

Slash didn't indicate surprise or concern that the Pope had released Father Armando from his vow. I guess he must have expected it. He just looked ready to have this conversation over. Honestly, I couldn't blame him.

"Just tell me who my father is, Emilio."

I looked between the two men. Their eyes were locked onto each other, neither willing to be the first to look away.

"Your father is the Savior of Salerno, Cristian Descantes," Father Armando finally said, his voice resigned.

Slash half-laughed, but there was no humor in the sound. "Oh, the irony. I have a saint for a father. I'm not sure whether to be amused or genuinely concerned for my soul."

Father Armando watched him carefully. "You don't sound surprised. Did you already know?"

"Lexi figured it out last night. I wanted to see if you'd confirm it. Why all the secrecy? What's the point?" Slash's voice held a bitter edge. "Why couldn't you or the Holy Father just tell me?"

"I was bound by my vows, as I told you."

"But you weren't the only one who knew," Slash said. "You said the Holy Father granted you dispensation to tell me."

"Yes. He knew, as well. As you know, the Holy Father listens to confession. He heard mine, and I heard Cristian's and your mother's. However, my vows would not allow me to share your parents' confessions, even with their son."

I put a light hand on Slash's arm, feeling the muscles in his forearm contracting and tightening under my fingertips. I wondered what he was thinking. How many people knew his background and had kept it from him? And why?

"I tried to do right by Cristian with you, but I failed

miserably. I am not worthy of him or you. I'm sorry for what you've had to endure, Nicolo. I wasn't nearly the man your father was, but I knew he would have kept his vows even unto death. I could do no less." Father Armando cleared his throat, taking a moment to compose himself. "You have no idea how much you remind me of him. *Il sognatore*, the dreamer with the face of a Roman god. That's what we called him, to his great embarrassment. Cristian never wanted that kind of attention."

Father Armando paused, his expression softening, and I imagined he was remembering a time long ago when the boys teased each other in fun. "Your father was the godliest man I've ever known. He touched my life profoundly. We grew up together in Salerno—went to the same school, played on the same sports teams, dated the same girls. He was not just my friend, he was a brother to me. I entered the priesthood first, after I had my calling at sixteen. He came to the church later. Looking back, I believe he was called to the priesthood for the important mission of teaching humility, sacrifice and the grace of God to those of us who would someday rise in the church. He was given to us for that very purpose. I can't explain it, but there was something about Cristian—a beauty, a genuine goodness that came from inside. People from every walk of life were drawn to him. It was as if he had an inner light, a magnetism. People wanted to be near him, and he welcomed them all. I don't know what he saw in me or why I was chosen to be his best friend. I didn't deserve it—but he honored me anyway. And I wasn't the only one who loved him. As soon as he met the Holy Father, Cristian became like a son to him. That's just the way he was. And when he died, you became ours. A son to me and a grandson to the Holy Father. We both love you with all our hearts."

Father Armando's deep voice shook with emotion. I gripped Slash's arm a little tighter, but he said nothing.

Father Armando reached up and held the cross around his neck tightly. "I see God working through you. It's come full circle, don't you see? The Savior of Salerno's son has now saved others. You are his living, breathing miracle."

"If he were such a saint, why he did abandon me?" Slash finally spoke, his voice tight with emotion. "My own father?"

I glanced at Father Armando and winced at the deep lines of pain etched on his face. "He never knew about you. He never knew he had a son."

Slash recoiled, as if someone had punched him. I'd thought the situation couldn't get any worse, but I was wrong. A lump formed in my throat. I couldn't begin to imagine how Slash was feeling. I pressed my thigh tighter against his to let him know I was with him.

Always.

"Why?" Slash finally managed to ask. "Why didn't he know about me?"

Father Armando paused, as if readying himself for the revelation. "Your mother didn't want him to know."

I hadn't meant to get involved in the conversation, but my indignation slipped out anyway. "Why? How could she keep something like that from him?" I asked. "What could possibly justify not letting him know he had a son?"

Father Armando didn't meet my accusing gaze. Instead he looked at Slash. "Your mother and Cristian were no longer engaged when she discovered she was pregnant, not long after the second incident."

"What second incident?" Slash asked.

"It was a few years after his rescue of the children on the bus at Salerno. Cristian was already a national hero, but he'd not yet had his calling to the church. Cristian once again came upon another life-and-death situation with a half-dozen lives at stake. This time, he didn't save everyone, he couldn't. He believed himself to be a failure. No one blamed him, but the souls of those who died weighed heavily on him. He came to me confessing he thought God had used a similar incident to lead him back to the church, believing it was a lesson for him to learn how to save people, not just those whose lives were in immediate jeopardy. *That* was his calling, and if he were ever required to face such a terrible dilemma again, he wanted to be ready to do God's will."

Father Armando pressed both hands over his eyes, as if they burned with weariness. My own breathing had become shallow, a tightness squeezing my chest. I glanced at Slash, but his face was a mask of stone. He sat with lethal calmness, not moving, not saying anything. It was impossible to tell how he was processing this information about his father, about his life.

"Cristian changed after that incident," Father Armando continued, his voice wavering. "He became deeply conflicted between his love for your mother and feeling led to devote his life to the church. Ultimately, he chose the church and the devout life of a priest. It was truly an anguished decision for him. When he and your mother parted ways, Cristian never knew your mother was pregnant, and it was her decision not to tell him. She believed it was too late. His heart belonged to the church, his life meant for a different purpose. Her path, too, led in a direction other than family. But before she left, she needed to confess. So, she chose me."

Father Armando picked up a glass of water from the coffee table and took a sip, his hand trembling. "For the rest of his life, Cristian made good on his promise to God. Not only did he save the children of Salerno, but over the years, countless others to whom he ministered. In the end, he sacrificed himself to save seventy-four more children and sixteen adults at Lombardy. I know it seems difficult to believe, but I assure you, Nicolo, God had a plan for him. Your father was truly a saint. In fact, he was the greatest man I've ever known…until I met his son."

In my opinion, it didn't seem a fair plan that God would put that kind of guilt and devotion into a man's heart and then give him a son he would never know and a mother who would give him away. Then again, if God hadn't brought the two of them together, Slash wouldn't have been born, I wouldn't have fallen in love with him and we wouldn't be here having this discussion. But it seemed like an awful lot of pain and anguish for a story that might have turned out a lot happier if different choices had been made. But I supposed that was the way life went—every decision we made took us down a road of our own choosing, impacting those who came after us in ways we might have never expected.

Slash leaned forward, resting his elbows on his thighs, clasping his hands in front of him. "So, you just agreed to keep his son a secret from him?"

"Never." Father Armando said shaking his head. "I didn't just agree. I bargained, pleaded and begged your mother to let me tell him. But she refused, and I was bound by my vows. She couldn't keep the baby, so she had considered…other options. I promised her that if she brought me the child, I would see he was protected and raised in a happy home. It was the only way I could save you. And then I lost you." His eyes filled with tears. "I'm sorry I failed you in so many ways. I beg for your forgiveness every day, but understand if you are unable to grant it."

Emotion caught in my throat. I dared a glance at Slash, but he was fixated on the picture of his father hanging from the wall illuminated by the candlelit shrine below. His expression indicated nothing of the emotions I knew had to be whirling like a firestorm within him.

"Is my mother still alive?" he finally asked.

Father Armando dipped his head. "Yes. But I remain bound by my oath and my promise to her. The Holy Father granted me dispensation to speak about your father's confession because Cristian Descantes is no longer alive and his legacy is secure. But I cannot, will not, reveal her name or what was in her confession. But I do ask you to find forgiveness in your heart for her, for she is an extraordinary woman in her own right, and the only woman your father ever loved."

Father Armando reached over and picked up the leather pouch on the coffee table. He pulled the tiny drawstring open and shook the contents of the pouch out into his hand. Looping a finger inside a chain, he held up a silver cross that was partially blackened and bent.

"I gave your father this cross as a present the day he took the vows of the priesthood. He told me he would always wear it as a reminder of all the people he couldn't save. He was wearing it the day he died."

Grief swept through me, a feeling of acute loss for

the life Slash might have had, and the father and mother he'd never known.

Father Armando stood and walked around the coffee table to stand next to Slash. He took Slash's bandaged hand and pressed the cross in his palm. "I'm giving you your father's cross, Nicolo. Children learn much about life from their parents. Sons especially learn from their fathers. You never knew your father, but you can still learn a most important lesson from his life. He was a hero to so many, yet he carried with him, every day, a reminder of those he felt he had failed. That failure drove him, but the pain never left him. I spoke at great length, and prayed with him many times about it, trying to help him find relief. But he couldn't let go. He didn't know how."

He put a gentle hand on Slash's shoulder. "I want you to take this cross, so you may learn from your father. Don't wear it as a reminder of the people you can't save. Wear it as a reminder of those you *have* and *will* save."

The room fell deathly silent. Tears slid down my cheeks, and I swiped at them with my fingertips.

Slash's fingers slowly closed around the cross, now hidden inside his bandaged fist. He remained utterly still, his dark head bowed and his shoulders hunched forward. After a minute—maybe more—he reached around his neck and unfastened the gold cross of the *sodalitium pianum*. For what seemed like an eternity, it dangled between his fingers before he finally released it onto Father Armando's coffee table. Then he carefully fastened his father's cross around his neck.

When it was secure, he rose and faced Father Armando.

"Emilio," he murmured. "I forgive you."

He stretched out his arms, and the two men embraced.

I don't know how long they stood like that, the man I loved and the only man who'd ever really been a father to him. As unconventional as it was, they were family. *We* were family.

Despite all the hurt, pain and secrets that had come between us, there was still love here. The Holy Father had been right. Forgiveness could heal hearts. Maybe someday Slash would find peace in that.

Maybe we *all* would find peace in that.

SIXTY

Lexi

SLASH STOOD ON the balcony of our hotel, gazing at the water below us. He'd taken me back to Salerno for our last night in Italy. It was the same hotel as before, the *Hotel La Lucertola*, the one built into the cliffs overlooking the sea.

His hands rested on the rail, shoulders straight, his dark hair blowing in the breeze. Standing there alone, he was the perfect picture of isolation. The ocean crashed against the rocks of the cliffs beyond the balcony. The smell of salt and brine wafted into the room on the warm afternoon air. Until this trip to Italy, I'd never realized how important the sea was to him—how it connected him to his home here. Now, it connected me to him so he was no longer alone.

I walked out onto the balcony and stood next to him, admiring the ocean. When he saw me, that sense of isolation vanished. Every time we were together, the pull between us got stronger and more resilient.

"Is everything fixed for Gio's wedding?" I asked.

"It is. It's amazing how fast things can move when the pope says he'll look into the matter."

He pulled me into his arms, held me snugly. I leaned back against him as we both enjoyed the view, his chin resting on top of my head. "Looks like we'll be return-ing to Sperlonga in a few months for Gio's wedding."

"I can't say I'm sorry about that," I said. "I'll get to see Nonna again, and finally meet your parents. Oh, jeez, I can't even wrap my head around that yet. Will we see Tito, too? I'm sorry I missed him this time around."

"I'll make sure we get together with him when we come back for the wedding. Did you know Tito was threatening to date you if I hadn't made my move yet?"

"Ha, ha. Did you tell him about our engagement?"

"I did. He's set to retire from the Swiss Guard soon."

"Life moves on."

"*Si*, it does."

A seagull screeched and circled above us. Suddenly it swooped down and skimmed its claws above the water, seemingly more interested in the simple pleasure of fly-ing than fishing.

"Salerno is such a beautiful place, and now it holds even more meaning for us," I said. "Not to mention, we're honorary residents."

"That we are, although I've yet to receive any hotel discounts."

I smiled, relaxing against the contours of his lean body. The clouds were beginning to show the first tinges of pink from the impending sunset. This time and space with him felt exactly right. A sense of con-tentment within me had been growing. It couldn't sweep away all our problems, but they felt more distant and less substantial when we stood together like this.

"I don't know why, Slash, but the most transforma-tive moments in my life keep happening near an ocean. Either it's you or it's an evolutionary thing."

"I'll keep that in mind," he said, his hand warm

against my cheek. "Either way, the next time we have a fight, I'm bringing you to the ocean."

I grinned. "I suppose there's hope yet that I'll embrace the sand, sun and salt someday. But I make no promises for suntan lotion, heat and oily beachgoers. Realistically, I don't see that part happening."

"Little steps," he said, and I could hear the amusement in his voice. "Progress can be gradual."

"True. For example, when I walked out onto the balcony just now and saw the sky, my first thought wasn't 'Look at that gorgeous turquoise sky.' Instead, I was thinking how blue light scatters in short, small waves across the atmosphere in tiny molecules to create an illusion of a turquoise sky. Then, when I viewed the ocean, instead of simply enjoying the view, I found myself studying the wave motion and position of the moon overhead to determine if the tide was ebbing or receding. That seagull's soaring over the waves made me think about how little discernment it has in regards to what it consumes. I mean, I've seen seagulls eating out of garbage cans."

He slid a hand down to the curve of my hip, resting it there. "I love how your mind works."

"Thank goodness," I said with feeling. "I've spent my entire life looking at the world and trying to figure out how it works. It's the main reason I've avoided people and relationships. People don't make sense to me. Within a time span of fifteen minutes, someone can act both altruistically and selfishly. People's moods are prone to change at random intervals, especially if feelings are involved. And don't get me started about predicting the actions of people in a relationship. It's totally confusing."

A rumble of laughter sounded in his chest, but he said nothing.

I turned around in his arms so I could see his face. "But that day when we visited the cathedral in Salerno, I saw beauty and peace. Maybe not for the first time, but uniquely in the context of my own personal journey of working out the complexities of our relationship. I guess my point is, I don't have to read music to enjoy the orchestra. Ever since I met you, I've become better equipped to *feel* a moment—like your strong arms around me right now. I can look at the water and *feel* relaxed, peaceful and loved. I think that's why some people come to the ocean, despite the crowds, sand and salty water. I am never going to understand the speedos, though."

He stroked a hand down my ponytail. "I adore you, *cara*."

"Likewise." I leaned my head against his chest, listening to his heartbeat.

"Slash, are you going to look for your mother?" I don't know why I asked, other than I happen to be the queen of blurting out awkward things at the most inopportune times.

The hand on my hair stilled and then lowered to rest on my shoulder. "I already have a mother. She's the only mother who matters to me. My biological mother made her choice regarding me a long time ago, and now I'm making mine. So, no, I'm not going to look for her."

"I understand. I just wondered."

He released me, slipping off his sunglasses and hooking them on the front of his shirt. Sitting down in the balcony chair, he rested his elbows on his thighs and regarded me. "She didn't want me then, so why would she want me now?"

The expression on his face was so vulnerable and unguarded, I wanted to throw my arms around him and hold him tight. Instead, I answered him as honestly as I could.

"People change," I said. "I'm the perfect example of that. I've also discovered that sometimes we hurt the people we love, intentionally and unintentionally, for many reasons. It's complicated."

"It's always complicated."

"So I've discovered." I turned and sat down in the chair next to him. He reached out to take my hand. We still had matching bandages, so we rested our fingertips against each other's. "You'll do what's right for you."

"What's right for *us*," he corrected.

"For us," I agreed.

We sat in companionable silence until he shifted in his chair, bringing my fingers to his lips and kissing them. "So, *cara*, when do you want to get married?"

I looked at him in surprise. "You're thinking about the wedding?"

"It's hard not to. Between Nonna, your parents and my family, it will be hard to avoid discussions regarding our plans. Especially now that Gio's wedding is on."

I glanced down at my engagement ring. "I guess you're right. I don't know. When do you want to have it?"

"Whenever you're ready." His hand brushed down my hair. "Technically, I already feel as if our life together has begun."

"I feel that way, too, Slash." That warm swell of contentment filled me again. "I'm not going to lie. I'm still nervous about the wedding—whatever we decide to do—

but I'm not scared about the marriage. After this, I know together we can handle anything that life throws at us."

"Truer words have never been spoken." He murmured something in Italian.

"What did you say?" I asked.

"I said you're the only one for me. You always have been." He stood again, pulling me to my feet, gently touching his forehead to mine. "And yet, why do I get the feeling you still want to tell me something?"

Wow. He did know me well. "Because I just made a decision. I know it's going to sound crazy, but given the fact the most important moments of my life seem to be happening near the ocean, I want to honeymoon near it. Are you okay with that?"

He leaned back and searched my expression, as if he didn't believe me. After a moment, he brushed my hair aside and whispered into my ear, "As long as you're there, *cara*, I can't think of a better place to be."

SIXTY-ONE

Cardinal Emilio Armando

THE HOUR WAS late in Italy, but it was early evening in America when Emilio picked up the phone and made the call. The phone rang several times before it was answered.

"Hello?" a female voice answered.

"It's Emilio," he said in English. "You've seen the news, I presume?"

"I have." She paused. "It brings back a lot of memories. I always knew he was a saint. Now it's official."

"Yes, it is. I also wanted you to let you know that Nicolo has been told Cristian is his father."

There was a long silence. "I see. What does he know about me?"

"Not much. Only that you brought him to the church in San Mauro, and you couldn't keep him. He also knows that, aside from the church, you were the greatest love of Cristian's life. I told him the truth about his father without betraying my vows to you. He deserved to know."

He was afraid she'd be angry, but instead she sighed. "Perhaps he did. He looks so much like Cristian, it takes my breath away."

"It is a bit unnerving how alike they are. He's even more like his father on the inside. Brilliant, complicated, fearless, compassionate and prone to feelings of guilt."

"Yet he chose computers over the church," she said. "That fascinates me. Perhaps there is more of me in him than I realized."

"He chose both," he corrected. "But unlike Cristian, he felt the greater opportunity for protecting others lay elsewhere. I am sure if he knew your role in facilitating that move, he would be grateful."

The photo of Cristian on the wall above the candlelit shrine caught his eye. Although his friend's face was serious, it seemed as though his eyes were smiling, benevolent and always watching. "Nicolo is his own man. A good man. He's found the love of his life. His fiancée suits him well, and is an excellent match. They're quite the couple when it comes to saving people. When you have a moment, check out the online newspaper in Salerno. You'll enjoy seeing what he's been up to in Italy."

"I'm at my desk," she said. "Give me a moment."

While he waited for her connect with the local Salerno news, he heard another phone ring in the background before it was silenced. He wondered how her research was going, and reminded himself to ask, as the pope would expect a report.

"I found it," she said. "He and his fiancée saved a crowd of paradegoers and children during a city-wide celebration of the saints? Oh, yes, he's truly his father's son."

She fell quiet, presumably reading further. "They are calling them the Second Saviors of Salerno? Oh my God, the irony is indescribable. It's like Cristian is up there in heaven, orchestrating this entire thing."

"Yes, it would have pleased him greatly," Emilio said. "And yet, Nicolo is your son, too. You've spent your entire life working to save millions of people in the poorest countries around the world. None of us should be surprised at Nicolo's passion for helping others. Which reminds me, how has the project been progressing? The pope's blessing and offer of assistance remains, if we can help."

He heard a thump and wondered if she had closed her laptop. "The vested interests that stand to lose a lot of money if we are successful are actively raising new obstacles and objections," she said. "But we are so close to being allowed to prove our claims. I'm deeply grateful for the church's offer. We're going to need all the advocates possible to counter the misleading fearmongering we will face. My biggest fear is our opposition will stoop to use any avenue to discredit our work or intentions. That surely includes trying to dig up dirt on the project leadership that they can spin and twist to sabotage decades of development. They are not being passive about it—it's an active threat. Several of our staff have reported that they are under occasional surveillance and they suspect that their cars and homes have been quietly searched. I have security cameras all over the place here and at the research center, using multiple monitoring services. Our IT security team reports regular attempts to break into our digital data archives, we believe to either delete or corrupt our work or introduce erroneous test data. We are backing up our data daily and to separate locations, being as cautious as possible. It is quite unsettling to say the least. I change my email password almost daily these days and still am very careful of what I communicate electronically."

"Be careful, we are praying for you. The world needs what you are developing."

"Thank you, Emilio. I appreciate that. We are concerned, but very determined. The potential is too great."

"I agree. There's one more thing, you need to know, however. If Nicolo ever wants to find you, he will leave no stone unturned in doing it. He's an extraordinarily gifted man, aided by an equally talented and courageous woman. Nothing will stop them."

She hesitated, perhaps considering the magnitude of that statement. "Does he have any reason to seek me out?"

"There are always reasons."

A long moment of silence passed before she spoke again. "Then I'll be prepared, as much as that is possible. If he does look me up, I hope it's after we've proven our claims." After another awkward pause, she spoke. "I wish them both great happiness. I really do. He deserves all the joy and contentment in the world. I will always regret my decision, but that's my cross to bear. It would be most difficult to share that with him."

He thought carefully before he offered some advice. "Be wary of holding secrets and guilt too close. They destroy lives, as you well know. May God help you find a way to your own peace. Be open to His guidance and assistance, no matter how unusual it seems."

He could almost see her wry smile. "Good advice, Cardinal. But forgiving is hard when the sin is great and the soul is too damaged. However, I'll try."

"No soul is too damaged for God," he assured her. "Godspeed and good luck."

He was about to hang up when she spoke softly. "Wait, Emilio. May I ask you one more favor? From time to time, would you occasionally let me know how he—they—are doing? I don't know anything about being a mother, but I love him in my own way. I often wish things had been different. While I don't deserve it, I would still like to hear about his life from someone who knows him like you do."

Emilio felt a twinge of sadness. "Of course. May I offer one more suggestion? Tomorrow is a new day. You've expended a great deal of energy to make amends for your mistakes."

"There isn't enough energy to make up for what I've done. You know that."

He sighed. "You sound a great deal like your son."

"I'd never wish this guilt on him." She paused a moment, perhaps collecting herself. "It was good to see you the other day, Emilio. It had been far too long. I wish we would have had more time to talk. But I appreciate you keeping me informed."

"Why wouldn't I? Just remember, all things are possible through God."

"Not *all* things." She paused. "Even God can't change the past. Anyway, the way things are going, we really need all the help we can get. Tell the pope we are counting on his prayers."

"You're already in them, but I'll mention it again for good measure. Just stay safe."

"I fully intend to do that. Goodbye, Emilio. Until we speak again."

"Until we speak again."

After he hung up, he sat for a long minute, staring at the picture of Cristian Descantes that hung on his wall. He let out a breath as his fingers rolled the rosary.

"Cristian, my friend, I beg for your intercession. Please send her the wisdom and guidance she needs. Pray for us all."

It wasn't an answer, but the flame on the votive candle below Cristian's photograph seemed to flicker with renewed life. He wouldn't be so bold to call it a sign, but he could call it hope.

For now, that was all they had.

* * * * *

ACKNOWLEDGMENTS

WRITING A NOVEL is a solitary effort for an author, except when said author has the amazing support of a fantastic group of people. I am so thankful for my brilliant brother, Brad, who helped me enormously during the plotting and writing stages of this book, as well as fantastic author and sister Sandy Parks (seriously, you guys should buy her books!), and my mom, Donna, who always have such thoughtful and insightful comments. I also have to thank Sandy, and her husband, Scott, for accompanying me on the most amazing vacation this summer to Italy and the Amalfi coast. It was a trip of a lifetime and permitted me to add a lot of special and unique detail to the story. I hope you enjoy it! I also want to acknowledge reader Jeannette Koenhein, the winner of my newsletter contest that permitted her to name a character for one of my books. She chose her son, Julian Koenhein, who became a character in this story. Lastly, but never least, I want to give a special shout-out to my editor, Alissa Davis, who is the most extraordinary editor EVER and always challenges me to do bigger and better every book. We've been together now for 11 books! Lexi and I couldn't do it without her!

ABOUT THE AUTHOR

JULIE MOFFETT is a bestselling author and writes in the genres of mystery, young adult, historical romance and paranormal romance. She has won numerous awards, including the Mystery & Mayhem Award for Best YA/New Adult Mystery, the prestigious HOLT Award for Best Novel with Romantic Elements, a HOLT Merit Award for Best Novel by a Virginia Author (twice!), the Award of Excellence, a PRISM Award for Best Romantic Time-Travel AND Best of the Best Paranormal Books, the EPIC Award for Best Action/Adventure Novel. She has also garnered additional nominations for the Bookseller's Best Award, Daphne du Maurier Award and the Gayle Wilson Award of Excellence.

Julie is a military brat (Air Force) and has traveled extensively. Her more exciting exploits include attending high school in Okinawa, Japan; backpacking around Europe and Scandinavia for several months; a year-long college graduate study in Warsaw, Poland; and a wonderful trip to Scotland and Ireland where she fell in love with castles, kilts and brogues.

Julie has a B.A. in Political Science and Russian Language from Colorado College, an M.A. in International Affairs from The George Washington University in Washington, DC, and an M.Ed from Liberty University. She has worked as a proposal writer, journalist, teacher, librarian and researcher. Julie speaks Russian and Polish and has two sons.

Visit Julie's website at juliemoffett.com.

Watch the Lexi Carmichael series book trailer at. youtube.com/watch?v=memhgojYeXM

Join Julie's Facebook Reader Group at facebook.com/groups/vanessa88

Follow Julie on Social Media:

Facebook: facebook.com/JulieMoffettAuthor.

Twitter: twitter.com/JMoffettAuthor.

Instagram: instagram.com/julie_moffett.

Pinterest: pinterest.ca/JMoffettAuthor.